ONE
NIGHT OF
SCANDAL

TERESA MEDEIROS

ONE NIGHT OF SCANDAL

AVON BOOKS
An Imprint of HarperCollinsPublishers

AVON BOOKS
An Imprint of HarperCollins*Publishers*
10 East 53rd Street
New York, New York 10022-5299

Copyright © 2003 by Teresa Medeiros

ISBN: 0-7394-3664-3

Printed in the U.S.A.

To Mama,
for getting out of bed every day,
whether you felt like it or not.
And for Daddy,
for being there when she did.

Acknowledgments

I would like to thank Claire DeAngelis, for giving me back my music; Jean Willett, for reading all of my different versions of Chapter One; tammy rae Cowan, for her faithful prayers, and the good Lord, for answering them; and my own "Mirabella," Buffy, who came into my life just when I needed her mischief the most.

My heartfelt gratitude goes to Carrie Feron, Andrea Cirillo, and my darling Michael, for believing in me.

Chapter 1

Gentle Reader, I'll never forget the moment I first laid eyes
on the man who planned to murder me . . .

LONDON, 1825

CARLOTTA ANNE FAIRLEIGH WAS COMING
out. Unfortunately, what she was coming out of at
the moment was both her elaborate ball gown and
the second-story window of her aunt Diana's Mayfair mansion. She might have managed the latter
without incident if the silk flounces adorning the
bodice of her gown hadn't become entangled in a
nailhead protruding from the inside of the windowsill.

"Harriet!" Lottie whispered frantically. "Harriet,
where are you? I'm in dire need of your assistance!"

She craned her neck to peer into the cozy sitting
room she'd inhabited quite comfortably until only a
few minutes ago. A fluffy white cat drowsed on the

hearth, but Harriet, like all of Lottie's good fortune, seemed to have vanished.

"Where has that silly goose of a girl gone?" she muttered.

As she struggled to work the ruffle free of the nail, the slick soles of her kid slippers danced and skidded along the tree branch that jutted out just below her, vainly seeking purchase.

She stole a reluctant glance over her shoulder, her arms aching from the effort. The flagstones of the terrace below, which had seemed so attainable only minutes before, now seemed leagues away. She considered bellowing for a footman, but feared it was her brother who would come running and discover her predicament. Although only two years her elder, George had recently returned from his first Grand Tour of the Continent and was only too eager to lord his newfound sophistication over his baby sister.

The discordant strains of a string quartet tuning their instruments wafted out of the French windows on the north side of the house. In a very short time, Lottie knew she would hear the clatter of carriage wheels and the murmur of voices and welcoming laughter as the cream of London aristocracy arrived to herald her debut into their society. They would have no way of knowing their guest of honor was hanging out of a window two stories above, having forfeited her one stab at respectability.

She might not have found herself in such a predicament if Sterling Harlow, her brother-in-law and guardian, had hosted her debut at Devonbrooke House, his sprawling West End mansion. But his cousin Diana had cajoled him into conceding the honor to her.

It took no great leap of Lottie's overactive imagination to envision her aunt's guests gathered around her broken body as it lay sprawled on the flagstones. The women would press their scented kerchiefs to their lips to muffle their sobs while the men "tsked" and "tutted" beneath their breath, murmuring what a terrible pity it was that they would be forever deprived of her vivacious company. She gave the rich violet poplin of her skirt a rueful glance. If the gown didn't suffer too much wear on the way down, perhaps her family could bury her in it.

It was only too easy to imagine their reaction as well. Her sister, Laura, would hide her tear-blotched face in her husband's lapels, her tender heart broken for the last time by Lottie's foolhardiness. But most damning of all would be the bitter disappointment etched on her brother-in-law's handsome features. Sterling had spent considerable time, care, patience, and money to mold her into a lady. Tonight had been her last chance to prove to him that all of his efforts had not been in vain.

Lottie might have still been sitting in front of the dressing table in the sitting room had her best friend Harriet not come trotting into the room just as her aunt's abigail was putting the finishing touches on Lottie's hair.

Recognizing the hectic patches of color staining Harriet's cheeks, Lottie had quickly risen from the dressing table. "Thank you, Celeste. That will be all."

As soon as the maid had departed, Lottie had rushed to her friend's side. "Whatever is the matter, Harriet? You look as if you've swallowed a cat."

Although Harriet Dimwinkle wasn't overly plump, everything about her gave the impression of roundness—her dimpled cheeks, the wire-rimmed spectacles shielding her fawn-colored eyes, the shoulders that remained slightly stooped despite hours of being forced to march around the parlor of Mrs. Lyttelton's School of Deportment for Fine Young Ladies with a heavy atlas upon her head. Her name alone had earned her merciless teasing from her fellow students. It hadn't helped that the girl was a tad bit . . . well, dim.

Never one to tolerate injustice, Lottie had appointed herself Harriet's champion. She was loathe to admit, even to herself, that it was the very thickness of Harriet's wits that allowed the good-natured girl to go along with most of Lottie's schemes without worrying about the consequences.

Harriet clutched at Lottie's arm. "I just overheard two of the maids whispering. You'll never guess who's been living right next door practically under your aunt's nose for the past fortnight."

Lottie glanced out the window. The darkened house that shared the square was barely visible through the falling shadows of dusk. "No one, would be my guess. The place is as quiet as a tomb. We've been here since Tuesday and I've yet to see a living soul."

Harriet opened her mouth.

"Wait!" Lottie backed away from her friend, holding up a warning hand. "Never mind. I don't wish to know. The last thing I need tonight is Laura chiding me for being such an incorrigible busybody."

"But you're not a busybody," Harriet said, blinking like an owl behind her spectacles. "You're a writer. You've always said your sister lacked the imagination to make the distinction. Which is why I simply must tell you—"

Lottie interrupted her again. "Do you know who Sterling asked my aunt to invite tonight? Miss Agatha Terwilliger."

Harriet paled. "Terrible Terwilliger herself?"

Lottie nodded. "The very same."

Agatha Terwilliger had been the one teacher at Mrs. Lyttelton's who had refused to grit her teeth and attribute Lottie's penchant for mischief to "high spirits" or a "passion for life." She'd been more interested in shaping her student's character than in placating Lottie's adoring and powerful guardian, the duke of Devonbrooke. The dour spinster had thwarted Lottie's will at every turn, earning her undying enmity as well as her reluctant respect.

"Sterling wants me to prove to Miss Terwilliger that I'm no longer the wicked little hoyden who stitched the fingers of her gloves together and rode the pony into her bedchamber. When I descend those stairs tonight, that shriveled old battle-axe"— Lottie winced at her lapse—"that dear, sweet woman will see only a lady, fit for entry into polite society. A lady who has finally embraced the noble notion that virtue is its own reward."

Harriet's expression turned pleading. "But even the most virtuous of ladies enjoys a nice hot sip of scandal-broth now and then. Which is why you simply *must* know who's been staying in that house. Why, it's—"

Lottie clapped her hands over her ears and began to hum the second movement of Beethoven's Fifth Symphony. Unfortunately, years of eavesdropping had honed her lip-reading skills to a fine art.

"No!" She slowly lowered her hands. "It can't be! The Murderous Marquess himself?"

Harriet nodded, her limp ringlets flopping about like a spaniel's silky brown ears. "The very one. And the maids swear this is his last night in London. He's leaving for Cornwall on the morrow."

Lottie paced the length of the faded Aubusson rug, her agitation growing. "On the morrow? Then this might be my last chance to catch a glimpse of him. Oh, if only I'd have known earlier! I could have climbed right down that tree outside the window and slipped into his courtyard with no one ever the wiser."

Harriet shuddered. "And supposing he'd caught you spying on him?"

"I'd have nothing to fear," Lottie said with more conviction than she felt. "From what I can gather, he only murders those he loves." Seized by inspiration, she hurried to her trunk and began pawing through its contents, tossing kid gloves, silk stockings, and hand-painted fans left and right until she found the pair of opera glasses she'd been seeking. "I don't suppose it would hurt to steal a little peek, do you?"

With Harriet nearly trodding on the scalloped hem of her gown, Lottie crossed the room and threw open the window. She leaned out and pointed the tiny gold binoculars at the house next door, thankful the tender green buds on the linden tree hadn't yet sprung into full leaf. Although no more than a stone wall separated them, the two houses might have existed in different worlds. Unlike her aunt's home, there was no lamplight spilling from the house's windows, no bustle of servants, no boisterous laughter as children and spaniels clattered up and down the stairs and romped across the parquet floors.

Harriet rested her round little chin on Lottie's shoulder, giving her a start. "Do you think your uncle might have invited him to the ball?"

"Even if Uncle Thane invited him, he wouldn't come. He's an infamous recluse," Lottie explained patiently. "And recluses are notorious for scorning invitations to even the very best of soirees."

A dreamy sigh escaped Harriet. "You don't suppose he's innocent, do you? The scandal sheets may have convicted him, but he was never even tried in a court of law."

Lottie shooed away a curious robin that had alighted on the branch above her head and was trying to peck at her golden topknot of curls. While it was all the fashion to adorn one's coiffure with feathers, she doubted an entire bird would go unnoticed. "What more proof do you require? He returned one night to his London town house to discover his beautiful young wife in the arms of his best friend, where she'd no doubt been driven by his callous indifference. He called her lover out, shot him dead, then whisked her back to the wilds of Cornwall, where she died only a few months later after taking a most suspicious tumble over a cliff and into the sea."

"If I were him, I'd have shot her instead of the lover," Harriet said.

"Why, Harriet, how delightfully bloodthirsty!" Lottie exclaimed, twisting around to eye her friend with new appreciation. "Only last week *The Tatler* ran a very cryptic tidbit implying that his wife's ghost still roams the halls of Oakwylde Manor, wailing for her dead lover. They say she won't rest until justice is done."

"I would think that would be most distracting to the digestion. Perhaps that's why he chose to spend a fortnight conducting business in London."

"Blast him anyway! The contrary creature has drawn all the drapes." Lottie lowered the opera glasses. "I had every intention of modeling the villain of my very first novel in his dastardly image." Sighing, she tugged down the window sash. "But I suppose none of that matters now. After tonight, I'll be officially on the marriage mart, which means all of London will be abuzz with gossip every time I use the wrong fork or sneeze without using my handkerchief. Before you know it, I'll be cloistered away in some country estate with a dull squire of a husband and a passel of brats."

Harriet sank down on an overstuffed ottoman, reaching to stroke the cat napping on the hearth. "But isn't that what every woman wants? To marry a wealthy man and live the life of a lady of leisure?"

Lottie hesitated, at a rare loss for words. How could she explain the unease that had been creeping through her heart? As her debut into society approached, she had the suffocating sense that her life was about to come to an end before it had even begun.

"Of course that's what every woman wants," she said, as much to reassure herself as Harriet. "Only a featherbrained girl would dream of becoming a celebrated Gothic novelist like Mrs. Radcliffe or Mary Shelley." She slid onto the stool in front of the dressing table, dipped some rice paper in a jar of powder, and dabbed at her fashionably *retroussé* nose. "I can't very well disappoint Sterling again. He and Laura have welcomed me into their home, seen to my education, and bailed me out of all my scrapes. He's been more of a father to me than a brother-in-law. When I walk down those stairs tonight, I want to see his face shining with pride. I want to be the lady he dreamed I would become."

She sighed, wishing the regal young woman in the mirror didn't look quite so much like a stranger. The doubt shadowing her features made her wide blue eyes seem much too large for her face. "We might as well resign ourselves to our fate, dear Harriet. Our hellion days are behind us. After tonight, there will be no more grand adventures for either of us."

Lottie's eyes met Harriet's in the mirror. "After tonight," she whispered. The next thing Lottie knew, she was hiking up her skirts and hooking one leg over the windowsill.

"Where are you going?" Harriet cried.

"I'm going to steal one look at our notorious neighbor," Lottie replied, swinging her other leg over the windowsill. "How can I ever hope to write about a villain with any conviction if I've never seen one?"

"Are you sure this is prudent?"

Her friend's concern gave Lottie pause. It was unlike Harriet to have reservations about anything Lottie suggested, no matter how outlandish. "I have the rest of my life to worry about being prudent. But I have only a few precious moments left to be me."

She lowered herself out the window. By stretching, she could just touch her toes to the branch below. During her years at finishing school, she'd gained ample experience scrambling both down and up trees to elude unreasonable curfews and diligent headmistresses.

"But what will I do if your sister and aunt come to fetch you?" Harriet called after her.

"Don't fret. With any luck, I'll be back before the musicians strike up the notes of the first waltz."

And so she might have been had the stubborn nail not snagged her flounces and Harriet hadn't abruptly vanished. Still dangling between window and tree, Lottie gave the fabric one last hopeless tug. Without warning, the flounce ripped itself free. She swayed, torn between grabbing for the tree and grabbing for the fluttering silk. Her hesitation cost her the last of her balance. She went plunging backward through the branches, a shriek lodged in her throat.

Fortunately, she didn't plunge far.

She landed in a prickly cradle formed by three branches misted with delicate spring greenery. She was still dizzily trying to absorb the fact that the gentlemen of London would have to mourn her loss another day when Harriet's shoulders and head appeared in the window above her.

"Oh, there you are!" Harriet said brightly.

Lottie glared up at her. "What did you do? Slip out for a spot of tea?"

Oblivious to Lottie's sarcasm, Harriet held aloft a dark garment. "I went to fetch your mantle. It's only May, you know. There's still a bit of a chill in the air. You wouldn't want to catch an ague. It might be the death of you."

"So might plunging thirty feet to the ground," Lottie informed her grimly. She gave her tattered bodice a rueful glance. "You might as well toss it down. It appears I'll have need of it."

The mantle came billowing down over her head, momentarily blinding her. Lottie batted the soft woolen folds away from her face, then balled up the garment and tossed it over the stone wall.

Harriet glanced nervously over her shoulder. "What am I to do while you're gone?"

"Be a dear and fetch a needle and some thread." Tucking one wayward breast back into her drooping bodice, Lottie muttered, "I don't think this is quite what Laura had in mind when she said my coming out would be the talk of the *ton*."

Grasping the limb above her head, Lottie hauled herself to her feet. Once she regained her balance, it was no challenge to swing down to the broad branch that stretched over the wall and into the courtyard next door. As she dropped to the ground on the other side of the wall, she heard a carriage rattle to a halt at the front of her aunt's house, followed by the murmur of voices as its occupants alighted.

She had even less time than she had hoped. The first guests were beginning to arrive.

As she bent to retrieve the mantle, an acerbic and all too familiar voice drifted over the front wall, sending a chill spilling like ice water down the back of her neck. "It's a miracle the child survived to her debut. I always used to warn her that someday she was going to get herself into a scrape she couldn't charm her way out of."

"Someday, Miss Terwilliger," Lottie whispered, whipping the soft woolen folds of the mantle around her shoulders. "But not tonight."

Hayden St. Clair sat all alone in the study of his rented house, reading by candlelight. " 'The mysterious M.M. himself was spotted ducking into a Bond Street haberdashery yesterday,' " he read aloud from the most recent edition of the *Gazette*. "A fine trick, that," he muttered, "considering I haven't left the house since Monday." He flipped the page of the newspaper, seeking the next column. " 'There are some who speculate his rare visit to London might have been timed to coincide with the start of the Season and the recent influx of blushing young belles eager to join the Husband Hunt.' "

Hayden shuddered, picturing some poor fox in

evening clothes being run to ground by a pack of giggling debutantes.

" 'If indeed the M.M. has decided to seek a new bride, may this humble observer suggest an appropriate hue for her bridal gown—*black.*' "

A snort escaped him—half laughter, half disgust. "Devilishly clever, aren't they? The entire miserable lot of them."

He held the pamphlet over the candle, waiting patiently until the edges began to curl, then burst into flame. Leaning forward in the brocaded wing chair, he tossed it on the cold grate, watching with no small satisfaction as it burned to ash along with that day's editions of *The Times*, the *St. James Chronicle*, the *Courier*, and the *Spy*. Disposing of them might have been easier had he bothered to light the fire one of the footman had laid in the hearth, but compared to the stinging winds that whipped across Bodmin moor, the chill damp of London felt positively balmy. He'd only been in London for a fortnight, but he already missed the salty tang of the sea and the shrill cry of the kittiwakes that wheeled over the foamy breakers.

He wondered what the scandalmongers would write if they knew he had come to London to seek a woman, but not a wife. Had they been less successful in their mission to discredit him, he might even have found her.

The Tatler had gone so far as to accuse him of fleeing Cornwall to escape his ghosts. Unlike the professional gossips, he wasn't fool enough to believe that ghosts could be confined to craggy cliffs and windswept moors. They were just as likely to lurk within a melancholy snatch of Schubert drifting out an open window on Bedford Square. They hovered in a whiff of floral perfume that stubbornly clung to his coat long after he'd brushed past its wearer on the crowded pavement. They stalked the fresh-faced young beauties who strolled past the shops of Regent Street, their bouncing curls and exuberant chatter bringing a smile of delight to every man who passed.

Every man too innocent to realize that one man's delight might very well prove to be another man's doom.

Hayden had caught a glimpse of just such a creature only that morning—a golden-haired sprite who had descended from a crested carriage and flitted into the house next door, calling out a teasing challenge to the girl who plodded along behind her. He had watched them from the second-story window of his bedchamber, his fingers frozen in the act of knotting his cravat. Although he'd slammed the window and jerked the heavy drapes shut before he could catch more than a tantalizing glimpse of her face, her laughter had haunted him for the rest of the day.

He rose, moving to the elegant leather trunk perched on the edge of the desk. It had been delivered only that morning. Opening the trunk, he eyed the offering nestled in its velvet-lined interior. It seemed a poor consolation for the treasure he had hoped to find. He would have done just as well to remain in Cornwall, he supposed, but his quest had seemed too significant to trust to a secretary or solicitor, however discreet. He started to lower the brass-banded lid, then stopped, oddly reluctant to hide away the trunk's contents.

He was stuffing books and ledgers into the valise yawning open on the other side of the desk when a knock sounded on the door. Hayden ignored it, knowing from experience that if he did so long enough, whoever it was would go away. He had dismissed the servants shortly after tea, deciding they might as well enjoy their last night in London even if he chose not to.

The rapping on the brass knocker persisted—firm, steady, and unrelenting. His patience taxed beyond endurance, Hayden shoved the last of the ledgers into the valise. He stalked across the foyer to the front door and flung it open.

His lingering skepticism regarding the existence of ghosts was dispelled in that moment.

An apparition from his own past lounged against the stoop's iron rail, his silvery-blond hair haloed by the misty glow of the gas streetlamps. Hayden hadn't laid eyes on Sir Edward Townsend since the blustery autumn day four years ago when Hayden had laid his wife to rest in the Oakleigh family crypt. Although Justine's interment was supposed to be private, Hayden hadn't had the heart to turn Ned away. After all, Ned had loved her, too.

He hadn't denied Ned that last farewell, but he had left the cemetery without exchanging a single word with him.

Once his friend might have thrown his arms around him and given him a hearty thump on the

back. Now Hayden's rigid posture made such a gesture impossible.

"Ned," Hayden said flatly.

"Hayden," Ned replied, his own expression
faintly mocking.

Before Hayden could protest, Ned had pushed his
way past him and into the foyer, twirling his walking stick between deft fingers. He cut much the same
figure as the boy of twelve Hayden had met at Eton
all those years ago—long-limbed and impeccably
groomed from the tips of his polished Wellingtons
to his short-cropped Grecian haircut.

"Do come in," Hayden said dryly.

"Thank you. I believe I will." Ned turned, tapping
the tip of his walking stick against the oak floor. "I
couldn't very well let you sneak out of London without seeing me again. Perhaps your butler has been
remiss. I've called on you every day for the past
week and have yet to receive a response." His gaze
fell on the hall table, where a silver bowl sat overflowing with calling cards and creamy vellum envelopes, none of which had been opened. "Ah . . . I
see it's not the butler who's been remiss, but I. I pre-
sumed too heavily upon the manners your mother
taught you, God rest her dear soul."

Hayden leaned against the door and crossed his
arms over his chest, refusing to look guilty. "My
mother taught me that it was ill-mannered to med-
dle in the private affairs of others."

Ignoring him, Ned picked up a stack of the cards
and invitations and began to shuffle through them.

"Lady Salisbury. Lady Skeffington. The duchess of Barclay." He shifted his gaze to Hayden, cocking one silvery eyebrow. "These are all from hostesses *par excellence*. Tell me—how does it feel to once again be one of the most sought-after bachelors in all of London?"

Hayden snatched the invitations from his hand and tossed them back on the table. "I've no interest in keeping company with those who pride themselves on their manners but not their kindness. They're not looking for a fourth for their card parties or a waltz partner for their daughters. They're seeking someone their guests can whisper about behind their fans and cigars—a curiosity to be both pitied and reviled."

"Ah, yes, the 'Murderous Marquess.' He cuts quite the villainous figure through the pages of the newspapers and scandal sheets, doesn't he? It's astonishing that I even worked up the courage to pay you a social call." Ned studied his neatly manicured fingernails. "But since I've no intention of sleeping with any of your future wives, I shan't worry about you calling me out or flying into a homicidal rage and stabbing me in the throat with a jam spoon."

Hayden stiffened, stung by his friend's boldness. "Nor should you. I have no intention of marrying again."

"More's the pity." But it was sadness that touched Ned's cool gray eyes, not pity. "You were one of the most devoted husbands any woman could hope to have."

They were both silent for a long moment. Then Ned's teeth flashed in a ghost of his old grin. "Come out with me tonight, Hayden! Harriette Wilson's been bought off by the duke of Beaufort and retired to Paris to tantalize everyone with her memoirs, but her sisters still know how to throw a party. We can get thoroughly foxed, plant a pretty bit of muslin on our laps, and pretend we're eighteen again and fresh from Eton. Come with me! You'll see. It will be just as it was."

Despite Ned's insistence, they both knew it would never be just as it was. Instead of three wild and handsome young bucks sampling the city's many illicit pleasures, there would be only two.

Hayden dredged up a smile of his own from somewhere in his memory. "I'm afraid you'll have to woo the winsome Wilson sisters on your own tonight. I plan to retire early and make an early start for Cornwall."

Ned peered into the gloomy study just behind him. "I can't bear the thought of you entombed in this rented mausoleum on your last night in civilization. At least let me send over some small bit of comfort to warm you."

"That won't be necessary. The cook left a nice fat quail on the stove and a bottle of Madeira. That will be all the comfort I require." Hayden swept open the front door.

Ned didn't waste time taking offense or pretending to misunderstand. But he did pause and turn on the stoop, a speculative gleam lighting his eye. "You really shouldn't be so hasty to dismiss my offer.

Even the juiciest of quails can benefit from a dash of spice."

Hayden watched Ned stroll to his carriage, troubled by the spark of mischief in his friend's eyes. At Eton, that look had always meant trouble, usually of the female variety.

Shaking his head at his own fancies, he firmly shut the door, dismissing both the night and its ghosts.

Lottie picked her way through the shadows cast by the overhanging tree branches, thankful that she hadn't allowed Harriet to accompany her. Harriet had never been any good at sneaking. She had an unfortunate tendency to clump about like a plow horse, no matter how soft the turf or how delicate her slippers.

Tendrils of mist rose from the damp earth, glowing ghostly pale beneath a wan scythe of moon. As she emerged from the shadows, Lottie drew up the mantle's hood to shield her hair from the moonlight.

The narrow, three-story house towered over her, dark and forbidding. Had it not been for the maidservants' gossip, Lottie would have sworn the house was deserted.

She studied the darkened row of third-story windows, wondering which one hid the marquess's bedchamber. It was only too easy to picture him sprawled atop a satin coverlet, a snifter of brandy cupped in his long, aristocratic fingers, a sardonic glint in his eye and a cynical sneer curving his lips.

Before wooing and wedding his now deceased

wife eleven years ago, Hayden St. Clair, the marquess of Oakleigh, was purported to have been one of the most eligible young bucks in all of England. The announcement of his engagement to the youngest daughter of a minor French viscount was said to have been greeted with hysterical fits of vapors and brokenhearted sobs. Although his marriage to the girl had ended in tragedy, fond recollections of their whirlwind romance could still bring a wistful sigh to the lips of even the most prudish of matrons. Despite his rather spectacular fall from society's grace, Lottie had no doubt that those same matrons would still welcome him into their drawing rooms today, if only out of morbid curiosity.

But he had chosen instead to exile himself to the wilds of Cornwall. His brief and infrequent visits to London were shrouded in secrecy. Ironically enough, his attempts to escape notice had only whetted society's curiosity and kept the scandal sheets churning out their lurid speculations.

Lottie waited for several minutes, bouncing up and down on her toes with impatience, but there were still no signs of life from the darkened house. Perhaps the marquess wasn't the recluse everyone believed him to be. Perhaps he was even now at some gentleman's club or gambling hell, indulging himself in some of the city's seamier pleasures.

She was turning away, prepared to make the arduous climb over the wall and back up to the sitting-room window, when a flicker of light drifted past the French windows at the far corner of the house.

Her heart skipped into an uneven cadence. It was

probably only a maid or a footman, she told herself, securing the doors for the night. But she moved forward anyway, skirting the shadows along the wall. By the time she reached the corner of the stucco terrace, the light was gone.

Lottie glanced toward her aunt's house. The rattle of carriage wheels was growing more frequent, the whine of the violins more insistent. She didn't dare linger much longer. Her brother-in-law might adore her, but the *ton* hadn't christened him the "Devil of Devonbrooke" for naught. If she missed the first dance of her debut, there would be hell to pay.

The light appeared again, a faint wink too tantalizing to ignore, then simply vanished. Lottie tiptoed across the terrace, promising herself she'd allow only one quick peek into the marquess's lair before she fully surrendered herself to virtue's chaste embrace. Lifting one hand to block out the glare of the moonlight, she sidled closer to the glass.

The adjoining window flew open. A masculine hand shot out, caught her wrist in its powerful grip, and dragged her into the house. Too startled to scream, she found herself gazing mutely up into the face of the Murderous Marquess himself.

Chapter 2

His face was both terrible and irresistible, its dark beauty reflecting the blackness of his soul . . .

ALTHOUGH THE CANDLELIGHT CLOAKED HIS face in shadows, there was no mistaking her captor for a manservant. Above his scuffed Hessians, he wore only a form-fitting pair of black trousers, an unbuttoned waistcoat, and a cream-colored lawn shirt, collarless and open at the throat. Only a gentleman would dare to be so careless in his dress. The rich aroma of bayberry wafted from his skin, mingling with the intoxicating warmth of the wine on his breath. He stood nearly a foot taller than Lottie, his broad shoulders blocking the moonlight.

"Damn that Ned anyway! I suppose this is his idea of discretion—sending you around the back of the house to skulk about the bushes like a burglar." His voice was silky, yet gruff, managing to soothe and incite her rioting senses in a single stroke. "Thank God I gave the servants the evening off."

"Y-y-you did?" she stammered, keenly aware that she'd never been alone with any man who wasn't a servant or relation. Nor had any man dared to handle her with such shocking familiarity. Although his grip had gentled, he showed no sign of relinquishing her wrist.

His thumb grazed her madly skittering pulse. "At least there won't be any witnesses."

"There w-w-won't?" Lottie echoed, beginning to feel like her aunt Diana's parrot.

Her prolific imagination immediately began to conjure up several dark scenarios for which a man would prefer there be no witnesses. Most of them involved strangulation and Harriet weeping over her mottled corpse.

His fingers weren't long and aristocratic, as she'd imagined, but blunt, powerful, and lightly dusted with calluses. As he chafed her icy hands between them, she tried not to envision them fixed around her throat.

"You're shivering. You shouldn't have lingered so long in the damp, you silly little fool."

Normally, Lottie would have taken loud vocal exception to her intelligence being questioned, but at the moment, she was questioning it herself.

"I didn't see a carriage out front. I suppose Ned left you stranded here?" When she didn't respond, he shook his head. "I knew he was up to no good. And to think, that meddling rapscallion had the nerve to accuse me of having no manners. Well, there's no help for it, is there? You might as well come with me. There's a fire laid in the study."

He secured the window with brisk efficiency, then retrieved a silver candlestick from a cherrywood occasional table. Lottie recognized the elusive flame she'd seen bobbing past the windows. As he started from the room, she hesitated, knowing this might be her last chance to bolt. But it might also be her last chance to taste adventure before settling down to a steady diet of tedium. If she stayed, what a tale she would have to tell Harriet! Provided she survived, of course.

As he disappeared around a corner, she found herself following, drawn forward by the inexorable tide of his will. He didn't seem the sort of man who was accustomed to being defied.

As she followed him deeper into the heart of the house, she peered about, straining to see. She wouldn't be able to tell Harriet much about his lair. The fluttering candlelight did little more than deepen the murky shadows. White sheets draped every stick of furniture, giving the deserted rooms a ghostly ambience. The hollow echo of their footsteps against the polished oak floor was the only sound.

He cast a curious glance over his shoulder. "Not much of a chatterbox, are you?"

Lottie had to bite her lip to keep from laughing aloud. If only George could have heard that! Her brother had always sworn that she only paused for breath between utterances because blue didn't suit her fair complexion.

"Perhaps it's just as well. I'm not much of a conversationalist myself these days. In truth, I'm barely fit for my own company." He stole another glance at her. "It's certainly rare to find a woman who knows when to hold her tongue."

Lottie's mouth fell open. She quickly snapped it shut, refusing to be goaded into a retort.

As her host ushered her through an arched doorway, her shoulder brushed his chest. She drew in a sharp breath, unprepared for the sweet sting of awareness that brought a flush to her cheeks.

Although the heavy mahogany furniture was unshrouded, the study was no more welcoming than the rest of the house. The floor-to-ceiling bookshelves along the back wall were empty of all but a thick layer of dust. He rested the candlestick on the desk, sending light flickering over the small leather trunk that sat open on the blotter. Following the direction of Lottie's gaze, he quickly moved to close and latch it, his features guarded. The protective gesture only multiplied her curiosity. What could he be so eager to hide? The freshly inked pages of a juicy memoir where he confessed all of his dastardly deeds? His latest victim's severed head?

Lottie remained frozen into place by her own misgivings while he crossed to the hearth and crouched to ignite the fire that had been laid there. His efforts with tinderbox, kindling, and poker soon had a fire crackling on the grate, creating a cozy oasis of light in the gloom of the house.

The fire cast his broad shoulders and narrow hips into silhouette. It wasn't until he moved to light the lamp on the desk that she caught her first clear look at him.

Between her guardian, her brother, and her uncle Thane, Lottie had spent so much of her life surrounded by handsome men that if one passed her on the street, she rarely spared him a second glance. But if she had caught a glimpse of this man as he strolled past, she would have walked into the nearest lamppost. His face wasn't so much handsome as it was utterly arresting. For once, her imagination had failed her. Although he looked even more wary than she felt, there was no sardonic glint in his eye, no cynical sneer to his lips. He was far younger than she'd envisioned. The deep grooves bracketing his mouth had been carved by wear, not time. He'd grown out of a baby face and into a creased brow and strong jaw. A rakish hint of beard-shadow defined its rugged arc. His tousled hair was such a deep, velvety brown that she nearly mistook it for black. He was in bad want of a haircut. Lottie's fingers tingled with the irrational urge to brush a rebellious lock from his brow.

His smoky green eyes beneath their thick, dark brows were his most compelling feature. Their luminous depths seem to shift from flame to frost, then back again, based upon the fickle whims of the firelight.

Lottie's head reeled. *This* was the Murderous Marquess? *This* was the vile villain who had dispatched both best friend and wife to early graves?

He cleared his throat and gestured to a pedestal

table where a half-eaten quail and a half-empty bot-tle of wine spoke of a lonely supper. "My coachman may not return for a very long while. Would you care for something to eat? A glass of Madeira to take the edge off your chill?"

Lottie shook her head, still afraid to speak, for fear of revealing herself.

He looked a bit nonplussed. Perhaps the wine was poisoned. "Then at least allow me to take your mantle."

Before she could deny him again, he closed the distance between them. With surprising gentleness, he smoothed the hood away from her hair.

Lottie squeezed her eyes shut, waiting for him to realize she wasn't whomever he had been expecting. Her family probably wouldn't even be able to hear her screams over the wailing of the violins.

His hand lingered against her hair. She dared to open her eyes. He was fingering one of the bright strands that had escaped her topknot, gazing down at it as if mesmerized.

A musing note softened the gruff timbre of his voice. "At least Ned had the good sense not to send me a brunette." His gaze shifted to her face. "So where did he find you? Are you a cousin of Fanny Wilson's? Or did he pay a visit to Mrs. McGowan's?"

The names struck an off-key chord in Lottie's memory, but with his touch playing havoc with her senses, she could barely remember her own name.

He shifted his hand from her hair to the curve of her cheek. His thumb caressed the softness he found there, straying dangerously near to her lips. "Who would have thought a devil like Ned could have found an angel like you?"

Lottie had been called a hellion, an imp, and a mischievous fiend. After setting off a Roman candle in his potting shed, she'd even been called a "wee divil" by Jeremiah Dower, the cranky, but beloved, old gardener at their country house in Hertford-shire. But she'd never once been mistaken for divine.

"I can promise you, sir, that I'm no angel," she murmured, blinking up at him.

He slipped his hand beneath the stray curls at her nape, his warm fingers settling against the vulnerable skin as if they belonged there. "You may not be an angel, but I'd wager you could give a man a little taste of heaven."

As their eyes met, he jerked himself away from her, an oath exploding from his lips. He strode back to the hearth, running a hand through his hair. "Sweet Christ, what am I doing? I knew I should have never let you in the house." He stood in profile, utterly still except for the rhythmic clenching of a muscle in his jaw. "I'm afraid you are owed an apol-ogy, miss, as well as whatever coin you were prom-ised. It seems that you and I have been the victims of a tasteless jest."

Lottie was nearly as shaken by his withdrawal as she'd been by his touch. "You don't seem particu-larly amused," she noted.

Fisting one hand against the mantel, he stared into the leaping flames. "Oh, I have no doubt that Ned convinced himself he had only my best interests at heart. He still fancies himself my friend and he knows that I don't dare visit certain establishments with those vultures from the scandal sheets dogging my every footstep. Sending me some nameless, faceless woman could only be a kindness." He slanted her a glance, the smoldering regard in his eyes warming every inch of her exposed skin. "But that doesn't explain why in the bloody hell he sent you."

His casual profanity should have shocked her, but she was too riveted by the raw loneliness in his gaze. The scandal sheets hadn't lied. This man was being haunted. But not from without. From within.

He took one step toward her, then another. "I can't do this," he said fiercely, but he was already closing the distance between them, already reaching to frame her face in his hands. His voice deepened to a husky whisper. "Can I?"

Lottie had no answer for him. As his head dipped downward, she began to tremble. Her situation was far more dire than she'd imagined. This dangerous stranger wasn't going to murder her. He was going to kiss her.

And she was going to let him.

She held her breath without realizing it as his lips brushed hers. They were softer than they looked, yet firm enough to mold her mouth to his will with nothing more than a feathery caress. Her lips tingled, parting just a fraction as he exerted a coaxing pressure that was more plea than demand.

After a moment of that delicious tension, he drew away from her. Lottie's eyes fluttered open just in time to see his mouth curve into a bemused half-smile. "If I didn't know better, I'd almost swear you'd never been kissed before." Before she could decide if that was an insult or a compliment, his smile faded. "I don't know what instructions you received," he said gruffly, "but there's no need to play the innocent with me. I'm not one of those leering gents who fancies silly young chits fresh from their debuts."

Lottie's mouth fell open in outrage.

"There now. That's better." Before she could sputter a retort, his mouth slanted over hers, accepting a surrender she had not offered.

Well! Lottie thought. She'd just show him how silly a young chit could be! She might not have been kissed before, but she'd caught her sister and brother-in-law at it often enough to gain a firm grasp of the rudiments. Without pausing to ponder the folly of her actions, she twined her arms around his neck and pressed her lips firmly to his.

Her affronted bravado lasted only until the scorching sweetness of his tongue delved between her lips. She should have been repulsed, not beguiled, but the tender swirl of his tongue against hers was irresistible. He explored the yielding softness of her mouth until she was clinging to him not to prove her mettle as a woman, but to keep from melting into a puddle at his feet. He didn't kiss like a murderer; he kissed like an angel—deep and hot and sweet, all leashed power and coiled delight.

When the tip of her own tongue touched his, he groaned deep in his throat and wrapped his arms around her waist, drawing her against the hard, muscled planes of his body. He guided her backward until her knees struck the padded cushions of the Grecian couch languishing in the shadows. The mantle slipped away, baring her throat and shoulders.

Lottie had forgotten all about her torn bodice, forgotten how easy it would be for a man to slip his hand beneath the shattered fabric and cup the weight of her breast in his palm. When Hayden St. Clair did just that, she froze, torn between shock and pleasure.

At first Lottie thought the sound she was hearing was her heart slamming against her ribs. Then she realized it was someone banging on a brass door knocker.

They broke apart, both breathless. Their gazes collided—hers guilty, his troubled.

He swore. "If this is Ned's idea of a prank, I'll strangle him."

Lottie opened her mouth; nothing came out but a squeak.

"Stay here," he commanded. "While I send whoever it is on their way."

With his departure, both her breath and her reason returned. What if his caller was the mysterious woman for whom he had mistaken her? Or worse yet, what if Sterling had discovered her absence and come looking for her? Either way, she was the one who was most likely to be strangled. Desperate to escape, Lottie began to cast frantically about for a way out of the study. She swept aside the heavy velvet drapes, gazing upward. Although there was no sign of Harriet, the cozy lights of her aunt's second-story sitting room beckoned to her from across the courtyard. It might just be possible to drop out of this first-floor window and vanish into the moon-dappled shadows while her host was otherwise occupied.

But before Lottie could do more than snatch up her mantle, a woman in a wine-colored pelisse came sweeping into the room, her shimmering auburn hair piled high atop her head. There could be no denying her beauty, even if it was of the rouged and powdered Covent Garden variety, better suited to trodding the boards than gracing the pages of *La Belle Assemblee.*

The marquess was fast on her heels. "I do believe you've made a mistake, miss. You can't just barge in here as if you own the place.

"There's been no mistake," the woman retorted. "This is the address what was given to my driver." She drew off her black, lace-trimmed gloves and began to unfasten the silk frogs of her pelisse, her sophisticated appearance at keen odds with her East End cant. "We'd best make haste, you know. It's damp as a morgue out there. The poor chap won't wait all night." She looked Hayden up and down like a wharf rat eyeing a particularly succulent piece of cheese before drawling, "More's the pity."

Lottie must have made some sort of sound without realizing it. The woman's head jerked in her direction. "What's she doing here?"

Hayden refused to be distracted. "Perhaps the question should be, 'What are *you* doing here?' "

The woman blinked at him. "Why, Mrs. Mc-
Gowan sent me."

Mrs. McGowan. Fanny Wilson. The names clanked
into Lottie's consciousness like badly struck notes
on the pianoforte. She'd read them often enough in
the scandal sheets. They were both notorious mem-
bers of the demimonde, women who peddled flesh
only to those wealthy enough to afford the most expensive and exotic of pleasures. Her face burned
with dawning horror as she realized exactly who—
and what—Hayden St. Clair had mistaken her for.
She clutched the mantle to her tattered bodice, but
still felt naked.

The woman began to circle Lottie, looking her up
and down much as she had Hayden only minutes
before. "The gent who hired me made no mention of
your lady."

Your lady. The words sent a curious shiver down
Lottie's spine. She waited for the marquess to deny
her, but he held his tongue.

"With all that creamy skin and those big blue eyes,
she's a tasty little bit of baggage, ain't she?" To Lottie's intense relief, the woman finally returned her
attention to Hayden, avarice gleaming in her eyes.
"But it makes no difference to me how tasty she is. If
you want to watch me with her, it'll cost you double.
Pleasures like that don't come cheap, not even for a
gent."

Hayden cocked his head to the side and studied
Lottie, his expression thoughtful. For one dreadful
moment, Lottie thought he might actually be considering the doxy's vile proposition. Then he finally

said, very softly, as if he and Lottie were the only two in the room, "If she's from Mrs. McGowan's, then you would be . . . ?"

"Just leaving." Lottie pasted on a bright smile as she began to inch toward the door. "Since your butler has been dismissed for the night, I'll just see myself out."

He took a single step, neatly blocking her path. "That won't be necessary. I believe it's my other guest who will be leaving."

"Then I'll see her out," Lottie volunteered, clutching at the woman's arm as if she was drowning in the Thames and someone had just tossed her a rope.

"Just one minute there, guv'nor," the woman protested, snatching her arm from Lottie's grip. "I don't want you ruining my fine reputation. In all her days—and nights, Lydia Smiles ain't never left a gentleman unsatisfied."

Without once taking his eyes off Lottie, Hayden retrieved a fat wad of pound notes from the open valise on the desk and tossed them to the woman. "I believe that should compensate you for both your time and your trouble, Miss Smiles. And I can assure you that nothing will give me more satisfaction than your imminent departure."

Despite the woman's sulky pout, she wasted no time in stuffing the pound notes down her bodice. As she drew on her gloves, she shot Hayden a regretful look and Lottie a sympathetic one. "A pity I couldn't have stayed, dearie. He looks to be more man than you can handle."

As the woman swept out of the room, Lottie could

find no argument for that. The front door slammed, sealing her doom.

Hayden St. Clair leaned against the desk, folding his arms over his chest and looking every inch as murderous as society claimed him to be. "You're a writer, aren't you?"

"Why on earth would you think that?" Lottie stole a guilty look at her hands, then tucked them behind her back. She'd taken great care to scrub every trace of ink from beneath her fingernails in honor of her debut.

"Let's just call it an educated guess, shall we?" His eyes narrowed. "So which one of those wretched scandal sheets sent you to spy on me? Was it *The Tatler*? *The Whisperer*? Or has even *The Times* stooped to such despicable measures?" He shook his head. "I can't believe they were foolhardy enough to send a woman. Especially a woman like you." He looked her up and down, his uncompromising gaze sending a frisson of heat over her skin. "Why, if I were a certain sort of man . . ." He left the observation unfinished, as if even he wasn't entirely sure what sort of man he might be.

She drew herself up. "I can assure you, my lord, that I'm no spy."

"Then perhaps you'd care to explain why I found you peering into my window."

She opened her mouth, then closed it. He arched one eyebrow.

All of the starch went out of Lottie's shoulders. "Oh, very well! If you must know, I *was* spying. But not for the tabloids. Only to satisfy my own curiosity."

"And have I succeeded in satisfying you?" The unspoken challenge in his gaze reminded her that only minutes before she had been in his arms, sharing his kiss, feeling the scorching heat of his palm against her naked flesh.

Feeling her cheeks heat, Lottie began to pace back and forth in front of the window. "I don't know why you're in such a foul temper. Why, there I was, just minding my own business—"

He arched the other brow.

"Well, I had the noble intention of minding my own business until Harriet overheard the maids gossiping and learned that my aunt's neighbor was the Mur—" She snapped her mouth shut, shooting him a nervous look.

"The Murderous Marquess?" he gently provided.

She decided it would be safest to neither confirm nor deny. "The next thing I know, I'm stuck in a tree with my lovely gown all ruined and my aunt's cat making smug faces at me." She paused in her pacing. "Are you following this?"

"Not in the least," he said pleasantly, crossing one booted ankle over the other. "But please don't let that stop you."

She resumed her pacing, tripping over the hem of the mantle draped over her arm. "So after narrowly avoiding Terrible Terwilliger herself, I catch a glimpse of a mysterious light in your window. The house could have been on fire, you know. Why, I might have saved your life! And what thanks do you offer me in return? You snatch me into the house, call me a silly, little fool, and then you—

you—" She swung around to face him, her chin held high. "You kiss me!"

"Surely the most vile of all my transgressions," he murmured, looking far more amused than ashamed. "Even murder pales in comparison."

She flung out her arms, not even noticing when the mantle slid to the floor. "Don't you understand? I can't be kissed yet. I'm coming out!"

"You most certainly are."

Warned by the downward flick of his gaze and the gruff note that had returned to his voice, Lottie glanced down to discover that her feverish pacing had caused her bodice to slip south. One seashell-pink nipple was peeping over the tattered silk.

Mortified, she gave the fabric a jerk, wincing as she heard yet another seam give way.

Determined to reclaim her wits, if not her dignity, she threw open the window, pointed across the courtyard to her aunt's house and announced, "I'm coming out. Tonight. Over there."

The mansion blazed with light. The jingling of harnesses, clip-clop of hooves, and clatter of carriage wheels had been joined by a steady stream of laughter and chatter. The string quartet had progressed from tuning their instruments to warming up, each note sounding more like music than the last. Since it appeared that everything was proceeding according to schedule, Lottie could only pray her absence had not yet been detected.

Hayden's expression slowly changed, going from dangerous to deadly. "You," he breathed, drinking in her features as if for the first time. "You're not from one of the scandal sheets, are you? You're the child from next door. The one I saw this morning." He ran a hand through his hair, raking it back from his brow. "Sweet God in heaven, what have I done?"

"Nothing!" she assured him, more alarmed than gratified by his reaction. "And I'm hardly a child. I'll have you know that I'll be one-and-twenty in less than two months. Why, Mary Shelley was only sixteen when she first eloped to France with Percy Bysshe Shelley."

"Much to the chagrin of the first Mrs. Shelley, whom he had neglected to divorce." Hayden paced behind the desk, as if searching for any shield to place between them. "I'm relieved to know you're no longer wearing napkins, but isn't twenty-one a bit old for a debut?"

Lottie sniffed. "I'm hardly on the shelf yet, if that's what you're implying. We spent the Season in Greece the spring I was eighteen. Then last year, I came down with an unfortunate case of—" she hesitated, realizing her confession would hardly make her sound like a mature woman of the world "—measles. But it was quite a severe case," she added, "and had it gone into scarlet fever, I could have died."

"And what a tragedy that would have been. We might never have met."

Lottie had misjudged him. He was quite capable of being sardonic.

Ignoring her glare, he planted both palms on the desk. "Have you any idea what an untenable situation you've placed us both in, Miss . . . Miss . . . ?"

"Fairleigh," she offered, bobbing him a one-handed curtsy that would have done Miss Terwilliger proud if Lottie hadn't been trying to hold up the bodice of her dress with the other hand. "Miss Carlotta Anne Fairleigh. But my family and friends call me Lottie."

His disparaging snort told her what he thought of that. "Yes, they would, wouldn't they? So, *Miss Fairleigh*, have you no care for your good name? Your reputation? No one ever truly appreciates their reputation until they've lost it. Trust me. I should know."

"But I haven't lost anything," she protested.

"Yet," he bit off through clenched teeth. As he came around the desk and started toward her, Lottie began backing toward the open window. "Just what would you propose I do with you now, *Miss Fairleigh*?"

She mustered up a hopeful smile. "Since chopping me up and hiding my body in the ash bin would be far too much bother, you might try smuggling me back into my aunt's house before Sterling misses me."

"Sterling?" he echoed disbelievingly, continuing to advance on her. "That wouldn't be Sterling Harlow by any chance, would it? The Devil of Devonbrooke himself?"

She waved away his concern. "Oh, he's not nearly so fiendish as all that. My parents died in a fire when I was only three. Sterling's mother, Lady Eleanor, took us all in, but she died when I was ten and Sterling has been both a brother and a father to me ever since he married my sister, Laura."

The marquess glowered at her. "Then you won't mind if I drag you over there by the ear and demand he give you the sound spanking you deserve."

She swallowed, her smile growing more wan. "Maybe the ash bin wouldn't be such a terrible fate after all."

His shadow fell over her. She half expected him to pitch her out the window, head first, but he simply scooped up the fallen mantle and swept it around her shoulders. She could feel the heat of his hands even through the soft, woolen folds.

"There's one thing you failed to explain, *Miss Fairleigh*. Why did you let me . . . ?" He lowered his gaze to her lips, a fringe of thick, dark lashes veiling his smoky green eyes. "Was that to satisfy your curiosity as well?"

Unable to resist the compulsion, Lottie moistened her lips with the tip of her tongue. "No," she said softly. "It was to satisfy yours."

He was going to kiss her again. The knowledge darkened his eyes a heartbeat before he admitted it to himself. This time, he gently framed her face in his hands and kissed her as if it was her first kiss and his last. As he swirled his tongue through the warm, honeyed depths of her mouth, the most extraordinary thing happened. An array of golden notes poured through Lottie's veins, glorious and sweet, soaring on wings of melody. It took her a dazed moment to realize the music wasn't coming from her heart, but from the ballroom of her aunt's mansion.

"Oh, no!" She clutched at Hayden's muscular forearms, blinking up at him in wide-eyed horror.

"The musicians just struck up the first waltz! I should have already descended the stairs! Everyone should be admiring me! Sterling should be leading me out onto the ballroom floor for the first dance!"

Hayden was gazing over her shoulder and out the window, his expression inscrutable. "I'm afraid he might be otherwise occupied."

Lottie slowly turned to the window and gazed upward, an icy ball of dread already forming in the pit of her stomach. Even from their angle, she could see that the sitting room was no longer deserted. On the contrary, it appeared to be thronged with people.

But Lottie only had eyes for the pale, spidery figure garbed all in black who was hunched in front of the window with Lottie's own opera glasses pressed to her eyes. Lottie held her breath as Agatha Terwilliger handed the tiny binoculars to the tall, golden-haired man standing rigidly at her side.

It was too late to slam the window and jerk the drapes closed. As Sterling lifted the opera glasses, all Lottie could do was stand frozen in Hayden St. Clair's embrace.

Chapter 3

*I fear my innocence was exceeded
only by my impetuosity...*

"THE GIRL IS RUINED. UTTERLY RUINED."
Agatha Terwilliger lifted her quizzing glass and surveyed the occupants of the elegant drawing room of
Devonbrooke House with a jaundiced eye. "It's just
as I feared. I always knew she'd come to a bad end."

At that dour pronouncement, Harriet's sniffling
spilled over into a sob. She was stretched out on a divan upholstered in green-and-gold striped damask,
her face blotchy from weeping, her ankle propped
on a bolster and swollen to twice its normal size.
"You mustn't blame Lottie. It's all *my* fault! I'm the
one who ruined everything! If I hadn't got scared
and gone after her, then stepped in that hole in the
side yard and made such a muddle of things, no one
would have ever known she was missing."

"And if I and my companions hadn't heard you

whimpering and moaning, you might still be lying in the grass like a beached cod," Miss Terwilliger snapped.

Duly chastened, Harriet subsided into hiccups.

Lottie's brother, George, fished a monogrammed handkerchief out of his waistcoat and handed it to Harriet. Having been named after St. George, he never could resist coming to the rescue of any damsel at the mercy of a dragon. "You mustn't blame yourself, Miss Dimwinkle," he said. "Miss Terwilliger was the one who raised the alarm when she failed to find Lottie in her room. If she hadn't been so persistent, none of Aunt Diana's guests would have even known my sister was missing." He leaned against the mantel with the world-weary grace he had affected in Europe, raking a lock of sandy hair out of his eyes. "Perhaps the situation isn't as grave as we fear. This is hardly the first scrape Lottie has gotten herself into."

"But it may very well best be the last." Miss Terwilliger folded her tiny, birdlike hands over the top of her cane and fixed him with a withering glare. "Tell me, son, does impudence run in your family?"

George's jaw tightened, his sullen expression making him look more twelve than two-and-twenty. He opened his mouth, then snapped it shut, plainly aware that any reply he could make would only prove her point.

From an overstuffed wing chair in the corner, Lottie watched the drama unfold. She sat with her bare feet tucked beneath the hem of her nightdress, a cashmere shawl draped over her shoulders, and a fluffy gray kitten curled up in her lap. Cookie, the beloved old maidservant who had practically raised her from a babe, had shuffled in only minutes ago and pressed a mug of warm chocolate into her hands. So far, being nearly ravished by a nefarious murderer wasn't much different from having a nasty head cold.

But that was only because her guardian had yet to make an appearance since bundling her into a carriage and having her whisked away from her aunt's house. The last she'd seen of Sterling, he had been striding back up the walk toward St. Clair's house, her babbled explanations still ringing in his ears. She took a nervous sip of the chocolate, trying not to imagine what might be transpiring between the two men.

The ormolu clock on the mantel ticked away several more tense minutes, accompanied by Harriet's incessant sniffling. Miss Terwilliger's fuzzy white head drooped, her black lace cap sliding over one ear as she lapsed into a doze.

They all jumped when the front door slammed. There was no mistaking the resolute click of Sterling's heels as he crossed the marble foyer. The kitten leapt out of Lottie's lap and scurried under the nearest ottoman. Lottie wished she could do the same.

She sat up as Sterling and Laura appeared in the arched doorway. Although a few stray threads of silver tarnished Sterling's tawny hair, his golden good looks had lost none of their gleam in the ten years since he'd wed her sister. And if not for the worried frown creasing her brow beneath its cascade of rich brown curls, the willowy Laura could have easily been mistaken for a debutante herself instead of a mother of two. Even as a child, Lottie had always been round and curvy, where Laura was slender.

Lottie kept her voice as bright as possible. "Oh, there you are! I thought you were going to stay out all night. Where are Nicholas and Ellie? Didn't they come home with you?" She had hoped the presence of her exuberant niece and nephew might temper the pall of dread that had fallen over the house.

Laura handed her mink-trimmed pelisse to a waiting footman, refusing to look at Lottie. "The children will be spending the night with their cousins. Under the circumstances, Diana felt it was the very least she and Thane could do."

Lottie sank back in the chair. Harriet's snuffling was torment enough. She didn't think she could bear anyone else blaming themselves for her bad judgment.

While Laura perched on the edge of a cream-colored sofa, still avoiding Lottie's eyes, Sterling crossed to the towering secretaire in the corner and poured a generous splash of brandy in a glass. He drained the glass in one swallow, his broad shoulders beneath his black tailcoat rigid with tension. Lottie's heart sank even further. Knowing his wife didn't approve of them, Sterling rarely indulged in strong spirits.

Cookie bustled into the drawing room, carrying a tray. She leaned over Lottie, her plump face wreathed in a tender smile. "There now, pet. Would you care for some nice warm gingerbread to go with your chocolate?"

Sterling swung around, clutching the glass in his white-knuckled grip. "For God's sake, would you stop pampering her! That's what got us into this bloody mess in the first place!"

Lottie froze, her hand halfway to the tray. Even Harriet stopped sniffling. The echo of Sterling's shout hung in the silence. In the ten years since he'd been Cookie's master, Sterling had never once raised his voice to her.

The old woman slowly straightened, her quivering chins held high. "As you wish, Your Grace." She bobbed a formal curtsy, her knees creaking from the effort, then turned and marched from the room.

Sterling's shoulders slumped as he watched her go. But it was Laura who finally spoke. "You might as well stop torturing yourself and everyone else, darling. You refused to breathe a word to me all the way home. But you can't keep what happened between you and the marquess to yourself forever."

Sterling rested the empty glass on the secretaire before facing them all. For the first time, he looked every minute of his thirty-eight years. "Lord Oakleigh says he has no intention of taking another wife. He claims he did not compromise your sister and he refuses to offer for her."

Harriet gasped, going so pale that George was compelled to exchange his handkerchief for the bottle of smelling salts Miss Terwilliger tossed to him.

Lottie drew in a shaky breath of her own, trying to convince herself that the emotion coursing through her was relief. "That's all very well and good," she announced, tired of everyone talking about her as if she were invisible. "Because I wouldn't have had him anyway. He's nothing but a stranger to me. And an ill-tempered stranger at that."

They all turned to look at her.

"You needn't look so shocked. I told you that I tore my dress while I was climbing out the sitting-room window. The man may be a boor, but he's not a liar. He's innocent. He did not compromise me."

Laura's soft brown eyes sharpened as she studied her sister's face. "And can you deny that he kissed you?"

To her horror, Lottie felt her cheeks heat. Her sister's challenge summoned up other unbidden memories. Hayden St. Clair caressing a lock of her hair as if it were spun from the finest gold, the aching loneliness in his voice as he had gazed at her, the beguiling tenderness with which he'd cupped her breast.

It took a tremendous effort, but she forced herself to meet Laura's gaze. "And what's the harm in an innocent kiss? I dare say that George has stolen a few of them in his day. And no one is forcing him to marry anyone."

Her brother took a sudden and intense interest in the carved molding around the chimneypiece.

Sterling shook his head, his expression grave. "I'm afraid this man stole more than just a few harmless kisses. He also robbed you of any hope you might have had of making a decent match."

The certainty of his words made even Laura blanch. "Perhaps we shouldn't be so hasty to judge,

Sterling. What if Lottie's right and it was nothing but a harmless kiss? Surely there will be other offers."

"Oh, there will be offers, all right," Sterling replied bitterly. "But not the sort we'd hoped for. By tomorrow morning, all of London will be reading about your sister's ruin in the pages of the scandal sheets."

Lottie exchanged a sheepish look with Harriet. Perhaps this was to be her punishment for all the hours the two of them had spent poring over those very newspapers, giggling over others' indiscretions.

"I don't see why I should have to wed at all," she said. "Surely there are other fates for a woman besides matrimony."

Miss Terwilliger banged the tip of her cane on the floor. "For once, the chit is right. Just look at me. I'm living proof that a woman doesn't require a man to lead a long and satisfying life."

As the shriveled little husk of a woman drew a yellowing handkerchief from her reticule and honked loudly into it, Lottie tried not to shudder.

"We appreciate your point, Miss Terwilliger," Laura said gently, "but no respectable family or establishment is going to hire a governess or teacher with a scandal in her past. Especially not one as lovely as our Lottie."

"I don't have to be a wife or a governess," Lottie protested, feeling her first twinge of genuine excitement. "Why, I could be a writer just as I've always dreamed! All I would require is some ink, some paper, and a small cottage by the sea somewhere."

Miss Terwilliger snorted. "I'd hardly call that ridiculous scribbling you do writing. Not with all of those wailing white ladies and vengeful dukes wandering around castles with their heads tucked under their arms. That sort of drivel is suitable only for lining birdcages."

Before Lottie could object, the timid Harriet piped up in her defense. "I like Lottie's stories . . . even if they do give me nightmares and make me sleep with the covers over my head."

"Carlotta's talent is not at issue here," Sterling said sharply. "Her future is." When he dropped to one knee in front of Lottie and took her hands in his, she almost wished he'd go back to yelling. His anger had always been easier to bear than his disappointment.

"You still don't understand, do you, poppet? This isn't like the time you tied the basket of frogs to Lady Hewitt's train or the time you hid the fox from Lord Draven's hunt beneath your bed. I can't fix this. I can't make it go away. All of my wealth, my titles, my political weight, my social standing—it's all worthless in the face of a scandal such as this. A reputation isn't a torn gown that can be mended with a needle and thread. Once ruined, it's forever lost." He reached up to stroke her hair, his amber eyes stricken by regret. "In all these years, the only thing I've never been able to protect you from has been yourself."

Lottie pressed his hand to her cheek, overwhelmed by the sense of helplessness that had brought this powerful man to his knees at her feet. As Laura bit her lip and Harriet reclaimed George's handkerchief and buried her face in it, Lottie was forced to blink back her own tears. "I'm so sorry. I wanted to make you proud tonight. Truly I did."

The effort Sterling put into his tender smile broke her heart anew. "I know, sweetheart. Now why don't you run along to bed and get some sleep while your sister and I decide what must be done."

. . . while your sister and I decide what must be done.

The utter finality of Sterling's words made even the thought of curling up in her cozy canopied bed impossible. She couldn't shake the suspicion that Sterling had already reached some irrevocable decision about her fate. Just as soon as George had escorted Miss Terwilliger to her carriage and two footmen had carried Harriet to a guest bedchamber, Lottie came creeping back downstairs, thankful that all the lamps in the foyer had been dimmed for the night.

The towering drawing room doors were still open. She slipped behind one of them and peeped through the crack between door and hinge.

Sterling was seated at the secretaire, his hand moving rapidly as he scrawled something on a piece of stationery.

Laura was pacing behind him, her lovely face shadowed by agitation. "We should be relieved, shouldn't we? After all, this Lord Oakleigh is hardly the husband we would have chosen for Lottie. What do we know of him besides what's been written in the scandal sheets?"

"One can hardly rely on the tabloids for taking an accurate measure of a man's character."

Lottie wondered if Sterling was remembering the scandal his and Laura's own hasty wedding had ignited. The scandal sheets had refused to believe a notorious rakehell like the 'Devil of Devonbrooke' could have lost his heart to an orphaned rector's daughter without some subterfuge on her part. Of course, the true story was twice as shocking as what they'd printed.

"Perhaps it's just as well that he refused to offer for her," Laura said. "How could we have asked Lottie to marry a man who didn't want her?"

Her sister wasn't entirely right, Lottie thought with a dark shiver. Hayden St. Clair did want her. Just not for a wife.

"A man who might never love her?" Laura finished.

Sterling dipped his pen in a bottle of ink and continued writing. "Many long and solid marriages have been built on far more stable foundations than love."

"Not ours," Laura reminded him softly. "And not Thane's and Diana's. Or even Cookie's and Dower's. We're the ones who taught Lottie that love is the *only* foundation for a marriage. How could we be so cruel as to ask her to live the rest of her life without it?" Laura rubbed his rigid shoulders. "Why don't we just skip the Season and all go back to Hertfordshire in the morning? We've always been our happiest there. With enough time, some new scandal should drive all thoughts of Lottie and this marquess from everyone's mind."

Sterling reached back to pat her hand. "Time will solve nothing, my dear. I'm afraid that society has a very long and unforgiving memory. Hayden St. Clair should know that better than anyone," he added bitterly. "On the contrary, it will only be a matter of time before the less scrupulous gentlemen of our acquaintance come beating a path to our door, whether it be right here in London or in Hertfordshire. They will murmur their regret over our *difficult situation*. They will offer our Lottie their *sympathy*, their *kindness*, their *protection*. But they will not offer her their good names."

Laura shook her head in dismay. "Surely that can't be her only possible future."

He folded the sheet of stationery, dribbled sealing wax along its seam, and pressed his ducal seal into the warm wax. "It won't be. Not if I can help it." Rising, he gave the bell rope hanging over the secretaire a sharp tug.

Lottie huddled deeper behind the door as Addison, the duke's butler, emerged from a darkened corridor and came striding past. From his bright-eyed alertness and the impeccable state of his attire, one would never guess that he had been jarred from a sound sleep. Lottie had always suspected that he slept in his crisply pressed trousers, starched shirt, and waistcoat.

"You rang, Your Grace?" he intoned.

When Sterling turned, he was holding two missives, nearly identical. "I want you to see that these are delivered immediately."

Lottie frowned, chilled by his resolute expression. What missive could possibly be so urgent that it required delivering in the middle of the night? She squinted at the clock on the mantel. Or in the first wee minutes of the morning?

Laura grabbed his arm, a panicked note creeping into her voice. "Sterling, what are you doing?"

"What I must." He gently shook off her grip. "And Addison?"

"Yes, Your Grace?"

"I also need you to insure that my pistols are made ready by dawn."

Lottie clapped a hand over her mouth to muffle her horrified gasp.

For once, Sterling had succeeded in ruffling the manservant's composure. Addison hesitated before slowly saying, "Yes, Your Grace. I shall see to it myself."

The manservant's bow lacked its usual crisp flair. He exited the drawing room, leaving Laura staring at her husband in open-mouthed disbelief. "In the name of all that's holy, what have you done?"

He turned back to the secretaire, busying himself with capping the ink and shoving the wax sealing sticks back into a cubbyhole. "In defense of my sister-in-law's honor, I've challenged Lord Oakleigh to a duel. And I've asked Thane to serve as my second."

"Thane won't do it. Diana won't allow it." Laura

shook her head, her expression fierce. "And neither will I."

Giving up all pretense of efficiency, Sterling slammed both palms against the hinged desk, his back still to his wife. "None of us has been left with any choice in this matter, including you!"

Tears began to spill down Laura's cheeks. "This is madness, Sterling! You know how much I adore my little sister, but you've already said it's too late to salvage her honor. So what can this possibly prove?"

"That she is of value. That she is worth fighting for."

Laura tugged at the back of his sleeve. "And is she worth dying for?"

Sterling turned to face her, his own eyes damp. "Yes. She is."

Laura gazed up at him for a long, helpless moment before throwing herself into his embrace. He wrapped his arms around her, closing his eyes as he buried his face in the softness of her hair.

Lottie slowly backed into the shadows of the foyer, the full enormity of her folly weighting her steps and making her stomach churn. This was no thrilling melodrama crafted by her clever pen. This was her brother-in-law's life, her sister's heart, her niece's and nephew's futures. She'd not only disgraced herself this time. She'd brought ruin down upon them all.

Any man who would kill his best friend in a duel would surely suffer no qualms of conscience about gunning down a stranger. Her overwrought imagination quickly provided an image of Hayden St.

Clair standing on some dewy common, his dark hair blowing in the wind, smoking pistol still in hand. She could see Sterling lying in a pool of his own blood, Laura cradling his lifeless body in her arms, her pale face streaked with tears, her gentle brown eyes bitter with accusation as she lifted them to Lottie. An accusation that would inevitably harden into hatred as she realized just what her sister's recklessness had cost them all.

Lottie closed her eyes to blot out the terrible image and for one traitorous heartbeat, it was St. Clair lying in a crimson pool of blood, his sooty fringe of lashes resting against his pale cheeks. Only there would be no one to weep for him, no one to cradle his lifeless body in their arms and mourn his loss.

When Lottie opened her eyes, they were dry and burning. Despite all of his noble intentions, Sterling had been wrong. One of them had been left with a choice.

She crossed the foyer with sure strides, breaking into a run before she reached the stairs.

Chapter 4

I blushed before his bold proposal . . .

HAYDEN HAD JUST SUNK DEEP INTO THE feather mattress of his rented bed, his exhausted muscles groaning with relief, when an all too familiar banging sounded belowstairs.

"Surely you jest," he muttered, throwing himself to his back and glaring up at the underside of the bed's wooden canopy. The one thing he'd looked forward to in London was a few nights of uninterrupted sleep. But it seemed even that was to be denied him.

Not even that rascal Ned could have devised a torture this diabolical. Hayden was a man who valued his solitude above all other comforts, yet in the space of a few hours his privacy had been besieged by a snooping virgin, an insolent strumpet, and an irate duke. Perhaps Ned had returned to confess that the entire nightmare had been one colossal joke, that the delectable debutante and her infuriated brother-in-law were only actors hired to perform in some ridiculous farce of which he'd become the unwitting lead.

But if that were true, then the woman he'd held in his arms tonight had been an accomplished actress indeed. Any Fleet Street doxy could mimic passion, but the innocence he'd tasted in her kiss was not so easily feigned.

The banging ceased. Hayden soaked in the blissful silence, afraid to breathe. Perhaps it had just been his valet or one of the other servants, stumbling back from their night of revelry at one of the local gin shops.

He rolled to his side and plumped up his pillow, determined to steal at least a fitful nap before sunrise.

The banging resumed—sharp and persistent.

Throwing back the covers, Hayden jumped out of the bed. He jerked on his dressing gown, yanking the sash in a careless knot. Snatching up a candlestick, he went storming down the stairs, cursing himself for having ever given the servants the night off in the first place. For a man who wanted nothing more than to be left alone, his company was certainly in very high demand these days.

As he flung open the door, the last person he expected to find standing on his stoop was Carlotta Anne Fairleigh.

She opened her mouth.

He closed the door.

There was a brief pause, then the banging resumed, twice as forceful as before.

Hayden threw open the door, using the full advantage of his height to glare down at his uninvited guest. She'd changed out of her torn gown and now looked less ravished than ravishing in a maroon skirt and a fur-trimmed spencer of emerald green velvet. The short jacket hugged her trim waist and accentuated the gentle curves of her bosom. She'd even crowned her curls with a saucy felt hat topped with a pink feather. Oddly enough, it was the defiant angle of that jaunty little feather that gave Hayden's heart an unexpected tug. If she was nonplussed at being confronted with six feet, two inches of angry male wearing nothing but a burgundy dressing gown and a ferocious scowl, she hid it well.

"Good evening, Miss Fairleigh. Or should I say good morning?" He searched the empty street behind her. A public hack was just disappearing around the corner, crushing his hopes of ridding himself of her quickly. "Are you alone or should I expect an outraged uncle or second cousin to come leaping out of the bushes at me at any minute, brandishing a rapier?"

"I'm alone," she replied, although she did flick a nervous gaze over her shoulder.

"That's what I was afraid of. Shouldn't there be a nursemaid or a nanny to see that you're tucked safely away in your bed? Hiring one would prevent a great deal of bother—especially for me."

Hayden was struggling to forget that only a short

while ago, he had come dangerously close to tucking her into his. Although if he had got her off her feet, he doubted they would have made it any farther than the Grecian couch in the study. At least the first time.

She sighed. "As I tried to explain to you earlier, Lord Oakleigh, I've been out of the nursery for quite some time now."

"Which means you should be old enough to understand the perils of engaging a public hack and visiting a lone gentleman in the privacy of his home in the middle of the night without a chaperone."

Clutching her silk reticule as if it were a talisman, she drew herself up. "According to my family, my reputation is already in ruins. I have nothing left to lose."

"If that's what you believe, Miss Fairleigh," he said softly, "then you are far more young and naive than I first thought."

Although she forced herself to hold his gaze, a becoming blush tinged her cheekbones.

Feeling like the worst sort of bully, Hayden sighed and stepped out of the doorway. "You may as well come in before someone sees you. There might still be one or two people in London who aren't aware that I've added debauching debutantes to my catalogue of vices."

She wasted no time in accepting his reluctant invitation. Before he could close the door, she was already heading for the study. "Do make yourself at home while I dress," he called after her. "Again."

If she could ignore his sarcastic pleasantries,

surely he could ignore the hypnotic sway of her hips beneath the rippling skirt. He returned to the study a few minutes later to discover she'd stirred the dying flames in the hearth to life and settled herself in the chair before the desk as if she belonged there. If nothing else, she was resourceful.

Hayden sank into the chair behind the desk, studying her. Although there were countless poets and romantics who would doubtlessly classify her heart-shaped face as angelic, it was the spark of devilment in the heavenly blue shade of her eyes that intrigued him. Her honey brown lashes and brows provided an irresistible contrast to her golden hair. Her mouth was a lush Cupid's bow, uptilted at the corners. Her slender nose was stylishly *retroussé*, but her pointed little chin betrayed more determination than was strictly fashionable.

Just as he had feared, that determination was directed toward him. Tugging off her gloves and stuffing them into her reticule, she said, "I'm sure you must be wondering why I would disturb you at such an ungodly hour."

Hayden suspected that she could disturb him at any hour. "I'm simply atwitter with curiosity." He drummed his fingertips on the desk blotter, his dry tone implying the opposite.

She leaned forward, her expression alarmingly earnest. "This is a bit awkward, but I was wondering if I might somehow persuade you to marry me."

For a long moment, Hayden couldn't speak at all. He leaned back in the chair, clearing his throat once,

twice, a third time before asking, "Are you propos-
ing to me, Miss Fairleigh?"

"I suppose I am. Although it might make a more
romantic story to tell our grandchildren if you pro-
posed to me."

Her hopeful tone prompted him to gentle his
voice. "I'm afraid there won't be any grandchildren.
As I explained to your guardian in no uncertain
terms, I have no intention of taking another wife.
Not now. Not ever. I also assured him that it would
not be necessary for you and I to wed because, despite appearances to the contrary, I did not compromise you." As Hayden recalled the velvety softness
of her breast against his palm, a pang of guilt
stabbed him. Perhaps he wasn't being completely
honest, even with himself.

Undaunted by his rejection, Lottie asked, "What if
you had compromised me? What then?"

He considered his reply very carefully. "Then I
would have been compelled upon my honor as a
gentleman to offer you the protection of my name."

She bowed her head. Given his past experience
with women, Hayden expected wheedling, recrimi-
nations, perhaps even a few artful tears. He did not
expect her to reach up and draw off her hat. The
feather drooped as she rested the scrap of felt on the
edge of the desk. Her hands went searching through
her hair, drawing out the pearl-tipped pins one by
one until a cascade of shimmering curls came tumbling around her slender throat.

She lifted her head, giving him a look that was a

smoldering mixture of invitation and innocence. Hayden felt his mouth go dry, the victim of a hunger too long denied. Her sensual boldness might have been even more affecting if he hadn't noticed the trembling of her fingers as she reached for the cloth-covered buttons of her jacket.

Hayden was around the desk before he even realized he'd moved. He closed his hand over hers, hoping she wouldn't notice that his own fingers were none too steady. He could feel the pounding of her heart through the heavy velvet of her jacket.

His voice was far rougher than his grip. "Forgive my bewilderment, but have you come here to persuade me to marry you or to compromise you?"

"Either. Both. Does it really matter as long as the outcome is the same?" She gazed up at him, desperation shining through her eagerness. "You can't deny that you want me. You were perfectly willing to compromise me when you thought you were paying for the privilege."

"But the price you're asking now is far too high." He studied her face through narrowed eyes. "Your guardian is one of the wealthiest men in all of England. You no doubt possess a generous dowry. Given your fairness of face, I'm sure you'll have no lack of suitors either now or in the future. So why on earth would you seek to wed a man with my reputation?"

She swallowed nervously, her tongue darting out to moisten her lips. "Because I find you . . . irresistible?"

This time when the knock on the front door sounded, Hayden didn't even start. But Lottie nearly jumped out of her skin.

"Stay right here," he commanded, giving her a warning look.

When he returned, she was sitting exactly as he had left her, staring into the leaping flames on the hearth. He tossed the missive he'd just received in her lap, making sure her guardian's broken ducal seal was plainly visible.

Her shoulders slumped, her breath escaping her in a defeated sigh. "If you don't agree to marry me, then my brother-in-law will be compelled to avenge my honor on the dueling field." She lifted her eyes to him. "I can't bear the thought of Sterling risking his life over such a worthless trifle as my reputation."

Hayden leaned against a corner of the desk. "What makes you so sure your guardian wouldn't win this duel?"

She drew in a shaky breath, but refused to relinquish his gaze. "You do have a reputation as an expert marksman."

Although Hayden's expression didn't so much as flicker, he heard the deafening report of two pistols fired in nearly perfect synch, smelled the bitter stench of gunpowder, saw Phillipe crumpling to the grass, stunned disbelief clouding his boyish face. But when he spoke, it was with icy calm. "Even an expert marksman can miss when faced with an opponent of equal skill. Who's to say that it wouldn't be my heart's blood spilled in this contest of yours?"

He chuckled, the dry sound devoid of humor. "Oh, yes, according to the scandal sheets, I haven't any heart."

"Prove them wrong," Lottie challenged, that stubborn little chin of hers every bit as troublesome as he'd feared. "By marrying me and sparing my brother-in-law's life."

He cocked his head to the side. "So you have no care for your own life, only for his?"

Although her hands fitfully crumpled the piece of stationery, she managed a small, self-mocking smile. "I just overheard Sterling talking to my sister. It seems that after tonight, all I have to look forward to is a steady parade of licentious gentlemen seeking to dandle me on their knees."

Hayden might have smiled at the image himself if it hadn't stirred up the brackish waters of his conscience. What if Devonbrooke was right? What if, by refusing to wed her, he had condemned her to a life spent lurking in society's shadows? He knew just how cold those shadows could be.

It certainly wasn't unheard of for a young woman of quality to enter the demimonde after savoring her first taste of scandal. Nor would it be difficult for a beauty such as Lottie to find a wealthy protector to pamper and cherish her. At least until some fresh new face caught his eye and he decided to pass her along to the next man. And the next. And the next . . .

Hayden wasn't aware his hands had curled into fists until he felt his fingernails bite into his palms.

He circled behind Lottie's chair and leaned over her shoulder, close enough for his breath to stir the downy ringlets over her ear. "And what if I'm one of those very men your brother-in-law was talking about? How do you know I won't take you to my bed tonight, then send you back to your family in the morning in genuine disgrace? What's to stop me from making you my mistress instead of my wife?"

She turned her head, the coral softness of her lips only a breath away from his. "Your word."

Hayden gazed into her unflinching eyes. It had been a very long time since anyone had trusted in his word. To protect her precious guardian, she was willing to sacrifice both her virtue and her pride. She would even allow his hands, bloodstained though they were, to sully her tender young flesh.

He slowly straightened and returned to the desk, where the elegant little trunk that was supposed to be making its way to Cornwall in only a few hours still sat. He should have stayed there, Hayden thought bitterly, far away from lovely young women and their meddling relatives.

This time, when he cast his gaze on his guest, it was with cool appraisal. "Tell me, Miss Fairleigh, has your guardian provided you with a sound education?"

Although she looked somewhat taken aback by the question, she nodded. "I spent two years at Mrs. Lyttelton's School of Deportment for Fine Young Ladies. While there, I memorized several letters from Mrs. Chapone's *Improvement of the Mind* such as 'Politeness and Accomplishments' and 'The Regulation of the Heart and Affections.' " She shrugged apologetically. "I must confess I never completely mastered 'The Government of the Temper.' "

"Nor did I," he murmured.

She ticked off the womanly graces so highly valued at such establishments on her fingers. "I can paint a pastel watercolor, sketch a recognizable likeness, work a sampler." Her face brightened. "Oh, and I've always excelled at the pianoforte."

"No music," he said, shaking his head. "I've no use for it."

She looked even more taken aback. "Well . . . then I can speak fluent French, sew a straight seam, dance the minuet, the waltz, and the—"

"Can you decline a Latin noun?"

She blinked up at him, obviously having never considered that a required skill for a wife. "Excuse me?"

"Can you decline a Latin noun?" he repeated with just the faintest trace of impatience. Giving the leather globe sitting beside the desk a forceful spin, he asked, "Can you locate Marrakesh on a globe? Can you tell me in which year the Ostrogoths conquered Rome? Have you any useful knowledge at all that doesn't involve hemming handkerchiefs or trodding all over your dancing master's poor aching feet?"

Her jaw had gone taut with the effort it was taking to govern her temper at that moment. "First, second, third, fourth, or fifth declension?" Without awaiting his reply, she snapped, "Marrakesh is the capital of southern Morocco, which lies in the north-west corner of Africa. And the Ostrogoths never conquered Rome, the Visigoths did. In 409 A.D., if I'm not mistaken."

It was all Hayden could do not to growl at his own folly. If she had turned out to be a silly young miss with her head stuffed full of useless trifles, he might have dismissed her to her fate without a moment's regret.

As he grabbed her hand and tugged her to her feet, her guardian's challenge went tumbling un-heeded to the rug. He started for the door of the study with her stumbling along behind him, taking three steps to every one of his long strides.

"Where are you taking me?" she demanded breathlessly. "Are you going to compromise me?"

He came to an abrupt halt in the doorway, wheeled around, and dragged her back to the desk. He retrieved her hat and slapped it on her head. The feather drooped over her pert nose, making her sneeze.

"No, Miss Fairleigh," he said through clenched teeth. "I'm bloody well going to marry you."

As the marquess's elegant chaise went rolling through the deserted avenues of the West End, the shuttered windows of the town houses and man-sions gazed back at Lottie like sleepy eyes. The first pink fingers of dawn had yet to streak the sky. Even the most diligent of servants would still be abed at this time of the morning.

Which was why Lottie's stomach sank when they

rounded the corner to find Devonbrooke House ablaze with light. She stole a glance at Hayden, but his set features revealed nothing.

The front door of the mansion stood ajar. Lottie and Hayden slipped inside. The servants were scurrying back and forth across the foyer in such a blind panic that no one even seemed to notice their arrival.

Sterling came striding out of the drawing room, his face haggard with exhaustion. "What do you mean she's missing?" he shouted. "How can she be missing? I sent her to bed hours ago."

Cookie trotted after him, looking close to tears. "Her bed is empty, Your Grace. And it doesn't appear to have been slept in at all."

Laura trailed behind them. "Do you think she might have run away? Perhaps she was afraid we were going to force her to marry that monster."

Beneath her hand, Lottie felt Hayden's arm stiffen. Before she could think of something clever to say, Addison came marching in from the library, a burnished mahogany case resting on his extended palms.

The butler stopped in front of Sterling with a click of his heels, his face reflecting the gravity of his mission. "Your pistols, Your Grace, freshly oiled and loaded."

"Perhaps we should go," Lottie whispered, trying to tug Hayden back toward the door. "This might not be the best time to share our joyful news."

"On the contrary," Hayden whispered back. "Your guardian appears to be in dire need of some joy." Before Lottie could protest, he captured her hand and marched forward, tugging her along behind him.

Warned by Cookie's gasp, Sterling turned. "You!" he exclaimed. "What in the devil are you doing here? Haven't you done enough harm to this family for one night?" As Lottie stumbled into view, Sterling added softly, "No. It appears you haven't."

"If you'll just give me five minutes to explain—" Lottie began.

"I'm only interested in the answer to one question," Sterling said. "Did you spend the night in his bed?"

Keenly aware of the warm fingers laced through hers, Lottie felt a flush creep into her cheeks.

"Now see here," Hayden said, stepping forward. "I won't have you impugning the young lady's honor."

"It's not her honor that concerns me!" Sterling shouted. "It's your lack of it. But there's no need to discuss that here. What's between us can be settled on the dueling field."

"I came to inform you that there won't be any need for a duel," Hayden said.

Sterling gave him a long, level look before saying coolly, "No, I don't suppose there will."

As he flipped open the lid of the case in Addison's hands, Cookie shrieked and Laura lunged for his arm. Easily shaking off his wife's grip, Sterling drew out one of the loaded pistols and leveled it at the marquess's heart.

Although Hayden didn't so much as flinch, Lottie threw herself in front of him as if her slight form could protect him from a pistol ball. "Put away the gun, Sterling! His intentions toward me are honorable. He came here to ask for my hand in marriage."

Although Sterling slowly lowered the pistol, his narrow gaze never left the marquess's face. "Is that true?"

"It is," Hayden replied.

"Why the sudden change of heart? When I spoke to you only a few hours ago, you swore you'd never take another bride."

Hayden's hands closed over Lottie's shoulders, their possessive heat making her shiver. "I'm sure I don't have to tell you how persuasive your sister-in-law can be."

Sterling's gaze shifted to Lottie. "And what about you? I suppose next you'll be trying to convince me that you've fallen madly in love with him."

For some reason, Lottie was thankful Hayden couldn't see her face as she looked her guardian in the eye and said, "Many long and solid marriages have been built on far more stable foundations than love."

Sterling's shoulders slumped in defeat, as he realized she had overheard his own damning words. Handing the pistol back to a dazed-looking Addison, he snapped, "Come with me, Oakleigh. We'll discuss this in the drawing room."

As the door slammed behind the two men, Lottie looked over to find Laura gazing at her through a sheen of helpless tears. "Oh, Lottie, what have you gone and done now?"

Lottie drew herself up, forcing a shaky smile. "I seem to have landed a marquess."

Chapter 5

*But he refused to relent. I would be his bride
or no man's at all!*

"THE MARQUESS OF OAKLEIGH," THE BUTLER
announced as he appeared in the doorway. Although the wizened old fellow managed to keep his
expression remarkably impassive, his bushy white
eyebrows appeared to be in imminent danger of taking flight.

Ned Townsend nearly choked on a mouthful of cigar smoke as Hayden St. Clair came striding into the
smoking room of his Kensington town house. Although Ned made an instinctive grab for the pamphlets and newspapers scattered across the writing
table, it was too late to do more than lean across
them and hope his shadow would blot out the most
damning of the headlines.

"So you've decided to pay a call on me after all,"

Ned said, mustering up his most affable smile. "Perhaps your manners aren't as rusty with disuse as I feared. To what do I owe the honor of this visit? I thought you were leaving for Cornwall this morning and here it is well after noon."

"I would have already been gone if it weren't for you and your infernal meddling," Hayden replied, leveling a glacial glare at him through his frosty green eyes.

Ned couldn't help but wonder if that had been the last look Phillipe has seen across the grassy field of Wimbledon Common nearly five years ago.

Hayden's appearance was in stark contrast to Ned's own short-cropped hair, starched cravat, and polished brass buttons. Hayden's boots were scuffed and at least three years out of fashion, his cravat loosely tied and ever so slightly askew. His coat hung loose over his rangy frame, as if he'd scorned more than a few meals recently. As was his habit, he was carrying his beaver top hat instead of wearing it, which had left his shaggy hair at the mercy of the wind. Despite his noble birth, there had always been a hint of the savage about the man, a vaguely uncivilized quality most women, both ladies and lightskirts, seemed to find irresistible. When forced to choose between Ned, Hayden, and Phillipe, they had invariably chosen Hayden.

Just as Justine had done.

Ned took a deep drag on the cigar, affecting an air of wide-eyed innocence. "I have no idea what you're talking about."

"Oh, come now. Surely you can't be the only soul in London who hasn't heard about last night's debacle." Hayden's gaze fell on the scattered newspapers. His jaw tightened. "No, I can see you're not."

Before Ned could protest to the contrary, Hayden had jerked that morning's copy of *The Times* out from under his elbow. He held it up to the early afternoon sunlight streaming through the bow windows and read the bold headline with dramatic relish. " 'M.M. Claims Another Victim in Crime of Passion.' " As Ned sank back in his chair, admitting defeat, Hayden scooped up two more papers. " 'M.M. Gives Kiss of Death to Innocent's Reputation.' Oh, and we mustn't forget that bastion of responsible journalism, the *St. James Chronicle*—'Debutante Succumbs to Lord Death's Irresistible Embrace.' "

" 'Lord Death,' " Ned repeated musingly. "You have to admit it does have a much more poetic ring than the 'Murderous Marquess.' "

Hayden slapped the papers back down on the table. "I hope you're satisfied. This drivel has probably sold more copies than the last installment of Harriette Wilson's memoirs."

Ned leaned forward to tap a wand of ash into a copper bowl molded to resemble an elephant's foot. "A regrettable incident, to be sure. But I still fail to see why I am to blame."

"Because it never would have happened if not for you. When this girl came snooping around my house, I mistook her for the woman from Mrs. McGowan's. The woman *you* hired."

Ned's mouth fell open, leaving the cigar to hang

limp from his bottom lip. Catching it before it could fall, he collapsed in the chair, unable to suppress a hearty swell of laughter. "Oh, that's just too rich! That poor, dear child. Please tell me you didn't . . ."

"Of course I didn't," Hayden growled. But even as he proclaimed his innocence, he seemed to be having some difficulty meeting Ned's eyes, an observation Ned found particularly fascinating. "I'm not given to ravishing every woman who comes knocking at my door. Or my window, for that matter."

"Perhaps if you were, you'd soon find yourself in a better temper." Ned stabbed a finger at *The Times.* "So just who is this girl? The papers dropped some tantalizing hints that some are bound to recognize, but they weren't bold enough to come right out and print her name."

Hayden sank into a sateen-covered wing chair, propping one ankle atop the opposite knee. "Carlotta Anne Fairleigh," he said, tolling the name as if it heralded his doom.

Although Ned had been on the verge of gaining control over his laughter, tears of fresh mirth sprang to his eyes. "Little Lottie Fairleigh? The Hertfordshire Hellion herself?"

Hayden's expression grew even more wary. "You've heard of her?"

"Of course I've heard of her. You'd be hard-pressed to find anyone in London who hasn't."

"I don't understand. How can she be so notorious when she's yet to make her debut into society?"

"And why do you think that is?" Ned queried, unable to suppress his broad grin.

"She told me that two Seasons ago her family was abroad and last spring she was afflicted with a nasty bout of the measles."

Ned snorted. "Afflicted with an acute case of embarrassment, more likely. Her guardian was probably waiting for the gossip from her last attempt at a debut to die down." Knowing he had all of Hayden's attention, Ned leaned forward in the chair. "Devonbrooke brought her to town the Season she was seventeen, fully intending to unleash her on society then. Prior to the ball he was hosting in her honor, as is the custom, she was to be presented at Court."

It was Hayden's turn to snort. They both knew that King George, formerly the licentious Prince of Wales, had turned the once noble tradition into an opportunity to ogle eager-to-please young beauties in the first blush of their womanhood.

Ned continued. "So picture if you will the lovely Lottie waiting in a crush of dizzy young belles for her royal summons. When it finally comes, she makes her way toward our gallant monarch, her fair bosom dripping a king's ransom in diamonds, the ostrich plumes adorning her hair swaying with each graceful step. But when she lifts her hoops to make her curtsy, she leans too close and those elegant plumes tickle poor George's nose. He proceeds to sneeze, popping every last button off his waistcoat." Ned shrugged. "Of course, that might not have happened if he hadn't been poured into it like an overripe pork sausage."

"The poor girl can hardly be blamed for the king's gluttony," Hayden pointed out.

"A sentiment the fair-minded George apparently shared, for much to everyone's relief, especially the young lady's, he simply burst out laughing. While the royal guard scrambled around on hands and knees to retrieve the buttons, George spotted a particularly tantalizing glint of gold himself. Unfortunately, it was buried deep in the hallowed and heretofore unbreached recesses of Miss Fairleigh's bodice."

"Oh, hell," Hayden muttered, resting his elbow on the arm of the chair and covering his eyes with his hand as if to ward off what was coming.

"Well, when the intrepid Miss Fairleigh felt that pudgy little hand groping between her nubile young breasts, she defended her virtue as only a true lady can."

Hayden peeked at Ned between his fingers. "Please tell me she didn't slap him."

"Of course not." Ned's grin spread. "She bit him."

Hayden slowly lowered his hand. "She bit the king?"

"Quite savagely, I'm told. It took three guards to pry her pearly little teeth out of his arm."

Despite his scowl, there was an unmistakable twinkle of amusement in Hayden's eyes. "I'm surprised she didn't end up in the Tower."

"If not for the impassioned intervention of her guardian, she might very well have. Which is exactly why Devonbrooke waited until George's ill health drove him into seclusion at Windsor before placing her back on the marriage mart. From what I hear, the girl has always been something of a wild child, given to much mischief and bluestocking notions about women in the arts." Ned waved the cigar. "But if you didn't compromise her, then I fail to see why any of this should matter to you."

"Unfortunately, her guardian doesn't share your progressive views," Hayden replied dryly. "He's procuring a special license from the archbishop even as we speak."

"Ah," Ned said, sobering abruptly. "I've heard Devonbrooke has had some experience in that area." Although it had been nearly ten years ago, the delicious scandal of the duke's own hasty wedding was still whispered about in some circles. "So am I to assume that congratulations are in order?"

"Condolences, more likely, since I'm about to be leg-shackled against my will to a child bride."

Ned chuckled. "You're barely one-and-thirty, Hayden. You're hardly in your dotage yet. I should think you'd still have the stamina to satisfy her."

Hayden gave him a dark look. "It's not my stamina I'm worried about. It's my patience. My last bride exhausted the modest amount with which I was blessed."

"But you were little more than a lad yourself when you married Justine."

And buried her.

The unspoken words hung in the air between them until Ned reached over and stubbed out his cigar. "So to what do I owe the honor of this visit? Do you mean to call me out after all? Shall I send for my second?"

Hayden rose, turning his hat over in his hands. Although he appeared ready to choke on his words, he finally managed to grind them out. "The wedding is to take place tomorrow at ten o'clock in the morning at Devonbrooke House. I thought perhaps . . . well, I've come to ask you to stand up with me."

Ned leaned back in the chair, touched in spite of himself. "Why, I would be honored!"

"Don't be," Hayden retorted, a spark of his old devilment lighting his eyes. "I had no other choice. You're the only friend I have left."

As he turned and went striding toward the door, Ned couldn't resist getting in a dig of his own. "Don't despair, Hayden. It's only until death do you part."

Hayden paused in the doorway, but didn't turn around. When he finally went marching past the gaping butler to the front door of the town house, it was with Ned's laughter ringing after him.

"Lord Death," Lottie repeated thoughtfully, everything but her topknot of curls disappearing behind a copy of the *St. James Chronicle*. "Hmmm, that does have a nice ring to it, doesn't it? Perhaps I should title my first novel *The Bride of Lord Death*." She peered at Harriet over the top of the newspaper. "Or does *Lord Death's Bride* sound even more sensational?"

Harriet shuddered. "I don't see how you can be so glib about all of this. Especially not when you're going to *be* the bride."

The two of them were huddled together on Lottie's bed, nearly buried beneath an avalanche of newsprint. Apparently, Sterling had rescinded his "no pampering" rule, for Lottie had been allowed to languish in bed until after noon. Since awakening, her every wish and whim had been granted with astonishing speed and efficiency. A pair of footmen had delivered Harriet to her bed while a bevy of maids hovered around to prop the girl's bandaged ankle on a pillow. Cookie had plied them with all of Lottie's favorite sweets, including scrumptious little heart-shaped French cakes soaked in rum and honey. Even George had popped his head in the door to volunteer himself for a game of whist should they grow bored with poring over the newspapers and scandal sheets that continued to arrive with amazing regularity, their ink barely dry. Lottie might have enjoyed all the attention were it not for Cookie's fretful "tsking" and the other servants' pitying sidelong glances.

Instead of having become engaged to a wealthy marquess, one would think she'd been stricken with a fatal disease. She was beginning to understand how a condemned man must feel when presented with a sumptuous banquet just prior to his march to the gallows.

Which was exactly why she'd decided to put on a brave face. She refused to feel sorry for herself when everyone else was taking such morose satisfaction in pitying her. She might have disgraced Sterling during her debut, but she had no intention of disgracing him during her wedding. If it was to the gallows she must go, then she would go with head held high. Fortunately, Harriet was too caught up in the melodrama of the situation to realize just how brittle Lottie's good cheer was.

Tossing aside the *Chronicle*, Lottie plucked the last French cake from the tray resting on Harriet's lap. "I must confess that it's rather unsettling to be reading about myself as the tragic heroine of my own story." She licked a drizzle of honey from her upper lip. "Perhaps I should simply consider my impending nuptials as research for my first novel. A chance to delve into the shadows of the marquess's heart and solve the mystery of his first wife's demise."

"That's all very well and good," Harriet said glumly, "but who's going to solve the mystery of his second wife's demise?"

Shooting her friend a chiding glance, Lottie swept up the afternoon edition of *The Whisperer*. "Oh, this is rich. The article describes our desperate, secret love for each other and paints Sterling as the heartless villain seeking to keep us apart."

"How terribly romantic!" Harriet exclaimed, pressing a hand to her heart.

"How utterly ridiculous." Lottie snapped the pamphlet closed, ignoring a curious pang of wistfulness. "I can promise you that the marquess harbors no love for me, secret or otherwise. Although I must admit that Sterling did look rather villainous last night when he started brandishing that pistol around." She scanned a particularly lurid account of last night's scandal in one of the cheap broadsides distributed on the docks. "Good heavens!" she exclaimed, feeling her throat heat. "According to this writer, you'd think we'd been caught *in flagrante delicto*."

"Smelling delicious?" Harriet asked, Latin having been one of her least favorite subjects, right before geography and after ladylike deportment.

Sighing, Lottie cupped a hand over her friend's ear and explained the phrase.

"Oh my!" Harriet breathed, blushing to the roots of her mousy hair. "Surely you won't be expected to do something so horrid. With *him*."

Before Lottie could elaborate, a gentle rap sounded on the door. She settled back against the mountain of pillows, hoping for more French cakes. But it was her sister, Laura, and her aunt Diana who came sweeping in, a pair of footmen trailing after them. Laura's eyes were red-rimmed from weeping, while Diana's were ringed with shadows.

Although Sterling's cousin wasn't truly Lottie's aunt, her easy affection and brisk common sense made her a natural for the title. Despite the elegant severity of her forest green gown and tightly wound chignon, the kiss Diana pressed to Lottie's brow was as tender as a mother's. "Hello, pet. If your dear Miss Dimwinkle will excuse us, your sister and I need to have a little chat with you."

"Can't Harriet stay?" Lottie asked, just beginning to realize how lost she was soon going to be without her devoted friend. Upon Hayden's insistence, the two of them were to depart for his home in Cornwall immediately after tomorrow morning's wedding.

"We'd rather she didn't," Laura replied, exchanging an odd look with Diana.

Lottie waited in curious silence as a disgruntled Harriet was borne away by the footmen. After carefully securing the door behind them, Laura sank down on one side of the bed, Diana on the other.

Diana reached over and took Lottie's hand. Fortifying herself with a deep breath, she said, "Your sister and I both feel we would be remiss if we did not seek to prepare you for the days—"

"And the nights," Laura added, blushing furiously.

"And the nights," Diana concurred, "to come."

Lottie's apprehensive gaze traveled between the two of them. Perhaps it wasn't too late to burrow beneath the pillows and feign sleep.

Diana was squeezing her fingers so hard that one of Lottie's knuckles popped. "As I'm sure you know, a woman's most cherished duty is to her husband."

"And never is that duty more cherished than on that most joyous of all occasions—her wedding night," Laura said, her bottom lip beginning to quiver.

Diana shot her a warning look. "For then comes the long awaited moment when a man and woman's *affection*," she stumbled over the word, her own impeccable composure beginning to desert her, "for one another is finally free to manifest itself in a physical manner."

"And thus will begin a tender initiation into a lifetime of commitment and hap—hap—happiness." The last word rose on a wail as Laura collapsed against Lottie's shoulder, bursting into tears.

"Oh, for heaven's sake, Laura, stop blithering!" Diana dabbed at her own overflowing eyes with her handkerchief. "You're going to frighten the poor child to death."

"There, there, now," Lottie murmured, squeezing her aunt's hand and stroking her sister's fine brown hair. "There's really no need for a lecture on the rigors of earthly love. I did grow up on a sheep farm."

Lottie knew her sister and aunt were probably thinking about how her marriage bed would differ from their own. They had both been blessed with husbands who adored them, a luxury she would never know. Instead, she would be expected to go willingly into the bed of a stranger—a man who bore her no long-standing affection, a man who had been coerced into a marriage he did not want to a woman he did not know, a man whose animal passions might very well override his tenderness. The thought of Hayden St. Clair on top of her, inside of her, awakened a dark thrill deep inside her soul, the shadow of an emotion that frightened her even more than he did.

Diana swiped away the last of her tears, determination sharpening her features. "There are things you can't learn on a sheep farm, my dear. Things that can bend even the sternest and most intractable of men to your will."

Lottie leaned toward her aunt, suddenly giving the woman's every word her rapt attention. Laura jerked up her head, so scandalized, her tears dried up mid-sob. "Diana, surely you can't mean to . . ."

"I most certainly do. If Lottie is to march into this enemy's camp to do battle, then she'll not go unarmed. And you and I know just the weapons to give her."

From the mournful mood hanging over Devonbrooke House the next morning, one would have thought its residents had gathered to witness a funeral instead of a wedding. Laura and Diana huddled together, handkerchiefs at the ready, while Thane and George stood side by side, their posture nearly as rigid as their expressions.

Rather than wearing black as the drollest of the scandal sheets had suggested, the bride wore pink. There had been no time to consult a seamstress, so Laura and Diana had helped Lottie choose a rose satin gown draped with an overskirt of ivory lace from her extensive wardrobe. To hide the trembling of her hands, she clutched a posy of purple hyacinths Cookie had hastily plucked from the house's courtyard garden. Cookie's teardrops still shimmered like dew on the velvety petals.

Lottie nearly popped the blooms off the hyacinths when Hayden St. Clair appeared in the arched doorway. He was accompanied by a tall, slender gentleman whose short-cropped blond hair was tinted more silver than gold.

As the men took their places before the marble hearth that was to double as an altar, the stranger boldly assessed her, then winked at her. Caught off

guard by the impish charm of the gesture, Lottie
nearly returned it before remembering to scowl back
at him. It would hardly do for her bridegroom to
think she was engaging in a flirtation right beneath
his nose. She might not even make it to Cornwall
alive. She could already see her family weeping over
his hastily scrawled note informing them of her
tragic demise after the train of her gown became entangled in the spokes of his carriage wheels.

A lone violin sobbed out a melody, Lottie's cue to
take her guardian's arm and allow him to escort her
to her bridegroom's side. She took a deep breath. If
this was indeed her march to the gallows, then the
time had come to face her executioner.

Garbed all in black except for the crisp white of
his shirtfront, cuffs, collar, and cravat, Hayden St.
Clair looked even larger and more imposing than
she remembered. She was touched to note that he'd
made some effort, however futile, to tame his unruly
hair. Without the stubble shadowing the hollows of
his cheeks and the curve of his jaw, he looked closer
to George's age than Sterling's.

As Lottie drew nearer to him, a thousand tiny
heretofore unnoticed details reminded her that he
was a stranger to her: the nearly imperceptible cleft
in his chin, the thin white scar just below his left ear,
the faint shadow above his upper lip even the keen-
est of razors would never dispel.

As she took her place at his side, she almost
wished her aunt and sister had kept their counsel.
Although her insatiable curiosity had driven her to

drink in their every word, she could hardly imagine doing some of the shocking things they had described with this man.

Or *to* him.

She lowered her eyes, hoping he would attribute her blush to maidenly modesty.

When the bishop commanded Sterling to give her hand into her bridegroom's keeping, Lottie had to tug her small hand out of his possessive grip.

The pleasant smile frozen on Sterling's face never wavered, not even when he leaned close to Oakleigh and growled in a voice audible only to the three of them, "If you break her spirit, I'll break your neck."

As Lottie and Hayden knelt before the bishop, her bridegroom's hand was warm and dry, his voice deep and unwavering as he vowed to forsake all others, keeping himself only unto her so long as they both should live. As Lottie echoed the lyrical words, she could not help but wonder if he was thinking of another woman who had made the same promise, only to betray both it and him.

The rest of the ritual passed in a blur. Before Lottie knew it, the bishop was closing the Book of Common Prayer and instructing them to rise. His eyes twinkling behind their wire-rimmed spectacles, he gave her new husband permission to seal their vows with a kiss.

Under the pretense of offering Hayden her cheek, Lottie whispered, "I'm sorry I got you into such a dreadful fix."

"I'm just grateful you found my attentions more

tolerable than the king's," he murmured, his breath warming the sensitive shell of her ear. "At least you didn't bite me."

Lottie drew back to gape up at him, so shocked she forgot to whisper. "Who on earth told you—"

Before she could finish, her husband's lips descended on hers, silencing her with a kiss.

Chapter 6

Dared I hope for some shadow of tenderness from such ruthless hands?

WHEN HAYDEN EMERGED FROM THE STRAINED wedding breakfast hosted by his new brother- and sister-in-law, it was to discover his carriage so weighted down with trunks, boxes, valises, and bags that it was nearly unrecognizable. An army of liveried footmen was still swarming all over it, securing endless lengths of rope and seeking any overlooked nook or cranny into which they might stuff another parcel or case.

"Good heavens, man," Ned said, eyeing the sagging struts. "Your new bride certainly doesn't believe in traveling light."

"Her guardian already sent two baggage carts ahead of us." Hayden shook his head disbelievingly. "If I hadn't sent my own servants with them in another coach, I would have had to hire an extra team of horses just to get us out of London."

"Isn't that . . . ?" Ned pointed to the contraption strapped upside down at the very peak of the mountain of luggage.

Hayden squinted at what appeared to be the wooden wheels of a hobbyhorse—the trendy new conveyance invented by a German baron to propel himself around the paths of the royal gardens. "Yes, I do believe it is."

Lottie emerged from the house at that minute, staggering beneath the weight of a woven basket three times as big around as she was. Hayden moved to relieve her, but she quickly wrestled the basket out of his reach.

"There's no need to trouble yourself. I can manage quite nicely, thank you," she insisted, huffing and puffing her way to the carriage. She'd been eyeing him suspiciously ever since he'd mentioned her ill-fated encounter with the king.

An alert footman swept open the carriage door, allowing her to heave her burden onto one of the seats. Hayden peered over her shoulder, fascinated by the mysterious "mmmrrrwwwing" sound that seemed to be coming from the basket.

Although he was completely at a loss as to where they would find another inch of space, he suggested, "Perhaps we should have the footmen tie it on top."

The basket growled, shuddered, and made a little hop, as if in protest.

Lottie stepped back and slammed the coach door in his face. "That won't be necessary. It's my lunch."

Hayden arched one eyebrow, but did not think calling his new wife a bald-faced liar would start their marriage off on an auspicious note.

She had changed into a bottle-blue carriage dress topped by a collar of stiff white lace and a fur capelet. Her topknot of curls was gone, replaced by a tidy cloud of ringlets and a wide-brimmed straw hat crowned with a towering array of crepe, ribbons, and tiny silk rosebuds. He supposed she'd chosen the sophisticated style to make her appear more matronly, but she looked more like a little girl playing dress-up in her mother's clothes. She certainly didn't look old enough to be any man's wife.

Especially his.

"Wait, Lottie! You forgot Mr. Wiggles!"

Hayden stood aside as Miss Dimwinkle came limping out of the house, a squirming black cat held at arm's length.

Lottie accepted the offering, draping the furry little beast over her arm like a live muff. "You don't mind if I bring my cat, do you?" she asked him, a curious flush staining her cheeks.

"Of course not," Hayden assured her. "I'm sure he'll feel right at home at Oakwylde. The barns are overrun with mice."

"The barns?" Lottie echoed, a dangerous glint appearing in her eye.

Before she could say anything more, the rest of her family emerged from the house. Lottie's guardian looked as if he was already regretting trusting his precious ward into Hayden's hands. Devonbrooke doubtlessly would have liked nothing better than for them to spend their wedding night beneath his roof. But Hayden had no intention of remaining under the man's thumb for a minute longer than was necessary. One untoward moan from Lottie's luscious lips and the duke would be calling for his dueling pistols again.

As his bride's brother, sister, aunt and uncle, and even the servants thronged around her, smothering her in a noisy round of hugs and kisses, Hayden stepped back into the shadow of one of the portico columns. In their eyes he knew he would never be anything but an interloper—the wicked ogre who had spirited away their beloved fairy princess.

As Hayden moved back, Ned started forward. Hayden clapped a hand on his friend's shoulder. "Just where do you think you're going?"

"Why, to kiss the bride, of course! As your groomsman, I consider it my sacred duty."

"Over my dead body," Hayden retorted. "Or yours if my bride discovers that you're the one who shared that little snippet of gossip about the king."

Conceding defeat, Ned leaned against the column. "If her teeth are as sharp as her wits, our monarch is lucky to be alive."

Lottie was keenly aware of her husband's retreat, but before she could draw him back into their circle, Harriet threw her arms around her in a crushing embrace, earning a protesting squeak from the cat.

Tears fogged up the thick lenses of the girl's spectacles. "I so wish I could come to Cornwall with you! I haven't any prospects of my own, you know. Who's going to want to marry a plain, dull-witted magistrate's daughter with no fortune to speak of?"

"Don't be silly," Lottie chided her. "By the end of the Season, you'll be writing to tell me you've received a dozen offers and can't decide whose heart to break first." Handing the cat off to her brother, Lottie held her own handkerchief to the girl's nose and ordered her to blow.

Shooting Hayden a narrow look, George leaned over and whispered, "If the two of you don't suit, you can always poison him, you know."

In spite of her jangled nerves, Lottie's lips twitched. Neither one of them had forgotten the time a jealous ten-year-old Lottie had tried to permanently remove Sterling from Laura's life by baking deadly toadstools into his cake.

"Given the marquess's reputation, he's more likely to poison me," she informed George from the corner of her mouth.

Her brother gave her shoulder a heartening pat. Although their relationship had always been a prickly mix of exasperation and affection, he probably knew her better than anyone. And loved her in spite of it. Although she knew it would mortify him, Lottie flung her arms around his neck. To her surprise, he didn't duck her kiss, but returned it with a hard squeeze of his own.

"You should be happy for me, you know," she whispered in his ear. "It's not every day a humble rector's daughter becomes the bride of a marquess."

George tweaked one of her curls. "There's never been anything humble about you."

"Which is exactly why there's no need for you to

worry. I can make him love me if I want. I can make anyone love me, can't I?"

"Of course you can," George assured her. He reluctantly released her, his crooked smile reflecting both of their misgivings.

Then Cookie was there to press a package wrapped in waxed paper and string into her hand. From its warmth and the spicy aroma wafting to her nose, Lottie quickly deduced it was gingerbread, fresh from the oven. Although Cookie's nose was red and swollen, her smile was radiant as she enfolded Lottie in her ample arms. "That handsome rogue had best take care of my little lamb or I'll make him a batch of my crumpets, I will."

Lottie burst out laughing. Cookie's crumpets were so notoriously dry her husband had been known to use them to patch holes in the plaster.

As the maid withdrew, dabbing at her eyes with her apron, Lottie was faced with the moment she had been dreading the most. Although she had managed to retain her cheery demeanor through all the other farewells, the eyes she turned to Laura and Sterling were suspiciously bright.

The responsibility for their little family had fallen on Laura's slim shoulders when she was only thirteen years old, yet she'd never once made Lottie or George feel like a burden or a nuisance.

Laura drew Lottie into a quick, hard hug, her eyes dry but fierce. "If you ever have need of me, you have only to send word and I'll come running."

"Then you'd best keep your bags packed," Lottie replied, "for I'll always have need of you."

As Laura withdrew, seeking solace in Diana's arms, Sterling rested his hands on Lottie's shoulders. Her lips trembled upward in a smile. "I promise I'll be the best wife I know how to be. I'll make the two of you proud this time. I swear I will."

Sterling shook his head, his own smile none too steady. "You always have, poppet. You always have." As he pressed a tender kiss to her brow, the rest of her family fell into an awkward silence.

Sterling reluctantly stepped back. George handed her the cat. There was nothing left for Lottie to do but allow the waiting footman to usher her into the carriage and wait for her husband to take his place by her side.

Hayden signaled one of his own groomsmen. The man came forward, leading a handsome bay. As Hayden mounted, even his friend, Sir Ned, looked taken back.

Hayden brought the horse alongside the open carriage door. "I never much cared for the crush of a carriage," he said. "I hope you won't mind if I ride with the outriders."

"Of course not," Lottie murmured, stroking the cat in her lap. "Mr. Wiggles here should be all the company I need."

Her bridegroom despised her.

Why else would he insist on traveling league after punishing league on the back of a horse instead of in the relative comfort of the carriage if not to avoid her company? With the plush velvet squabs cushioning her from all but the worst of the road's rigors, Lottie leaned toward the window, craning her neck to catch a glimpse of her new husband. She had to admit he cut a fine figure on horseback with the shoulder-cape of his coat flapping behind him and his dark hair tossed by the wind. He was every bit as grim and dashing as the title character in her own short story "The Villainous Vicar of Vinfield Village." At the end of that tragic tale, Lottie's noble heroine had chosen to fling herself from the highest tower of the abbey ruins rather than surrender her virtue to the lecherous clergyman. Lottie could only hope such a sacrifice would not be required of her.

Her fingers itched for pen and paper to capture Hayden's image, but her writing case was packed safely away. She'd learned of the perils of writing in a moving carriage after she'd accidentally dumped an entire bottle of indigo ink down George's brand-new collar. Her brother had refused to speak to her for over a fortnight.

Fighting a wave of melancholy, she settled back in the seat. Although she'd left them many leagues and hours behind, her family's farewells still echoed in her ears. For the first time in her life, she was truly alone. Even in those first difficult years after their parents had died, she and George and Laura had always had each other. Now she had no one. The cat in her lap nudged his broad head against her palm, as if to remind her that wasn't entirely true.

She scratched his whiskered cheeks, coaxing a rumbling purr from his throat. "You're fine company, aren't you, big fellow, if not much of a conversationalist."

She tipped her head back, hoping a nap would wile away the long hours still to come. But before she could close her eyes, a glint of brass beneath the opposite seat caught her eye. She leaned forward, catching a glimpse of burnished leather banded by shiny brass. It was the trunk she'd seen in Hayden's study, the one he had hastened to close the moment she had walked into the room. Whatever its contents were, he had refused to trust them to the care of his servants or to the elements outside the carriage.

Wondering what could possibly be so precious to a man who was rumored to hold so very little dear, Lottie stole a look out the window. Hayden was riding well ahead of the coach in an easy lope, his broad shoulders braced against the wind.

She would not succumb to temptation, she told herself sternly, folding her gloved hands in her lap. She was a lady now, a marchioness. And a marchioness would never stoop to snooping, no matter how tantalizing the mystery that presented itself.

" 'Virtue is its own reward. Virtue is its own reward,' " she muttered to herself. Perhaps if she quoted Miss Terwilliger's favorite proverb often enough, she would begin to believe it.

As if to test her resolve, a shaft of sunlight pierced the clouds and came streaming through the carriage window, transforming the glint of brass into the beckoning gleam of gold. Lottie bit her lip and moaned beneath her breath. Had she been Percival himself, the Holy Grail could have looked no more enticing.

Dumping the startled cat on the seat beside her,

she scrambled to her hands and knees on the carriage floor. She tugged eagerly at the small trunk, sliding it out of its hiding place. She ran her hands over the banded lid, but it took no more than a cursory examination to determine that it was locked.

Having had a fair amount of experience wiggling her way into places she hadn't been invited, Lottie simply plucked a hatpin from her bonnet and went to work on the lock. She was so engrossed in her task that she didn't realize the vehicle had ceased its rocking or that the carriage door had swung open until someone just behind her cleared their throat with a distinctly masculine edge.

She froze, only too aware that her new husband was enjoying an unfettered view of her backside. Thankful for her voluminous skirts, she gave the trunk a hasty shove, sliding it back beneath the seat.

Holding up the pin, she smiled at Hayden over her shoulder. "I dropped my hatpin. But I found it."

"That's fortunate," he drawled, eyeing the colorful tower of ribbons and flowers affixed to her head. "We certainly wouldn't have wanted you to lose that hat."

Before he could say anything more, he was distracted by the sight of the ginger-colored cat reclining on the seat like a plump pasha enjoying a chariot ride.

He frowned at the cat. "That's odd. I would have sworn your cat was black."

Rising to slide into the opposite seat, Lottie shrugged. "It must have been a trick of the light. If he was black, I never would have named him Pump-kin, now would I?"

"Pumpkin?" Hayden's eyes narrowed further. "I thought his name was Mr. Wiggles."

"And so it is," she replied without missing a beat. "Mr. Pumpkin Wiggles."

The cat indulged himself in a long, languorous stretch, looking far too fat and lazy to have ever wiggled.

Blowing out a deep breath, Hayden reached beneath his collar to rub the back of his neck. "We've stopped at a coaching inn to change teams. I thought you might care for some refreshments." He nodded toward the basket on the seat next to her, a wicked light dawning in his eyes. "Unless, of course, you'd rather share your lunch with me."

"Oh, no!" Lottie scrambled for the door. "I'll save it for tea. Cookie only packed enough for one."

She accepted the hand he offered her, feeling the warmth of it even through her glove as she stepped down from the carriage. She was almost to the door of the inn before she realized he wasn't following.

She turned. "Aren't you coming?"

He was still gazing into the carriage, his expression thoughtful. "No, I don't believe I will. I seem to have lost my appetite."

When Lottie returned to the coach a short while later, determined to sneak the basket out for a brief respite while Hayden was occupied in the stables, both the basket and Pumpkin were right where she had left them.

But the trunk was gone.

* * *

Lottie tried not to think of the night to come. But when the shadows of dusk came drifting over the hedgerows, painting the swiftly passing meadows in shades of lavender and gray, she could no longer pretend the day or her innocence would last forever. When they reached the coaching inn where they were to spend the night, she would be expected to go to her husband's bed, just as countless brides before her had done.

By sending the servants ahead, he had ensured their privacy. There would be no valet to prepare his bath, no maid to help her undress. Perhaps he planned to attend to that task himself. She could only too easily imagine him slipping the pearl buttons that lined her bodice from their moorings, easing the fabric apart to expose the delicate lace of her chemise, the pale swell of her breasts.

Or perhaps he would wait until she was already in bed, extinguish the candles, and come to her out of the darkness. He might lift her nightdress to her waist—gently if he was a patient man, roughly if he was not—then climb atop her and . . . and . . .

Despite Diana's and Laura's thorough tutoring, Lottie still could not bring herself to follow that image to its inevitable conclusion. When they had informed her that there would be far less pain and far more pleasure if her bridegroom took the time to make her ready for him, she had quipped that perhaps they should be having their conversation with him instead of her.

Her aunt and sister had also felt compelled to

warn her that they'd heard tell of men who were quite primitive in their lovemaking. Men who would climb atop their wives, rut them like a ram turned loose in the sheep pen, then roll off of them and collapse in a snoring heap. Understandably, their wives were more likely to consider the marriage bed an unpleasant duty to be endured, not enjoyed. If Hayden turned out to be such a man, they'd given Lottie several suggestions to woo him to tenderness, to offer him pleasure so that he might be coaxed into pleasuring her in return. An array of shocking, yet undeniably seductive, images danced through her head, making it ache. Lottie rubbed her brow, wondering how she could possibly remember all that they had told her. Perhaps she should have taken notes.

She was having no trouble remembering how masterfully Hayden's broad fingers had stroked her nape, how his tongue had glided like warm honey over her parted lips and into her mouth. She was almost more afraid that her husband would have no need of instruction. That he would know exactly what wicked deeds to perform and which soft, secret places to touch to bring her to a place where she could deny him nothing.

Rocked by a shiver, Lottie hugged her capelet tighter around her shoulders. It was full dark now and still the carriage showed no sign of halting. As the moon rose in the sky, they passed one inn, then another, their welcoming lights fading back into the night as swiftly as they'd emerged.

Although Lottie was determined to remain vigilant, the soothing purr of the cat in her lap and the relentless rocking of the carriage soon lulled her into a dreamless sleep.

As the beckoning glow of the Alder Tree Inn came shining through the trees, Hayden reluctantly signaled the outriders and coachman. He'd had every intention of driving himself to the ragged edge of exhaustion, but the horses did not deserve to share the same fate.

The coach rolled to a halt in the yard of the cozy little inn. Rubbing sleep from their eyes, the inn's post boys came loping out of the stable to unhitch the carriage team. Tossing the reins of his horse to one of them, Hayden dismounted, barely resisting the urge to groan aloud as his stiff muscles absorbed the shock of the landing. While the coachman lumbered down from his perch to swing open the carriage door, Hayden strode toward the inn, determined to secure lodgings for what little was left of the night.

The coachman awkwardly cleared his throat. "M'lord?"

Hayden turned to find the man standing beside the open door of the carriage. Warned by the pointed way he was studying his boots, Hayden warily approached the vehicle and peered inside.

Lottie was sprawled sideways on one of the plush seats, her hat askew, her lips parted in a delicate snore, and a tiny gray ball of fluff with a snowy white bib and socks nestled in the crook of her arm. Nonplussed, Hayden blinked at the sleeping kitten, but his gaze was swiftly drawn downward. The skirts of Lottie's carriage dress had ridden up to mid-calf, providing a tantalizing glimpse of gartered silk stockings and lace-trimmed pantalettes. Prodded by the rush of raw heat to his groin, Hayden was forced to admit that his efforts to exhaust himself had failed miserably. He could ride to hell and back and still not be unmoved by such a sight.

But he had succeeded in exhausting Lottie. The dim glow of the carriage lamp only accentuated the dark smudges beneath her eyes. Hayden muttered a curse under his breath. He'd shown more concern for the horses than for his bride. He should have realized the grueling pace he'd set would eventually take its toll.

Although the dewy flush of her skin and the hand curled beneath her chin made her look like a little girl, the rhythmic rise and fall of her gently rounded breasts reminded him that she was no child. She was a woman.

His woman.

He stiffened, wondering where that traitorous thought had come from. If his seven years with Justine had taught him anything, it was that no one could ever truly possess another human being. The tighter you tried to hold on, the more you had to lose.

"Shall I wake her, m'lord?"

Hayden jerked down the hem of Lottie's pelisse, having nearly forgotten the coachman standing at his elbow. That would be the prudent thing to do.

Let the man rouse her while he made provisions for their lodgings.

"That won't be necessary," he heard himself saying. He handed the kitten to the coachman before reaching to gather his bride in his arms.

Chapter 7

*As I caught my first glimpse of his fortress, I realized
I had wed the Master of Hell himself . . .*

AS HAYDEN CARRIED LOTTIE THROUGH THE
common room of the inn, she settled deeper into his
chest and curled her arms around his neck. The
innkeeper's wife, already garbed in dressing gown
and nightcap, had bustled ahead of them to light a
fire in her finest chamber while her beaming husband had informed him that it wasn't every night
they had the privilege of playing host to a gent and
his lady. The woman was waiting in the doorway,
candlestick in hand, when Hayden reached the top
of the stairs. He slipped her an extra pound note to
ensure they would not be disturbed until morning
and she left them alone with a wink that was dis-
armingly girlish despite the snowy white braids that
dangled to her rump.

Hayden kicked the door shut, then tugged off Lottie's hat and gently laid her back on the bed they were to share. Like the rest of the inn, the quilt beneath her was faded, but clean. She sank into the feather tick with a sigh, but refused to relinquish her grip on his neck until Hayden gently reached around and unfastened her arms. Making a disgruntled face, she turned her cheek to the pillow and murmured something about French cakes and Mr. Wiggles, all without ever opening her eyes.

Hayden took a step backward, warily eyeing her fully clad form. Perhaps he shouldn't have been so hasty to dismiss the innkeeper's wife.

It wasn't as if he was a stranger to the mysterious web of laces, buttons, ribbons, and silk that comprised a female's attire. He'd undressed his fair share of them before falling beneath Justine's spell.

Shrugging away his misgivings, he tugged off Lottie's fur capelet and dainty half-boots, then slipped the pearl buttons of her carriage dress out of their moorings one by one. As he reached beneath her chemise to loosen the constricting laces of her corset, he reminded himself that he had every right to do so.

So why did he still feel like the worse sort of lech?

Despite Lottie's bravado, everything about her seemed smaller than him. Her vulnerability stirred a long dormant desire to protect. He had tried to protect Justine. He had failed.

The side of his palm brushed the gentle swell of one creamy breast. His gaze drifted to her face. As he freed her from the pressure of the whalebone stays, her lips parted in a blissful sigh.

Hayden's own mouth went dry. He remembered just how sweet those lips could taste. How tender and yielding they'd felt beneath his own. He wanted to taste them again, to dip his tongue between those ripe coral petals and steal a sip of nectar.

But it wouldn't be stealing, he reminded himself grimly. He had every right to claim her kisses and so much more. There would be no overprotective guardian to stop him should he choose to slide his hand beneath the skirts of her carriage dress and seek out the narrow slit in the silk of her pantalettes. No scandal sheet reporter to denounce him for breaching both the silk and her tender body until his questing fingers coaxed forth a nectar even hotter and sweeter than her lips could provide, until her breathless sighs deepened into moans and her thighs fell apart in invitation. No gossipmongers to whisper rumors and lies about him for pushing her skirts to her waist and covering her pleasure-wracked body with his own.

He should have made her his mistress instead of his wife. If he had, there would have been no danger of her delving into his past or his heart. Cursing himself as the worst sort of fool, Hayden leaned forward until his mouth brushed the softness of Lottie's skin.

Lottie rolled to her side, a satisfied sigh escaping her lips. Perhaps Sterling was going to let her sleep past noon again or at least until Cookie came banging on her bedroom door with a tray of warm rolls and a pitcher of hot chocolate. She burrowed deeper into her pillow, hoping to return to the hazy sweetness of her dreams. She vaguely remembered strong arms lifting her as if she were weightless, a broad chest cradling her cheek, warm lips brushing first her brow, then her parted lips with delectable tenderness.

Her eyes flew open. The milky light of dawn poured through the warped glass of an unfamiliar window. Rough-hewn beams lined the walls and served as rafters for the plastered ceiling. She could have been in any room in any inn anywhere between London and Cornwall. The last thing she remembered was being lulled into a drowsy stupor by the rocking of the carriage. Blinking the fog of sleep from her eyes, she struggled to separate dream from reality.

She would almost swear those strong arms had belonged to her husband. But Hayden could just as well have ordered the coachman or one of the stable boys to perform the onerous task of carrying her to bed.

She drew in a deep breath. The aroma of bayberry clung to her skin. It was his scent. Enveloping her. Intoxicating her. Marking her as his own.

Lottie slowly rolled over, biting her lip so she wouldn't scream if she found a tousled dark head on the pillow next to her.

The bed beside her was cold and empty. She was alone.

She sat up and buried her face in her hands, torn between relief and mortification. She had slept through her own wedding night, putting all of Laura and Diana's marvelous tutelage to a shameful waste. What an utter ninny her husband must think her!

But what about the kiss? Had that been a dream or a memory? As she touched her fingertips to her lips, she was struck by an even more startling thought.

What if she had slept through more than just the night?

Fighting panic, she peered around her. The tumbled bedclothes revealed nothing. She'd always been a restless sleeper, given to flinging legs and arms in every direction and churning her blankets into a storm-tossed sea. She slowly lifted the edge of the quilt and peeked beneath. Although her dress, shoes, and corset were gone, she still wore her chemise, pantalettes, and stockings.

"I can't decide what's more insulting," drawled a voice that was equal parts silk and rust. "That you thought I would avail myself of a sleeping woman or that you believed you'd have no memory of it if I did."

Lottie's first instinct was to tug the quilt over her head. She forced herself to lower it instead. Hayden was standing in the open doorway, leaning against the doorframe. With typical perversity he had chosen that moment to look as if he'd just stepped out of a gentleman's fashion plate. Although he could have never been mistaken for the dandy Sir Ned was, his cravat was neatly knotted and his waistcoat pressed. A pair of buff trousers hugged his lean hips. His jaw was freshly shaven, his hair damp from a recent wetting and slicked back from his brow. His sudden inclination toward tidiness only made Lottie's own dishabille seem more tawdry.

Shaken that he'd divined her thoughts so accurately, she clutched the quilt to her chest, glaring up at him through a tangled skein of hair. "My dress seems to have gone missing. I was just making sure that I hadn't lost anything else of value as well."

"You were utterly exhausted last night so I asked the innkeeper's wife to help you out of your garments." He nodded to a ladder-backed chair in the corner draped with a faded blanket. "I slept over there."

Lottie winced. The chair must have been excruciatingly uncomfortable, especially after a hard day spent in the saddle. "So you were the one who carried me in?"

He nodded. "Fortunately, it was well after midnight and there were only a few stragglers in the common room. It would hardly do for rumors to reach London that I'd strangled my bride before the wedding night could even commence."

She narrowed her eyes at him, but it was impossible to tell if he was mocking her or himself. He still hadn't answered all of her questions. He might not rob a sleeping woman of her virtue, but would he steal her kiss? Or had that provocative brush of his mouth against her parted lips been nothing more than a dream?

He straightened. "If you'd like, I'll send one of the maids up to help you dress. I thought you might wish to breakfast in the common room." He arched one eyebrow. "Unless, of course, you'd prefer to dine on the basket Cookie packed for you."

"The basket? The basket! Oh, no, I forgot about the basket!" Heedless of her state of undress, Lottie threw back the blankets.

Betraying his first sign of alarm, Hayden crossed the room in two long strides and tossed them back over her. "There's no need to panic. Pumpkin, Mr. Wiggles, and their charming young female traveling companion are all downstairs in the inn kitchen, lapping up a saucer of fresh cream."

"Oh." Eyeing him sheepishly, Lottie settled back in the bed, hugging her knees to her chest. "I suppose I should have confided in you sooner, but I was afraid you were the sort of man who wouldn't care for cats."

"Nonsense," he said crisply. "I adore cats. They make the softest, most supple gloves."

She gasped. He was halfway to the door before she realized he *was* mocking her. At least this time. She sat up on her knees. "You must think me an ungrateful wretch. I haven't even thanked you properly for marrying me and sparing Sterling's life."

"There's no need," he replied without turning around. "I no longer believe in dueling. I would have never accepted your brother-in-law's challenge."

As a stunned Lottie sank back against the pillows, he drew the door shut behind him, leaving her with yet another mystery to solve.

*   *   *

They'd been back on the road to Cornwall for less than an hour when a chill curtain of rain began to fall from the leaden sky. Lottie opened a window of the carriage and leaned out, welcoming the sharp slap of the raindrops against her face. Now Hayden would be forced to share both the carriage and his real reasons for wedding her. Was it possible that he might actually be entertaining some sort of affection for her? That he hadn't wed her out of pity or duty, but out of desire?

As he drew his horse to a halt, her spirits soared. But he paused just long enough to drag an item from one of his saddlebags. As he shook out its voluminous folds and slipped it over his head, Lottie saw that it was an oilcloth cape, designed to shield its wearer from even the cruelest of elements. Although it left his head exposed, he simply shook the rain from his hair and rode on.

It seemed her husband preferred riding in the cold, pouring rain to spending a few meager hours in her company. Lottie sank back in the seat, wishing she could blame the stinging of her eyes on the rain.

Late that afternoon Lottie started from a fitful doze to discover a boneless Pumpkin draped across her lap. Mr. Wiggles and her gray and white kitten, Mirabella, were curled up together on the opposite seat. Now that they were no longer being smuggled like so much French contraband, the cats were enjoying the run of the carriage.

Although the patter of the rain on the carriage

roof had ceased, the sky continued to brood. Feeling overheated and out of sorts, Lottie eased the napping cat to the seat and leaned forward to shove open the window. Her breath caught in her throat.

The orderly patchwork of meadows, hedgerows, and stone fences had vanished, leaving the landscape as alien as the pitted surface of the moon. The wind wailed across the sweeping sea of grass and marsh like a chorus of ghosts, swirling around the standing stones that littered the barren moor. It was as if this place would never know the kiss of spring, but would slumber forever beneath a winter sky. Yet its very desolation gave it a sort of bleak beauty, a thrilling wildness Lottie had never encountered in the tidy squares of London or the rolling hills of Hertfordshire.

Exhilarated, she leaned into the wind. It wasn't hard to understand how Cornwall had become the stuff of legend. She could almost see the towering Cormoran striding over the standing stones as if they were pebbles, massive club in hand and Jack the Giant Killer dogging his heels. The wind carried to her ears the clash of swords as Arthur met his bastard son Mordred for the last time on the field of battle. And was that the shadow of a cloud drifting across the marsh or hordes of nasty little spriggans streaming out of an ancient burial mound, looking for a traveler to terrorize or a baby to steal?

She caught a glimpse of Hayden riding well ahead of both the carriage and the outriders. If only she were pounding along on horseback beside him instead of cooped up inside the carriage! The scent of the sea tickled her nose and it was then that she caught her first glimpse of Oakwylde Manor.

Her first impression was of brooding gray stone perched against a stark backdrop of sky. With the moor behind them and the cliffs ahead, it was as if they had truly arrived at the end of the earth.

Hayden wheeled his mount around, his powerful thighs steadying the horse's flanks. With his dark hair whipping in the wind, he seemed as much a part of this place as the vast sky and the churning sea. If this was the end of the earth, then he was its master.

As well as her own.

The carriage made a sharp turn onto a long, curving drive paved with rough stones. As Lottie tilted her face skyward, her new home loomed in her vision. Hayden might be this house's master, but she would soon be its mistress.

Even by Sterling's standards, the Elizabethan manor with its sprawling wings and central court was a grand house. Although its steeply gabled roof was peppered with a plethora of brick chimneys, only a few plumes of smoke drifted skyward to mingle with the clouds. With no sunlight to reflect, its generous expanse of mullioned windows gleamed with the dull ennui of half-shuttered eyes. The house didn't appear to be dead, but simply slumbering beneath the same dark spell as the bruised sky and the windswept moor. Lottie shivered, wondering if the sun ever shone in this place.

As the carriage rocked to a halt, the front door of the house swung open and over two dozen servants came marching out, dutifully taking their places at the foot of the front steps to welcome home their master and his new bride. Lottie wondered at their numbers. A house this size should boast a staff of at least fifty.

Shyness had never been one of her failings, but she was suddenly reluctant to emerge from the snug cocoon of the carriage. Being a marquess's bride was one thing, but taking her place as his wife was quite another. She took her time securing the cats in their basket, smoothing the wrinkles from her skirt, straightening her hat. Finally, the carriage door swung open. It wasn't the coachman or a footman extending a hand in invitation, but Hayden himself.

Pasting on a brave smile, she took his hand and descended the carriage steps. The wind whipped the maidservants' aprons into a flapping frenzy and forced Lottie to secure her hat with her other hand. As they approached the house, Hayden scanned the rows of servants, a troubled expression on his face. Aside from their scant numbers, Lottie could find nothing amiss. From the distinguished butler and tall, scrawny head housekeeper with the ring of keys at her waist to the liveried footmen and blushing, apple-cheeked maidservants, they might have been the staff of any nobleman's country estate.

"Welcome home, my lord," the butler intoned, stepping forward. "The baggage carts have already arrived and been unloaded."

"Very good, Giles," Hayden murmured, although his expression lost none of its edge.

Several of the younger maids were gaping at Lottie with open curiosity. Surely Hayden had instructed the servants traveling with the baggage carts to prepare the rest of the staff for his bride's arrival.

Hadn't he?

Before he could formally introduce her, a plump, sun-browned partridge of a woman came striding around the corner of the house. Her arrival wouldn't have been so remarkable if she hadn't been dragging a young lady of approximately ten years of age . . . by her ear.

Hayden went rigid and Lottie could not help staring. The servants all gazed straight ahead, as if this were an ordinary, everyday occurrence in their lives.

Although her jaw was set in sullen defiance, the girl didn't let out so much as a squeak of protest as her captor marched her to the front of the servants, halting her directly in front of Hayden. The woman planted her beefy hands on the girl's shoulders to keep her from bolting.

The child was tall, yet painfully thin, with sharp features that might one day be considered striking. Her mane of dark hair was the largest thing about her, framing her face like a hedgerow allowed to grow wild. Lottie's fingers itched for a comb and a ribbon, although a garden hoe and a rope might produce more satisfying results. If Cookie were here, she'd insist upon force-feeding the child a steady diet of gingerbread and plum puddings to fatten her up.

Although it appeared considerable effort had been wielded to make the girl presentable, one of her stockings had slipped down around her ankle. Her blue pinafore was rumpled and marred by grass stains while its matching ribbon had slid halfway down her back, freeing her hair to fall in her face.

There was something oddly familiar about that face. Something about the stubborn set of her jaw, the wary look in her striking violet eyes, the sulky curl of her lip . . .

Lottie shook off the fancy. Judging from her disarray, she must be one of the servants' children or perhaps an orphan adopted from some nearby village. Sterling had taken in such waifs upon occasion, providing charity and an education until they were old enough to take their place in the servants' hierarchy.

The woman beamed up at Hayden as if the jovial twinkle in her brown eyes could somehow offset the child's petulance. "Welcome home, Master Hayden. We're glad to have you back. I trust you found everything on your journey that you were seeking?" She shifted her smile to Lottie, her freckled nose crinkling.

Although the woman's familiarity caught her off guard, Lottie could not help returning the warm smile.

"On the contrary, Martha," Hayden replied, the

trace of irony in his voice unmistakable. "I found far more than I was seeking."

"We can see that," the girl blurted out, shaking the hair out of her eyes with a defiant toss of her head. "So who is she? Is she my new governess?"

Before Lottie could even react to the absurd question, Hayden drew her gloved hand into the crook of his arm. "No, Allegra. She's your new mummy."

Chapter 8

*Had his wife returned from her moldering grave
to frighten me . . . or to warn me?*

LOTTIE WOULD HAVE BEEN HARD PRESSED TO
say who looked more horrified by Hayden's announcement—she or the girl. They both gaped at
each other for a startled moment, then shifted their
disbelieving gazes to Hayden. Lottie tried to snatch
her hand away from him, but he held it fast, his profile impenetrable.

A stunned buzz had risen from the servants. Apparently, his daughter wasn't the only one caught
off guard by the news of Hayden's nuptials. One of
the maidservants even dared to giggle, only to find
herself sharply shushed by the head housekeeper.
The woman's quelling glare could have frozen a
waterfall.

Studiously avoiding Lottie's eyes, Hayden said,

"Lottie, I'd like to introduce you to my daughter, Allegra."

"Daughter?" Lottie blurted out, too flabbergasted for discretion. "You made no mention of a daughter."

The minute the words were out of her mouth, she wished she could snatch them back. Although she would have believed it impossible, the girl's expression grew even more stony. "And why would he? Since he prefers to pretend I don't exist."

Hayden's jaw tightened until it was practically a mirror of the girl's. "You know that's not true, Allegra. I just don't choose to expose you to unnecessary scrutiny."

"Because you're afraid I'll embarrass you," Allegra shot back.

"No. Because I'm afraid someone else will seek to embarrass *you*," he retorted.

Lottie felt compelled to intervene before the exchange deteriorated into a full-out row. "Now, Allegra, you mustn't be angry at your papa for not warning us of each other's existence. Had our . . . um . . . *courtship* not been such a whirlwind one, I would have had time to brush up on my *Debrett's*." Digging her nails into Hayden's arm, Lottie beamed up at him. "You simply didn't want to spoil the surprise, did you, darling?"

Allegra folded her bony arms over her chest, looking even more like her father. "I hate surprises."

"Now, young lady, I don't believe that's entirely true," Hayden said, his expression softening.

Although he could have set one of the footmen to the task, he strode back to the carriage himself and unlatched the rear boot. Resting at the very top of the deep storage compartment was the mysterious trunk that had taunted Lottie since the first moment she had laid eyes on it. While Allegra watched his return with wary indifference, Lottie bit her lower lip in anticipation.

At Hayden's command, one of the footmen stepped forward to steady the trunk while Hayden drew a small gold key from his waistcoat pocket and inserted it into the lock. Lottie and all of the servants craned their necks as he threw open the lid, displaying its contents for Allegra.

Lottie couldn't contain her gasp of delight. Instead of a severed head, nestled within the plush velvet lining was one of the most exquisite dolls Lottie had ever seen. She wore a lavender frock of dotted swiss sprigged with pink flowers, silk stockings, and a pair of dainty kid slippers. Her rich sable hair coiled around her shoulders in shimmering curls. A master craftsman had carved and painted her delicate features. A smile played around her rosebud lips, while her violet eyes seemed to twinkle with mischief beneath their lavish fringe of lashes.

Lottie's gaze slowly traveled between the doll and Allegra. Hayden had obviously gone to great trouble and expense to commission a flawless miniature replica of his daughter—not a replica of the child she was, but of the woman she might someday become.

Hayden awaited Allegra's response, so stiff Lottie would have sworn he wasn't even breathing. Allegra continued to gaze into the trunk, her expression inscrutable. The silence stretched until Lottie could no longer bear it.

"What an amazing piece of workmanship!" she exclaimed, smiling at Allegra as she reached to stroke the doll's cheek. "Why, she looks exactly like you!"

"Don't be silly," the girl said, sparing her a contemptuous look. "It looks nothing like me. It's beautiful."

With those words, she wrenched herself from Martha's grip and went pelting away, her dark hair streaming behind her. This time, no one tried to stop her. The servants either studied their shoes or stared straight ahead.

Hayden watched her disappear around the side of the house, his face no less expressionless.

Although she couldn't have said what possessed her to be so bold, Lottie gave his arm a comforting squeeze. "Don't take her words to heart, my lord. I was a very precocious child myself."

"You still are," he replied, slamming the lid of the trunk and thrusting it into her arms. Before Lottie could respond, he had turned on his heel and strode into the house.

"Don't mind the master," Martha told Lottie as she led the way up a broad, curving staircase to the third floor of the manor. "Even as a boy, his temper sometimes got the best of his tongue."

"You knew him as a boy?" Lottie asked, trailing her fingertips along the iron balustrade.

"That I did. I was his nurse, you see. His and his

father's before him. God rest his soul," the woman added, signing a cross on her ample bosom. "Being his only child and heir, Master Hayden was the apple of his papa's eye. I've often thought it a blessing that both his father and his mother passed shortly before he decided to wed that flighty French girl. The scandal probably would have killed them anyway."

A blessing for whom, Lottie wondered, eyeing the woman askance. Surely not for Hayden, who had been left all alone to face society's censure.

Martha seemed to have no qualms about usurping the head housekeeper's duties. Duties such as escorting a new bride to her chambers after she'd been soundly slighted by her groom.

Although the old woman's faded brown hair was streaked with white, she had an abundance of energy for her age. Even when she was standing still, she seemed to bustle. With her leading the charge, there was no time for Lottie to get her bearings as they traversed the winding maze of galleries and corridors, no time to examine the heavily carved mahogany cornices or faded portraits that scowled down at her from the landings. Even the footman following them was forced to trot to keep up or risk being left all alone with the trunk containing Allegra's doll and a basket of angry cats.

"Did Allegra inherit her father's temper?" Lottie asked.

Martha snorted. "Along with her mother's temperament, I'm afraid. Although there's some that might try, no one could argue that the child is a changeling."

At the end of a long corridor, the woman threw open a door, revealing a room so stuffed with trunks, hatboxes, valises and other assorted items that there was very little room left to walk.

Clucking like a mother hen, she used her broad hips to clear a path. "This is just what I feared. When the baggage carts arrived, Mrs. Cavendish, the housekeeper, had your things sent to this room because it was next to the schoolroom. I'll ring for the maids and have them removed to the marchioness's chambers immediately."

"Just where would those chambers be?"

Martha blinked at her. "Why, adjoining the marquess's, of course."

Lottie gazed around the room. From what little she could see of its whitewashed iron bedstead, cast-off furniture, and faded ivy-patterned wallpaper, it bore a comforting resemblance to the chamber she had shared with her sister in Hertfordshire before Sterling had swept them all into the lap of luxury.

"That won't be necessary, Martha," she said firmly. "I believe this chamber will suit me just fine."

It was the woman's turn to look at her askance. "Very well, my lady," she said slowly. "Then I'll have Mrs. Cavendish send up some of the maids to help you unpack."

"That won't be necessary either," Lottie assured her. She didn't believe her raw pride could withstand their giggling scrutiny. "I'm quite accustomed to looking after myself," she lied. "I can manage very well on my own."

"As you wish, my lady." Although a trace of reproach darkened Martha's nut-brown eyes, she dutifully departed, shooing the footman ahead of her.

Three hours later as the sky outside the window faded from gray to black and a shy moon came peeking out from between the scudding clouds, Lottie was still exactly where she'd claimed she wanted to be—on her own. She was perched on one of the many trunks she had yet to unpack, wearing one of her most elegant dinner dresses and awaiting a summons to supper.

After a brief romp in a small roof garden Lottie had discovered at the opposite end of her corridor, Pumpkin had laid claim to a fluffy bolster while Mr. Wiggles went exploring among the maze of luggage with Mirabella nipping at his heels. The kitten was still young enough to employ only two modes of locomotion—bouncing and pouncing. Her chief source of amusement was derived from jumping out at unsuspecting passersby and snagging their stockings, which was why Lottie kept her feet drawn up and resting on one of the trunk's hinges.

She smoothed the watered silk of her skirt. She had already changed her gown three times—no easy feat without a maid to assist her. But she'd been too proud to ring for one after rejecting Martha's earlier offer. She'd finally settled on a dinner dress with a square-cut bodice and full skirts the same shade as her eyes. Although it had taken an entire paper of hairpins and several oaths that would have made her pious father turn over in his grave, she had finally managed to wind her curls into a passable chignon, leaving only a few stubborn tendrils free to tumble about her cheeks.

She pinched a bloom of color into those cheeks, determined to look every inch the lady of the manor when her husband laid eyes on her again. He would soon see that she was no precocious child, but a woman to be reckoned with.

Her stomach rumbled. She consulted the watch suspended from the delicate gold chain worn around her neck. Surely there were more practical ways to dispatch an unwanted wife than by starving her to death. Resting her chin in her hand, she pictured Laura and Sterling's consternation when they received a package that contained nothing but her bleached bones and her husband's regrets. Given that she'd never willingly missed a meal in her twenty years of existence, at least they'd *know* it was murder.

A knock sounded on the door, startling Lottie so badly she nearly went tumbling off the back of the trunk. She rushed to the door, then paused to steady her breathing and smooth her hair before opening it, not wanting to betray her eagerness to the footman who had been sent to escort her to dinner. After all, there was no need for *her* to be nervous. Hayden was the one who should be hanging his head in shame after giving her the cut direct.

She swung open the door. It wasn't a footman, but a red-haired, freckle-faced young maid who stood there, carrying a tray laden with food and wearing an apologetic smile. "Miss Martha thought you might be hungry after your journey, m'lady."

"How very kind of her." Smiling wanly, Lottie accepted the offering.

The girl bustled around the room, lighting several tall beeswax candles and kindling the fire that had been laid in the hearth. She offered to help Lottie dress for bed, but Lottie declined and soon she was all alone again.

It seemed her bridegroom was perfectly content to let a servant see to her comfort. Perhaps somewhere in the manor in some elegantly appointed dining salon, he and his daughter were enjoying an opulent supper. Refusing to let him spoil her appetite, Lottie ate with savage relish, choking down every last bite of the freshly baked bread and hearty bean soup. Martha had even been thoughtful enough to send up a generous portion of shredded kippers and chicken for the cats. At least her heartless husband hadn't yet ordered them banished to the barn. Or summoned his tailor to measure him for three new pairs of gloves.

After she'd eaten, Lottie tore down her chignon and struggled her way out of the dinner dress, carelessly ripping an expensive tatting of Venetian lace from the hem. She dug through the trunks one by one until she finally located the one that contained her nightclothes.

Resting on top was a gown she'd never seen before. As she held it up to the candlelight, the diaphanous silk ran like a waterfall through her fingers, a sensual delight to the touch. It was a garment fashioned for one purpose and one purpose only—the pleasures of loving between a man and a woman.

Overcome by a wave of loneliness, Lottie pressed the gown to her cheek. She could just see Laura and Diana tenderly folding it into the trunk, along with all of their hopes and dreams for her future.

Shoving the garment deep into the trunk, she fished out one of her oldest and rattiest nightdresses. The familiar fabric enveloped her as she blew out all the candles but one and climbed into the cold, strange bed. While Pumpkin and Mr. Wiggles curled up at her feet, Mirabella hunkered down on the pillow behind Lottie, indulging in another of her favorite pastimes—biting Lottie's hair. The kitten was still so small that half the time Lottie was afraid she'd roll over and smother her and so vexatious that half the time she was afraid she wouldn't.

Lottie lay there, watching the flickering shadows cast by the firelight dance on the walls. The wind soughed mournfully around the windows, rattling the beveled panes.

Her gaze strayed to the unlocked door.

What if Hayden wasn't neglecting her, but was simply biding his time until the rest of the household fell asleep? Perhaps that was why he'd denied himself her bed at the inn last night. Perhaps he was waiting until they arrived at his kingdom by the sea where both his word and his will were law.

Now that he was finally free of the constraints of society, what if he was making his way to her room at that very moment, intent upon ravishing her? Lottie shuddered, the thought making her blood run both hot and cold. For the first time, she realized how truly at his mercy she was. Here in this place, there would be no Laura to warn her away from danger, no George to rush to her rescue, no Sterling to protect her from herself. She had only her own wits to rely on.

Throwing herself to her side, she squeezed her eyes shut, wishing desperately for sleep.

She lay there for a long time, listening to the house creak and sigh around her. She was just beginning to doze off when an unearthly wail sent her bolting upright in the bed. For a long moment, all she could hear was her heart pounding in her ears. Then the eerie cry came again, so fraught with anguish that there was no mistaking it for the wind.

As if from another, far more innocent, lifetime, Lottie heard her own voice: The Tatler *ran a very cryptic tidbit implying that his wife's ghost still roams the halls of Oakwylde Manor, wailing for her dead lover.*

She jerked the covers over her head, her teeth chattering with fright. Although she'd been reading and writing about them for most of her life, Lottie wasn't even sure she had believed in ghosts until that very moment. But it was impossible to imagine that mournful sound coming from a human throat.

She cowered beneath the blankets for what felt like an eternity before a thread of shame came creeping through her terror. She was hardly behaving like the intrepid heroine she had always fancied herself to be. If this were a Gothic novel or even one of her very own stories, the plucky young heroine would be only too eager to take up her candlestick and go exploring the menacing shadows of the gloom-shrouded manor.

Summoning every ounce of her will, Lottie threw back the blankets and slid her icy feet to the floor. Harriet might quail before the prospect of encountering a ghost in the flesh, or lack thereof, but she, the marchioness of Oakleigh, was made of sterner stuff.

Hayden wandered the deserted corridors of Oakwylde Manor like a phantom. Full dark had fallen hours ago. By now even the boldest of the servants would be safely barricaded behind the locked doors of their quarters. He would not encounter another soul until morning—at least not a living one.

He was already wondering what madness had possessed him to bring his bride to this place. He should have allowed her to set up housekeeping in the rented house in Mayfair where she could have remained safe and secure in the bosom of her family. They certainly wouldn't have been the first married couple in the *ton* to maintain separate households.

Or separate beds.

Martha's eyes had glinted with disapproval when she'd come to inform him that Lottie had rejected the marchioness's luxurious chambers in favor of a lowly bedroom near the schoolroom. When he had ordered that a hearty supper be sent to her room, along with some choice morsels for her cats, he'd almost thought the old nurse was going to defy him. What did Martha expect him to do? Starve his bride out? Or march to the east wing and drag her back to his chambers by the hair?

Martha might not realize it, but Lottie was right where she needed to be. Far away from the west wing of the house. And far away from him.

But that still didn't ease his temptation. Lottie's chamber might be out of earshot of the west wing, but it was also out of earshot of the servants' quarters. If he was so inclined, he could go to her there and take his pleasure at his leisure with no one, not even the ever-vigilant Martha, ever the wiser.

Hayden rubbed his brow, trying to clear it of the images that thought provoked. Images of Lottie's rosy limbs entwined with his own, her shimmering golden curls spread across his pillow, her generous lips parted in a gasp of pleasure.

His fantasies had only been fueled by spending most of his wedding night watching her sleep, admiring the abandon with which she had kicked at the blankets and thrown one lithe thigh over her pillow as if it were a lover. It had taken every ounce of his meager control not to drag those blankets off of her and slide into the place of that pillow. It hadn't helped his embattled resolve to know that some might consider bedding her both his right and his duty.

But he had more pressing duties, he reminded himself, as his long strides slowed outside Allegra's chamber. A thin sliver of light shone from beneath the door. Ever since she was a tiny child, his daughter had been prone to nightmares. He had ordered that a lamp always be kept burning in her bedchamber in case she woke in the night and was afraid.

Once she might have come running to him. Once she would have trusted him to chase away her monsters. But that was before he'd become one of them. He touched his fingertips to the burnished oak. He wanted to imagine her snuggled safely in her bed with her new doll tucked in her arms. But she had rejected his offering and any comfort it might have provided. He listened outside her door for several minutes, but didn't hear so much as a restless whimper.

As he turned away, determined to seek the cold comfort of his own bed, the first wild wail shattered the sleeping silence of the house.

Hayden froze, the hackles on his neck rising. Was it his imagination or was the cry louder than usual? More agonized? Angrier? Or had his fortnight in London simply sharpened his senses? Made his every nerve ending even more exquisitely attuned to the subtle nuances of loss and pain? When the second wail came, he didn't even flinch. Because he knew that as jarring as those unearthly cries were, the worst was still to come.

Someone was playing the piano. Lottie's steps faltered as the distant melody drifted to her ears, slow and haunting and sweet. At first she couldn't place the piece, but then she recognized it as the first movement of a Beethoven sonata, the one they'd began calling the "Moonlight Sonata" after his death.

The song was beautiful, yet seemed to be mourning some unspeakable loss. Lottie felt her throat tighten. For a disjointed moment, she wondered if perhaps she had never left her bed to go in search of a ghost, but had somehow drifted into a dream. A dream where she was doomed to wander the lonely corridors of Oakwylde Manor forever with only the flickering flame of her candle and that haunting melody to guide her.

Following its siren song, she glided down a curving flight of steps to the main floor. She hadn't heard a single wail since she'd come creeping out of her bedchamber, clutching the candlestick in her trembling fingers. She drifted through the moonlight-dappled entrance hall and turned to the right, wandering for several minutes until she finally found herself in a broad corridor lined on both sides with closed doors. She paused to listen, cocking her head to the side. The plaintive notes seemed to be coming from both everywhere and nowhere all at the same time. Cupping a hand around the guttering flame of her candle, she worked her way down the hall, trying each door in turn. They all opened effortlessly to her touch, revealing rooms that were dark and silent.

Just as the movement climbed to its passionate crescendo, she reached the double door at the far end of the corridor. As soon as her fingers curled around the brass doorknob, the music abruptly stopped. Lottie jerked back her hand. The silence cut a dark hole in the fabric of the night, leaving nothing but the ragged sound of her own breathing.

She slowly reached for the doorknob again, holding her breath as it began to turn. Then stopped. She gave it a sharp rattle. Nothing. The door was locked.

She slumped against it, thinking that if she were as brave as she'd always fancied herself to be, she would be feeling disappointment, not relief.

She drew in her first even breath only to find it clouded with the perfume of night-blooming jasmine, heavy and cloying. A chill draft whipped through the corridor, snuffing the flame from the candle and leaving Lottie in darkness.

She had feared being alone in the dark. But *not* being alone was far worse. She could sense a presence lurking just behind her, dangerous and feral.

A low growl came out of the shadows. "Damn you to hell! Why can't you stay where you belong?"

The candlestick clattered to the floor as a pair of hands seized her and spun her around, pinning her roughly against the door.

Chapter 9

*If I was to survive his treachery, I would have
to take matters into my own hands . . .*

THERE WAS NOTHING SPECTRAL ABOUT THE
hands that gripped her. They dug into her shoulders, radiating a raw heat that stirred the gooseflesh
on Lottie's arms more surely than any icy draft.

It took her a dazed moment to realize she hadn't
been abandoned to complete darkness. Moonlight
spun a pale web through a stained-glass fanlight set
high in the wall above the double doors. But until
her eyes adjusted, it was only enough light to reflect
the wild gleam of her husband's eyes.

Hayden looked more than capable of doing murder in that moment. With each ragged breath, his
nostrils flared and his heaving chest brushed hers.
His knee was flexed between her thighs, making escape, or even struggle, impossible. As his gaze slid
down to her trembling lips, all she could do was

hang limp in his embrace and wait for him to either kiss her or kill her.

Reason slowly returned to his eyes, chasing the shadows of madness before it. "You?" he rasped, shaking his head. When he lowered his mouth to her throat, she could only turn her head aside, helpless to resist. He nuzzled the silky flesh of her throat, breathing her in like a stallion scenting a mare he was about to mount. "I don't understand. Why are you wearing that cursed perfume?"

Lottie shook her head, her own breath growing short. He seemed to be consuming all of the air in the corridor. Instead of pushing him away, her traitorous fingers clung to the front of his shirt, drawing him even closer. "What perfume? I'm not wearing any scent at all."

He released her abruptly and took a step backward. For some reason, she felt even more vulnerable without his hands on her.

He swiped an unsteady hand over his face. "What are you doing here?" he demanded, his voice gruff. "Why aren't you in your bed where you belong?"

Lottie thought it might be a less than prudent moment to remind him that she now belonged in his bed. "I *was* in my bed. But how was I to sleep with all of that frightful noise? It was enough to wake the dead."

She regretted the words the instant she said them, but it was too late to summon them back. Although she would have thought it impossible, Hayden's face grew even more closed. "I don't know what you're talking about."

"Why, of course you do! You must have heard it. The wailing?" She waved a hand at the door behind them. "Then someone in there playing the piano as if their poor heart was breaking?"

"I heard nothing," he said flatly, refusing to so much as glance at the door.

"What about the jasmine? You can't deny that you smelled the jasmine."

He shrugged. "One of the maids must have passed through here earlier with some fresh cut blooms from the garden. I simply mistook their fragrance for your perfume."

Lottie didn't waste her breath reminding him that in this barren and windy clime, jasmine probably wouldn't bloom until June, if then. "And I suppose the wailing I heard was just the wind whistling down a crack in one of the chimneys."

"Have you a better explanation?" he asked, his gaze a direct challenge.

Lottie moistened her parched lips with her tongue before blurting out, "I thought perhaps it might be a ghost."

Hayden simply stared at her for a long moment, then snorted. "Don't be a silly goose. Despite what the scandal sheets print to sell their miserable rags, there are no such things as ghosts. What did you think?" he asked. "That my dead wife had returned from the grave to warn you away from me?"

"I don't know. You tell me. Was she given to fits of jealousy?" As Lottie surveyed the pagan beauty of his thick brows and unshaven jaw, it was hard to imagine any woman not being jealous of such a man.

"When she didn't get her way," he replied softly, "Justine was given to all manner of fits."

Shamed by his candor, Lottie pressed a hand to her still thudding heart. "It wasn't the ghost who nearly frightened me to death. It was you."

"Well, that's one method of murder no one's ever accused me of. I doubt your family would have been amused, but I'm sure the gossipmongers would have found it a novelty." He leaned against the wall, giving her a mocking glance from beneath his dark lashes. "So tell me, Carlotta, if I *had* frightened you to death, would you have come back to haunt me?"

She considered the question for a moment before nodding. "I most certainly would. But I wouldn't drift about moaning and wailing or play some pretty piece on the piano. I'd bang on the bottom of a kettle and sing all seven verses of 'My Wife's a Wanton Wee Thing' at the top of my lungs."

Her reply startled a laugh out of him. His open smile transformed his face, deepening the boyish crinkles around his eyes and restoring a wayward dimple to his cheek. As he studied her, the lingering warmth in his eyes suddenly made her acutely aware of her own appearance.

He had a rare gift for catching her at a disadvantage. While she had wanted to appear the very height of sophistication the next time they came face-to-face, here she stood in her ragged cotton nightdress and bare feet with her hair tumbling around her shoulders like a little girl's. But he wasn't looking at her as if she were a little girl. He was looking at her as if she were a woman.

"You really ought to be ashamed of yourself," she told him. "This is the second time today that you've ambushed me."

His smile faded, leaving Lottie with a keen sense of loss. He picked up a delicate vase from a marble-topped pier table, turning it over in his hands. "If I could have sent word of our nuptials ahead, I would have. But I didn't dare risk Allegra finding out I'd taken a wife from one of the servants. She would have run away before we even arrived." He spoke as if that were a common occurrence.

"Why didn't you tell *me* about *her*? Were you afraid I'd run away as well?"

"Would you have?"

"I don't know," she responded truthfully. "But I do know that I might have handled the situation with a bit more grace if you had warned me that I was to become a mother as well as a wife."

"If you'll recall, when we met I wasn't looking for either."

What Lottie recalled was that moment in Mayfair when he had turned to look at her in front of the fire. Whatever he'd been looking for, in that moment she would have almost sworn he'd found it. If the woman from Mrs. McGowan's had arrived a few minutes before she had, would he have looked at her the same way? Would he have framed her pow-dered face in his hands and kissed her rouged lips as if she were some long lost piece of his soul he'd never known he was missing? Lottie wondered if he would ever look at her that way again and what she might do if he did.

He returned the vase to the table. "As you may have guessed by now, I traveled to London to seek a governess for my daughter. She's getting to be too much for even Martha to handle."

Remembering the woman's firm grip on Allegra's ear, Lottie found that doubtful.

"She's always been a difficult child, but in the past few months, she's grown utterly impossible."

"I seem to recall hearing the same thing about myself on occasion," Lottie confessed.

"Imagine that," he replied dryly.

"There are some fine establishments that specialize in making the impossible possible. Have you ever considered sending her away to school?"

"Of course I have." He raked a hand through his hair, the gesture fraught with frustration. "I'd like nothing better than to get her away from this place, this house . . ." *Me.* Lottie heard the word as clearly as if he'd said it aloud. "But she simply won't hear of it. Every time the subject is broached, she throws such a terrible tantrum that I fear for her health. Last month when I mentioned a school in Lucerne, she nearly stopped breathing altogether and the doctor had to be summoned. Which is why I decided to journey to London and take matters into my own hands." A bitter smile twisted his lips. "But thanks to the efforts of the gossipmongers and scandal sheets, I met with little success. After all, what respectable woman would accompany a man with my reputation to Cornwall?"

Lottie gazed at him, realization slowly dawning. "No respectable woman, I suppose, but perhaps one who'd lost her respectability? One whose reputation was in ruins?"

Without replying, he shifted his gaze to the shadows.

After a moment of awkward silence, she asked softly, "Why marry me at all? Why didn't you simply hire me?"

"Even with a chaperone, I could hardly bring an unmarried young woman into my home to teach my daughter." The uncharacteristic gentleness of his words only deepened their sting. "Especially one I'd allegedly compromised."

Lottie told herself she should be grateful for his honesty. At least he'd disabused her of any girlish romantic notions before she could make even more of a fool of herself than she already had.

Thankful that she'd always landed the leading role in the amateur theatricals at Mrs. Lyttelton's, she managed a brittle smile. "I'm gratified to learn that you gained something from our little marriage of inconvenience besides an unwanted bride. Now, if you'll excuse me, I'd like to get back to my bed before the wind starts whistling down the chimney again or playing the 'Hallelujah Chorus' on the piano."

As she made to brush past him, he closed his hand over her arm, tugging her to a halt. "If you expected more from our union, my lady, then I'm deeply sorry."

Gently but firmly disengaging her arm from his grip, Lottie tipped her head back to meet his gaze. "Don't be, my lord. After all, the only thing you promised me was your name."

*　*　*

Without so much as a candle or a ghostly melody to guide her, it took Lottie four tries to retrace her path back to her bedchamber. A wailing white lady would have been a welcome distraction, but she encountered nothing more frightening than a small, forlorn mouse who looked as lost as she felt. For the first time it occurred to her how curious it was that not a single servant had come to investigate the mysterious noises. They would all have to be stone deaf or drunk in their beds not to have heard those rending cries.

By the time she finally found her chamber, Lottie was feeling quite cross. Tripping over Mirabella, then stubbing her bare toe on one of the unpacked trunks hardly improved her temper. She had no right to be angry, she told herself as she limped back to the bed. Hayden had promised her his name, not his heart.

Stroking Mr. Wiggles, she huddled against the headboard and gazed into the waning flames of the fire. At least she wouldn't have to waste any more of her precious time lying around waiting for a wedding night that would never come. Hayden could deny believing in ghosts all he liked, but when he had snatched her up in his arms with that unholy light glowing in his eyes, he had only proven that his passion would never be for her, but only for his dead wife. She would never be anything more to him than a glorified governess.

Miss Terwilliger's puckered face rose in her vision. Was she to share the old woman's fate after all?

Was she to squander her youth trapped in a musty schoolroom until both her blood and her passions ran as dry as chalk dust through her veins?

Her own eager words to her family came back to haunt her: *I don't have to be a wife or a governess. Why, I could be a writer just as I've always dreamed! All I would require is some ink, some paper, and a small cottage by the sea somewhere.*

Lottie sat up, gripped by a new excitement. Wasn't a mansion by the sea preferable to a humble cottage?

Even among the room's chaos, it didn't take Lottie long to find the small leather case she was seeking. Her movements brisk with determination, she unpacked paper, pen, and a brand-new bottle of ink. After stirring up the fire and lighting a fresh candle, she settled herself before the rosewood writing desk in the corner, a purring Pumpkin in her lap.

She nibbled on the end of the pen for a minute, then scrawled, THE BRIDE OF LORD DEATH *by Carlotta Anne Fairleigh* across the top of the paper, finishing her name with a majestic flourish. After another moment's contemplation, she drew a bold line through the whole thing and wrote just beneath it LORD DEATH'S BRIDE *by Lady Oakleigh*. If her husband had nothing to offer her but his name, then she might as well make use of it. Every publisher in London would be clamoring for such a manuscript. Even Miss Terwilliger would no longer be able to deny her talent.

Mercilessly squelching a pang of conscience, Lottie drew a clean page in front of her. It took no feat of imagination to conjure up Hayden's face in that moment when he had pinned her against the door, both his eyes and his hands blazing with passion. Her pen all but flew across the page as she wrote, *I'll never forget the moment I first laid eyes on the man who planned to murder me. His face was both terrible and irresistible, its dark beauty reflecting the blackness of his soul . . .*

Chapter 10

If he was the Master of Hell, then I was now its mistress . . .

LOTTIE DECIDED THE NEXT MORNING THAT IF it was a governess her husband wanted, then it was a governess he would have. Scorning the shimmering rose poplins and rich blue velvets that she adored, she unearthed a silvery gray morning gown from one of the trunks. By ripping away the striped sash and popping off the silk rosettes that trimmed the hem, she created a frock as unrelentingly gray and stark as the sky outside her window.

She tugged her hair into a painfully tight chignon, ruthlessly stripping it of its curls. Not a single tendril was allowed to escape.

She surveyed her reflection in the cheval glass that stood in the corner, her generous lips compressed into a stern line. All she needed was a pair of wire-rimmed spectacles and a fat hairy mole on her chin and she might be mistaken for Miss Terwilliger. She looked quite ancient—at least twenty-four.

While she waited for the breakfast hour to arrive, she began to dig through her boxes and trunks. Perhaps this place wouldn't feel so strange once she surrounded herself with familiar things. She had emptied two trunks and filled every nook and cranny of the walnut tallboy in the corner when she became aware of a most curious sensation. Although she'd read about it in numerous Gothic novels and even written about it a time or two in her own stories, she'd never truly experienced it.

The hair on the back of her neck actually stood on end.

The stocking she was holding slipped through her fingers as Lottie slowly turned, wondering if she was about to come face-to-face with the ghost of Hayden's first wife.

Judging from the hair hanging in its eyes and the dirt smudging its slender nose, the creature peeping around the doorframe was definitely mortal. Sensing that her visitor was only a friendly smile away from bolting, Lottie quickly returned her attention to the trunk.

"Good morning, Allegra," she said coolly. "Would you care to come in?"

From the corner of her eye, she saw the girl sidle into the room, her feet dragging in their unlaced boots. Lottie was thankful that the first chapter of her manuscript, finished shortly before dawn, was tucked beneath a false panel at the bottom of her writing case, safe from prying eyes.

After a moment of awkward silence, Allegra blurted out, "Do you love my father?"

Lottie couldn't have said why the question gave her pause. After all, she barely knew the girl's father. While she was struggling to frame a suitable answer, Allegra scuffed the toe of her boot against the floor. "I shouldn't blame you if you didn't. He's quite insufferable."

Lottie was spared from either scolding or agreeing by Mirabella, who came bouncing out from under the bed like a rabid dust bunny. She pounced on one of Allegra's bootlaces with demonical glee.

Lottie expected Allegra to fuss and croon over the kitten just as any other little girl would have, but the child was staring at the object Lottie had just fished out of the trunk.

Lottie held up the battered doll, a fond smile curving her lips. "My sister bought her for me on her very first trip to London when I was around your age. Laura thought she looked just like me. Can you believe the poor dear was once nearly as lovely as the doll your father had made for you?"

The doll had originally sported a topknot of long golden curls, but Lottie had scorched half of them away in an overzealous session with the curling tongs. The roses in her cheeks had faded. The ruffles of her petticoat were tattered and stained, her snub nose chipped. She wore a black silk patch over one eye.

"After she lost her eye in a tragic archery accident, my brother George and I used to play pirates with her," Lottie explained. "We used to make her walk the plank out of the barn loft—hence the chipped nose."

Allegra continued to study the doll, a thoughtful expression on her serious little face. "I like her," she finally said. "Might I play with her?"

Lottie was taken aback by the bold request. But Allegra's uncompromising gaze was impossible to resist. Despite what Hayden had told her about Allegra's tantrums, Lottie got the distinct impression that the child asked for little and expected even less.

Smoothing the doll's skirt, Lottie reluctantly handed her over. "I don't suppose you can do her any more harm than I already have."

"Thank you." Without another word, Allegra tucked the doll beneath her arm and marched from the room.

Lottie arrived at breakfast to find Hayden waiting for her at the head of a mahogany monstrosity of a table long enough to hold a cricket tournament atop its gleaming surface. Devonbrooke House had boasted just such a table, but when it was only the family dining, Sterling had insisted that they gather at one end or the other, the better to enjoy each other's company and conversation. As a footman escorted Lottie to the lone chair situated at the foot of the table, she could only assume that Hayden had no interest in either.

He did have enough manners to rise when she entered the room.

"Good morning, my lord," she said primly, sliding into her seat.

"My lady," he returned, surveying her staid attire through hooded eyes.

He dropped back into his chair, drawing a watch from his waistcoat pocket. At first Lottie thought the gesture was meant to reproach her for her tardiness, but then she realized there was one more place set at the table.

Exactly halfway between the two of them.

Hayden barely had time to snap his watch shut before Allegra appeared. Instead of dragging her feet, the girl was practically skipping. She'd dressed for breakfast by pulling up one grimy stocking and smearing the dirt from her nose to her cheek. Humming beneath her breath, she made a great production of shoving one of the heavy chairs closer to her own and settling her burden into it with the tender consideration usually reserved only for the aged or the infirm.

Hayden scowled at the chair, unable to hide his consternation. "What on earth is that *thing*?"

"She's my new doll. Mummy gave her to me." Allegra turned and beamed at Lottie. The sunny smile transformed her face. For an elusive instant, she wasn't just striking, she was beautiful.

The little monster.

As Hayden shifted his gaze to Lottie, she felt her stomach sink to the vicinity of her knees. "How very generous of Mummy," he said smoothly, his eyes glittering as he lifted his cup of coffee to her in a mocking toast.

Generous indeed for Lottie to give his child a well-worn and well-loved toy to pamper while his own lovely and expensive gift moldered in her plush coffin of a trunk.

"It's just one of my old playthings," Lottie hastened to explain. "Allegra came in while I was unpacking and took a fancy to her."

The girl folded her napkin into a makeshift bib and tucked it into the doll's ruffled bodice. "Mummy said the doll looks just like she did when she was my age."

Hayden thoughtfully studied the doll's fuzzy, scorched curls, chipped nose, and pirate's patch. Despite her many travails, her remaining blue eye had never quite lost its smug twinkle, nor her rosebud lips their smirk. "I, for one," he said, "can still see a marked resemblance."

Fortunately for him, the same little red-haired maid who had brought Lottie her supper came bustling in with a steaming tureen of porridge at that moment, blocking Lottie's outraged glare. As they ate, the tense silence was broken only by Allegra's crooning as she lifted her spoon to the doll's lips to offer her some porridge. Lottie downed her own hot chocolate in a single gulp, rather wishing it was strychnine.

As Allegra polished off the last of her porridge with a satisfied slurp, her gaze traveled between Hayden and Lottie. "So how did the two of you meet?"

Lottie choked on a mouthful of kipper.

"I believe I'll let Mummy answer that question." Hayden settled back in his chair, the wicked sparkle in his eyes warning her that he was anticipating her answer nearly as much as Allegra was.

Knowing that she couldn't very well blurt out, "I was peeping through your father's window when he mistook me for a courtesan," Lottie blotted her lips with her napkin to stall for time. "Well . . . although it may seem as if we wed in haste, I was well aware of your father even before we met."

"Is he famous?" Allegra asked, blinking innocently.

"Notorious," Hayden murmured, taking a sip of his coffee.

Lottie's smile felt frozen in place. "Let's just say that he's rather celebrated in certain circles. Which is why I was so very eager to make his acquaintance."

"And was he everything you hoped he'd be?"

"And more." Lottie gave Hayden a smile dripping with acid sweetness.

"So where did you meet?"

"Actually, we met during my debut," Lottie informed the girl, trying very hard not to lie. "Just before the first waltz."

She slumped with relief as Allegra's avid attention shifted to her father. "How did you know you wanted to marry her?"

Even down the length of the table, the look Hayden gave Lottie was as intimate as a caress. "As I'm sure you can see, your stepmother's charms were such that I didn't require much persuasion."

And he hadn't, Lottie supposed. Not unless you counted the dueling pistol Sterling had leveled at his heart. She tore her gaze away from his, shaken not only by his blatant deceit, but by its unsettling effect on her. She would have to guard herself more carefully in the future. Any man who could lie to a child, especially his own, was even more dangerous than she had believed.

To her keen relief, the maid reappeared at that moment to clear away the dishes.

Allegra wiped the doll's mouth, then rose. "May we please be excused, Father?"

"By all means," Hayden replied evenly.

As she departed, cradling the doll to her shoulder as if it were a cherished babe, the maid gaped after her, too engrossed to notice when a stream of chocolate dribbled out of a cup and into Lottie's lap.

"Meggie!" Hayden said sharply.

The girl snapped out of her daze. "Oh, m'lady, I'm so sorry!" She snatched up a napkin and smeared the chocolate deeper into the expensive fabric of Lottie's skirt.

"It's quite all right," Lottie assured the girl as she struggled to wrest the sticky napkin from her fingers.

When the maid had finished her clearing and gone, Hayden leaned back in his chair, a wry smile playing around his lips. "You'll have to forgive Meggie. She's not accustomed to hearing my daughter ask permission for anything. Especially not from me."

"Once we begin our lessons, I'll do what I can to polish her manners."

"I don't give a flying fig about her manners."

Hayden slammed his coffee cup down on the table, startling Lottie with his vehemence. "I didn't bring you here to stuff Allegra's head with a lot of rot and nonsense. I want you to teach her languages and history and geography and mathematics. I want you to give her knowledge that might actually be of benefit to her if she ever has to make her way in this world alone."

"Most of society considers the grace to make a proper curtsy and the ability to fill out a dance card correctly the only knowledge necessary to snare a wealthy husband," Lottie pointed out.

"Those skills will be useless to Allegra. She'll never be able to take her rightful place in society or make an advantageous match." Bitterness edged his voice. "Her mother and I made sure of that."

"She's still several years away from her debut. Perhaps if enough time passes . . ."

His pitying gaze silenced her. "I could keep her cloistered here for the next thirty years, but when she emerged into society, she would still be known as the daughter of a cold-blooded murderer."

Lottie swallowed, not entirely sure if he was referring to the duel that had killed his best friend.

"What I want you to do is develop her mind." An odd shadow passed over his face. "I want you to make it strong. Unbreakable."

Remembering the cunning the child had exhibited by fawning over the bedraggled doll, Lottie murmured, "That shouldn't be too difficult a task."

"I just need to know that after I'm gone, Allegra will be able to look after herself. As long as I'm alive, she'll never want for anything." He studied Lottie's face, his green eyes softening to the warmth of a sunlit glade. "If you'll help me protect her, my lady, nor will you."

He might be making a promise he couldn't keep, Lottie thought after he had sketched her a bow and taken his leave. She was afraid she was already beginning to want for something she could never have.

After a meandering search of the house turned up no sign of her young charge, Lottie wandered to the basement kitchen, hoping one of the servants might know where to find Allegra. She stepped off the stairs and rounded the corner only to discover Martha and Mrs. Cavendish in a heated discussion. Although their hissed whispers probably weren't carrying to the nervous-looking maids hovering near the fireplace oven, Lottie had only to sidle near enough to read their lips.

"I don't think we should hire the girl," Mrs. Cavendish was saying. The head housekeeper's pale flesh was drawn tightly over her prominent cheekbones, giving her face a sunken look. Had she been one of their teachers at Mrs. Lyttelton's, Lottie and Harriet probably would have unkindly christened her 'Mrs. Cadaver.' "After all, what do we know of the chit, other than that she just showed up on the master's doorstep this morning begging for a position?"

"Well, I say we can't afford not to hire her,"

Martha said. "We lost three girls last month and another two last night. They fled before dawn without
even bothering to pack their belongings. If this
keeps up, it'll be just you and me looking after the
entire house by summer."

"But the girl has no letters of reference, no experience, and she's blind as a bat. When Giles answered
the door this morning, she nearly strangled him
with his own cravat because she thought it was still
the door knocker. And did you see the way she handled the broom? Why, she stirred up more dirt than
she collected! When I handed her the feather duster,
she handed it right back to me, saying that both
feathers and dust make her sneeze."

"She'll learn quick enough if she wants to eat. If
she doesn't, I'll box some sense into her ears."

Mrs. Cavendish drew herself up, her thin nostrils
flaring. "Well, I still think it's a mistake."

Looking as if she'd rather like to box Mrs.
Cavendish's ears, too, Martha hissed, "Then it's a
mistake we'll have to make. What else are we to do?
It's only bound to get worse now that he's brought
another woman into this house. Even the men are
afraid to come out of their quarters after dark. No
one wants to risk running into that frightful—"

Lottie must have made some involuntary noise,
for both women jerked around to stare at her. They
could have looked no guiltier had they been caught
nipping from a bottle of cooking sherry.

Mrs. Cavendish was the first to rush forward, the
ring of keys at her waist jingling and her thin lips

pressed into a solicitous smile. "Oh, my lady, whatever are you doing down here? If you needed something, you had only to ring."

"She's right, dearie." Martha came bustling toward her. "You mustn't forget that you're a marchioness now and old Martha here is at your beck and call."

Before Lottie could catch her breath, the women had surrounded her. Clucking and scolding, they quickly herded her out of the kitchen, leaving her no more time to wonder about the nearsighted new maid who had only sneezing fits and boxed ears in her dismal future.

Since both Martha and Mrs. Cavendish denied any knowledge of Allegra's whereabouts, Lottie decided to brave the manor grounds. As she slipped out the front door of the house, the harsh wind stung her cheeks and made a mockery of her cashmere shawl. It was hard to believe that somewhere in England, a gentle breeze was coaxing the buds on the trees into full bloom while the tender petals of the late-blooming tulips poked their way through the sun-warmed soil. Here there was only moor, wind, sea, and sky, all battling to see who would claim dominion over this barren kingdom.

Although her first impulse was to duck right back into the house, she set off at a brisk pace, still thinking about the conversation she had overheard. Despite what Hayden had claimed, apparently she wasn't the only one who had been disturbed by that mournful wailing last night. Nor was it the first time it had occurred. If it happened again, Lottie promised herself she would not go fleeing into the night like those terrified maids. She would somehow find the nerve to return to the spot where she had heard that ghostly music, even if it meant risking another confrontation with her husband.

After a search of the deserted courtyard and neglected gardens yielded nothing, she finally found Allegra perched high in the gnarled branches of an apple tree at the edge of a dying orchard. Lottie's doll lay abandoned at the foot of the tree, sprawled facedown in the dirt.

Shaking her head ruefully, Lottie brushed off the doll's chipped nose and gently propped her against the tree trunk in a sitting position. "Halloo there!" she shouted up at Allegra. "Won't you come down and talk to me?"

The child's sunny demeanor had vanished. "No, thank you," she called out, continuing to gaze toward the distant horizon. "I'm quite content where I am."

Lottie absorbed that information for a moment. "Very well, then. If you don't want to come down, then I'll come up." Having learned her lesson on the night of her debut, Lottie took the time to strip off her shawl and knot her skirts between her legs, fashioning a makeshift pair of pantaloons, before starting up the tree.

She arrived at Allegra's perch, stockings snagged and slightly out of breath, to find the girl eyeing her suspiciously. "I didn't think ladies were allowed to climb trees."

"Ladies are allowed to do whatever they like," Lottie informed her. She leaned forward, lowering her voice to a conspiratorial whisper. "As long as there's no one else about to see them."

She settled herself between two branches, torn between the curving coastline on one side and the sweeping sea of marsh grass on the other. Even with the wind snatching away each breath before she could take it, she had to admit it was a magnificent view.

Allegra continued to scowl at her. "What are you doing here? Shouldn't you be with my father?"

"Actually, your father was the one who sent me to find you. He thought that I might be able to help you with your lessons."

"I don't have lessons."

Taken aback by the child's brusqueness, Lottie said, "Well then, perhaps it's time you did. I brought some wonderful books from London—Raleigh's *The History of the World*, Linnaeus's *Philosophia Botanica*, Savigny's *History of Roman Law in the Middle Ages*."

"I don't like books."

It was Lottie's turn to look suspicious. She didn't trust anyone who didn't like books. "If you don't like books, then you've never read *Castle of Wolfenbach* by Mrs. Parsons. It was so thrilling that after I finished it, I refused to sleep without a candle burning by my bedside for over a week."

Allegra sniffed disdainfully. "Martha says that books are a waste of both paper and time and I'd be better served learning how to plant potatoes."

Horrified, Lottie couldn't speak at all for a moment. "Well, if Martha had ever read *The Midnight Bell, The Mysterious Warning,* or *The Murderous Monk,* she might not be so quick to dismiss *all* books as a waste of time and paper!" Remembering that she was supposed to be providing a model of decorum for the child, Lottie struggled to rein in her temper. "Since I haven't had any experience with planting potatoes, why don't we meet this afternoon in the schoolroom before tea for our very first lesson?"

"Very well. It's not as if I have a choice, do I, *Mummy*?" This time the name was delivered with withering scorn.

"I'm not your mummy, Allegra," Lottie said quietly, "and you needn't pretend I am."

"Then you needn't pretend to like me." The girl hugged one knee to her chest, gazing in the direction of the sea. "Nobody else does."

"I wouldn't say that's entirely true. Your father seems to like you a great deal."

"Ha! He doesn't like me. He only buys me expensive gifts like that silly doll because he pities me."

Lottie frowned, disturbed by the absolute conviction in the child's voice. "You're his daughter. Why on earth would he pity you?"

Allegra turned to look at her, her dark hair blowing in the wind. "Can you keep a secret?"

"No," Lottie responded truthfully.

Allegra rolled her eyes and went back to studying the jagged cliffs scarring the coastline. "He pities me because my mother was mad and I'm going to be mad, too."

Although she was the one who was supposed to

be giving the lessons, Lottie suddenly realized there was much she could learn from this child. She wasn't entirely surprised to learn that Hayden's wife had suffered from insanity. Surely only a madwoman would cuckold a man who could kiss like that.

"Did your father tell you that you were going to be mad?"

"Of course not," Allegra said scornfully. "He won't talk about it at all. He won't talk about anything that matters. But I hear the servants talking about it all the time when they think I can't hear. 'Poor child. She's just like her mama,' they whisper, looking at me and shaking their heads as if I'm blind as well as mad."

"Do you feel mad?" Lottie asked, studying the little girl's sullen face.

Allegra looked taken aback by the question, as if she'd never really considered it before. "No," she finally replied, blinking as if surprised by her own answer. "But I feel angry a great deal of the time."

Lottie laughed as she swung down to the next branch and began to make her way to the ground. "So did I when I was your age. Don't worry. It will pass."

Reaching the ground, Lottie shook out her skirts. She briefly considered rescuing her doll, but after a moment's thought decided to leave her to Allegra's dubious care. Draping her shawl around her shoulders, she started for the house.

"He'll never love you, you know." The wind carried Allegra's voice to her ears. "He'll never love anyone but her."

Lottie tripped over a hillock of grass. Hoping the girl hadn't witnessed her stumble, she resumed her brisk pace, muttering, "We'll just see about that, won't we?"

Chapter 11

*I soon learned that there are more frightful horrors
in this world than wailing white ladies...*

May 25, 1825

Dear Miss Terwilliger,

I am writing to express my profound sorrow for any embarrassment or distress I might have caused you during our
years together at Mrs. Lyttelton's. After much earnest
soul-searching and painful reflection, I have come to realize
that I was not nearly half as clever as I believed myself to be.

While there is a certain amount of vulgar amusement
and social cachet among one's peers to be derived from leaving livestock in a bedchamber for an indeterminate amount
of time, the cost in both personal belongings and dignity is
far too high to be borne. (You really ought to be thankful I
only left a pony! I can assure you that a goat has a much
heftier appetite, especially for silk undergarments and any
blossom or ribbon that might adorn one's favorite hat.)

I can also promise you that having the fingers of your gloves stitched together is not nearly so unpleasant as having the seams of your pantalettes tightened so that your first attempt to sit results in a noise so odious and mortifying it cannot be referred to in polite (or impolite) company.

As I struggle to emulate your unfailing composure, I am beginning to develop a new appreciation for the depths of your restraint. When I feel a scream of outrage bubbling up in my throat or when I find my fingers curling into the precise shape of a dainty little female throat, I think of you and grit my teeth into an indulgent smile. When I find myself testing the blade of my butter knife against my thumb with more attention than is duly necessary, I remember your forbearance and find the strength to carry on without slapping a single soul.

I like to think that you would be proud of the model of virtue and maturity that I have become. Please know that I will always be . . .

> *Ever your humble servant,*
> *Carlotta Oakleigh*

P.S. Can you recommend something that will take raspberry currant stains out of boot leather?

≈

May 30, 1825

Dear Aunt Diana,

Although we are parted, I know you haven't forgotten that I've a birthday coming up this summer. I was rather hoping you might send me a new bonnet and some lovely

unmentionables? (Oh, and a charming little pair of nan-
keen half-boots would not be looked upon with disdain.)

Your doting niece,
Lottie

P.S. Give Uncle Thane and the twins my love, but please
don't mention the unmentionables.

❦

June 4, 1825

Dear George,

How you must have laughed when you learned that your
baby sister had become—oh, I can hardly bear to contem-
plate it!—a mother! You, who always said that I never
cared for any child except myself. (Although we both
know that's not entirely true, for I've always been very
fond of the twins and my own dear niece and nephew,
Nicholas and Ellie. And contrary to what you've always
said, I don't just adore Ellie because she is the mirror image of myself at that age. She has many other winning
qualities, not the least of which is her unshakable belief in
her own wit and beauty.)

I'm sure you'll also be surprised to learn that I am
conducting myself with the mature refinement and decorum expected from a woman of my station. I strive to set
a positive example for my impressionable young stepdaughter, guiding her actions with a firm, but loving
hand.

So hold that image of the carefree girl you once called

"Sister" (among other things) in your heart, for the tender joys "of motherhood have finally made a woman of her!

Maturely,
Carlotta

P.S. You were wrong about brown spiders. Their bite is not fatal. Not even if one inadvertently finds its way into your shoe.

❦

June 8, 1825

Dear Laura and Sterling,

Please forgive me for not writing sooner, but I've been too busy basking in the tender affections of my husband and stepdaughter. They are such a joy to me that I find it difficult to tear myself away from their company to perform even the simplest task!

I'm well aware that you had reservations about this marriage, but I want to assure that I have gained not only an adoring husband, but a loving daughter as well. Please don't suffer a single moment's remorse or regret on my account. I could not bear it if you did!

I promise to write more soon. Until then, picture me surrounded by the convivial bliss that only a joyous union between man, woman, and child can bring.

Ever your adoring,
Lottie

P.S. Could you please send me another yellow parasol? I seem to have sat on mine and broken all of its spokes.

❧

June 10, 1825

Oh, my dearest Harriet,

Forgive my cramped and crooked handwriting, but I am penning this missive in the relative privacy of a broom cupboard. (Picture your once fashionable and elegant friend reduced to sitting in the gloom on an overturned bucket, paper balanced on one knee while a mop handle pokes her in regions best left unnamed.) Why am I in the broom cupboard, you ask? Be patient, my dear friend, for in time all will be revealed!

I was quite dismayed when George wrote to tell me you had chosen to return to the bosom of your own family immediately after I departed for Cornwall. Sterling and Laura would have been delighted to have you finish out the Season as their guest. It gave me great solace to picture you making the rounds of the afternoon teas, taking phaeton rides in Hyde Park, flirting and dancing the night away at all of the balls and soirees I might have attended had I not squandered my own Season for the price of a kiss. (Although it was admittedly a very fine kiss.)

Lest you picture me cowering in this cupboard to escape some hulking brute of a husband, let me assure you that the marquess has been the very model of solicitousness. Sometimes I wish he would shout and rail at me if only to prove he is aware of my existence. Although he plays the gentleman with unfailing courtesy, he tends to look through me rather than at me. *(And as you well know, I've never excelled at being ignored.)*

No, it is his daughter I seek to escape—the ten-year-old step-bratling who plagues every waking moment of my existence. I know I can't hide in here forever, as our afternoon "lessons" are due to begin in an hour. On most days, those lessons consist of me patiently conjugating French verbs while the cunning little imp yawns and taps her foot and gazes out the window, plotting her next nefarious deed. Only yesterday, I returned to my chamber to discover that all the precious ink in my bottles had been replaced with boot polish. While my first inclination was to hunt her down and dump them over her smug little head, I refused to give her the satisfaction.

What does the marquess make of his daughter's mischief, you ask? Although I suspect our little clash of wills is a secret source of amusement to him, he acknowledges it with nothing more than a raised eyebrow or the most imperceptible twitch of his lips as he ducks behind the most recent edition of The Times. He seems perfectly content to let the two of us battle it out, with all the spoils going to the victor.

My only solace lies in settling myself before my writing table each evening and penning some more glimmering shards of prose for my novel. *(I did mention my novel, didn't I?)* Fortunately, the nights have been peaceful, as the ghost has yet to make another appearance. *(I did mention the ghost, didn't I?)*

Wait! What's that I hear? Is it a stealthy footstep on the stairs? A shudder of dread courses down my spine as I crack open the cupboard door and steal a peek into the corridor. Ah, sweet relief! It's not the step-demon, but only the new maid, fleeing Martha's wrath. I've yet to catch a good look at the poor clumsy creature. She spends all of her time scuttling like a nearsighted crab from one domestic disaster to another. You can follow her progress through the house simply by listening for the sound of breaking crockery and Martha's bellowing.

There is so much more I want to tell you, but it's only a matter of time before I am discovered. Oh, dear, sweet Harriet, my friend and confidante, how I wish you were here!!!

Eternally yours,
Lottie

P.S. If I find one more bug in my shoe, I fear my husband won't be the only one in this house guilty of murder.

Two days after Lottie posted her letter to Harriet, the late afternoon sun came peeking out from behind the clouds in a rare appearance. Craving a taste of spring, Lottie decided to escape both the house and Allegra for a little while. She was strolling past the stables when she felt a now familiar prickling at the nape of her neck. Weary of being toyed with, she swung around, fully intending to blast Hayden's sullen little snoop of a daughter into next week.

A tiny yellow kitten was teetering after her on unsteady legs.

Lottie began to back away as if it were a Bengal tiger. "Oh, no, you don't! The last thing I need right now are more cats cluttering up my life. You just toddle right back where you came from." She continued to walk backward, making shooing motions with her hands.

Undaunted by her rejection, the kitten simply increased its pace until it ran full tilt into her ankles. Groaning, Lottie reached down and scooped the creature into her palm. With its hoarse mews and tufted yellow fur, it was more like holding a baby duck than a baby cat.

A gangly lad with a thick shock of black hair drooping over his brow came rushing out of the stables. When he saw her cradling the kitten, he skidded to a halt and doffed his battered cap. "Sorry for the trouble, m'lady. It's mum has gone missing. Left this wee one and three others just like it to fend for themselves."

Lottie barely resisted the urge to groan again. "Three others, you say, Jem?"

" 'Fraid so." The boy shook his head sadly. "And the poor mites barely big eno' to feed themselves."

As if to underscore his words, three more kittens of varying shapes and colors came waddling out of the stable, looking like a motley pack of overgrown rats.

As the yellow kitten scrambled up Lottie's arm and onto her shoulder, she blew out a sigh of defeat. "I don't suppose you have a basket in there as well, do you?"

Hoping to smuggle the kittens back to her bedchamber without being spotted, Lottie ducked through an open French window on the side of the house facing the sea. She batted her way through the smothering weight of the velvet drapes, finally emerging only to find herself facing an imposing mahogany desk stacked high with leather-bound ledgers.

A desk her husband just happened to be sitting behind.

He was eyeing her with detached interest, as if she were some exotic worm that had just tunneled its way out of the woodwork.

She clutched the basket to her chest, thankful that she'd had the presence of mind to tuck a kerchief over it. "Why, hello there!" she boomed, hoping to drown out the kittens' sporadic squeaking. "It's a grand day, isn't it? I've been out gathering . . ." she struggled to think of any sort of fruit or vegetable that might grow in such stony and inhospitable terrain ". . . walnuts. I've been out gathering walnuts."

Smiling pleasantly, Hayden reached for the tasseled bell pull dangling behind his chair. "Why don't I summon Martha? Perhaps she can ask Cook to bake them into a pie."

Lottie couldn't quite hide her horror. "Oh, no! Please don't do that! I much prefer to eat them right out of the shell."

"Suit yourself," Hayden murmured, returning his attention to the ledgers.

She crept toward the door.

"Carlotta?"

"Yes?"

Without looking up, he said, "They're bound to be hungry. You might as well stop by the kitchen for some kippers and cream."

Lottie froze in her tracks. Allegra was right. The

man *was* insufferable. She gazed down at the undulating kerchief on top of the basket. What was it Laura and Diana had told her on the night before her wedding? That it was not uncommon for lovers to exchange small thoughtful gifts to woo one another outside of the bedchamber?

"You should be ashamed of yourself, my lord," she scolded, turning to face Hayden.

He at least did her the honor of glancing up from his work. "I should?"

"Yes, you should. Because now you've gone and spoiled my surprise." She approached the desk, inordinately pleased that she had succeeded in stirring some emotion in him, even if it was only suspicion. "I was hoping to tie a pretty ribbon around your gift before I presented it to you."

Plopping the basket down on the desk, Lottie whipped away the kerchief with a flourish. The kittens came spilling out in all directions, teetering about the desk on unsteady legs. Hayden could have looked no more horrified had she dumped a nest of poisonous vipers onto his blotter. A calico kitten began to gnaw on the end of his pen while a black one darted toward an open bottle of ink.

He snatched up the ink in the nick of time. The kitten went careening over the side of the desk and into a wooden wastebasket, where it proceeded to set up a shrill mewing.

"Oh, look!" Lottie pointed to the yellow kitten. It had pounced into Hayden's lap and was sucking blissfully on one of the cloth-covered buttons of his waistcoat, its purr audible even over the other kitten's piteous pleas for rescue. "Isn't that darling? The little fellow thinks you're his mother."

Grimacing, Hayden gingerly detached the kitten, holding it at arm's length. "Well, I most certainly am not!" He shifted his glower from the cat to Lottie. "I appreciate your generosity, my lady, but what exactly am I to do with these . . . these . . . creatures."

Lottie backed toward the door, feeling as if she'd just lapped up a saucer of fresh cream herself. "Oh, I don't know. Maybe you should ring for Martha and have her bake them into a pie."

"Don't tempt me," he growled, shaking his leg in a futile attempt to dislodge the black kitten, who had finally managed to turn over the wastebasket and was now clawing its way up the leg of Hayden's doeskin trousers.

"I wouldn't dream of it," Lottie assured him, flashing a saucy smile before ducking out of the room.

Lottie was still smiling as she strolled through the entrance hall, heading for the kitchen. She figured she should at least help scrounge up some kippers and cream, although she couldn't have said whether it was out of pity for Hayden or the kittens. Perhaps she should even consider implementing some more of her aunt's and sister's suggestions. If nothing else, she had finally succeeded in getting her husband's undivided attention.

As she started down the corridor that led to the basement stairs, Meggie was approaching from the opposite direction, her coppery braids poking out from beneath her mobcap. Instead of pausing to bob a deferent curtsy as she usually did, the young maid brushed past Lottie with barely a mumbled pardon, her reddened face averted.

Lottie stared after her, shaking her head in puzzlement before proceeding.

Even before she reached the bottom of the stairs, the buzz of excited voices and merry laughter assailed Lottie's ears. Ducking beneath the rack of copper pots hanging from the plastered ceiling, she peeked around the corner to discover a group of servants gathered around the battered pine table, all gazing at something scattered upon its surface. Neither Giles, Martha, nor Mrs. Cavendish were anywhere in sight.

"Read that one again, Cook," one of the scullery maids demanded, pointing over a footman's burly shoulder.

"Read it yerself," Cook snarled, leaning forward until her bony nose practically touched the table. "I ain't done with this one yet."

"She can't," the footman said. "Her mum never taught her how to read."

The maid gave his liveried bottom a firm pinch. "But she taught me other things, didn't she, Mac?"

As they collapsed on each other's shoulders in a giggling heap, Cook handed a cheap broadside over her shoulder. "Here. Take this one. It's got pictures."

"Oooooh!" Cooing in unison, they snatched the broadside out of her hand, nearly ripping it in two in their eagerness. Lottie inched forward, her own curiosity getting the best of her. She turned her head this way and that, but could only make out a crude caricature of a man and woman.

"Will you just listen to this?" One of the maids who evidently *could* read held up a rumpled newspaper, her eyes glittering with excitement. " 'Before trapping him into marriage, she was rumored to have enjoyed a number of liaisons with other men, including a brief dalliance with the king himself.' " Several of the servants gasped. " 'Her former lovers claim that her lusty appetites were exceeded only by her ambition.' "

Lottie winced in sympathy. Once she might have pored over the broadside with a lurid hunger even greater than theirs, but now she felt nothing but compassion for its ill-used victim. No woman, however impure, deserved to have her reputation tarred with such a black brush.

Cook snorted. "Whirlwind courtship indeed! More like a spider spinning a web for the fattest, juiciest fly it could catch."

"Ha! Listen to this!" Another pamphlet emerged from the fray. " 'After one torrid night of sin, the resourceful rector's daughter found the randy nobleman to be the answer to all her prayers.' "

"She don't look to be prayin' in this picture!"

The footman held up the broadside, bringing the drawing into vivid focus. It depicted a young woman with enormous eyes, an exaggerated topknot of curls, and a jutting bosom, down on her knees before a sneering gentleman. The footman was right. She was most definitely *not* praying.

Lottie touched a hand to her stomach, feeling suddenly ill. Her hasty marriage might have placated the more reputable papers, but not these common rags. This was exactly what Sterling had sought to protect her from. He'd been willing to kill or risk being killed to silence these ugly voices forever.

"No wonder the master don't seem in no hurry to welcome her into his bed," one of the gardeners said. "He's probably afraid he'll catch the French pox."

"Or he might be waitin' to make sure she ain't got some other gent's get in her belly!"

They all burst out laughing, but the scullery maid's cackle died on a shrill note as she turned. The color drained from her ruddy cheeks, leaving them white as chalk. At first Lottie thought she'd caused the violent reaction, but the woman's horrified gaze was riveted on something just over Lottie's left shoulder. One by one, the servants nudged each other into silence.

"Would anyone care to explain the meaning of this?" Hayden's measured words cracked like gunfire in the sudden hush.

Lottie must have swayed without realizing it, for her husband's hands closed firmly over her shoulders, steadying her. Although her first instinct was to sink into him, to absorb both his warmth and his strength, she forced herself to remain upright. He was accompanied by a scowling Martha and a white-faced Mrs. Cavendish.

Newspapers and pamphlets quickly began to disappear under the table. "We was just havin' a bit o' fun, m'lord," Cook whined. "We meant no harm by it."

As the footman sought to tuck the broadside behind his back, Hayden reached for it.

"No!" Lottie darted forward and snatched the paper from the servant's beefy fist, wadding it into a ball before Hayden could see it.

Catching her by the wrist, Hayden tugged the broadside from her rigid fingers. As he unfolded it, she was tempted to close her eyes before he could realize what he was holding, but pride kept her burning gaze fixed firmly on his face.

As Hayden studied the crude drawing, a flush slowly crept up his throat. He lifted his dark-lashed eyes to hers, crumpling the paper in his fist. Despite the violence of the gesture, his voice was gentle as he said, "I'm so sorry. I had hoped to spare you this."

Every trace of that gentleness vanished as he returned his attention to his staff. "Who brought this rubbish into my home?"

No one even dared to breathe.

Moving to Cook, he held out his hand. After a moment's hesitation, she drew the yellowing newspaper out from under the table and laid it across his palm. He tossed it on the kitchen fire without even bothering to glance at it. The other servants wasted no time in rising to file past the hearth, casting each newspaper, pamphlet, and broadside on the flames until the stench of burning newsprint filled the air.

Hayden swung around, his eyes pitiless. "Mrs. Cavendish, I hold you personally accountable for the actions of your staff. Would you care to identify the culprit who brought this . . . this refuse into my house?"

The housekeeper actually took a step backward. "B-b-but, my lord, I knew nothing of this until Meggie came to fetch me, just as she did you. How on earth am I to find the guilty party?"

Martha was scanning the servants' downcast faces one by one, her eyes narrowed. "You just leave that to me," she muttered, disappearing down the darkened corridor that led to the servants' quarters.

As the painful silence stretched, the footman ducked his head sheepishly and jerked his thumb toward the hearth. "Everybody knows they make up half that rot, m'lord. We meant no disrespect to her."

Hayden took a step forward, tension coiled in his every muscle, and for one dark moment, Lottie thought he might actually lay hands on the man. "*Her?* Do you mean *my wife*, perchance?" The possessive gleam in his eye gave Lottie a delicious little thrill. "*Your* mistress? The marchioness?" Hayden's frosty gaze swept over the rest of the servants. "The lady who has the power to dismiss the whole sorry lot of you with neither references or wages?"

They all looked so wretched that Lottie was about to reassure them she had no intention of doing any such thing when Martha came marching back into the kitchen, dragging a sobbing young maid. The girl's ill-fitting mobcap had slid down over her eyes. All that was visible of her face were two quivering lips and one very red nose.

"I've found our culprit!" the old nurse announced triumphantly. "All it took was a sound pinch and she confessed to having those nasty scandal sheets squirreled away in her valise. Well, you wicked girl, have you anything to say to your mistress before she sends you packing?" Martha gave the maid a shove toward Lottie, snatching away her mobcap.

The girl squinted at Lottie through her tears, her limp brown hair plastered to her head and her round face blotchy from weeping.

Lottie gaped at her. "Harriet?"

"Lottie!" With a broken wail, Harriet came barreling into Lottie's arms, nearly knocking her off her feet.

Chapter 12

*His cruel, yet handsome, visage began to haunt my
dreams, as well as my waking hours . . .*

MARTHA LOOKED UTTERLY AGHAST. "MY LADY,
whatever are you doing? Surely you don't know this
creature?"

"I most certainly do." Still reeling with shock, Lottie wrapped a protective arm around the sobbing
girl and glared at the nurse. "This *creature* is my
dearest friend in all the world—Miss Harriet
Dimwinkle. Her father is a magistrate in Kent."

"A magistrate?" As Martha went stumbling backward, Cook shoved a chair beneath her.

The old woman sank heavily into it. Judging from
the bruises on Harriet's arms, some faded and some
fresh, it wasn't the first time she'd been pinched for
one infraction or another. And judging from
Martha's glazed eyes, she was already entertaining

visions of herself imprisoned in the stocks of some idyllic English village.

Although Mrs. Cavendish clucked disapprovingly, her eyes glinted with triumph. "You should have listened to me. I warned you that nothing but trouble would come from hiring the silly—" As Lottie turned her glare on the housekeeper, Mrs. Cavendish smiled through clenched teeth. "—the dear girl."

Two more chairs were quickly provided for Lottie and Harriet. Lottie gently guided her friend into one of them and sat down across from her.

She chafed Harriet's trembling hands between her own. "I thought you'd gone home to Kent. How on earth did you come to be here?"

"I'd be very interested in hearing the answer to that question myself," Hayden said, fishing a handkerchief out of his waistcoat pocket and handing it to Harriet. He leaned against the stone hearth, looking even more infuriatingly masculine than usual in this feminine domain.

"I ran away," Harriet blurted out between breathless hiccups. "I let the duke and duchess believe I was returning to my family, but I just couldn't bring myself to go back there. I knew how disappointed my parents would be to find me back on their doorstep. They were so hoping I'd find a husband in London to take me off their hands!"

"But how did you get all the way to Cornwall without even a servant to look after you?" Lottie asked.

"Your sister put me on the coach to Kent, but I

crawled out the other door and traded my best brooch for a ticket on a mail coach traveling to Cornwall." Harriet honked loudly into Hayden's handkerchief. "I knew no one would miss me."

"You poor dear." Lottie brushed a limp lock of hair from Harriet's eyes. "What happened to your spectacles?"

"I took them off on the coach to polish them and this rather large gentleman climbed in and sat right on top of them. Instead of apologizing for crushing them, he yelled at me for being stupid and careless." Fresh tears flooded Harriet's eyes.

Lottie squeezed her friend's hands before she could start wailing again. "Why didn't you come to me right away? Why did you feel you had to masquerade as a maid?"

Harriet shot Hayden a furtive glance. "I was afraid he'd send me back to my family." She leaned closer to Lottie, lowering her voice to a stage whisper clearly audible to everyone in the room. "Or make me disappear."

Hayden rolled his eyes. "As fascinating as your adventures may be, Miss Dimwinkle, you still haven't explained how you came to be in possession of those broadsides and scandal sheets."

Harriet lifted her damp brown eyes to him. "They were selling the horrid things in the street in front of the inn while I was waiting for my coach. I spent my last shilling buying up as many as I could afford so no one else would see them. I was going to burn them the first chance I got."

"But you didn't," Hayden gently reminded her.

"To be honest, I forgot all about them. What with all the dusting and sweeping and shouting . . ."

"And pinching." Lottie shot Martha a reproachful look.

Harriet shrugged helplessly. "I've no idea who stole them out of my valise and left them out for the other servants to find. Who would do such a cruel and wicked thing?"

"Who indeed?" Lottie murmured, feeling her mouth tighten.

Too late, she realized Hayden's speculative gaze was locked on her face. When he pushed away from the hearth and strode from the kitchen without a word, she had no choice but to follow.

They found Allegra in the schoolroom, sitting at her little wooden desk in a pool of sunshine. She was copying numbers from her primer into a blank ledger in neat columns. Her dingy stockings were both pulled up and a faded lavender ribbon held her cloud of dark hair out of her face. Lottie's doll was propped at the desk beside her, wearing a matching ribbon in her scorched yellow curls.

As Lottie entered the schoolroom, Allegra beamed up at her. "Good afternoon, Mummy. Is it time for my lesson?"

"You might say that," Hayden said, stepping around Lottie in the doorway.

As his imposing figure cast a shadow across her desk, Allegra's smile faded.

"Have you anything to say for yourself, young lady?" he asked.

Allegra slowly closed the primer before rising to face her father. She didn't waste her breath denying his unspoken accusation. "I won't say I'm sorry because I'm not. I thought they should know. I thought everyone should know just what sort of woman you'd married."

Lottie fought to keep her temper in check. "You might be too young and naive to realize this, but the stories they print in those sort of papers are not only unkind, but untrue. The only way they can turn a profit is by spreading lies about innocent people."

The girl reached beneath her primer and pulled out another pamphlet. Judging from its ragged condition and the dirty little fingerprints that stained it, it appeared to have been read more than once.

"What about this story? Is it a lie as well?" She began to read, both her voice and her hands shaking. " 'Many still remember when Oakleigh employed his lethal charms to woo and win the heart of the exquisite Justine du Lac. His new bride had best beware. It seems that falling in love with the Murderous Marquess is only one short step away from falling over a cliff. Or being pushed.' "

For one terrible moment, Lottie couldn't even look at Hayden. All she could do was hold her breath and wait for him to burst out laughing, to rumple his daughter's hair and scold her for paying any heed at all to such nonsensical rubbish. All it took was one look into Allegra's stricken eyes to know that she was waiting for the same thing. And that she'd been waiting far longer than Lottie had.

Lacking the child's patience, Lottie turned and boldly looked at him.

"Go to your chamber, Allegra," he ordered, his face as striking and expressionless as a mask. "And remain there until I send for you."

A strangled sob tore from Allegra's throat. Hurling the pamphlet to the floor, she went tearing past them and out the door. Shooting Lottie an unreadable glance, Hayden turned on his heel and followed.

Hayden drove his horse across the moor through the gathering dusk. He knew he could ride until they were both lathered with sweat, but there would be no escaping that moment in the schoolroom when Lottie had turned to look at him. In the years since Justine's death, he'd grown accustomed to every sort of look imaginable—curious peeks, sly glances, suspicious glares. He'd even managed to steel his heart against the shadow of doubt that bruised his daughter's eyes every time she lifted them to his face.

But when Lottie had turned her uncompromising blue eyes on him, begging—no, demanding—the answer to the one question no one else had even dared to ask, he had felt the defenses around his heart shudder as if from some terrible blow.

Shifting his weight and tugging on the reins, he wheeled the bay around at the edge of a dank bog and sent him thundering back toward the manor. He might be willing to risk his own neck by charging through the marshy turf, but he was not willing to risk the horse's.

He should have known Lottie wouldn't flinch from any challenge. To a man who'd spent the last four years measuring his every breath by what it would cost him, her reckless courage was both infuriating and irresistible.

Hayden almost wished he'd seen some damning trace of fear or loathing in her eyes. Perhaps then he could dismiss her as coolly as he'd dismissed the rest of his passions. But the possibility that she might believe whatever he told her—might believe *in* him—posed a temptation he had not anticipated. A temptation even sweeter and more dangerous than the luscious curves of her body.

Leaning low over the horse's neck, Hayden drove his mount past the house and toward the cliffs, seeking to remind himself just how high the cost of surrender would be.

She stood at the very edge of the cliff, gazing down into the churning cauldron of the sea. Wave after wave crashed against the jagged rocks below, flinging sprays of spume high into the air. A cool cloud of mist rose to envelop her, clinging to her skin and molding the gossamer silk of her nightdress to her breasts and thighs. Although she shivered, she did not retreat. She'd dreamed of such unbridled wildness all of her life. While one part of her longed to escape the dark and windy night, another part of her yearned to throw her arms wide and welcome it, to give herself over to its all-encompassing embrace.

She slowly turned. He was there, just as she knew he would be, a darker shadow against the inky blackness of the sky. As he reached for her, she took one step closer to the edge of the cliff. But they both knew she would not flee. She could resist him no more than the tides could resist the relentless tug of the moon. Melting into his arms, she turned her face up to receive his kiss.

He took her mouth, softly and tenderly at first, then wild and rough, his tongue plundering its eager sweetness. She clung to him, returning his ardor with desperate abandon, knowing it would never be enough until every inch of their flesh was joined, until she surrendered to his will and took him deep inside of her. She ached everywhere he touched—her lips, her breasts, the hot, damp flesh between her thighs. Once he might have been content knowing he possessed both her body and her heart, but tonight his kiss demanded no less than her soul.

The wind grew even wilder, seeking to wrest her from his arms. But she knew she had nothing to fear, for he would never let her go. At least that's what she believed until he tore his mouth away from hers and gave her a gentle shove. As she teetered there on the edge of that precipice, her arms still reaching for him, the last thing she saw was his face—both beautiful and chilling in its utter absence of regret.

Then she was falling, falling, falling into a vast abyss of nothingness, her own anguished scream echoing in her ears.

Lottie jerked upright at the writing table, her fevered flesh drenched in icy sweat.

Still trembling, she shoved aside the crumpled

pages of her manuscript and buried her face in her hands. The dream must have been her punishment for writing so late into the night and dozing off in the middle of a chapter. After helping Harriet move her meager belongings from the servants' quarters to the bedchamber across the hall, Lottie had retreated to her writing table to pour all of her doubts and suspicions into another scene of her novel. A scene where her heroine first begins to suspect that the man to whom she has entrusted her heart is a heartless killer.

But the dream had been more vivid than anything Lottie had ever written. Although she'd never caught a clear glimpse of the lover's face, she could still taste his kiss on her lips, still feel the unfamiliar ache between her thighs.

She pressed her fingertips to her temples, struggling to make sense of it all. Had the woman on the edge of the cliff been her or had she been poor doomed Justine, betrayed by a faithless kiss? Had the dream been a vision from the past or a premonition of the future? Or had it simply been a product of her own distraught imagination, fueled by that disastrous encounter between Hayden and Allegra in the schoolroom.

Lottie started as her bedchamber door flew open. Harriet came rushing in, her nightcap sliding down over one bleary eye. "Can't you hear those terrible screams? What on earth could make such an ungodly noise?" She bounded into the middle of Lottie's bed, barely missing Mr. Wiggles, and tucked her bare feet beneath her nightdress. "Could it be

the ghost the servants are always whispering about?
Is the manor truly haunted?"

For the first time, Lottie realized she hadn't
dreamed the bloodcurdling scream that had awakened her. As she cocked her head to listen, the distant
screaming evolved into shrill screeches punctuated
by the sound of breaking glass.

Lottie shook her head. "That, my dear Harriet, is
no ghost."

Harriet blinked like a frightened owl. "Then what
is it? Are we being set upon by smugglers? This is
Cornwall, you know. Are we going to be ravished in
our beds?"

Still suffering the feverish aftereffects of the dream,
Lottie muttered, "We should be so lucky."

But she knew perfectly well that no ghost or
smuggler could set up such a dreadful racket. As
those outraged shrieks continued, she felt her own
temper mounting. She'd spent the last three weeks
keeping it in check—striving to be a genteel wife, a
patient stepmother, a long-suffering governess. And
what had it gotten her? She'd been defied at every
turn by a ten-year-old tyrant, mocked and insulted
by her own servants, and left aching for the touch of
a man who refused to so much as deny that he may
have shoved his last wife over a cliff in a fit of jealous
pique. As far as she was concerned, virtue had yet to
reveal any rewards at all.

She rose, shoving the pages of her manuscript
back into her writing case and snapping it shut.

"Where are you going?" Harriet demanded as

Lottie snatched her dressing gown off a chair and stormed toward the door.

Lottie spun around, her eyes glittering with a look her friend recognized only too well. "I'm going to show a certain young miss why they call me the Hertfordshire Hellion."

As Lottie hurried down the stairs to the second floor, tightening the sash of her dressing gown as she walked, the long-case clock on the landing chimed midnight. Usually at this time of night, there wasn't a servant to be found anywhere outside of their quarters, but tonight maids and footmen scurried like frightened mice through the corridors of the manor. Several of them slanted her curious glances as she passed, plainly startled to find their mistress marching through the house in her nightclothes with her hair unbound and streaming down her back.

Lottie rounded a corner only to nearly collide with the burly footman who had taken such delight in that cruel caricature.

As he stumbled backward, his broad cheeks flaming, Lottie tossed her curls. "If you'll excuse me, I'm off to rendezvous with the king for a romantic interlude." She touched a finger to her lips, lowering her voice to a whisper. "But please, whatever you do, don't tell the master."

Leaving him leaning against the wall with his mouth hanging open, she continued on her way. On this night she had no need of a candle or a ghostly melody to guide her. The corridors blazed with light, as if every lamp in the house had been lit to ward off a terror even more chilling than a spirit from beyond the grave. Several servants had gathered in the corridor outside of Allegra's bedchamber, their faces white with strain. The floor beneath their feet was littered with broken porcelain, and Jem, the stable boy, was leaning against the wall, clutching a bloody rag to his head. Allegra's door was closed, but inside the room, the storm raged unabated.

Before Lottie could even reach the door, little Meggie threw herself in front of it, bobbing an awkward curtsy at the same time. She had to shout to be heard over the screaming. "Oh, m'lady, we don't dare open it again!" The maid flinched as something heavy struck the door from the other side. "She's already blackened Girt's eye and given poor Jem here the very devil of a headache."

The stable boy nodded in agreement, the motion making him wince.

"I know you're only trying to protect me, but I can look after myself. Please stand aside," Lottie commanded.

Meggie cast the bleeding stable boy a frantic look. "Go fetch the master, Jem. And hurry!"

Groaning, Jem shoved himself away from the wall and went loping down the corridor.

"I appreciate what you're trying to do, Meggie. Truly I do," Lottie assured the maid. "But as your mistress, I insist that you step aside and allow me into that room."

She was still arguing with the girl when Hayden came striding down the corridor. With his hair uncombed and his eyes ablaze with determination, he looked so much like the lover from her dream that Lottie felt her skin flush and her heart start to beat faster. Not even the two kittens trotting at his heels could make him look any less forbidding.

"What in the devil do you think you're doing?"

Although he loomed over her, Lottie stood her ground. "Your daughter is disturbing everyone's sleep, including mine. I'd simply like to have a little chat with her."

Casting a grim glance toward the servants, Hayden caught her by the wrist and dragged her into the deserted bedchamber across the hall. The room was lit only by moonlight, just as that windswept cliff in Lottie's dream had been.

Pausing just long enough to sweep the kittens out of harm's way, Hayden slammed the door behind them, muffling the din to a bearable level. "You can *chat* until you're blue in the face, but I can assure you that you'll be wasting your breath. There's no reasoning with Allegra when she gets like this. I've already sent Martha to the village for the doctor."

"And just what do you expect him to do?"

"Keep her from harming herself. Or anyone else." He ran a thumb along the thin scar beneath his left ear, probably not even aware he was doing it. "If he can get some laudanum down her throat, she might even sleep until morning."

Lottie wondered exactly how he'd gotten that scar and just how many sleepless nights he had endured waiting for the doctor to come pour laudanum down the throat of someone he loved.

Steeling herself against a rush of empathy, she said, "It sounds to me as if Allegra needs a dose of laudanum less than she needs a sound thrashing."

As he backed her up against the door, Hayden looked utterly capable of doing violence. "I'll have you know that I've never once laid a hand on my child!"

As Lottie gazed up at him, big and angry and dangerous in the moonlight, she was startled to realize that she desperately wanted him to lay a hand on her. She wanted him to lay his hand against her breast, to tenderly cradle its softness in the cup of his palm as he slowly lowered his mouth to hers and . . .

An outraged shriek pierced the thick wood of the door, shattering the shocking fantasy.

"Yes, that much is evident, isn't it?" Lottie retorted, struggling to gather her wits. "Perhaps if you had, we'd all be in bed asleep right now. So would you care to tell me what set her off this time? I trust it didn't go well when you summoned her."

"Not particularly." Stepping away from her, Hayden rubbed the back of his neck, his reluctance to confide in her nearly palpable. "I told her that if she didn't offer you an apology in front of the servants, I was going to send her away to school. And I told her I meant it this time."

A tendril of warmth unfurled low in Lottie's belly. The last thing she had expected him to do was champion her. But then another thought occurred to her. If he sent Allegra away to school, he would have no further need of her. Although she couldn't have said why, that realization flooded her with an emotion dangerously close to panic.

She turned around, closing her hand around the doorknob.

"I'm warning you," Hayden said. "You won't be able to reason with her. Not when she's seized in the grips of this madness."

Lottie cast him an exasperated look over her shoulder. "Oh, she's mad, all right. She's absolutely furious!"

Throwing open the door, she marched into the corridor. Meggie watched her approach, her eyes wide with alarm.

Following fast on Lottie's heels, Hayden snapped, "Let her in."

Although the maid's eyes widened even further, she clearly had no intention of defying her master. She threw open Allegra's door, then quickly sought shelter in young Jem's arms.

Lottie's steps never faltered, not even when a porcelain washbasin went whizzing past her head and smashed into the corridor wall, only a few inches away from where Hayden was standing. She simply reached behind her and closed the door in his face. Judging from the shambles the room was in, Allegra was rapidly running out of things to throw.

The girl crouched in the middle of an enormous four-poster, her hands gripping the tumbled bedclothes. Her face was mottled with rage, her long, dark lashes clumped together by tears. As Lottie calmly surveyed her, Allegra let out an earsplitting shriek and reached for the only object still left on the bed—which just happened to be Lottie's doll. Snatching the doll up by one foot, Allegra drew it back over her head.

"I wouldn't do that if I were you." Although Lottie's voice was low, it was laced with enough threat to give the girl pause. Especially when Lottie reached behind her once again and turned the key in the lock.

Allegra slowly lowered the doll, her eyes wild and her chest heaving. "Didn't they warn you? You shouldn't come near me when I'm like this. I'm quite mad, you know. I-I-I can't control myself. I might hit you or kick you or scratch you . . . or . . . or . . ." She bared her pearly little teeth. "Why, I might even bite you!"

"If you do, then I shall bite you back. I've had experience, you know. I once bit the king."

Allegra's jaw dropped. "Of England?"

"The very same. It took six of his guards to pry my teeth loose from his arm. Or was it eight?" Actually, it had only been three, but Lottie felt a little exaggeration was never amiss, either in literature or in life.

She meandered over to the bed. Allegra scrambled backward until her shoulders were pressed against the headboard. "I'm warning you! Don't come near me. If you do, I'll . . . I'll hold my breath until I turn blue."

"Go right ahead. Don't let me stop you." Lottie sank down on the foot of the bed, smiling pleasantly at the child.

Looking more irritated than enraged now, Allegra gulped in a deep breath, pursed her lips, and puffed out her cheeks. As the child's eyes bugged out and her color slowly shifted from pink to purple, Lottie counted beneath her breath. She had only reached thirty-five when Allegra collapsed on the pillows, gasping for air.

"Not very impressive, I'm afraid," Lottie said, shaking her head. "Once when my sister gave the last tea cake to my brother, I held my breath for almost two minutes. By the time I was done, my sister was weeping and George was on his knees, begging me to eat the cake."

Allegra sat up, lowering her head like a bull about to charge. She'd obviously saved her most dire threat for last. "If you don't leave my room this very instant, I'm going to scream."

Lottie simply smiled.

Allegra opened her mouth.

Lottie screamed.

It was a full-throated, operatic masterpiece, designed to pierce every eardrum within a fifty-league radius. If there had been an unbroken piece of porcelain left in the room, it would have shattered into a thousand pieces.

Only as the scream tapered off did Lottie become aware of fists pounding frantically on the door and a masculine voice shouting her name. The door came crashing inward, splintering right off its hinges. Hayden quickly followed, stumbling to a halt and looking utterly flummoxed to find Lottie sitting on the foot of the bed, a serene smile curving her lips while Allegra cowered against the headboard, her hands clamped to her ears.

Martha and a white-bearded gentleman Lottie assumed must be the village doctor hovered behind Hayden, their own expressions equally bewildered.

Sobbing hoarsely, Allegra went bounding off the bed. She ran right past her father and into Martha's arms.

Throwing her arms around the woman's ample waist, she cried, "Oh, Martha, please make her go away! I'll be good, I swear I will! I'll do whatever Father wants! Just please don't let her bite me or make that dreadful noise again!"

As Allegra buried her face in Martha's bosom, still sobbing, Lottie rose from the bed. Hayden was staring at her as if she were Attila the Hun and Joan of Arc all wrapped into one.

"I believe she'll sleep now," Lottie told him. She gave the doctor a pointed glance. "*Without* the laudanum."

Tightening the sash of her dressing gown, she sailed past them all and out of the bedchamber. She emerged into the corridor to find Meggie, Jem, and the rest of the servants eyeing her with a newfound mixture of trepidation and respect.

"Oh, m'lady, we thought the young miss was murderin' you, we did," Meggie blurted out. "I've never seen the master in such a state. Why, he shoved Jem right out of the way and broke down the door hisself!"

As Lottie passed, biting back a smile as she imagined Hayden battering down that door like a knight rushing to the rescue of his lady fair, each of the servants in turn offered her a bow or curtsy. She knew

Allegra's apology could wait until morning. Now that they were free to finish out their night in peace, it no longer mattered to the servants if she was rumored to have been the mistress of every nobleman in London.

They were simply grateful that she was now theirs.

Chapter 13

How was I to discover what terrible secrets lurked behind the locked door of his heart?

AFTER THAT NIGHT, ALLEGRA BECAME A MODEL pupil. She showed up for her lessons each morning promptly at ten o'clock, pinafore starched and stockings neatly gartered. She would stand beside her desk, hands clasped in front of her, and decline one Latin noun after another, then follow that with a matter-of-fact recitation of her multiplication tables. She could locate Marrakesh on the globe and deliver an oral history of both the Ostrogoths and the Visigoths that would have made the Romans weep with envy.

Lottie no longer had to shake out her shoes each morning before donning them or hide her bonnets just in case a stray goat wandered into her bedchamber. With both Allegra and the ghost holding their silence, they were all able to enjoy several blissfully peaceful nights of sleep. It seemed a truce had been declared at Oakwylde Manor, albeit a wary one.

But without the challenge of foiling Allegra's schemes, Lottie soon found herself plagued by another malady—boredom. If anything, Hayden was even more distant than before, treating her with the remote courtesy one might accord to a second cousin thrice removed. And although she was grateful for her friend's loyal companionship, Harriet's company had never been overly scintillating. Her chief topic of conversation was usually whatever they'd had for tea the day before.

One gloomy Tuesday morning found both her and Allegra gazing out the schoolroom window, watching rain trickle down the mullioned panes. As one raindrop merged into another, Lottie felt her eyelids growing heavy. Allegra's yawn was quickly echoed by one of her own.

Catching herself before she could slump into a full-blown doze, Lottie closed the book on her desk with a decisive snap.

Allegra started guiltily and began scribbling madly in her ledger.

Lottie rose. "We've been studying Magellan and de Soto for the past week. Well, I say what better way to understand the mind of a great explorer than to go exploring."

"Exploring?" Although Allegra looked no less wary than usual, a spark of interest lit her eyes.

"Rumor has it that this manor has over fifty rooms and I've probably only seen half of those. Why don't we start with the attic and work our way down? We might even find some of those priest holes and secret passages Meggie and Jem are always whispering about."

"But what about Father? If I don't finish my lesson for today, he won't be pleased, will he?"

Lottie felt an impish smile curve her lips. "Rumor also has it that your father rode over to Boscastle with his steward this morning to settle some accounts and he won't return until late afternoon. Even Martha has gone off to the village for the day to visit her sister." Although Allegra still looked doubtful, Lottie held out her hand. "Come, my little conquistador, there are new worlds for us to conquer."

On such a dark and windy day with the rain beating against the gabled roof, there was no better, more cozy, place to be than a sprawling attic. The interconnected warren of rooms with their trunks full of moth-eaten clothes and abandoned toys kept Lottie and Allegra occupied for most of the morning. In one corner, Lottie found a speckled rocking horse. She gently ran a hand over its rough-hewn neck, wondering if it had once belonged to Hayden.

They finally emerged from the attic near noon with dirt-smudged stockings and cobwebs in their hair. Although Allegra clung to her stony reserve, Lottie kept up a stream of chatter amiable enough for the both of them.

They wandered the second and third floors for a

while, finding only bedchambers and sitting rooms dusty from disuse. They had reached the end of a long portrait-lined gallery when they heard footsteps approaching.

Lottie snatched up Allegra's hand and darted toward a back staircase. Although she knew very well that it was probably only Meggie carrying an armful of fresh linen, she hissed, "Come, de Soto! It's those cursed English seeking to plunder our ships and steal our booty!"

By the time they reached the ground floor, Lottie was breathless with laughter and even Allegra seemed to be struggling to hold back a smile. They emerged from the stairwell and stumbled to a halt in the middle of a broad corridor lined with doors.

Her expression darkening, Allegra began to back toward the mouth of the corridor. "We shouldn't be here. It's not allowed."

Lottie slowly turned, recognizing the double doors at the far end of the corridor. They were in the west wing, standing in the very spot where she had heard the ghostly strains of piano music her first night at the manor.

Allegra cast a guilty glance over her shoulder, her voice growing more urgent. "We really should go. I'm not supposed to play here."

But Lottie's gaze was drawn back to those mysterious doors. The doors Hayden had pinned her to with his hot, hungry hands. The doors he had refused to so much as look at when she had mentioned the music.

She began to walk toward them, her steps measured. "What sort of explorers would we be," she asked softly, "if we fled at the first sign of danger?"

She reached for one of the doorknobs, her fingers trembling ever so slightly.

"There's no use." Allegra drifted toward the doors, almost as if she couldn't help herself either. "They've been locked for over four years. Martha's the only one allowed a key."

Lottie knew it was wrong to encourage Allegra to disobey her father. But curiosity was fast overcoming her conscience. If he had nothing to hide, why would Hayden insist that the doors be kept locked?

Allegra crept nearer as Lottie reached into her chignon, tugging out a hairpin. Since she wasn't wearing a hat, it would have to do. After several minutes of poking, jiggling, and muttering, she finally felt the lock surrender to her touch.

She straightened. Allegra was hovering so close Lottie could hear each rapid, shallow breath the child took. She reached behind her and clutched Allegra's icy hand, not sure if she was doing it to reassure Allegra or herself.

As Lottie eased open the door, an involuntary sigh escaped her lips. The octagonal-shaped room was exquisite—airy, delicate, and feminine, without a trace of the dark mahogany that brooded over the rest of the manor. It had been decorated in the Greek revival fashion so favored by the cream of society only a few years ago. The walls were paneled in white wainscoting trimmed with gold leaf. Hand-painted flowers adorned every cornice and frieze. Slender columns graced the perimeter of the room, soaring toward a domed skylight that defied the gloom by coaxing every last drop of light from the weeping sky. The lower panels of the dome had been painted an ethereal shade of blue and splashed with fluffy white clouds.

"I've always imagined that heaven would look something like this," Lottie whispered, reluctant to disturb the hush.

Except for the gentle patter of the rain against the skylight, the only sound was the shuffle of their slippers as she and Allegra drifted across the parquet floor, hand in hand.

If this was heaven, then the woman in the portrait hanging over the white marble mantel must surely be an angel. As soon as Lottie had been old enough to crawl out of her cradle and toddle over to a mirror, she had recognized herself as an Incomparable Beauty. But this divine creature with her flowing sable curls and laughing violet eyes was beyond comparison.

At least Ned had the good sense not to send me a brunette.

As Hayden's rueful words echoed through her memory, Lottie absently touched a hand to her own hair. For the first time, it seemed washed out to her, a pale shadow of some more vibrant hue.

The woman in the portrait didn't have the alabaster complexion of an English rose, but a sultry

Gallic glow. She was gazing at someone just to the left of the artist, someone who coaxed a teasing pout to her lush lips and made her eyes sparkle with unspoken promises. It was difficult to believe such a spirit could ever be snuffed out of existence. Even frozen forever on canvas, Justine was more alive than most women could ever hope to be.

She was the sort of woman a man might die for. The sort of woman he might kill for.

Lottie was so shaken that she didn't feel Allegra's fingers slip away from hers until they were gone. She turned to find the child gazing up at the portrait with an almost eerie detachment.

"Your mother was very beautiful," Lottie said, struggling to hide her own unease.

Allegra shrugged. "I suppose so. I don't really remember her."

Hoping to break the portrait's seductive spell, Lottie turned her back on it, realizing as she did so that the chamber wasn't a drawing room, but a music room. A gilded harp sat in one corner next to a low-slung divan. In the opposite corner was a clavichord that would have probably been more comfortable in a music room of a century ago. But the centerpiece of the room was a Viennese piano that had been hand-painted white to match the wainscoting. Its wing-shaped lid was propped upright, its curved cabriole legs a study in grace.

Lottie moved to the instrument and gently ran one finger along its gleaming bone and ebony keys. There wasn't a speck of dust to be found anywhere on it. If Martha was the only one allowed a key to this chamber, then she was a very diligent keeper of her former mistress's memory.

Catching a flicker of movement out of the corner of her eye, Lottie asked Allegra, "Do you play?"

The girl snatched her hand away from the keys and tucked it behind her back. "Of course not. Father would never allow it."

Lottie frowned. There were several yellowing pieces of music scattered across the music stand, almost as if their mistress had simply excused herself to indulge in afternoon tea and might return at any moment. As Lottie slid onto the bench, she felt as if she were profaning a sacred altar.

She flexed her fingers, toyed with a few awkward chords, then began to play. The piano had a beautiful tone—rich, sweet, and majestic. Lottie had always enjoyed banging away on just about any instrument. Long before Sterling had engaged her first music master, she, George, and Laura had spent many a happy evening gathered around the battered pianoforte in Lady Eleanor's drawing room.

After a stumbling start, her fingers danced nimbly over the keys in a sprightly passage from Handel's "Water Music" that had always been one of her favorites. She stole a glance over her shoulder at Allegra.

The child was gazing at the keys with a rapt hunger Lottie had never before seen on her face. Shifting tempo, Lottie launched into a merry Scottish jig. Grinning over her shoulder at Allegra, she sang in a exaggerated Scottish burr—

> *"My wife's a wanton wee thing,*
> *She winna be guided by me.*
> *She sell'd her coat and she drank it,*
> *She sell'd her coat and she drank it,*
> *She row'd herself in a blanket,*
> *She winna be guided by me."*

Before long, Allegra was humming along and tapping her foot in time to the rousing rhythm. After the third verse, she joined in on the chorus, shyly at first, but gaining confidence with each note. Her voice was a dusky alto, the perfect complement to Lottie's soprano.

For some reason, Lottie couldn't bear the thought of watching Allegra retreat back into her wary shell. After she had exhausted every verse of the song, she began to make up verses of her own. Her absurd improvisations soon had them both laughing so hard they could barely gasp out the words to the chorus. Neither one of them realized that they had left the door to the music room ajar.

Music and laughter.

Two sounds Hayden had thought never to hear again at Oakwylde Manor. Yet when a washed-out bridge cut his journey to Boscastle short, he had returned to find them both ringing through his home.

He stood in the entrance hall, rainwater dripping from the brim of his hat, and listened to that ghostly echo. For a dazed moment, he actually believed that time had somehow gone skipping backward in his absence.

He saw himself striding along the corridor that led to the music room, his steps not weighted with dread, but light and eager. He threw open the doors to find Allegra, not tall and gangly, but small and chubby, perched on her mama's lap.

Their dark heads merged into one as Justine patiently arranged Allegra's pudgy little fingers on the piano keys, singing an airy nursery rhyme in her sweet contralto. Hayden leaned against the door-jamb for a long time, content just to watch the two of them together. To his keen relief, there were no shadows beneath his wife's eyes that might bode ill for his homecoming.

"Papa!" Allegra squealed, her eyes lighting up as she spotted him. She slid out of her mama's lap and came scrambling over to be swept up into his arms. As she pressed her plump little cheek to his, he closed his eyes and breathed deeply of her baby-sweet scent.

When he opened them again, he was still standing in the drafty entrance hall, his arms empty and his heart aching with loss.

"My lord?" queried a puzzled-looking Giles. "You're quite thoroughly drenched. May I take your coat and hat?"

Hayden didn't even reply. He simply brushed the man aside and started for the music room.

Lottie and Allegra were so engrossed in their merriment that they never heard his clipped footsteps cross the room, never realized they were no longer alone until the lid of the piano came slamming down with a mighty crash, revealing him behind it.

Chapter 14

*Alas, every word that fell from his lips was a pretty lie,
designed to seduce me!*

RISING FROM THE BENCH, LOTTIE FACED Hayden across the gleaming expanse of the piano's lid, her ears still ringing.

He hadn't even taken the time to doff his coat or hat. Rain dripped from the shoulder-cape of his coat to the parquet floor, while the brim of his hat shadowed his eyes. From the corner of her eye, Lottie could see Allegra visibly shrinking, her shoulders hunching inward, her lips growing narrow and pinched. The sight made Lottie want to stamp her foot in frustration.

"Who let you in here?" Hayden demanded.

"No one," Lottie replied, truthful and defiant all at once.

He shifted his accusing gaze to his daughter. "Allegra?"

The child shook her head violently. "I certainly don't have a key."

He swept off his hat. After catching her first clear glimpse of his eyes, Lottie almost wished he'd left it on. "Then how in the devil did the two of you get in here? You know it's forbidden."

"We were playing at explorers," Lottie confessed, hoping to divert his attention from the child.

Her ploy worked a little too well. Hayden rounded on her, his narrowed eyes and taut jaw challenging her to continue.

She lifted her shoulders in an apologetic shrug. "And as I'm sure you know, there's nothing more enticing to an explorer than the lure of the forbidden."

For just an instant, something else flickered through his frosty green eyes—something both dangerous and alluring. "So what did you do? Steal the key from Martha?"

"Of course not! I would *never* encourage Allegra to steal." Lottie folded her hands primly in front of her. "I simply picked the lock with one of my hairpins."

Hayden gazed at her in disbelief for a moment, then let out a harsh bark of laughter. "Oh, that's rich! You won't encourage my daughter to steal, but you have no qualms about teaching her how to pick a lock." Allegra came around the piano and tugged at the sleeve of his coat, but he was too busy glaring at Lottie to notice. "What do you plan to do for your next lesson? Show her how to hold up a coach at gunpoint?"

Before Lottie could sputter a retort, Allegra gave

her father's sleeve another tug, this time succeeding in getting his attention. "She didn't teach me how to pick the lock. She picked it herself." Her voice rose. "And do you know why? Because she saw that I was lonely and bored and unhappy and she was the only one in this house who cared enough to do anything about it!"

Both Hayden and Lottie gaped at the child, astonished by her passionate outburst. Never in a million years would Lottie have dreamed that Allegra would come to her defense. As she studied the girl's fierce little face, she felt an unexpected rush of tenderness.

Hayden, however, did not seem to be suffering any such sentimental pangs. "Your stepmother might not be well acquainted with the rules of this house, young lady, but you are. There's absolutely no excuse for your disobedience." He shook his head, his expression grave. "I'm deeply disappointed in you."

"Well, that's nothing new, is it, Father? You always have been." Somehow, it would have been less damning if Allegra had burst into tears and fled. Instead, she turned and strode stiffly from the music room, her small hands clenched into fists.

Biting off an oath, Hayden swung away from the piano only to find himself face-to-face with the portrait of his first wife. Lottie was almost thankful that she couldn't see his expression in that moment. With an intuition she hadn't even known she possessed, she suddenly knew exactly who had been standing just to the left of the artist when that portrait was painted. Justine's laughing eyes and teasing pout were for Hayden alone.

"After she died," he finally said, his voice as dry as grave dust, "I spent over a fortnight in this room—refusing to eat, refusing to sleep, refusing to see my daughter. The day I finally found the strength to walk out those doors, I swore I'd never set foot in here again as long as I lived." He stiffly turned away from both the portrait and Lottie, as if he could no longer bear to look at either of his wives.

"I'm sorry," Lottie whispered, suffering the full ramifications of her mischief for the first time.

"For what?" he asked, turning his hat in his hands. "Making a mockery of my wishes? Deliberately encouraging my daughter to defy me? Driving yet another wedge between the two of us with your meddling?"

"If you think me such a terrible influence on your daughter, then I don't understand why you brought me to Oakwylde in the first place."

Hayden slammed a fist down on the top of the piano. "Because I wanted her to be like you!"

Lottie gazed at him, stunned by his words.

"I wanted her to use her mind to think her way out of situations instead of being a slave to her moods. I wanted her to be clever and strong and resourceful and confident!"

As Lottie gazed into his fierce, dark-lashed eyes, she felt a curious melting sensation in her midsection—as if she'd just swallowed a mouthful of Cookie's warm spice pudding. She came around the piano, drawing as near to him as she dared. "I swear to you that I didn't mean any harm by bringing her here. Didn't you hear her when you walked in? She was singing and laughing like any ordinary ten-year-old child. For just a few short minutes, she was happy!"

"Her mother liked to sing and laugh, too. Unfortunately, Justine's happiness invariably preceded everyone else's misery, including her own."

"And yours?" Lottie ventured.

Hayden did not reply.

She sighed. "So how are you going to punish me for my transgression? Send me to bed without supper?"

"Don't be ridiculous. Although you persist in behaving like one, you're not a child."

"I'm not a servant either," she shot back. "Although you persist in treating me like one."

As he turned and started for the door, coolly dismissing her challenge, Lottie suddenly wanted to throw an Allegra-sized tantrum. She wanted to snatch up one of the exquisite porcelain shepherdesses smirking down at her from the mantel and hurl it at the back of his head.

"Maybe it wasn't madness that drove your wife into another man's bed," she called after him. "Maybe it was your own insufferable indifference."

Hayden froze, allowing Lottie only about half a second of regret. Then in one abrupt motion, he turned and came striding back toward her, the fire in his eyes scorching away the frost. She wouldn't have been surprised to see steam come rolling off the damp wool of his coat. He backed her right up against the piano with his hard, muscular body, curling the powerful fingers of one hand around her nape.

But instead of strangling her, he brought his mouth down hard on hers. She expected him to punish her with his kiss, not pleasure her. Which was why it was even more affecting when its violence was tempered by the beguiling swirl of his tongue through her mouth. He kissed her as if she belonged to him, as if she always had and always would. He was the lover from her dream and the dark power of his kiss left her teetering on the edge of a dangerous precipice, on the brink of taking a fall that would surely prove fatal to both her body and her heart.

She was still clinging helplessly to him when he tore his mouth away from hers. Tangling his fingers in her tumbled chignon, he gazed down at her, his eyes heavy-lidded and glittering with desire. "I can assure you, my lady, that it's not indifference keeping me from your bed."

He freed her as abruptly as he'd seized her, striding from the room and slamming the door behind him with such a thunderous bang that the harp strings twanged in protest.

As Lottie collapsed against the piano, shaken to the core, Justine gazed down at her, her knowing eyes sparkling with amusement.

Lottie huddled in her bed that night, her every nerve tingling with tension. A peaceful hush had fallen over the sleeping house, but perversely enough, the quiet only deepened her growing sense of unease. Even one of Allegra's tantrums would have been a welcome distraction. She briefly considered wandering across the hall, but the last time she'd peeked in on Harriet, her friend had been sleeping like a lamb.

She threw herself to her side, kicking away both her blankets and a startled Mr. Wiggles. She grabbed for the cat, but it was too late. He'd already jumped down from the bed in a feline huff, his tail jutting straight into the air. He nudged open the door and trotted from the bedchamber, obviously in search of better company.

Lottie flopped back among the pillows. "It seems I can't make anyone happy these days," she muttered to Mirabella, who was curled up on the pillow beside her. "Especially not anyone of the male persuasion."

She closed her eyes, then quickly opened them again. In truth, she was more afraid of sleep than wakefulness. For with sleep would come dreams. And in those dreams, she just might find herself back on the edge of that windswept cliff in a stranger's arms. A stranger whose kiss tasted exactly like her husband's.

She gazed up at the shadows flickering across the ceiling. Perhaps she should add a new scene to her novel. A scene where her feisty heroine fights off the carnal advances of the blackguard who has tricked her into marriage. A scene where she haughtily informs him that she'd rather die than suffer his kiss. For surely a noble death would be preferable to enduring the indignities of his hard, hungry mouth on hers, the dark and delicious thrust of his tongue, the caress of his fingertips against her throat as he coaxed her to open wider, take him deeper . . .

Biting her bottom lip to stifle its treacherous tingling, Lottie flung herself to her stomach. She'd nearly drifted into a fitful doze when, without so much as a plaintive wail to herald it, the first notes of piano music came drifting to her ears.

Lottie's eyes flew open. Her first instinct was to dive beneath the blankets. But all she could do was hold her breath and listen.

The distant music was at once both beautiful and terrible—an uncontrollable deluge of passion, its every note shadowed by madness.

"Justine," she whispered. Seeing the woman's portrait had somehow made it impossible to think of her as simply "the ghost."

What force could be powerful enough to drag a woman back from the grave? Was Justine trying to frighten her away because she believed her to be a rival for Hayden's affections? Or was she trying to warn Lottie not to make the same mistake she had, not to trust her heart or her life into Hayden's hands?

Lottie dragged her pillow over her head and pressed it to her ears. But there was no escaping the music's relentless fury. It could not and would not be ignored.

As the piece reached a fiery crescendo, she tossed aside the pillow. Rising, she strode to her dressing table and pawed through the tangled snarl of rib-

bons and garters until she found what she was looking for—a long and particularly lethal-looking silver
hatpin.

She held it up to the firelight, admiring its gleam.
Apparently, Justine had forgotten one thing. Lottie
now possessed the keys to the kingdom. And if that
kingdom turned out to be hell, then running into the
devil himself was a chance she'd have to take.

Hayden was in the very devil of a temper. He wandered the lonely corridors of the manor, cursing
himself for being such a fool. He might have sought
to punish Lottie with his kiss, but he had succeeded
only in punishing himself. Even his bed had become an instrument of torture, its icy embrace a bitter contrast to the beguiling warmth of Lottie's
arms.

She had released these demons herself when she
had dared to throw open the door of the music
room. It was almost as if some part of him had been
entombed in that room right along with Justine's
memory. But Lottie hadn't been content to let him
rot there in the shadows with the rest of the ghosts.
She had marched in with her silly songs and giddy
laughter and dragged him into the light.

Even Justine had fled before her bold determination. In that moment when they'd kissed, there had
been only Lottie—her mouth a living flame beneath
his—hot and sweet and irresistible. When her small
hands had clutched at the front of his coat, urging
him closer instead of pushing him away, he'd felt

dangerous stirrings of life, not just in his body, but deep in his soul.

Even more damning than their kiss had been that moment when he had confessed that he wanted Allegra to be like her. That he admired her courage, her cleverness, and her unwillingness to abide by the stifling rules of society. He might have just as well blurted out that he was falling in love with her.

Hayden stopped in his tracks, the notion more horrifying than any wailing specter from the past. The last time he'd lost his heart, he'd nearly lost his mind right along with it.

As if to remind him of the cost of such folly, a wild torrent of piano music came rushing down the corridor toward him, its raw power derived from both its beauty and its madness.

Hayden moved inexorably toward the sound, fearing Lottie had unwittingly unleashed a force that could destroy them both.

Lottie strode through the darkened manor, the skirt of her nightdress billowing out behind her. Knowing the servants would all be cowering in their beds by now, she hadn't even taken the time to don her dressing gown. The music swelled with each step that brought her closer to the west wing. But she refused to be dissuaded from her mission. She was no longer driven by courage or curiosity, but by a fierce desire to confront the woman who refused to relinquish her claim on Hayden's heart.

In truth, Lottie was more terrified than she'd ever been in her life. By the time she reached that long, lonely corridor, not even the surging music could completely drown out the chattering of her teeth. As she approached the doors at the end of the hall, she half expected them to swing open all on their own, a trap disguised as an invitation.

Her numb fingers failed to budge the knob. The doors were locked, just as she and Allegra had found them earlier. Lottie's hands were sweating so badly that she dropped the hatpin twice before finally managing to pick the lock.

Still she hesitated. If she threw open the doors without warning, would she find some malevolent vapor hovering over the piano? Or would the keys simply play themselves, guided by an unseen hand?

Utterly unnerved by that image, she slowly turned the knob, halfway hoping the music would cease as abruptly as it had her first night at the manor. But as she eased open the door, it swept over her in such a thundering wave that Lottie could feel her very heart take up its rhythm.

Shadows draped the spacious room. The rain had ceased hours ago, but clouds still scudded across the circle of sky visible through the skylight, veiling the alabaster face of the moon and casting Justine's portrait in shadow.

The lid of the piano was up, shielding its keys from her view.

Lottie slowly circled the instrument, promising herself she would not scream no matter who—or what—she found on the other side. The heady fragrance of night-blooming jasmine swept over her, making her feel dizzy and slightly drunk.

She rounded the piano to find a woman garbed all in gauzy white, her long, dark hair rippling down her back.

Justine.

Lottie could not have screamed if she had wanted to. Her throat was paralyzed with fright.

A gust of wind scattered the clouds. Moonlight came streaming through the skylight to reveal not a woman, but a child wrapped in a nightdress twice her size.

Allegra.

Awestruck by the beauty and power of the child's playing, Lottie had to grip the edge of the piano to keep from staggering.

Allegra's small fingers flew over the piano keys, pouring out a litany of fury and heartbreak no child her age should ever have to know. Tears streamed down her pale cheeks as she played, yet her fierce concentration never wavered from the sheet of music before her, not even when Lottie came drifting into her view, unable to stop herself from creeping closer to the source of that astonishing music.

Allegra's hands pounded the keys, bringing the nocturne to a close with a crashing flourish.

"How?" Lottie whispered into the ringing silence that followed.

Allegra curled her hands in her lap. They were suddenly the hands of a child again, clumsy and unsure of themselves. "There's a secret passage behind the mantel that leads up to the second floor. Mama and I used to play hide-and-seek there all the time. Papa"—she stumbled, but quickly recovered—

"Father could never find us when we hid there."

"I meant how did you learn to play the piano?" Lottie gestured toward the keys, shock robbing her of all eloquence. "Like *that*?"

"Mama was teaching me when she died." The girl shrugged her slender shoulders. "It was never hard for me the way it is for some people."

Lottie shook her head. The child was a prodigy and she didn't even realize it. "I thought you didn't remember your mother."

"Oh, I remember her!" Allegra's gaze grew fierce again. "He doesn't want me to, but I do. She was kind and funny, always laughing and singing. She would spend hours just sitting on the floor with me, drawing pictures or teaching me a new song. She would let me wear all of her hats and we would serve tea to my dolls together."

Lottie smiled wistfully, wishing she had such memories of her own mother. "You must miss her very much."

Allegra rose from the piano bench. She paced back and forth across the parquet floor, bunching up handfuls of the fine linen to keep from tripping over the hem of the oversized nightdress. "I never meant to become a ghost, you know. Whenever Father would go away, I would sneak in here and play the piano. I didn't even realize the servants could hear me until one morning when I overheard Meggie and Martha whispering about the manor being haunted."

"But you didn't stop."

"No," Allegra admitted, her gaze openly defiant.

"I didn't. After a while, I even started playing when Father was home. He was in Yorkshire on business when I first found the trunk in the attic where he kept Mama's things locked away. I put on her nightdress because it smelled like her."

Lottie nodded. That must explain the jasmine, although oddly enough, the fragrance seemed much weaker than it had only a few minutes ago.

Allegra turned pleading eyes to Lottie. "I didn't have anything of hers, you see. He'd hidden it all away. And he refused to speak of her at all. It was as if she had never existed, and I couldn't bear it!" The girl's voice broke as fresh tears spilled down her cheeks. "Oh, I hate him! I hate him with all my heart!"

Lottie didn't even realize she'd opened her arms until Allegra ran into them. The girl flung her arms around Lottie's waist, sobbing as if her heart was breaking anew. As she stroked Allegra's soft, thick hair, Lottie lifted her head to find Hayden standing in the doorway of the music room, his face ashen in the moonlight. Before she could reach out a hand to him, he had vanished back into the shadows.

Lottie drew a blanket over the sleeping child. Although Allegra's face was still stained with tears, she slept with the open-mouthed abandon of the very young. She probably wouldn't awaken until morning. Even so, Lottie was reluctant to leave her all alone. She glanced around the child's bedchamber until she spotted her old doll perched on the windowsill, smirking affably at them both. Lottie gently tucked the doll in the crook of Allegra's arm, then drew the bedchamber door shut behind her, leaving the lamp burning.

She found Hayden exactly where she thought she would—standing in the middle of the music room, gazing up at Justine's portrait. The moon had shifted in the sky, bathing the portrait in a luminous glow.

"Why shouldn't my daughter hate me?" he asked bitterly as he heard Lottie's hesitant footfall behind him. "After all, I took her mother away from her."

For just an instant, Lottie would have sworn her heart stopped.

"Look around this house," he continued. "Outside of this room, there are no portraits of her, no samplers she stitched, no watercolors she painted—not even the smallest remembrance that she ever walked these corridors. Allegra was so young when her mother died. I suppose I thought it would be better if she could just . . . forget."

Lottie's heart started beating again, if unevenly. She sank down on the edge of the divan, her knees betraying her. "How could you expect Allegra to forget? You obviously haven't."

Turning away from the portrait, Hayden moved to the piano. Using only one finger, he picked out the first few notes of the second movement of Beethoven's "Pathetique." "I even denied her the piano after her mother died. I suppose I always believed that somehow the music and the madness went hand in hand, that she couldn't have one without the other. Justine was brilliant. Had she been a man, she would have been invited to play for the king. She adored music."

"And you adored her." Lottie refused to insult either of them by pretending it was a question.

Hayden's finger hit the wrong note. He withdrew his hand from the keys. "We were very young when we wed. I wasn't yet twenty-one and she was seventeen. At first I thought her mercurial moods were just part of her charm. She was French, after all, and much less reserved than the women I was accustomed to. One minute she'd be laughing, the next sulking over some imagined slight, the next goading you into a shouting match. But then she'd cry and beg you to forgive her so prettily." He shook his head wryly. "It was impossible to stay angry at her for more than a few minutes."

Lottie stole another look at the portrait, then almost wished she hadn't.

Hayden straddled the piano bench, facing her. "It wasn't until after Allegra was born that Justine's moods took a darker turn. She would go for days without sleeping, then take to her bed for weeks at a time."

"It must have been very difficult for you."

He shook his head, refusing her pity. "There were dark days, but there were good days, too. When Justine was well, we were all happy. She adored Allegra. Being a mother gave her so much joy. Although she would sometimes turn her wrath against me, I never once saw her lift a hand to our baby." His face darkened so dramatically that Lottie glanced at the skylight to see if a cloud had passed over the moon. "When Allegra was six, Justine lapsed back into one of her black moods. I thought perhaps a Season in London would lift her spirits. We married so young that I'd always felt a little guilty for depriving her of the social whirl she loved." A bitter smile twisted his lips. "My dear friends Ned and Phillipe had both courted her before we married. At our wedding, they laughed and swore they'd never forgive me for stealing away their treasure."

A tarnished treasure indeed, Lottie thought, but she managed to hold her tongue.

Hayden rose from the bench and began to pace the floor much as his daughter had done earlier. "At first London seemed to be the answer to all of my prayers. For over a fortnight, Justine was the toast of the town, the belle of every ball. Then things started to go wrong. I knew the signs only too well. She stopped sleeping. Her eyes grew too bright, her laugh too shrill. She would pick quarrels with me over anything—or nothing at all. We started having terrible rows. We both said things that were . . . unforgivable. She began staying out until the wee hours of morning, wearing too much powder and rouge, flirting shamelessly with other men in my presence."

"What did you do?" Lottie asked, fighting the urge to reach out and grab his hand as he passed.

"What could I do?" He spun around to face her. "When one of my sympathetic friends sent over his private physician—a most reputable fellow who had treated our former king during some of his darkest days—the man simply shook his head and suggested I send her to Bedlam. Bedlam!" Hayden dropped to one knee, closing his hands over Lottie's shoulders. His eyes searched her face, their dark-fringed depths fierce with anguish. "Do you know what they do to the inmates at Bethlem Hospital, Lottie? They chain them to the walls in tiny cells. The attendants charge the public a fee to come and gawk at them. Why, Justine wouldn't have survived the night!"

Now Lottie couldn't bear to look at him or the portrait. Couldn't bear to imagine that vibrant young creature chained to a wall like a feral animal while spectators paraded past, laughing and pointing. She didn't realize she was crying until Hayden gently brushed a tear from her cheek with the pad of his thumb.

"After the physician left, I informed Justine that we'd be returning to Cornwall in the morning." He fingered the scar beneath his left ear, managing a rueful smile. "She did *not* take the news well. I was afraid she might do some mischief to herself so I gave her a generous dose of laudanum. Her physician from home had sent a bottle with me, just as a precaution. Before long she was sleeping like a babe.

"There were arrangements to make. Friends to bid farewell to. So I left her there in the care of a servant."

Hayden rose to his feet. Once Lottie might have begged to hear the end of such a story. But suddenly she wanted to press her fingertips to his lips, wanted to implore him not to utter another word about that night.

When he spoke again, all the passion had drained from his voice, leaving it as remote as the moon. "When I returned, I found her with Phillipe." His uncompromising gaze pinned Lottie to the divan. "Do you want to know what the worst of it was?"

"No," she whispered. But it was too late. They both knew it.

"He let her believe it was me. She was sick and drugged and confused and she thought I'd returned so we could make up our quarrel. If she hadn't been watching, half out of her mind, when I dragged him off of her, I wouldn't have waited for the duel. I would have killed him with my bare hands." He flexed those hands now, reminding Lottie of their power.

"If you had, you'd be rotting away in Newgate right now and Allegra would be without a father." But would she still be without a mother? It was the one question Lottie couldn't bring herself to ask.

Hayden raked a hand through his hair, shaking his head. "After Phillipe fled, everything was a blur. I was half crazed myself. I remember sweeping Justine up in my arms and carrying her through the town house. All I could think about was getting her out of that bed where she had ... where they had ..." His hands clenched into fists. "She still didn't realize what had happened. I remember the feel of her cuddled against my chest, the way her arms curled so trustingly around my neck just as they had a hundred times before. She gazed up into my eyes and told me how sorry she was for the cruel things she'd said, the hurtful things she'd done. She told me how much she loved me, how grateful she was to me for giving her the chance to prove that love."

He unclenched his hands, studying them as if they belonged to a stranger. "For one fleeting instant, as I gazed down into those beautiful eyes of hers, I wanted to strangle the life from her, if only to spare her the knowledge of what she had done—what she'd done to us."

"But you didn't," Lottie said fiercely, rising from the divan.

He watched her approach, his eyes wary. "I have no need of your pity, my lady, and I certainly don't deserve your absolution."

"I don't pity you," she said calmly. "I envy you."

"Envy?" He snorted in disbelief. "Are you mad as well?"

She shook her head. "Most people go through their entire lives and never know a love like the one you and Justine shared."

Hayden rolled his eyes toward the skylight. "Dear Lord in heaven, deliver me from the romantic notions of schoolgirls. If that was *love*," he all but spat, "then I want no part of it ever again. It does nothing but destroy everything in its path."

"It hasn't destroyed you or your daughter. Yet."

"Are you so sure of that? You heard Allegra tonight. She despises me."

Lottie rested her hands on her hips. "Oh, really? Is

that why she goes into hysterics at the mere mention of being sent away from you? Is that why she snuck into this room and masqueraded as a ghost in the desperate hope that *you* would be the one to walk through those doors, not me? Why, the only way she knew how to get your attention was by dressing up as her dead mother!"

For a long moment, Hayden could only blink at her in disbelief. "That's ridiculous! Whenever I try to give her my attention, she flings it back in my face, just as she did the doll I had made for her."

"That's because she doesn't want dolls or expensive toys from you. She wants you to look at her! She wants you to *really* look at her, just once, without seeing Justine!"

Lottie couldn't have said when her voice rose to a shout. She just knew that somehow they'd ended up standing toe-to-toe, so close she could feel the heat roiling off of his body and smell the crisp, rich scent of his bayberry soap.

Hayden reached down and twined one of her long, golden curls around his fingertip, his voice growing dangerously soft. "What about you, Carlotta? What do *you* want?"

Lottie wanted him to look at *her,* just once, without seeing Justine.

She wanted him to assure her that she wasn't falling in love with a murderer.

But most of all, she wanted to kiss him. She wanted to stand on tiptoe and claim that wary mouth of his for her very own. She wanted to kiss him until all the ghosts—both Justine and that phantom of his younger self—had been banished from the room. She wanted to twine her arms around his neck, press herself against him, and remind him just how warm and giving living flesh could be.

So she did.

Chapter 15

How could my treacherous flesh
crave the touch of a murderer?

HAYDEN STIFFENED IN SHOCK AS LOTTIE'S lips brushed his jaw, scattering soft kisses all along its rigid curve. He closed his eyes, a muscle working in his throat, as her lips sought the corner of his mouth. But it was the bold flick of her tongue against that vulnerable spot that made him groan, coaxed his mouth into melting against hers, no longer able to resist the carnal innocence of such a kiss.

Wrapping his arms around Lottie, Hayden slanted his mouth over hers, thrusting his tongue deep into the silky heat of her mouth. Her tongue curled around his, maddening him with its wordless promise of pleasure. Pleasure he had denied himself for far too long. Somewhere in his mind, love and loss had become inextricably intertwined.

But Lottie was seeking to give, not take, and he was powerless to resist such a generous offer.

Until he glanced up to find Justine laughing down at him, mocking him for succumbing to the very temptation that had once proved his ruin.

Hayden thrust himself away from Lottie, struggling to catch his breath. If he dared to look at her in the moonlight with the spun gold of her hair tumbling down her back, her lush lips moist and swollen from his kisses, her misty blue eyes imploring, he knew they'd both be lost. He'd have her beneath him on the divan, her nightdress rucked up around her waist, before she could draw another breath.

"I already told you once," he said, his voice so harsh he barely recognized it himself, "I neither want nor deserve your pity."

"Is that all you think I have to offer you—pity?"

Hayden closed his eyes, steeling himself against the husky catch in her voice. "I'm sure you have much to offer, my lady. But I have nothing to give you in return."

"Because you gave it all to *her*."

Even as his silence condemned him in her eyes, Hayden could not resist stealing one last look at Lottie.

Although her eyes glistened with unshed tears, that stubborn little chin of hers had lost none of its determination. "Then I hope the two of you will be very happy together. I'm beginning to believe you deserve each other."

With those words, his wife turned and walked

stiffly from the room, much as his daughter had done earlier in that cursed day.

Biting off an oath, Hayden swept one of the porcelain shepherdesses off the mantel and hurled it at Justine's portrait with all of his might. The figurine shattered against the canvas without leaving a single mark on her angelic face.

The next morning Lottie sat on a rock near the edge of the cliff, the hem of her skirts whipping in the wind. She wanted to cry, but she knew the wind would only snatch the tears from her face before they could fall. So she simply gazed out to sea, her heart aching and her eyes burning with unshed tears. She wondered if Justine had ever sat in this very spot, gazing down upon the jagged rocks that would end her life.

Lottie was beginning to realize just what a colossal fool she had been since coming to Oakwylde. She had thought to banish all the ghosts from the manor, never taking into consideration that it wasn't Hayden's house that was haunted, but his heart. Despite all of her bravado, she did not know how to fight an enemy she could not see.

Watching the breakers swirl around the rocks, she wondered how it must feel to be loved with that kind of all-consuming passion. How could a man destroy something he loved so much? But passion and jealous rage often went hand in hand, she reminded herself. The hunger to possess was all too often coupled with the drive to destroy what refused to be possessed.

"Justine," she whispered bitterly, searching the cloudswept sky. "Why did you have to take all of his secrets to your grave?"

She closed her eyes, wondering if she was imagining the faint hint of jasmine that perfumed the wind.

When she opened them, Allegra was standing there, clutching Lottie's doll in her arms. As usual, she didn't bother with pleasantries, but simply blurted out, "Father says I'm to be allowed into the music room to practice the piano whenever I like."

Although her expression was no less dour than it normally was, the girl somehow managed to look as happy as Lottie had ever seen her. Perversely enough, it was Hayden's kindness, not his rebuff that finally prompted the tears in Lottie's eyes to well over.

"That's marvelous," she said, dashing away a tear before Allegra could see it. "I'm so happy for you."

"Then why are you crying?" the child asked, creeping nearer.

"I'm not crying," Lottie insisted. "The wind just blew a speck of dirt in my eye." But to her dismay, the tears began to spill down her cheeks faster than she could dash them away.

"No, it didn't," Allegra said accusingly. "You're crying."

No longer able to dispute the obvious, Lottie buried her face in her hands to muffle her sobs.

She was startled to feel the weight of a small hand on her shoulder. "Why are you crying?" Allegra asked, sounding genuinely curious. "Was someone mean to you? Someone besides me?"

That earned her a strangled hiccup of laughter. Lottie lifted her head, smiling at the child through watery eyes. "No one was mean to me. I'm just feeling a little sad today."

"Here." Allegra shoved the doll at Lottie. "When I'm sad, sometimes I squeeze her very tightly and it makes me feel better."

Caught off guard by the child's unexpected generosity, Lottie took her old doll and gave it a wary squeeze. Surprisingly enough, she did feel a little better. But not nearly as good as she felt when Allegra slipped one small hand into hers.

"The two of us were just about to have breakfast," Allegra informed her. "Why don't you join us? Unless you're too sad to be hungry, that is."

Lottie stared at their joined hands. Hayden might not have need of her, but perhaps his daughter did.

Wiping away the last of her tears, she allowed Allegra to tug her to her feet. "Don't be silly," she said, swinging the girl's hand in hers as they started for the house. "I'm never too *anything* to be hungry."

Hayden St. Clair was being haunted.

This spirit was much more tenacious than any found between the pages of a Gothic thriller. It didn't wail like a banshee or shine mysterious lights from the window of some deserted chamber. It never rattled chains after midnight or drifted up and down the corridors of the manor in the moonlight with its severed head beneath its arm. Nor did it play ghostly melodies on the piano in the music room or wake him out of a sound sleep with a whiff of fragrance that should have dissipated years ago.

On the contrary, it haunted his every waking moment, boldly laying claim to each room of his home until there was nowhere he could flee to escape it.

He had his first inkling of its presence a few days after his moonlight encounter with Lottie in the music room. He was passing by the drawing room when he heard a most astonishing sound. He froze in his tracks, cocking his head to listen. The sound wasn't completely foreign to him. He had heard it many times before, but so long ago that it was like a song remembered from a dream.

His daughter was giggling.

Unable to resist the siren lure of the sound, he retraced his steps and warily peered around the archway that framed the drawing room door.

Lottie, Harriet, Allegra, and Lottie's scruffy old doll were all gathered around a teak-inlaid table, partaking of afternoon tea. They each wore elaborate hats festooned with a colorful array of feathers, ribbons, flowers, and cobwebs. Hayden did a double take when he spotted the stuffed parrot perched on the shoulder of Lottie's doll. The mangy bird perfectly complemented both her eye patch and her leering smirk. The doll required only a cutlass in her dainty little hand and she would be ready to sail the bounding main.

Even Mirabella wore a hat—a baby bonnet of ivory lace, its satin bow tied beneath her furry chin. Allegra held the squirming kitten in her lap to keep it from bolting, giggling every time the creature reached up to bat at the ribbons dangling from her own hat.

Apparently, Hayden was the only one who hadn't received a formal invitation to the tea party. Three of the kittens Lottie had given him stood on the table, lapping cream from a china saucer, while their yellow sibling chased its own tail around a table leg.

As Allegra added a ruffled petticoat to Mirabella's elegant ensemble, Pumpkin and Mr. Wiggles went streaking past Hayden, obviously fearing they were in danger of being subjected to similar indignities. Hayden knew he would be wise to follow. Yet still he lingered, reluctant to abandon the charming chaos of the scene.

He hadn't counted on the yellow kitten spotting him. Before he could slip away, it came trotting toward him, mewing at the top of its tiny pink lungs.

"Traitor," Hayden muttered, nudging it away with his foot.

But it was too late. The smiles had vanished. The merry chatter had ceased. Miss Dimwinkle looked as if she were trying to choke on a mouthful of scone. If she succeeded, Hayden assumed he'd be required to add the burden of another untimely death to his conscience.

Lottie blew a wayward feather out of her eyes, surveying him coolly and looking every inch the lady of the manor in her tulle-and-cobweb draped hat and her fingerless lace mittens. "Good afternoon, my lord. Would you care to join us?"

Allegra buried her sullen face in Mirabella's fur as if she could care less whether or not he accepted Lottie's invitation. Hayden was the only one who knew it hadn't been an invitation, but a direct challenge—one Lottie obviously expected him to refuse.

He returned her mocking gaze with one of his own. "You won't make me wear a bonnet, will you?"

"Not unless you choose to."

Lottie drew the only remaining stool up to the table and poured him a cup of tea. Hayden dutifully sat, but bounded quickly back to his feet when the stool let out a protesting yowl. Gritting his teeth, he swept the yellow kitten off the stool and onto the rug. It immediately clawed its way back up his leg, snagging his doeskin trousers, and curled up in his lap, purring madly. Hayden draped a napkin over it and tried to pretend it wasn't there.

The stool was far too short for him. Every attempt he made to fold his long legs beneath it failed miserably. He finally had to content himself with stretching his legs to the side, which brought them in dangerous proximity to Lottie's trim ankles. Her shapely limbs might be swathed in layers of petticoats, pantalettes, and stockings, but that didn't stop him from imagining how sleek and warm they would feel wrapped around his waist.

"Would you care for some cream?" Lottie asked.

Jerking his gaze away from the curve of her calf, Hayden eyed the cream pitcher askance. The black kitten was teetering on its lip. Even as he watched, it lost its balance and went plunging into the milky froth. Before Allegra could rescue it, it scrambled back out and gave itself a dazed shake, scattering drops of cream all over the front of Hayden's waist-coat.

"No, thank you," he murmured, watching it lick its whiskers clean with fastidious care. "I believe I shall pass."

"We borrowed the hats from the attic." Lottie offered him his teacup, her haughty tone all but daring him to protest. "I hope you don't mind. Allegra said they belonged to her mother."

"Not all of them." Hayden pointed to the lace-trimmed bonnet framing Mirabella's cantankerous little face. "If memory serves me correctly, that one once belonged to me."

Allegra cupped a hand over her mouth to suppress an involuntary giggle. "You wore a bonnet?"

"I most certainly did. But it wouldn't have been so mortifying if your grandmother hadn't insisted on having my portrait painted in it while she dandled me on her knee. I must confess that at the time I had curls that would rival your own."

Allegra looked doubtful. "I've never seen such a painting."

"Nor will you," Hayden assured her, taking a sip of his tea. "I 'accidentally' spilled some lamp oil on it and set the hateful thing afire when I was around your age."

"That was quite clever of you," Allegra blurted out. Ducking her head so that her hair shielded her face, she returned her attention to stuffing Mirabella's hind legs into a pair of doll's pantalettes.

"Have you any other youthful indiscretions you'd care to share with us?" Lottie asked, her blue eyes all innocence as she pinched off a bite of scone and tucked it between her lips.

Hayden fought the overpowering urge to lean over and lick away the dab of clotted cream at the corner of her mouth. "One doesn't have to be a youth to commit indiscretions," he replied, refusing to surrender her gaze. "Some temptations, however foolhardy, only sweeten with age."

Blinking at them both from behind a pair of over-sized spectacles loaned to her by one of the servants, Harriet snatched up a handful of iced tea cakes, obviously hoping that if she kept her own mouth full, Hayden wouldn't address her directly.

"So tell me, Miss Dimwinkle," he said pleasantly after she'd crammed them all in her mouth, "are you enjoying your stay in Cornwall?"

Harriet lowered her tea, her hand trembling so violently that the cup rattled against the saucer. "Oh, very much, my lord," she mumbled around a mouthful of cake. "I can't begin to tell you how grateful I am to you for writing my parents and asking them to allow me to stay on here as a companion to Lottie. Why, if you'd have sent me packing back to Kent, I would have simply di—" Harriet stopped talking and chewing at the same time, her expression horrified.

"Died?" Hayden gently offered, hoping to help her swallow before she did just that.

From out of nowhere, Allegra suddenly said, "Lottie's mama died when Lottie was only three. She burned up in a fire. Lottie doesn't even remember what she looked like. Isn't that sad?"

Hayden stole a look at his wife. She looked as puzzled as he felt. "Yes, it is," he agreed with utter sincerity. "Terribly sad."

Still refusing to look at any of them, Allegra rocked Mirabella in the crook of her arm like an ill-tempered, overdressed baby. "Lottie said I should be thankful that I remember my mama."

Hayden felt his throat tighten. "And so you should," he finally managed to choke out, speaking of Justine to his daughter for the first time since her death. "She loved you very much."

Awkwardly shoving back the stool, he stood. The yellow kitten rolled to the floor, shooting him a wounded look. "If you'll excuse me, ladies, I have business I must attend to. I'm sure you'll be eager to get back to your lessons after tea."

Hayden didn't linger long enough to deter-mine who looked guiltier at his mention of lessons— Allegra or Lottie. His only thought was of escape. But as he strode down the long corridor that led to his study, the merry music of their laughter pursued him more surely than any phantom.

Hayden soon learned that there was nowhere he could go to elude their happiness. In the days that followed, it echoed from the schoolroom in wild bursts as poorly muffled as the mysterious thumps that preceded it. It drifted through the open window of his study at dusk as Lottie and Allegra chased the kittens through the garden. It came rippling out of the drawing room after supper as Lottie read aloud from one of her treasured Gothics, her dramatic delivery generating more giggles than shivers. When Hayden caught Meggie and Jem lurking behind the drawing room door, hanging on to her every word, he didn't even have the heart to rebuke them. Especially not since they'd stolen his own hiding place.

Even more haunting than the laughter was the music. Now that the doors of the music room had been thrown wide open, Hayden never knew when it would come spilling through the house, shattering the walls of silence he'd spent the last four years building around himself. It was the one manifestation he could not endure. Whenever Allegra played, he would find some task to take him from the house, whether it was striding to the village on some poor excuse of an errand better suited to his steward or driving his bay across the moor at a breakneck pace.

Although it was a joy to watch his child blossom beneath his bride's attentions, their growing bond only made Hayden feel more isolated. He sought refuge in the library one damp, rainy evening only to encounter a sight he'd never witnessed before— his daughter . . . reading.

Allegra was curled up in a large leather chair before the fire in stocking feet, her nose buried in a book and Mirabella dozing on her lap.

Hayden hesitated in the doorway, unable to resist taking advantage of the rare opportunity to study her. If Allegra knew he was there, she would doubtlessly bolt.

Her face had lost its sallow cast. Her daily romps with Lottie and Harriet had coaxed a flush of color into her cheeks, while their elaborate afternoon teas had begun to ripen the flesh on her bones. A blue velvet ribbon held her glossy mane of dark hair out of her eyes. He'd seen Lottie tending to it before the fire in the drawing room each night, chattering away as she dragged a brush through the stubborn tendrils until they crackled and shone.

As startling as those changes were, the greatest transformation had taken place in his daughter's expression. Her eyes were no longer shadowed by wariness, her lips no longer pinched in a sullen pout.

As Hayden traced the purity of her profile, he shook his head ruefully, realizing that he would soon have a young beauty on his hands. He had always believed she would never marry, when in truth, he might have to beat off her suitors with a stick.

Although Hayden's first instinct was to back out of the room before she saw him, some curious impulse made him clear his throat.

Allegra jerked her nose out of the book, her eyes widening and a guilty flush staining her cheeks. "Father! I didn't hear you come in. I was just... studying my lesson for tomorrow."

As Hayden approached, she attempted to slide the book behind her back.

Before she could succeed, he plucked it neatly from her hand. "What are you studying? History? Latin? Geography?" He held the book up to the firelight, recognizing the thin paperbound volume as one of the cheap chapbooks sold by vendors on the street corners of London. They'd succeeded in introducing the wicked pleasures of the Gothic to impoverished readers who couldn't afford genuine novels.

"*The Spectre of the Turret,* eh?" He thumbed through the pages. "Kidnapping, murder, ghosts, nefarious doings. It sounds very enlightening to me. And what's this?" he asked, spotting another volume tucked between cushion and chair arm. He picked up the book and flipped open the cover, studying a hand-colored engraving of a swordsman dressed as Death offering a severed head to his opponent. "Hmm? *The Cavern of Horrors.* Doesn't look like a place I'd care to visit."

Dumping a disgruntled Mirabella to the hearth rug, Allegra scrambled to her feet, snatching both books out of his hands. "I was just going to return these to Lottie. She must have left them here last night."

Hayden tucked his tongue into his cheek, silently applauding his wife's craftiness. If Lottie had left the chapbooks in the library, she had done so deliberately, hoping to whet Allegra's hunger for the printed word.

"Don't go!" he blurted out as Allegra turned away. "Please," he added softly to reassure her that it wasn't a command, but a request. "I was just looking for a book to wile away a few hours of the evening." He held out a hand, nodding toward *The Cavern of Horrors.* "May I?"

Still eyeing him warily, Allegra handed over the book and sank back into her chair. Hayden settled himself into the twin leather chair opposite hers, kicking off his shoes and propping his own stocking feet on an ottoman. He opened *The Cavern of Horrors*, pretending not to notice the bewildered scowls his daughter kept shooting him over the top of her own chapbook.

He didn't have to pretend for long. After only a few pages, he found himself curiously caught up in the convoluted tale of murder and mayhem.

Both Hayden and Allegra were so engrossed in their reading that they never saw Lottie pause in the doorway of the library to study the cozy tableau. With the rain beating against the mullioned windows and the cat dozing on the stone hearth, they could have been any father and daughter enjoying a quiet evening in each other's company.

Neither one of them heard Lottie go creeping away, still smiling to herself.

Although he didn't make the mistake of joining them again, not even Hayden's pride could stop him from wandering past the drawing room each day when Lottie, Harriet, and Allegra were taking tea. No matter how busy he was, he would find some excuse to linger in the doorway and drink in their merry chatter. His daughter might not welcome his company, but she did seem to be growing more accepting of it. She no longer sought to leave a room the minute he entered it.

As he strolled past one afternoon, he was surprised to find the expensive doll he'd had made for his daughter sitting across the table from Lottie's doll.

Apparently, Allegra was as surprised as he was.

She was standing with hands on hips, surveying the new arrangement with an all too familiar scowl clouding her face. "What's *she* doing here?"

"Harriet's not feeling well this afternoon," Lottie informed her smoothly, taking a sip of tea from a bone china cup. "She has a touch of the ague. We needed a fourth for our table so I didn't see any harm in inviting our little friend here. She's been buried in that box ever since she arrived at Oakwylde. I dare say it's frightfully stuffy in there."

Allegra slumped into the empty chair, still glaring at the interloper. With her immaculate white gloves and exquisitely coiffed sable curls, the doll appeared to be looking down her patrician nose at them all. Lottie's doll leered back at her, her eye patch askew.

Hayden continued on his way, barricading himself in his study until curiosity got the best of him. He peered around the drawing room archway a short while later to find Allegra wagging a finger in the new doll's face. "I'll not have you hogging up all the tea cakes, you wicked girl," she scolded. "And any proper lady knows you never wear gloves while you're eating."

As Allegra proceeded to peel off the doll's gloves and thrust a crumbling jam cake into her dainty hand, dripping strawberry preserves down the front of her costly lavender frock, he felt an involuntary chuckle well up in his chest. As Lottie glanced at the door and lifted her teacup to him in a mocking toast, Hayden realized that she hadn't dug the neglected doll out of its trunk for Allegra.

She had done it for him.

* * *

By the next week both Lottie and Allegra had abandoned all pretense of lessons while Hayden had abandoned all pretense of believing they were still having lessons. When they decided to celebrate a rare appearance of the sun one morning by dragging Lottie's hobbyhorse out to the drive, Hayden lounged on the front stoop of the manor to watch, his eyes shamelessly drinking in his wife's every move.

The wheeled contraption was designed to be propelled by the rider straddling its wooden frame and taking long gliding strides until the vehicle reached a hill steep enough to coast down. It's wooden wheels had been fashioned for paved garden paths, not cobbled drives, so at the moment poor Miss Dimwinkle was rattling past at a pace guaranteed to jar her teeth from her head. Lottie and Allegra ran along on either side of her, laughing and shouting encouragement.

As they disappeared over a hill, Hayden leaned back on his elbows and turned his face to the sun, basking in its warmth. The fine, windy day seemed determined to prove that spring might come late to this corner of Cornwall, but it was well worth the wait. The air smelled of warming earth and things growing wild on the moor. Tender wisps of greenery were beginning to sprout on the branches of trees one would have sworn were dead only a few days ago. A snowy blanket of hawthorn blossoms draped every hill, while the cliffs were coming alive in a blaze of bluebells, sea campion and gorse. The colonies of young kittiwakes roosting in their sheltering crags heralded spring's arrival with their chiming calls.

The hobbyhorse reappeared, this time with Lottie astride it and Harriet and Allegra trotting after her. Lottie's strong, lithe legs soon propelled the contraption into a fast clip. As she reached the top of the hill, she settled her weight on its frame and went sailing down the drive, shrieking with laughter. Her bonnet flew out behind her, bound only by its velvet ribbons. Frowning, Hayden sat up, unnerved by her fearless flight.

Before he could call out a warning, the hobbyhorse struck a rough stone and went bouncing off the drive and into the grass. Lottie's eyes widened.

As she went hurtling toward a grassy bank, Hayden came to his feet. He was off the stoop and sprinting down the drive before Lottie even hit the clump of earth that sent her flying head over heels through the air.

As he ran, Hayden was nearly blinded by a stark image of Lottie lying utterly still in the grass, her neck twisted at an unnatural angle as the roses faded from her cheeks.

He reached her crumpled form at the same time as Harriet and Allegra. They knelt across from him in a puddle of skirts as he gathered Lottie's warm body into his arms, gripped by icy panic. "Lottie! Lottie! Can you hear me?"

Her eyes slowly fluttered open. She blinked up at him. "Of course I can hear you. You're shouting directly into my ear, aren't you?"

As a teasing smile dimpled the downy curve of her cheek, Hayden was torn between kissing her and shaking her senseless.

Keenly aware of Harriet and Allegra's avid scrutiny, he had to content himself with scolding her. "You careless little fool, what did you think you were doing? You could have broken your bloody neck."

Across from him, Allegra's eyes widened with horrified delight. Realizing it was the first time he'd ever cursed in front of his daughter, Hayden added, "Damn it all."

Lottie wiggled to a sitting position in his arms, but made no attempt to extricate herself from them. "Don't be silly. It's hardly the first tumble I've taken on this thing. You should have seen poor George the week Sterling brought it home from Germany. He took a dive right into a patch of thistles and couldn't sit down for a week."

Hayden hauled her to her feet, still glowering at her. "If I catch you pulling another stunt like that, you won't be able to sit down for a week either."

Harriet and Allegra exchanged a scandalized look.

The hobbyhorse was lying in an ungainly heap a few feet away in the grass. Lottie moved to rescue it.

As she rolled it back toward the drive, Hayden rested his hands on his hips. "Surely you're not going to get back on that contraption after it almost killed you."

"I most certainly am," she retorted. A wicked light dawned in her eyes. "Unless, of course, you'd care to take it for a whirl."

Hayden couldn't let such a challenge pass. "I've got an even better idea."

He marched over to her. She squealed in surprise as he closed his hands around her trim waist and lifted her, setting her sidesaddle on the narrow wooden seat. She clutched at the handlebars to keep her balance. Before she could protest, he threw one long leg over the vehicle's frame, reached around her to close his hands over hers on the handlebars and began to propel the hobbyhorse forward with long, powerful strides. When they reached the top of the next steep incline, he sank down on the seat behind Lottie and stuck his legs straight out before them, sending the vehicle hurtling down the hill at a breakneck pace.

Lottie's terrified squeals quickly became screams of laughter. Harriet and Allegra pelted along behind them for several steps before finally giving up the chase. Then there was only the wind in his hair, the sun in his face, and Lottie's lush, warm body tucked against his.

Hayden had driven his bay across the moor a hundred times since Justine's death, attempting to outpace the shadows of the past. But with Lottie in his arms, he felt as if he wasn't just running away from something, but racing toward something.

Unfortunately, that something proved to be a ditch.

He tugged frantically at the handlebars, but the hobbyhorse continued to shoot straight for the ditch. "Why isn't it steering?" he shouted, fighting to be heard over the rush of the wind.

"Steering?" Lottie shouted back over her shoulder. "What steering?"

Thinking he'd surely misheard her, he tried again. "How do I steer the confounded thing?"

Given the mounting gravity of their situation, Lottie sounded entirely too cheerful as she bellowed back at him, "If its inventor had bothered to equip it with steering, do you think I would have crashed the first time?"

There was no more time to debate the inventor's lack of foresight. The ditch was only a foot away from snagging their front wheel. Wrapping his arms around Lottie's waist, Hayden launched them both off of the hobbyhorse. As they went flying through the air, he curled his body around hers, determined to bear the brunt of their landing.

The next thing Hayden knew, his head was being cradled against something seductively soft and a woman was crooning his name. He opened his eyes a fraction of an inch only to discover that the something soft was Lottie. He was stretched out across her lap, his head cradled against her bosom. It was such a pleasant sensation he rather wished he could stay there all day.

"Oh, Hayden, I feel terrible! If you hadn't been so smug, I would have warned you about the steering. I never meant for you to take such a nasty tumble." She stroked his brow, her fingers tenderly sifting through the vexatious lock of hair that always hung in his eyes. "Can you hear me, you poor dear?"

"Of course I can hear you," he murmured, gazing up at her through his lashes. "You're crooning in my ear, aren't you?"

She stood up abruptly, dumping him unceremoniously to the ground.

"Ow!" Rubbing the back of his head, he sat up and gave her a wounded look. "I'm certainly glad the turf is soft here."

"So am I," she snapped, avoiding his eyes as she brushed tufts of grass from her skirt. "If you'd have broken your neck, the gossips would have blamed me and I would have been known as the 'Murderous Marchioness' for the rest of my life." She sniffed. "Or at least until I found a more affable husband."

As she turned to march away from him, her skirts swishing with indignation, Hayden sprang to his feet and grabbed her by the hand, tugging her around to face him. "Nothing's sacred to you, is it?"

When she realized he was laughing down at her instead of scowling, the wary look in her eyes deepened. "Only the things that deserve to be."

As Hayden reached to gently pluck a blade of grass from her hair, he wondered what might have happened in that moment had they been any other man and woman standing on that sun-drenched hill. If they had met under different circumstances in a different lifetime. If he had been allowed to tenderly woo her before making her his bride.

They might have found out if the mayblossom-scented breeze hadn't carried to their ears the rattle of wooden wheels on cobblestone. Hayden frowned, shading his eyes against the sun's glare as he peered up the hill. A carriage was just turning into the drive, its lacquered shell gleaming like a raven's wing.

Visitors to Oakwylde Manor were hardly a common occurrence. He hadn't extended a single invitation to any of his neighbors since the day Justine had been laid to rest.

The hobbyhorse forgotten, he and Lottie hurried up the hill to join Harriet and Allegra. The carriage was just rattling to a halt in front of the manor. A footman rushed forward to throw open the door and a tiny creature emerged from the vehicle's shadowy interior, dressed from bonnet to boots in stark, unrelenting black.

Clutching at Lottie's arm, Harriet let out a strangled gasp. Lottie paled as if Grim Death itself was descending from the carriage.

"Who is it?" Allegra asked, tugging at Lottie's sleeve. "Is it the undertaker?"

"Worse," Lottie breathed. "It's Terrible Terwilliger herself."

Hayden might have laughed at their exaggerated reaction to what appeared to be a harmless little old lady if her traveling companion hadn't stepped down from the carriage in the next moment, his silvery-blond hair glinting in the sunlight.

As their visitor tucked his elegant walking stick beneath his arm, Allegra squinted toward the carriage. Suddenly a sunny smile broke over her face.

"Uncle Ned! Uncle Ned!" she shouted, breaking into a run.

Hayden could only stand and watch as his daughter went racing past him to throw herself into the arms of another man.

Chapter 16

*My only hope was to outwit him
at his own diabolical game . . .*

SIR EDWARD TOWNSEND SWEPT ALLEGRA UP
into his arms, giving her cheek a noisy kiss. "Why,
there's my girl! It's been so long I didn't know if you'd
even remember your old uncle Ned. Just look at you!"
He deposited her back on her feet and chucked her
under the chin. "When I saw you last, you were barely
out of napkins and now here you are a beautiful
young lady! So tell me, how many proposals have
you collected from lovestruck young swains?"

While Allegra ducked her head, blushing pro-
fusely, Lottie stole a look at Hayden. He was watching the tender exchange, his face utterly devoid of
expression.

Handing his walking stick to the footman, the
dashing knight offered one arm to Allegra and the
other to Miss Terwilliger. As the trio strolled toward

them, their progress slowed by Miss Terwilliger's cane, Lottie struggled to tuck her tumbled curls back into their pearl combs. There was nothing she could do about her attire. She'd worn her oldest dress to ride the hobbyhorse, a faded brown muslin more befitting a scullery maid than a marchioness.

Harriet was vainly trying to hide herself behind Lottie. "Do you think my parents sent her? Has she come to fetch me home?"

"Just who in the devil is she?" Hayden asked.

"She was one of our teachers at Mrs. Lyttelton's," Lottie hissed out of the corner of her mouth. "But for the past few years, she's been hiring herself out as a private governess."

"Oh!" he replied dryly. "*That* Terrible Terwilliger."

Stepping forward, Lottie clasped one of the old woman's black-gloved claws between her hands, smiling through clenched teeth. "Why, Miss Terwilliger, what an astonishing surprise! Whatever brings you to our little corner of the world?"

The woman scowled at Lottie over the top of her wire-rimmed spectacles, the mole on her chin sporting even more hairs than Lottie remembered. "Don't be impertinent, chit. You sent for me."

"I did?" Lottie squeaked.

"You did?" Hayden echoed, slanting Lottie a dark look.

"Of course you did. I might have had to read between the lines of your letter, but you made it abundantly clear that there was a child here in desperate need of my guidance." Miss Terwilliger cast Allegra a withering look, taking in the girl's windblown hair and the bonnet hanging halfway down her back. "And I can see I arrived not a moment too soon."

Allegra sidled out of sight, joining Harriet behind Lottie.

Miss Terwilliger drew Ned forward, fluttering her sparse lashes in a way that might have been construed as coquettish in a woman a hundred years her junior. "I would have been delayed even longer had this charming gentleman here not agreed to escort me."

Hayden appraised Ned with a cool gaze. "I suppose my wife sent for you as well."

Before Lottie could protest, Ned grinned. "Now, why would I need an excuse to visit such a dear old friend?"

"You don't need an excuse," Hayden retorted. "You need an invitation."

Ned sighed. "You always were such a stickler for the proprieties."

Baffled, Lottie glanced between Sir Ned and Miss Terwilliger. "How did the two of you even come to know each other?"

"You have only yourself to blame, my lady," Ned replied, retrieving his walking stick from the footman. "It was at your wedding breakfast that I struck up an acquaintance with your brother George. It didn't take long to discover we shared a number of common interests."

Lottie could hazard a guess as to what those interests might be—most likely riding, gaming, and seducing opera dancers.

"I just happened to be making a call on him at

Devonbrooke House when Miss Terwilliger arrived with your letter. After she shared its contents with your family, it was decided that she should journey here to offer you her services as soon as she could extricate herself from her current situation."

Miss Terwilliger tugged off her gloves with a snap that made Lottie flinch. "I shall expect room and board plus an advance on my wages within the week. And I'll tolerate absolutely no flirting from my employers. I'm too old to be chased around the schoolroom by some randy nobleman trying to steal a peek beneath my skirts." She wagged a bony finger in Hayden's face, the hairs on her mole quivering with indignation. "I'll expect a lock on my bedroom door, young man, and you can rest assured that I intend to use it."

Barely managing to conceal his shudder, Hayden sketched her a genteel bow. "You need have no fear for your virtue, madam. I shall strive to comport myself as a gentleman in your presence."

As he straightened, he shot Lottie a look that warned her he was making her no such promise. If he hadn't wanted to murder her before, he most certainly did now.

The gallant Sir Ned came charging to her rescue. "Come, my lady, and tell me how wedded bliss is suiting you." Linking his arm through hers, he drew her toward the house. "Your husband may delight in playing the ogre for those who expect it of him, but I'm sure you've already discovered that a prince's heart beats beneath that stalwart breast of his."

Since Lottie couldn't very well admit that she was beginning to wonder if any heart at all beat beneath her husband's breast, she simply cast Hayden a helpless glance over her shoulder and allowed herself to be drawn into the net of Sir Ned's charm.

By the time Hayden arrived at supper that night, Ned was regaling them all with stories of his and Hayden's misspent youth at Eton. Hayden sank into his chair only to be forced to spring stiffly back to his feet when it let out an offended squeak. Muttering "infernal creatures" beneath his breath, he swept a black kitten onto the floor.

Since it was the governess's first night at Oakwylde, Lottie had even invited Miss Terwilliger to join them for supper. Wearied by the arduous journey, the old woman was already nodding off in her soup. As Hayden settled himself in his chair, she emitted a snore that could just as easily have been mistaken for a death rattle.

"Don't mind her," Hayden said, accepting a helping of smoked herring from Meggie. "Ned's stories often have that effect on people."

It was impossible for him not to notice that Ned had positioned himself at Lottie's elbow. His wife was looking particularly delectable tonight in a high-waisted silk confection that shimmered like rosewater in the candlelight. Her curls had been swept up to bare the graceful curve of her throat. Hayden found himself wanting to press his lips there, to taste the pulse that beat just below the warm satin of her skin.

As Ned shifted in his chair, positioning himself at the perfect angle to ogle the creamy swell of her breasts, Hayden toyed with his butter knife, his eyes narrowing. Perhaps he had spoken too hastily back in London when he had vowed never to stab his friend in the throat with a jam spoon.

Harriet sat across from their guest, blushing and giggling and making calf's eyes at his every word. Hayden halfway hoped the simpering creature would fall in love with him. It would serve the rascal right to have her dogging his every step like a devoted puppy. Allegra sat next to Harriet, her own gaze equally adoring. Hayden slathered butter on a steaming roll, trying not to remember a time when his daughter had looked at him that way.

"So tell me, Ned," he said, "what time do you hope to be off in the morning? It's a long journey. You might want to get an early start. Perhaps you should have your valet awaken you before dawn."

"Hayden!" Lottie exclaimed, plainly appalled by his rudeness. "Why wait until morning? Why don't you just hand him his hat and escort him to the door right now?"

Hayden widened his eyes innocently. "Shall I ring for Giles?"

Ned laughed aloud. "There's no need to scold, my lady. I learned long ago not to take offense at your husband's boorish behavior. Actually, Hayden, I don't have to be back in London for a week. I thought I might linger on as your guest and take advantage of the opportunity to get to know your charming bride." He captured Lottie's hand and brought it to his lips, a devilish glint in his eye. "I'm hoping that in time she'll come to look upon me as something of a brother."

"She already has a brother," Hayden said flatly. "And a husband." Rising, he tossed his napkin to the table. "If you'll excuse us, ladies, Sir Ned and I are going to retire to the library for port and cigars."

"But the second course hasn't even been served," Lottie protested.

Ned also rose and tossed down his napkin, accepting Hayden's unspoken challenge. "Have no fear, dear ladies. We shall return in time to join you for dessert. As Hayden can tell you, I never could resist anything sweet."

He winked at Harriet, causing her to titter into her napkin. Then, sketching them all a gallant bow, he followed Hayden from the dining room.

Hayden stalked ahead of Ned, his long strides making short work of the crimson and blue runner that lined the corridor. He didn't utter a single word, not until they were both settled in the library, a glass of port in one hand and a lit cheroot in the other.

"You're playing a dangerous game, my friend," Hayden warned, leaning against the mantel.

"On the contrary." Ned sank into a leather chair and propped his gleaming boots on an ottoman. "As I see it, you're the one who's courting danger by neglecting your lovely young bride."

"What makes you think Lottie's neglected?" Hayden asked, frowning.

Ned took a puff on the cheroot. "Your rather unconventional sleeping arrangements, for one thing."

Hayden narrowed his eyes. "You've only been here for a few hours. Which maid did you seduce to obtain that juicy tidbit of gossip?"

Ned gave him a reproachful look. "You underestimate my charms. It took no more than a smile and a wink to coax that charming little red-haired baggage into spilling all of her secrets. It seems that you and the marchioness's marital relations, or lack thereof, have been an endless source of speculation in the servants' quarters."

Hayden tossed his cheroot into the cold fireplace, having lost his taste for it. "You know better than anyone that this wasn't a marriage sought by either one of us. Under such circumstances, it's not unusual for a husband and wife to maintain separate chambers."

"Nor is it unusual for one of them to take a lover." As Hayden gazed at him in disbelief, Ned swirled his port around the bottom of the glass. "Oh, come now, you can't tell me you haven't thought of it. She's a very fetching girl. If you don't want her, I can promise you that some other man will." He took a nonchalant sip of the port. "She seems to be far more level-headed than Justine. You needn't worry about scandal. I'm sure she'll be discreet in her choice of lovers."

Hayden calmly set his own glass on the mantel, then jerked Ned up by his flawlessly knotted cravat and slammed him against the nearest bookshelf. Ned's cheroot tumbled to the floor, but being the consummate gentleman, he didn't spill a single drop of his liquor.

Still balancing the glass in his palm, he thrust his sneering face into Hayden's. "What are you going to do, Hayden? Call me out? So what's it to be this time? Swords in the courtyard? Pistols at dawn? Have you chosen your second yet? If you'd like, I can check your pistol for you, then hand it over so you can shoot me with it."

The crimson veil of rage clouding Hayden's vision finally cleared enough to reveal that it wasn't fear glittering in his friend's eyes, but triumph.

Hayden slowly released him, fighting to control his ragged breathing. He rescued his glass from the mantel and lifted it in a mocking toast, hoping to hide the unsteadiness of his hand. "Congratulations, my friend. You succeeded in goading me into making a cake of myself over a woman. Again."

"What I did was goad you into admitting you were falling in love with your wife."

"Lest you've forgotten, the last time I fell in love with my wife, two people died."

A rare note of passion edged Ned's voice. "But isn't that both the beauty and the danger of love? It should be a prize worth killing for, even worth dying for if necessary."

"Noble sentiments indeed coming from a man whose idea of eternal love is a week spent in an opera dancer's bed. If Phillipe were here, I'm not so sure he would agree with you." Hayden gazed into the ruby depths of his port. "Is that why you came here? To punish me for his death?"

"I came here because I thought it was time you stopped punishing yourself. Phillipe needed kill-

ing," Ned said grimly, "especially after what he did
to Justine. If you hadn't shot him, some other husband would have."

Hayden lifted his head. "And what about Justine?
Did she need killing as well?"

Ned subsided, gazing at him through troubled
gray eyes. "I honestly don't know, old friend," he
said softly. "You're the only one who does."

Hayden reached over and gently smoothed Ned's
wrinkled cravat. "I believe there are some ladies in
the dining room waiting to share dessert with you.
Give my wife my regrets, won't you?" He gave
Ned's cravat a last fond pat, then turned and started
for the door.

"If you continue to deny your feelings," Ned
called after him, "then I'm afraid regrets are all
you'll have."

Allegra surprised them all by taking quite a fancy to
Miss Terwilliger. Since they both tended to blurt out
the first thing that popped into their heads, the two
of them were never at a lack for conversation. With
the crotchety old teacher occupying Allegra's morn-
ings with lessons, Lottie found herself at something
of a loss.

She wandered into the music room one morning,
searching for a book she'd mislaid the night before,
only to find Sir Ned gazing up at Justine's portrait,
hands in pockets.

Joining him, she sighed. "So have you come all the
way from London to worship at the shrine?"

He shook his head. "Most certainly not. The only offering that would satisfy a woman like Justine would be a man's heart—ripped from his chest while it was still beating."

Lottie glanced at him, surprised by the depth of his disdain. "Why so jaded? Didn't you once woo her as well?"

"Yes, I did." He returned his gaze to the portrait, a rueful smile curving his thin lips. "With all the passion and romantic fervor of any love-smitten twenty-year-old. I sought to fill up her dance card at every ball and composed laborious odes to the dusky sheen of her hair and the lushness of her lips."

"It must have broken your heart when she decided to marry Hayden."

He lifted his shoulders in an elegant shrug. "When she scorned my suit, I sulked and cried foul as I was expected to do, but if you must know the truth, in my heart I felt nothing but an overwhelming sense of relief."

Lottie frowned, bewildered by his confession. "But I thought you adored her. How could you give her up so easily?"

"I'm not sure. Perhaps even then I knew she was a tragedy waiting to happen. Besides, I'm not half the man Hayden is," he said frankly. "I would have never been strong enough to endure her capricious moods and demands."

Lottie struggled to keep her voice light as she asked, "Was Hayden's friend Phillipe equally smitten and equally relieved?"

A scowl clouded Ned's sharp features. "Phillipe was no friend to Hayden. I could have told him that, but he wouldn't have believed me. With that sunny temperament of his, Hayden was always determined to believe the best of everyone."

Lottie bit back a smile, bemused to hear her husband's temperament described as sunny. "He always seemed determined to believe the worst of me. The night we met, he thought I was a spy for one of the scandal sheets."

Ned snorted. "If he truly believed that, he probably *would* have tossed you off the nearest cliff."

"If Hayden believed Phillipe to be his friend, why did Phillipe betray him?"

"Phillipe was the second son of a viscount who had gambled away most of the family wealth, while Hayden was the cherished only son of a marquess, and heir to a generous fortune. Phillipe coveted everything Hayden touched, most especially Justine. He never forgave Hayden for winning both her heart and her hand."

"Hayden told me that he and Justine quarreled quite violently while they were still in London just before . . . before Phillipe. Do you know why?"

Ned sighed. "Justine desperately wanted to give him another child—an heir, but she'd suffered so after Allegra's birth that Hayden feared the strain of childbirth might destroy what was left of her mind."

"But how did he prevent . . . ? How did they . . . ?" Lottie faltered, hesitant to reveal her own ignorance.

"It was quite simple, my lady," Ned said gently.

"After Allegra was born, Hayden never returned to his wife's bed."

Lottie could only gaze at him, stunned by the revelation. She had believed she had nothing to offer her husband that could compare to the passion he had shared with Justine. Yet he had denied himself the woman's bed for over six years.

Ned continued. "Aside from being insane, Justine could be insanely jealous. She became obsessed with the notion that Hayden was seeking his pleasures in other women's beds."

"Was he?" Lottie met Ned's gaze boldly, hoping to conceal the cost of the question.

Ned shook his head. "Most other men, myself included, would have kept a mistress to relieve their baser needs. But not Hayden. He couldn't bear to do that to her. Or to them."

Lottie gazed up into Justine's mocking violet eyes. "Because he loved her."

When Ned spoke again, he seemed to be choosing his words with great care. "Hayden was thrust into the position of caretaker at a very young age. I often felt that his love for Justine was more the love of a parent for a child than that of a man for a woman. He knew in his heart that they could never truly be equals." Dismissing the portrait, Ned turned to appraise her, the challenge in his gaze unmistakable. "I always felt he needed a woman who would be his match, both in the bedchamber and out of it."

Sketching her a courtly bow, Ned excused himself, leaving Lottie alone with Justine to ponder his words.

Hayden was reviewing the accounts of his local properties the next day, his head awash in a sea of numbers, when a brisk knock came on the door of the study. He was forced to dislodge one kitten from his lap and another from his foot before he could even rise. He was halfway to the door when he stumbled over a third cat. Sighing with exaggerated forbearance, he nudged it out of his path with the toe of his boot.

He swung open the door. No one was there. He stuck his head out the door and looked both ways, but the corridor was equally empty. He glanced down to discover a folded sheet of vellum at his feet. Someone must have slid it beneath the door. He unfolded it to find an invitation lettered in a bold hand that could only belong to his wife.

It seemed that she had decided to host a musicale in honor of their guest. Lady Oakleigh and Miss Harriet Dimwinkle were to sing a duet of "Hark! Hark! The Lark!" while Miss Agatha Terwilliger had been enlisted to pluck out "I Kissed My Lover in the Greensward" on the harp. Hayden shuddered, thinking the image might very well tempt him to pluck out his eyes. Of course, the *pièce de résistance* of the evening was to be Lady Allegra St. Clair's rendition of the Beethoven sonata known as "Tempest" on the piano.

Hayden slowly lowered the invitation. "Tempest"

had been one of Justine's favorite pieces. He'd spent many a cozy evening in the music room with a fire glowing on the hearth and Allegra in his lap, listening to Justine master its rippling melody. But whenever she would stop sleeping and start burning with the fire that threatened to consume her from within, she would play the piece over and over, the notes so wild and discordant that Hayden feared he, too, might be in danger of losing his mind.

The thought of having to sit there and listen to that piece rendered by Allegra's small fingers made him break out in an icy sweat.

He could do this, he told himself, crumpling the invitation in his hand. For his daughter's sake, he could do this.

Which was what Hayden was still telling himself six hours later as he stood in front of the cheval glass in his bedchamber. He could have taken no more care with his appearance had he been invited to Windsor to dine with the king. His collar and cuffs were starched, his cravat as expertly knotted as Ned's, his unruly hair coaxed into some semblance of civilized behavior. Yet the man staring back at him from the mirror was as wild-eyed as any savage.

He drew out his watch and snapped it open. They were all probably already gathered in the music room, just waiting for him to arrive. It would hardly come as a shock to any of them, especially Lottie, if he sent Giles to deliver his regrets.

If you continue to deny your feelings, then I'm afraid regrets are all you'll have.

As Ned's warning echoed through his head, Hayden jerked his coat straight and turned his back on the man in the mirror.

Allegra flitted around the music room like a nervous butterfly in her pink dimity frock and kid slippers. With Lottie's help, her rebellious hair had been coaxed into gleaming spiral curls that cascaded halfway down her back. Although both of her dolls had been given seats of honor in front of the piano, she was beginning to look more like a young lady than a little girl.

Praying she hadn't made a terrible miscalculation, Lottie did her level best to keep from glancing at the door every three seconds. At any minute she expected Giles to appear and announce that his lordship had been called away on a matter that required his immediate attention. Such as prying a pebble from his horse's hoof or inspecting the washed-out stonework at the foot of the drive.

From her place beside Sir Ned on the divan, Harriet took a slurp of her punch. "I hope you won't be too disappointed by my warbling, sir."

"You needn't fret, Miss Dimwinkle," Ned replied, winking at Lottie. "One can hardly expect a lady to have both the face and the voice of an angel."

Burying her face in her punch cup, Harriet tittered with delight.

"It's a quarter hour past my bedtime," Miss Terwilliger announced to no one in particular. "I would have never agreed to lend my talents to this little bacchanalia had I known the revelry would extend until the wee hours of the morning."

Lottie glanced at her own watch. It was half past seven.

"We needn't wait any longer." Allegra sank down on the piano bench, surveying her slippers. "He's not coming."

"He most certainly is."

They all whipped their heads around to find Hayden standing in the doorway. His curt bow only underscored the casual elegance of his finery. As their eyes met, his wary gaze stole Lottie's breath away. With his set jaw and that stubborn lock of dark hair tumbling over his brow, he'd never looked more devastatingly handsome. Although she didn't acknowledge her father's arrival with a gesture or a greeting, Allegra's face went pink with pleasure.

Hayden claimed the chair next to Lottie's, warming her every breath with the masculine musk of bayberry. She could not resist leaning over and whispering, "You look as if you're about to attend a public execution."

"I am," he whispered back, the polite smile frozen on his face. "Mine."

With their audience complete, Lottie and Harriet moved to the music stand to begin their duet. While Lottie's voice was high and true, Harriet's voice could only be described as an off-key croak more suited to "Hark! Hark! The Toad!"

No doubt fearing an encore, the instant the last note died Ned leapt to his feet and gave them an enthusiastic round of applause, shouting, "Bravo! Bravo!"

Lottie took her bow, then dragged the beaming Harriet back to the divan.

Miss Terwilliger's solo was next on the program, but none of them had the heart to awaken her. Taking her cue from Lottie's nod of encouragement, Allegra slowly rose to take her place at the piano, her small hands trembling.

The minute those hands touched the keys, they lost their tremor as if by magic, their nimble grace casting a spell over them all.

As the first notes came rippling from the instrument, Lottie stole a glance at Hayden. Was she imagining the hint of panic in his eyes, the fine sheen of sweat on his brow? She had deliberately positioned the chairs so they would be sitting with their backs to Justine's portrait, but perhaps he could still feel those knowing eyes of hers boring into the back of his neck.

Allegra had just reached the dramatic climax of the piece when Hayden lurched to his feet. Her fingers stumbled to an awkward halt, the unfinished chord ringing in the silence.

"I'm sorry," he said, his voice a strangled rasp. "I'm desperately sorry, but I can't . . . I simply can't . . ."

Casting Lottie a beseeching look, he went striding from the room.

Lottie sat at the writing desk in her bedchamber, her pen poised over the page, but no words flowing. What had once been captured so easily in bold penstrokes of black upon ivory now seemed mired in shades of gray. The characters in her novel felt no more real to her than the garish caricatures sketched by some anonymous artist for the scandal sheets. Every time she tried to picture her villain, she saw that last helpless look Hayden had given her before fleeing the music room.

She had retreated to her desk after tucking a sub-dued Allegra into bed. Although they had all begged the girl to continue after Hayden's unceremonious exit, not even Ned's teasing charm could coax her into playing another note. She had insisted upon retiring, her face pinched and pale. Lottie would have much preferred that she sob and rant and throw one of her legendary tantrums. The child's stoic suffering reminded Lottie entirely too much of Hayden.

Realizing she had dribbled ink all over the page, Lottie snapped open her writing case, drew out a fresh sheet of paper and refilled her pen from the ink bottle. She'd been half-heartedly scribbling for several minutes when the first ghostly strains of piano music drifted to her ears.

Her hand jerked, upsetting the bottle of ink. It went spilling across the page, blotting out everything she'd written.

Listening to the heartbreaking beauty of those wild, impassioned notes, Lottie closed her eyes and whispered, "Oh, Allegra."

Hayden stood gazing down at the surf that foamed around the jagged rocks at the base of the cliff. Although his well-muscled legs were braced against the wind, its punishing gusts still battered him, making him sway dangerously close to the edge of the cliff. Above him, the clouds flirted with the moon, their shifting moods as fickle as Justine's had once been. Behind him, the house was dark and silent, its occupants long abed and dreaming of the morrow.

Hayden knew there would be no use in seeking his own bed tonight. Every time he closed his eyes, all he would see was the stricken look on his wife's and daughter's faces as he spoiled their fine evening.

He was still standing there when the wind carried to his ears the first distant notes of piano music. It was the same piece Allegra had played that night, the same piece Justine had once played over and over, her frenzied fingers attacking the keys. As Hayden slowly turned to gaze up at the darkened windows of the house, the music gathered in strength and fury, like an approaching storm.

Lottie strode down the shadowy corridor that led to the music room, the notes of the sonata crashing over her in waves. Once such a sound would have struck terror in her heart, but now she knew she had nothing to fear but a hurt and defiant child. The music room door stood open in invitation, just as it had ever since the night Lottie had discovered Allegra masquerading as the ghost.

Lottie slipped into the room, the hem of her nightdress brushing the floor. Moonlight streamed through the skylight, shrouding the piano in a hazy glow. Just as before, the lid of the instrument had been left propped open, sheltering its keys from her view.

She breathed in the dizzying fragrance of jasmine. Allegra must have been dipping into her mother's perfume again.

Sighing, Lottie rounded the piano. "You have every right to be angry with your father, Allegra, but that doesn't mean you can just—"

The bench was empty. Lottie's gaze slowly shifted to the keys, which continued to rise and fall for a full measure before falling still and silent.

Lottie opened her mouth, but nothing came out so she simply closed it again. She stretched out her hand to stroke a trembling finger down one of the keys.

"If this is your idea of a jest, my lady, I am *not* amused."

Lottie jerked up her head to find Hayden standing a few feet away, his face veiled in shadows.

Chapter 17

How was I to bear the secret shame of my surrender?

HAYDEN HAD STRIPPED AWAY BOTH HIS FIN-
ery and the civilized veneer it provided. He wore no
coat or waistcoat and his rumpled cravat hung loose
around his throat. His hair was wild, his eyes even
wilder. As he came striding out of the shadows, Lottie jerked her hand away from the piano.

"It's a bit late to play the innocent, don't you
think?" He stopped near enough for her to smell the
mingled scents of danger and sea air. "I just looked
in on Allegra. She's sleeping like a babe."

Lottie stole another look at the piano keys, torn
between terror and wonder. "Sh-sh-she is?"

"Yes, she is. And I already know you can play so
you may as well confess that it was you playing that
piece." His eyes narrowed to frosty slits. "Unless, of

course, you're going to try to convince me that there really *is* a ghost."

Lottie glanced at the portrait over the mantel. For once, Justine didn't seem to be laughing at her, but with her. Her violet eyes sparkled in the moonlight as if the two of them shared a secret only a woman could know—a secret she was urging Lottie to keep. Was it possible they were no longer rivals, but allies? Had Justine brought both her and Hayden to this place for a reason?

Curiously emboldened by the notion, Lottie faced Hayden. "The way you went running out of here tonight when Allegra was playing, I would have sworn you were the one being pursued by a ghost."

"The ghost of my own folly perhaps. I should have known better than to set foot in this accursed room."

"Yet here you are again," Lottie said softly, taking a step toward him.

He eyed her warily, the downward flick of his gaze taking in her tumbled curls, the worn folds of her nightdress, her bare feet. "Only because you played a cruel and heartless trick. Just why was that, Lottie? Didn't you think the disappointment I saw in my daughter's eyes tonight was punishment enough for me?"

Lottie shook her head. "I wasn't seeking to punish you."

He raked a hand through his hair. "Then why in the bloody hell did you lure me here?"

Moonlight bathed the rugged planes of Hayden's

face in its alabaster light as he gazed down at her, no longer able to hide his helpless hunger. Lottie had wondered what she might do if he ever looked at her like that again and now she knew.

"For this," she whispered, cupping his face in her hands and drawing his lips down to hers. Her kiss entreated him to drink deeply of the tenderness she had to offer. It was a heady brew, intoxicating them both with its sweetness.

"Oh, hell," he muttered against her lips. "You're feeling sorry for me again, aren't you?"

"Isn't that why you married me?" Lottie pressed her lips to the muscular column of his throat, savoring the warm, salty taste of his skin. "Because I'd gotten myself into a terrible scrape and you felt sorry for me?"

He twined his fingers through her hair and gently tugged, forcing her to meet his fierce gaze. "I married you because I couldn't bear the thought of another man making you his mistress . . . putting his hands on you . . . touching you the way I wanted to touch you."

His confession sent a primal thrill coursing through her. "Show me," she whispered.

Sweeping the smoky velvet of his tongue through her mouth, Hayden wrapped one arm around her hips and lifted her, bearing her backward until they came up against the piano. Swiping the stick away, he brought the lid crashing down, then set her atop it.

Lottie rested her small hands on his broad shoulders to steady herself, but she could do nothing to ease the ragged rhythm of her breathing. At last there were no servants, no Harriet, no Allegra to come between them. Even Justine had retreated to the shadows, leaving the two of them all alone with the moon.

Hayden gently enfolded her in his arms. For the moment he seemed content just to breathe in her sighs and nuzzle the downy skin of her throat. As the tip of his tongue traced the delicate curve of her earlobe, then delved into its sensitive shell, Lottie gasped, her knees falling apart of their own accord. He stepped between them, growling deep in his throat as he filled his hands with the softness of her breasts. He rubbed the calloused pads of his thumbs over her nipples through the worn cotton of her nightdress, sending a rush of sensation through her womb.

Adrift in a sea of delight, she barely felt him ease the nightdress from her shoulders, exposing her breasts to his heated gaze.

"Oh, Lottie, sweet Lottie," he said thickly, gazing down at her in the moonlight. "I've been dreaming of this moment since that first night in Mayfair."

Before she could absorb the wonder of that confession, he bent his dark head to her breasts, glazing first one nipple, then the other, with the nectar from their kiss. Any shyness she might have felt was banished by his boldness as he teased one of the throbbing nubs with his tongue, then drew it into his mouth, suckling deep and hard. This time the rush of sensation melted from her womb to the aching hollow between her legs.

When she tried to press them together to soothe that torturous tickle, her husband's hips were there, hard and unyielding, giving her no choice but to wrap her legs around him.

Hayden shuddered, fearing Lottie's innocent ardor was going to be his undoing. He leaned away from her, allowing himself a moment just to drink in the sight of her. She looked like a wanton angel with her eyes half shuttered with desire, her hair tumbled around her flushed cheeks, both her lips and her naked breasts glistening from his kisses.

"Lovely Lottie," he whispered, touching a hand to her hair. "I tried so hard to convince myself you were still a child, but I knew in my heart that you were a woman. All woman."

Keeping his eyes locked on hers, he slipped his other hand beneath her nightdress, breathing a silent prayer of thanksgiving that she did not sleep in drawers. His hand glided past her knee, to the downy satin of her thigh, then higher until the very tips of his fingers brushed the silky triangle of curls at the juncture of her thighs.

Her eyes drifted shut. Her chest hitched, her breath coming hard and fast. No longer able to temper his need with restraint, Hayden laid her back on the piano, shoving the skirt of her nightdress to her waist.

She was golden everywhere—gold-tipped lashes, golden skin, golden curls, both above . . . and below. His hungry gaze lingered there, the pace of his own breath quickening. He wanted nothing more than to sift his fingers through their gossamer softness, to search for a pearl even more priceless than gold.

Watching her face, he breached those nether curls with one finger, groaning at what he found. She was already wet for him, both inside and out. It was all he could do in that moment not to unfasten the front flap of his straining trousers and plunge deep into her melting core. But the shadows of delight dancing across her flushed cheeks captivated him, coaxed him to delay his own pleasure so he might linger over hers.

He stroked between those dusky petals until she began to writhe beneath his hand. Gently circling the sensitive bud sheltered by their folds with the pad of his thumb, he leaned over and touched his mouth to her ear. "Tell me, angel—do you taste as heavenly as you look?"

Lottie's eyes flew open, but Hayden was already cupping her rump in his big, warm hands, already dragging her to the very edge of the piano, where she would be completely at his mercy. Nothing Laura and Diana had told her had prepared her for the sight of her husband's dark head poised between her legs, for the delicious shock of his mouth pressing against that forbidden place she'd barely even dared to touch with her hand.

This is madness, Lottie thought wildly. To be lying atop a piano in the moonlight with her nightdress tangled around her waist, writhing beneath the mouth of a man who refused to offer her love, but gave freely of this devastating delight. In that moment, she was almost less afraid that he'd murdered his first wife than that she no longer cared if he had.

With each wanton flick of his tongue, pleasure coursed through her, dark and sweet and fulsome. She tangled her fingers in the rough silk of Hayden's hair as he made music on her with his mouth, drawing her as taut as any piano string. As that exquisite melody neared a crescendo, she arched against him, fearing she might snap altogether.

At the precise moment she began to spasm against his mouth, he slid his longest finger deep inside of her, sending her over the cliff and into a dazzling freefall. But he was there to catch her in his strong arms, to gather her against his chest and soothe her uncontrollable shivering with tender caresses and wordless endearments.

"For a minute there," he murmured against her hair, "I was afraid you were going to scream the way you did that night in Allegra's room."

Still breathless, she hid her flushed face against his throat. "For a minute there, so was I."

Capturing her mouth in a deep, drugging kiss, he lifted her and carried her to the divan. He settled her against the sateen cushions before dragging off her nightdress and tossing it to the floor. Although there was something undeniably wicked and thrilling about being naked while her husband was still fully clothed, Lottie was starved for the warmth of his flesh against hers. She tore at the studs of his shirt, parting the linen until they were skin to skin, heart to heart.

Hayden squeezed his eyes shut, thinking he would never feel anything as exquisite as the plush softness of Lottie's naked breasts against his chest. At least that's what he believed until that bold little hand of hers drifted down to cup the bulging front of his trousers.

As Hayden's hips rocked hard against her hand, Lottie's insatiable curiosity quickly shifted to wonder. When he had claimed he had only his name to offer her, he had lied. She stroked the rigid shaft beneath the thin layer of doeskin, tracing its generous outline with two fingers. A ghost might have his heart, but she would have the rest of him.

With a strangled groan, he bore her back against the divan, reaching between them to unfasten his trousers. A cloud drifted over the moon, sending shadows spilling over them. As he covered her, Lottie opened her arms and her legs, embracing both the darkness and him. He rubbed himself against her, bathing his rigid length in the luscious honey he had teased from her body.

Lottie moaned, dazed with delight. As far as she was concerned, he could have continued that maddening assault on her senses all night, but on the very next stroke, he shifted the angle of his hips, sliding deep inside of her.

Based on what Diana and Laura had told her, she knew Hayden had done everything in his power and more to make her ready to receive him. But there was no preparing for this. Her fingernails dug into the sweat-slicked muscles of his upper back.

She bit her lip to keep from crying out, but not before a distressed squeak escaped.

Still buried deep within her, Hayden froze, his powerful body held in check.

"Don't stop!" Lottie cried, struggling to blink away her tears of pain before he could see them. "You've been more than generous to me. Now it's time for you to take *your* pleasure."

"Thank you, Carlotta," he replied solemnly, even as his shoulders shook beneath her hands. He surprised her by planting a tender kiss on the tip of her nose. "That's very noble and self-sacrificing of you. I'll strive not to make the unpleasantness last any longer than necessary."

Bracing his palms against the divan to support his upper body, he began to glide in and out of her in long, hypnotic strokes. Squeezing her eyes shut, Lottie began to shiver with reaction. There was still the fullness, the tightness, the burning, but the pain was beginning to melt into something else. Something magical. Something extraordinary.

She couldn't pinpoint the exact moment his pleasure became her own. She just knew that one minute she was holding herself as stiff as a board in a desperate attempt not to shy away from him and the next her hips were arching up to meet him, urging him deeper.

"Have you had enough unpleasantness?" he murmured, his own voice none too steady. "Shall I stop now?"

"No," she moaned, clutching at the rigid muscles of his upper arms. "Never."

"Why, you insatiable little vixen! And to think, I once assured Ned that I had enough stamina to satisfy you."

Lottie dared to open her eyes then, dared to tangle her fingers in his hair and boldly drag his lips down to hers. "Then prove it."

He covered her mouth with his own, welcoming the challenge with an upward thrust of his hips that made her gasp. His hard masculine weight pinned her to the divan until there was nowhere for her to go but deeper into the cushions, nowhere for him to go but even deeper inside of her. If the melody he had played on her body with his mouth was an exquisite nocturne, then this was a thundering rhapsody, irresistible in its power and its passion. It seemed to go on and on, building to one majestic crescendo after another. When he added an unexpected grace note by reaching between them and touching her, Lottie shuddered beneath his clever fingers, rapture rocking her to her very core.

Squeezed in a vise of raw delight, Hayden felt the last of his own control crumble. As he buried himself to the hilt in his wife's willing young body, ecstasy came roaring through him in a relentless tide, sweeping away the past and all of its ghosts.

"Laura and Diana were right," Lottie murmured, her cheek pillowed against Hayden's chest and one leg thrown possessively over his thigh.

"About what?"

She twirled a sweat-dampened coil of chest hair around her finger. "They told me that it would go much easier on me if you made me ready to receive you first."

A deep chuckle reverberated through his chest. "They made it sound as if I was going to be paying you a social call."

Lottie giggled. "Perhaps we should have had Giles announce you." She deepened her voice to mimic the butler's dour inflections. "Lady Oakleigh is ready to receive you now, my lord. If you'll step into the music room and remove all of your clothing, you'll find her waiting on the divan."

"Sounds like a delectable prospect to me. If you'll hang on, I'll ring for him." The muscles in Hayden's chest rippled as he stretched one arm over his head, pretending to reach for the tasseled bellpull that dangled over the harp.

Lottie rolled over on top of him and snatched at his arm, squealing in protest. "Don't you dare! I can just see Mrs. Cadaver"—she winced—"I mean Mrs. Cavendish sneering down her long nose at us. If she caught us in such shocking disarray, she'd probably send Meggie in to dust us."

"And what would be the harm in that?" Hayden cupped her bottom in his hands, a wicked glint lighting his eye. "I can think of several clever uses for a feather duster."

"I dare say you can, my lord. But so can I."

As Hayden felt her soft curls, still damp with his seed, brush his swelling staff, he groaned aloud— half in pain, half in pleasure. Ned need have no fears about his stamina where his lusty little wife was concerned. All she had to do was look at him with those luminous blue eyes of hers and he was cocked and ready to fire again. And that didn't even take into account what the maddening gyrations of her rump were doing to him.

He swirled his tongue over her kiss-swollen lips, his breath growing short. "So tell me—what else did your aunt and sister tell you to prepare you for your duties in the marriage bed?"

"Well . . ." she replied thoughtfully, giving him a sultry look from beneath her gold-tipped lashes, "they warned me that there were some husbands so uncontrollable in their lusts, so savage in their appetites, that they would fall upon their wives like rutting beasts, seeking only to satisfy themselves."

"How horrendous." Hayden felt his lips slant into a devilish grin. "But just for a little while," he suggested, closing his hands around her waist and sliding out from under her so that she lay sprawled on her stomach among the soft cushions of the divan, "why don't we pretend that I'm exactly that sort of husband?"

As he rose up on his knees behind her, sliding a cushion beneath her hips, Lottie gazed at him over her shoulder, her eyes widening and her own breath quickening. "I suppose I could bear it if I must. I would never wish to shirk my wifely obligations."

"Nor I my husbandly duties." As Hayden pressed himself deep inside of her, she whimpered with delight, her fingernails digging into the divan. "Just close your eyes, angel," he murmured. "It will be over before you know it."

*   *   *

Through the skylight Hayden could see wispy pink clouds drifting across a canvas that was slowly shifting from slate to blue. Ignoring Lottie's drowsy protests, he tugged the voluminous folds of her nightdress over her head, then gathered her into his arms. She curled her arms around his neck without opening her eyes, her tousled curls tickling his nose. Unlike Justine, she didn't favor heavy floral scents. Instead, her clean, soapy scent mingled with the lingering musk of their loving, intoxicating him with each breath he took.

Although Hayden's first instinct was to carry Lottie to *his* chamber, *his* bed, he forced himself to turn toward the east wing. If he tucked her into his sprawling four-poster, he would only end up making love to her again. And again. He'd already been entirely too greedy in his attentions. All that remained of his wife's innocence were a few rusty stains on both of their thighs. Her ravished body needed time to recover from their passionate couplings.

He would inform Meggie that her mistress was not to be disturbed. As soon as she showed signs of stirring, he would have a hot bath sent to her chamber. An image of Lottie sitting in a brass tub with her golden curls pinned atop her head and her golden breasts glistening with moisture flashed through his head, making his loins quicken anew. Hayden swore, cursing his own noble intentions.

As he carried Lottie into her bedchamber and tucked her beneath the blankets, her large yellow tomcat glared at him accusingly from the foot of the bed.

"You needn't look so outraged," Hayden whispered. "I dare say you've done your share of prowling in your day. And without benefit of matrimony."

Mr. Wiggles was nowhere in sight, but as Hayden was settling an extra quilt over Lottie, Mirabella came skittering out from under the bed. With one of those inexplicable bursts of energy so common to baby cats, she dashed across the bed, then made three wild circuits of the room before bounding up on the rosewood writing desk in the corner.

"Now, look what you've gone and done," Hayden scolded, spotting the overturned ink bottle.

Looking utterly unrepentant, the kitten jumped down from the table and marched calmly to the hearth, where she proceeded to plop down and lick her furry little belly.

Stealing a look at Lottie to make sure she hadn't awakened, Hayden moved to right the bottle before the ink could spill over onto the rug. But it seemed the kitten was justified in its smugness. The ink was dry, spilled long before the cat had gone on its rampage.

As Hayden pried the bottle off the ruined page, his elbow hit the writing case perched on the edge of the desk. It tipped over, pouring out page upon page of vellum stationery, all filled margin to margin with Lottie's rather spectacular handwriting. She tended toward dramatic curlicues and majestic flourishes. She didn't dot her *i*'s so much as anoint them with splashes of ink. Picking up one of the pages, Hayden felt a smile curve his lips. His wife wrote much as she made love—with unfettered passion and a raw enthusiasm that more than made up for any lack of precision.

Assuming she was keeping some sort of household journal as most ladies did, he was moving to gather the rest of the pages and tuck them back into the compartment at the bottom of the case when the first sentence on the very first page caught his eye: *I'll never forget the moment I first laid eyes on the man who planned to murder me . . .*

Hayden's smile slowly faded as he sank into the desk chair and began to read.

Chapter 18

Disaster! I am found out!

"LOTTIE! LOTTIE, WAKE UP! IT'S NEARLY time for tea!" From the quaver of horror in Harriet's voice, one might have deduced that missing afternoon tea was equivalent to missing the last chariot to heaven on the Day of Judgment.

Groaning, Lottie dragged a pillow over her head. But Harriet was not to be dissuaded. She tugged the pillow away, then pried open one of Lottie's sluggish eyelids with her thumb.

"You need to wake up," she shouted, as if Lottie were suffering from deafness as well as drowsiness. "It's Sir Ned's last day here and you've nearly slept it all away." Lottie glared at her friend through one baleful eye as Harriet picked up the glass of water sitting on the table next to the bed and gave it a tentative sniff. "Oh, dear Lord, the marquess hasn't gone and poisoned you, has he?"

Despite Lottie's reassurances to the contrary, Harriet persisted in believing that Hayden was some sort of homicidal lunatic, just waiting for the perfect opportunity to murder them all in their beds.

Shoving Harriet's hand away, Lottie sat up. "Do stop fussing over me, Harriet. No one's slipped any arsenic into my tea. I just didn't get much sleep last night."

As Lottie flexed her limbs in a long, lazy stretch, she was keenly reminded of exactly what she'd been doing instead of sleeping. She was sore in muscles she'd never even known she had. But if not for that warm, tingly soreness, she might have wondered if the whole night hadn't been some delicious dream. Perhaps it would be easier to believe if she had woken up in Hayden's bed, in Hayden's arms.

"Tell me, Harriet," she asked, hugging her knees to her chest, "have you never thought it odd that the marquess and I don't share a bedchamber?"

Her friend shrugged. "Not really. My parents can barely stand to share a house. So what kept you awake last night? Was it the return of the ghost?" Harriet cast a nervous look over her shoulder. "Apparently, I slept right through the fracas, but the servants have been whispering about it all morning. Someone or *something* was playing the piano in the music room again. At first everyone thought it was Allegra, but when Martha looked in on her, there she was, nestled snug in her bed. Meggie said Martha came flying back into the servants' quarters as if her skirt was afire." Harriet looked rather pleased by that tidbit. "Oh, and there was no wailing this time, but after the music stopped, several of the servants claim to have heard the most frightful moaning."

"Indeed?" Hoping to hide both her smile and her blush, Lottie pretended to smother another yawn behind her hand.

Harriet's eyes grew even rounder. "Martha told me it sounded as if some poor soul was being tortured to death."

Lottie saw herself sprawled half-naked on top of the piano; lying limp and sated with pleasure beneath Hayden's powerful body; on the divan shivering with anticipation as he rose up on his knees behind her. The only death delivered by her husband had been the one the French so eloquently called *le petit mort*. And it was a death she would gladly die a thousand times at his skillful hands.

Unable to completely hide her shiver of delight, she said, "You can tell Meggie to stop fretting. I don't think we'll be hearing from the ghost again any time soon."

"What makes you say that?"

Lottie could not bring herself to betray Justine, not even to Harriet. She was too grateful to the woman for luring both her and Hayden to the music room with that haunting melody. "It's just a notion I have. And besides, who wants to dwell on the past all the time when the future is all that matters?" Driven by a surge of hope that she, Hayden, and Allegra might actually become a family, Lottie threw back the blankets and bounded out of the bed. "I'm ravenous. Didn't you say something about tea? I feel as if I could eat a whole tray of scones." Before Harriet could answer, Lottie strode to the window and threw up the sash. "How could I have slept so much of the day away? It's absolutely glorious out there!"

Outside the manor, the wind whipped across the endless expanse of moor, driving scudding gray clouds across an even bleaker sky.

Lottie turned around to find Harriet blinking at her as if she'd lost her wits. "Are you entirely sure you haven't been poisoned?"

Lottie laughed. "If I have, then I'm already craving more of the stuff, for it's the sweetest poison I've ever tasted."

Before she could close the window, a gust of wind went swirling around her, sending the papers scattered across the writing desk fluttering into the air. Both she and Harriet rushed to rescue them. Lottie had half of them stuffed back into her writing case before she realized something was amiss. Every page in her hands was blank.

She frowned down at them in confusion for a moment before snatching the remaining pages out of Harriet's hands. They, too, were as pristine as they'd been on the day she'd purchased them from the Bond Street stationers.

"Whatever is the matter?" Harriet asked, staring at Lottie's trembling hands. "You've gone as pale as a ghost."

Grabbing up the writing case, Lottie pried frantically at the false panel nestled in its bottom. The compartment below was empty.

"My book," she whispered, dread clutching at her stomach as every damning word she'd written since coming to Oakwylde Manor resounded through her brain. "It's gone."

After a fruitless search of the house, Lottie finally found Hayden sitting on a rock at the edge of the cliffs, framed by a misty canvas of sea and sky. Although the rocks below weren't visible from her vantage point, Lottie could almost feel them there, their jagged and glistening teeth yawning open to snag the careless or the foolhardy.

Hayden was studying the document in his hand and looking every inch the Gothic villain in his buff-colored trousers, open-throated ivory shirt, and scuffed boots. The restless fingers of the wind tossed his dark hair. As Lottie studied the terse line of his mouth, she marveled that it could be the same mouth that had curved into a tender smile before brushing her lips with a kiss, the same mouth that had given her such exquisite pleasure only a few hours before.

Feeling heat rush from her cheeks to other even more traitorous regions of her body, she said, "You had no right to go through my things."

Hayden lifted his head to meet her challenging gaze. They both knew she was bluffing. According to the laws of England, she had no things. Everything she owned belonged to her husband. Including her body.

"You're absolutely correct," he admitted, startling her. "I'm quite ashamed of myself. But you really should consider my ill manners a tribute to your literary skills. I stumbled upon the first page of your little masterpiece by accident, but once I started reading, I became so engrossed in the adventures of the 'Deadly Duke' and his fearless young bride that I couldn't bring myself to stop."

He withdrew an entire stack of pages from a cleft in the rock. With a sinking feeling, Lottie recognized her own handwriting. Oddly enough, she felt more naked before him now than she had last night. Then she had felt cherished and protected. Now she felt raw and exposed, as if Hayden was peering into the darkest, most cobweb-infested recesses of her soul with a quizzing glass. It was all she could do not to snatch up the pages and hide them behind her back.

She nodded toward the edge of the cliff. "I'm surprised you haven't scattered them to the wind."

"And deprive the world of such a burgeoning talent? I think not." Hayden tapped the manuscript with one finger. "Oh, you're given to the occasional lapse into melodrama, such as the chapter where your intrepid heroine discovers the feeble-witted daughter her dastardly husband keeps locked in the attic, but overall, it's a fine effort. You should be quite pleased with yourself."

Then why did she feel so wretched? "There's always some unfortunate soul locked in the attic in these books," she tried to explain. "Especially if the house has no dungeon."

"Perhaps I should consider having one built," he

murmured, the glint in his eye making him look every bit as devilish as Lottie's duke.

Weary of being toyed with, she snapped, "You know, this never would have happened if you had just carried me back to *your* bed."

He gave her a reproachful look. "But how could you have rested comfortably knowing that at any minute I might have strangled you in your sleep?" Despite his mocking good cheer, he rather looked as if he'd like to strangle her now. "So tell me, have you found a publisher yet?"

"Of course not!"

"But you had every intention of finding one." It was not a question.

"No. Yes. I don't know!" Lottie shook her head, desperate to make him understand. "Perhaps I did, but that was before."

Tucking the manuscript back into the cleft, Hayden rose, an admiring gleam in his eye. "And to think I accused you of spying for the scandal sheets. You had a much loftier goal in mind, didn't you? This way, you won't have to share any of your profit or your glory. 'Lady Oakleigh' should be quite the literary toast of London."

Lottie gaped at him, incredulous. "Is that what you believe? That I planned this from the start? That I trapped you into marriage for the sole purpose of using your life as inspiration for some ridiculous novel?"

"I don't know. You tell me." He stroked the backs of his fingers down her cheek, his touch sending a frisson of heat dancing over her skin. His voice deepened to a silky murmur. "Did you find last night to be an inspiration as well? Was it a way for you to find out just how the 'hands of a murderer would feel against your flesh?' "

Lottie closed her eyes briefly, unprepared for the shock of having him use both her words and his caress as a weapon against her. But when she opened them again, it was to meet his smoldering gaze with one of her own.

"I suppose there's no help for it, is there?" she said flatly, pushing his hand away. "I've been found out. If you must know the truth, I came peeping into your window that night just hoping I'd be mistaken for a common doxy and accosted in front of my family and most of London. Then, with my reputation in ruins, I hoped to be dragged away from the loving bosom of everyone I held dear and delivered to some drafty old mansion on the edge of creation where I could be treated as little more than a servant by some brooding nobleman and his bratty daughter. After determining that the brooding nobleman was still in love with his dead wife, who has a reputation for popping out of the grave whenever something doesn't suit her, I planned to entice him into making mad, passionate love to me on top of a piano." Lottie's voice rose. "And just as you suspected, this was all part of my diabolical scheme to further my literary ambitions!"

Hayden gazed down at her for a long moment, a muscle twitching in his cheek. "Would the clavichord have done or did it have to be the piano?"

Without a word, Lottie snatched the manuscript

from the rock and strode to the edge of the cliff. The wind tugged her curls from her topknot and whipped them across her face, nearly blinding her.

"Don't!" Hayden barked just as she prepared to feed the pages to the sea. His hands closed over her shoulders, drawing her away from the brink of the cliff. "Don't," he said more gently. "The literary world might survive such a loss, but I'm not sure either one of us would."

Hugging the manuscript to her chest, Lottie turned to face him. "I started writing the first night I heard the ghost," she confessed. "After you informed me that ours was to be a marriage in name only."

Hayden retreated a few steps, almost as if he didn't trust himself to remain near her. "I would have thought such a revelation would have been a relief, especially given that the 'icy touch' of my hand was enough to provoke 'shudders of dread in any innocent.'"

Lottie gave him an annoyed look. "Did you memorize the entire manuscript?"

"Only select passages," he assured her, folding his arms over his chest. "Mostly those dealing with my 'utter moral depravity' and the 'compelling grimness' of my 'sardonic countenance.'"

Lottie moaned. "Not *your* countenance, the *duke's* countenance. It's just a silly bit of fiction, you know, not a biography."

"So any resemblance between the 'Murderous Marquess' and your 'Deadly Duke' is purely happenstance?" he asked, the skeptical arch of one eyebrow making him look quite sardonic.

She swallowed, trying not to squirm. "Well, I might have borrowed a few elements of your life to enrich the story, but I'm reasonably sure you've never sold your soul to the devil in exchange for immunity for all your crimes."

"There might be some who would disagree with you," he said softly, all traces of mockery disappearing from his face.

As Lottie gazed at him, a thread of hope wound its way through her remorse. Perhaps it wasn't too late to atone for her own crimes.

Still shielding her heart with the half-finished manuscript, she took a step toward him. "Then why don't you let me prove them wrong?"

Hayden raked a lock of hair from his narrowed eyes. "Just what are you asking of me?"

Lottie drew in a deep breath, wishing she were half as fearless as her heroine. "I'm asking you to let me tell society *your* story—the one the scandal sheets will never print."

The look Hayden gave her was almost pitying. "It's a bit late in the tale to reform the Deadly Duke, don't you think?"

"It's never too late," she said, taking another step toward him. "Not if he has someone to believe in him."

Hayden stiffened. "I accused you of being given to melodrama, my lady, not maudlin sentimentality."

Lottie felt a pang of loss. So she was back to being "my lady" instead of "lovely Lottie" or "sweeting," was she? But it was the prospect of losing something even more precious that emboldened her. "I'm not talking about redeeming the Frankenstein monster. I'm talking about vindicating a man who's been wrongly accused of killing the woman he loved more than life itself."

Although Lottie managed to say the words without flinching, they slid like a blade through her tender heart.

Swearing beneath his breath, Hayden strode to the edge of the cliff a few feet away from her. He stood gazing out over the white-capped waves, his profile as stark as the sky.

Lottie drifted toward him. "All I need to clear your name is the truth about how Justine died. You told the authorities it was an accident. Was she drunk on laudanum? Did she wander away from the house and lose her way in the mist? Did she trip over a loose rock or the hem of her gown? All you have to do is tell me what happened that night on the cliffs. Let me give you the happy ending you deserve!"

She reached for his arm, somehow believing that if she could touch him, she might be able to reach him. After last night, she refused to believe that hands capable of such mesmerizing tenderness could also be capable of shoving a defenseless woman to her death.

As her fingertips brushed his sleeve, he wheeled around and caught her by the shoulders, his hands hard and ruthless as he backed her toward the edge of the cliff. "You say you want the truth, my lady, but what if the truth won't give either one of us a happy ending? What then?"

As her heels fought for purchase on the loose

rocks, sending several of them tumbling into the abyss behind her, Lottie shrank from her husband, frightened by the darkness in his eyes. She regretted it immediately, but it was too late. That all too familiar mask of wariness had already descended over his face.

Swinging her away from the cliff, Hayden released her, smoothing away the fingerprints his grip had left on her sleeves. "Go back to London with Ned, Lottie, and finish your story," he said gruffly. "Give your duke the nasty comeuppance he deserves. Rescue your foolhardy heroine from his clutches and give her a hero worthy of her regard. But please don't ask me to give you something I bloody well can't."

With those words, Hayden turned and went striding toward the house, leaving Lottie clutching the crumpled pages of her manuscript.

The day Lottie left Oakwylde Manor was much like the day she had arrived. A leaden bank of clouds brooded over the moor while a chill wind churned the sea into swirling whitecaps. If not for the tender haze of green veiling every hill and tree, Lottie might have believed that spring had been nothing more than a dream, as beautiful and fleeting as the night she'd spent in Hayden's arms.

Although the servants had gathered in the drive to bid her farewell, there was no sign of Hayden or Allegra. While Meggie dabbed at her eyes with her apron, Giles stood at rigid attention, his cravat starched, but his mouth drooping mournfully. When

Martha started sniffing, Mrs. Cavendish whipped a handkerchief from her pocket and handed it to her, her mouth pressed into a thin line, but her eyes suspiciously bright.

Ned escorted Harriet and Lottie to his waiting carriage, but even he couldn't come up with a suitable quip to lighten the mood. He was handing Harriet into the carriage when Allegra came sprinting around the corner of the house, Miss Terwilliger hobbling along behind her. Much to Lottie's relief, the crusty old governess had elected to stay on at the manor, realizing that her young charge would need her now more than ever.

Allegra stumbled to a halt in front of Lottie, clutching Lottie's doll. "Here," she said, thrusting the doll into Lottie's arms. "You take her." The girl's slender throat hitched, betraying how hard she was struggling not to cry. "I don't want you to be all alone."

Lottie tenderly smoothed down a scorched wisp of the doll's hair before handing her back to Allegra. "She never cared much for London. She always said it was too stuffy and civilized for a pirate queen. I'd rather you look after her until I get back." Drawing the child into a fierce embrace, Lottie whispered into her ear, "And I will be back. I promise."

Lottie straightened, giving Allegra into Miss Terwilliger's gnarled but capable hands. Handing her cane to a footman, the old woman rested those hands on Allegra's shoulders, urging her to stand straight and tall.

Ned held out a gloved hand, his expression

somber. Lottie took it and climbed into the carriage, sinking into the seat next to her basket of cats while Ned settled himself next to Harriet. When she had arrived at Oakwylde Manor all those weeks ago, her heart had still been longing for home. Now she was going home, yet leaving her heart behind.

As the carriage lurched into motion, she leaned out the window and gave the manor one last look. Although the mullioned windows reflected little but the cloudswept sky, she could feel Hayden there— watching, waiting. He'd given her no choice for now but to leave him to his ghosts.

"If you ever truly loved him, Justine," she whispered fiercely, pressing her eyes shut, "then set him free."

The sound that came drifting back to her ears might have been the cry of a kittiwake wheeling over the breakers or a woman's laughter rippling on the wind.

Chapter 19

Perhaps it wasn't too late to trade my soul for his . . .

"AUNT LOTTIE'S COME HOME! AUNT LOTTIE'S come home!"

As Lottie descended from the carriage in front of Devonbrooke House, her niece's jubilant cry greeted her from an upstairs window. The front door of the house flew open and her family came spilling out, all laughing and chattering at once.

For a few minutes, all was chaos as they enveloped her in a bruising round of hugs and kisses. Laura beamed as Sterling swung Lottie around in a wide circle, lifting her clean off her feet. Uncle Thane and Aunt Diana had been invited for supper, so their twins and their spaniels added to the noisy confusion by frolicking beneath everyone's feet. When Lottie heard a sharp yelp, she quickly moved her foot, unsure if she had stepped on a dog or a toddler.

George thumped her on the back, grinning like a drunkard. "I never thought I'd miss your prattling, sis, but I must say it's been deadly dull around here ever since you left."

"That's not what I heard," Lottie retorted, nodding toward her traveling companion, who was helping Harriet down from the carriage. "Sir Ned tells me that you've been courting a certain red-haired opera dancer for the past fortnight."

Scowling at Ned, George blushed to the roots of his sandy hair. "Balderdash! It's more like she's been courting me."

"Aunt Lottie! Aunt Lottie!" Eight-year-old Nicholas tugged at the sleeve of her spencer. "Is it true what they say about Cornwall? Do they have fearsome giants there who clean their teeth with children's bones?"

"I should say not, Nicky." Lottie raked a lock of wavy dark hair out of her nephew's brown eyes. "The giants in Cornwall eat the bones as well. You can hear them crunching in the middle of the night when you're trying to sleep."

As he squealed in delight, his nine-year-old sister rolled her eyes. "Boys are so silly. Everyone knows that there are no such things as giants in Cornwall. Or anywhere else, for that matter."

"You're right, Ellie," Lottie said, keeping her expression utterly serious. "But that's only because the sea monsters ate them all."

"See!" Nicholas shouted. "I told you there were sea monsters in Cornwall!" Hooting with triumph, he gave one of his sister's golden curls a sharp yank.

As he went dancing out of her reach, Uncle Thane scooped both a spaniel and a twin out of harm's way.

"Why, you wretched little—" Abandoning all pretense of sophistication, Ellie took off after her brother, chasing him down the tree-shaded block.

As Lottie gazed after them, Laura slipped an arm around her waist. "Why so wistful? You can't tell me you've missed their constant bickering."

"I was just thinking about how much I'd love to introduce them to someone I know."

"Your daughter?"

Realizing that she had never thought of Allegra that way until that very moment, Lottie felt her throat tighten. "Yes," she said softly. "My daughter."

Sterling gave the carriage a puzzled look. "So where is that doting husband of yours? If he's cowering in the carriage, afraid I'll shoot him, you should let him know that Addison has my pistols locked safely away."

Lottie took as deep a breath as her corset would allow. This was the moment she'd been dreading. Pasting on a cheery smile, she turned to her brother-in-law. "I'm afraid Hayden wasn't able to accompany me on this trip. He's quite busy with estate business this time of year. But he insisted that I come anyway. He knows how much I've missed you all and he didn't want to deprive me of your company."

Sterling chuckled. "From what I gathered from your letters, he's quite besotted with his beautiful young bride. I'm surprised the two of you can bear to be separated for more than a day."

George snickered. "Or an hour."

"George," Laura said softly, placing a warning hand on her brother's arm as she studied Lottie's face.

Lottie could feel her smile faltering. She hadn't shed a single tear since leaving Oakwylde, but a dangerous prickling was starting to build behind her eyelids. Painfully aware of Sir Ned's sympathetic gaze, she said, "Of course it's a terrible burden for us to be apart from each other for any length of time. I'm sure he'll be as lost without me as I will be without him."

Oblivious to his sister's mounting distress, George patted her on the shoulder. "So now that you have the poor fellow under your paw, how long is he going to let you stay with us?"

"Forever, I'm afraid," Lottie blurted out, bursting into tears and throwing herself into Laura's arms.

Alone at last, Lottie sat in her old bed, a mountain of snowy white pillows plumped behind her back. Although it was a balmy summer evening outside, a cozy fire crackled on the hearth, warming the spacious bedchamber. Cookie had even tucked a heated brick wrapped in flannel beneath the blankets at the foot of the bed to warm her toes. Pumpkin and Mr. Wiggles were currently glaring at each other, trying to determine who was going to have the privilege of stretching out on top of it.

Once Lottie might have taken shameless advantage of her family's pampering, but tonight she'd felt only relief when Laura had finally shooed them all from the room. She didn't think she could bear another minute of Diana and Cookie's sympathetic clucking or Sterling, George, and Thane's threats to hunt down her scoundrel of a husband and rip his heart from his chest for making her cry.

Laura had been the last to go, giving Lottie's hand a gentle squeeze before promising, "When you're ready to talk, I'll be here."

Throwing back the smothering weight of the quilt, Lottie climbed out of the bed. As pleasant as her family's cosseting was, she wasn't a little girl anymore. She was past the age where a broken heart could be mended with a cup of warm chocolate and a steaming hunk of Cookie's gingerbread.

It didn't take her long to find what she was looking for. Her writing case was the last thing she had shoved into her hastily packed valise. She perched on the end of the bed, her feet drawn up so Mirabella couldn't dash out from under the bed and attack them, and unlatched the case. She had crammed the pages of her manuscript back into it without ceremony, no longer caring if they got wrinkled or torn.

If Hayden hadn't found them, she might be settled in the marchioness's chamber at Oakwylde right now, awaiting her husband's pleasure. Lottie closed her eyes for an aching moment, knowing that Hayden's skillful hands and oh-so-clever mouth would have made sure that his pleasure was also her own.

Opening her eyes, she gazed down at the manuscript. Her brilliant prose now seemed like nothing more than the meanderings of some overindulged child who had been told her every scribble was a masterpiece. As she flipped through the pages, the silky rasp of Hayden's voice haunted her more surely than any ghost.

It's a bit late in the tale to reform the Deadly Duke, don't you think?

It's never too late, she had told him. *Not if he has someone to believe in him.*

But she hadn't believed in him. No one had. Not the scandal sheets, not society, not even his own daughter. And she had proved herself no different from any of them by demanding a truth she already knew in her heart.

Suddenly Lottie realized why her family's attention had made her squirm. She didn't deserve their pity, nor did Hayden deserve their contempt. She was just as much to blame for their parting as he was.

She also knew what she had to do. Dumping the pages out of the writing case, she gathered them into her arms. She'd never willingly destroyed a single jot of her handwriting, but her steps were steady as she rose from the bed and marched to the fireplace. She held the pages to her heart for the briefest moment before tossing them into the dancing flames.

She didn't linger to watch them burn. Instead, she returned to the writing case and drew out a clean sheet of paper, a pen, and a fresh bottle of ink. Using the case as a makeshift desk, she settled herself against the pillows and began to write, her hand flying across the page as if winged.

*　　*　　*

"What in the devil do you think she's doing up there?" Sterling stood with hands on hips, scowling up at the ceiling of the drawing room. "Burning her lamp until the wee hours of the morning, dressing like a charwoman, taking all of her meals in her room."

"At least she's eating," Laura pointed out from her place on the sofa. She smoothed the sampler she was stitching over her knee. "Cookie swears every tray comes back to the kitchen all but licked clean."

"It's not her appetite I'm worried about. It's her state of mind. She's been back in London for nearly two months and she hasn't attended a single tea or soiree. Poor George is so bored with entertaining Miss Dimwinkle that he's about to pull his hair out. Or hers. Yet still Lottie refuses to leave the house and the only caller she'll receive is that rascal Townsend." A pained frown clouded his brow. "She never did say why Oakleigh sent her away. You don't suppose . . ."

"No, I don't." Laura jabbed her needle firmly through the fabric. "And nor should you. Lottie's whims may be fickle, but her heart never has been."

"If I'd have known the scoundrel would send her back with it broken, I'd have shot him on sight." Raking a hand through his tawny hair, Sterling sighed. "I don't know how much longer I can bear all of this mystery. I only wish she would confide in us."

Laura rose to tenderly link her arm through his. "Be patient, my love," she said, giving the ceiling an enigmatic glance of her own. "Perhaps that's exactly what she's doing."

* * *

"Aunt Lottie! Aunt Lottie!"

Laying aside her pen, Lottie sighed. She might be able to shut out the rest of the world while she worked, but it was impossible to ignore her nephew's exuberant bellow. He rarely spoke in anything but a shout, but he had a particularly deafening bellow reserved for special occasions.

Rubbing her lower back, she rose from the writing desk and hurried to the window, sweeping the voluminous folds of Cookie's apron out of her way. She'd given up any hope of ever scrubbing all the ink out from under her fingernails, but she still possessed enough vanity to want to protect her pretty gowns.

She threw open the sash and leaned out, blinking as the bright afternoon sunshine blinded her. She'd only managed to steal three hours of sleep last night and she felt as dazed as a caterpillar emerging from its cocoon. She finally located her nephew dangling from the lowest branch of the elm tree that shaded the broad tree-lined street.

"What is it, Nicky? Have you caught another shiny bug?"

Grinning, the boy pointed down at the street. "This time I caught a shiny carriage!"

Lottie squinted down at the vehicle parked in front of the mansion. A crested carriage certainly wasn't an uncommon sight in this posh corner of London. Sterling maintained half a dozen of them in his own carriage house. But none of them had the heraldic emblem of an oak tree with spreading branches etched on their lacquered doors.

Lottie's heart doubled its rhythm.

The next thing she knew, she was flying down the broad staircase, whipping off Cookie's apron as she went. She shoved it into the hands of a startled maid at the foot of the stairs, then went barreling toward the wide-eyed footman standing beside the front door.

"Will you be going out, my lady? Shall I fetch your—"

When she showed no signs of slowing, he swept open the door, obviously fearing she was going to run right through it if he didn't. Lottie stumbled to a halt on the front stoop, frantically shoving a loose curl back into her untidy topknot.

If not for the black-garbed figure who accompanied her, Lottie might not have recognized the child descending from the carriage. Miss Terwilliger leaned heavily on her cane, but the girl stood straight and tall, wearing a fetching blue bonnet and frock. Her hair had been gathered into glossy dark braids. Despite the proud tilt of her chin, she clutched the doll in her arms in a white-knuckled grip, clearly uncertain of her welcome.

"Allegra!" Lottie raced down the front steps and swept Hayden's daughter into her arms.

As she crushed the child to her, she would have almost sworn she could smell the scent of the moor on her—that elusive breath of wild wind and growing things. Lottie inhaled deeply, praying she would detect a thread of bayberry winding through it.

"Just look at you!" Holding Allegra by the shoulders, Lottie set the girl away from her. "I swear you've grown two inches in as many months!"

Miss Terwilliger sniffed. "That shouldn't surprise you. Most children thrive on equally strict doses of affection, discipline, and fresh air."

Lottie glanced over Allegra's shoulder at the carriage, unable to completely disguise the hope leaping in her heart. "Surely you ladies didn't travel so far without an escort, did you?"

Instead of answering, Allegra reached into the reticule looped around her wrist and drew out a square of folded vellum.

She held it out to Lottie. "This is for you. He sealed it before I could read it."

Her heart sinking, Lottie took the note and drew her thumbnail along its seam, breaking the wax seal she recognized as her husband's. She slowly unfolded it.

My lady, it read in Hayden's tidy scrawl. *My daughter has done nothing but mope since you left. Her morose countenance is beginning to play havoc with my digestion. Please look after her.* As a postscript, he'd added, *You were a much better mother to her than I ever was a father.*

When she lowered the note, Allegra was gazing up at her, her violet eyes beseeching. "He's all alone now. I'm frightened for him."

"I know, sweeting," Lottie whispered, gathering the child into her arms. "So am I."

They might have remained that way for a long

time if Ellie hadn't come skidding around the side of the house at the precise moment Nicholas swung down from the tree and landed right in front of them.

"What on earth are you bellowing about now?" Ellie demanded of her brother, giving his shoulder a shove. "One of these days you're going to catch fire and no one is going to throw a bucket of water on you because you're always going on and on about nothing at all."

Before Nicky could shout a retort, Ellie spotted their visitors. Allegra was openly gaping at her, wide-eyed with astonishment at finding herself face-to-face with a living, breathing duplicate of the doll in her arms.

Scowling at the doll, Ellie planted her hands on her hips and tossed her topknot of golden curls, her snub nose fixed firmly in the air. "Where did you get that? Aunt Lottie would never let *me* play with her."

To Lottie's surprise, instead of snarling back at her niece, Allegra ran to the carriage and retrieved the doll her father had given her. "Here," she said, shoving the raven-haired beauty into Ellie's arms. "You can play with her if you'd like."

Ellie studied the doll, then stole a surreptitious glance at Allegra, caught off guard by the uncanny resemblance. Although she was younger than Allegra by at least a year, she finally sighed and said, "Well, I'm too old to play with dolls, but if you insist, I don't suppose it can do any harm. Would you like to see my kittens? I have a dozen of them in my bedchamber. They don't care for anyone but me, but perhaps they'll let you pet them if I tell them it's all right."

"I have kittens, too," Allegra said, running back to the carriage to fetch a woven basket. She flipped open the lid and four bewhiskered faces popped into view. Recognizing the cats she had given Hayden, Lottie knew Allegra had not exaggerated. Her father was well and truly alone now.

While the girls went off, hand in hand, each clutching a replica of the other, Nicholas was left standing forgotten on the pavement. He wrinkled his freckled nose and spat in disgust. "Girls!"

Lottie rumpled his hair. "They're not nearly as pleasant as bugs, are they? While the girls are playing with their dolls and kittens, why don't you escort Miss Terwilliger into the house and ask your mother to prepare two guest chambers?"

Dragging his feet, Nicky obeyed. As he and the governess disappeared into the house, Lottie unfolded the note again, gently smoothing her fingertips over Hayden's words. "I'll look after her," she whispered. "And I'll look after you, too. You just see if I don't."

Tucking the note in the pocket of her skirt, she hurried up the front stairs, more eager than ever to get back to her work.

A crisp autumn breeze drifted through the dormer windows of the fourth-story office, mingling with the acrid scent of soot from the nearby chimney pots. Lottie kept her gloved hands folded tightly over her reticule to keep them from fluttering all over the place and betraying her nervousness. She could hardly believe she was sitting in the offices of Minerva Press.

She had often frequented the legendary publisher's lending library and bookshop on the first floor of the brick building, but she'd never before dared to breach its inner sanctum. Here in this magical and somewhat shabby place, where the air was perfumed with the intoxicating aromas of dust, ink, leather and paper, one's dreams could be bound and sold to provide endless hours of pleasure. Perhaps Mrs. Eliza Parsons herself had once sat in this very chair while she nervously awaited the publisher's verdict on *The Mysterious Warning* or *Castle of Wolfenbach*.

Ned lounged in the ladder-backed chair across from Lottie, rhythmically tapping his walking stick on the hardwood floor. Catching her eye, he stopped tapping. "It's not too late for us to duck out of here, you know. Are you absolutely certain this is what you want to do?"

She nodded. "It's what I *have* to do."

"You realize he may throttle me for allowing you to do it? That is, if your brother-in-law doesn't throttle me first."

Lottie crinkled her nose at him. "That's a risk I'm willing to take."

They both sat up straighter as the door behind the desk swung open. A stoop-shouldered, balding man entered the room, a manuscript tucked under his arm. He wore an unadorned frock coat, a moth-eaten cravat, and a waistcoat and trousers of mis-matched plaid. Lottie found it somehow comforting that his neatly trimmed fingernails were rimmed with half-moons of ink.

Sinking into the chair behind the desk, he placed the manuscript in front of him, then drew off his spectacles to wipe his eyes.

"Come now, Mr. Beale," Lottie said with a half-hearted laugh. "Surely it wasn't as bad as all that."

The publisher pinched the bridge of his nose before slipping his spectacles back on. "My dear lady," he said, fixing her with an earnest look, "surely you must be aware that this is not the sort of novel we usually publish at Minerva. Our readers are accustomed to more . . . how shall I say it . . . ?" he steepled his fingers beneath his chin ". . . *sensational* fare."

Ned started to rise. "We're very sorry to have wasted your time, sir. I do hope you'll forgive us for—"

Glaring at him, Lottie cleared her throat pointedly. Sighing, he dropped back into his chair.

She leaned toward the desk, seeking to charm the publisher with her warmest smile. "As one of Minerva Press's most devoted readers, I can assure you that I am well aware of what you *usually* publish. But under the circumstances, I was hoping you might at least consider my manuscript. Surely you can't deny that it would be a profit-making endeavor for your company."

"But at what cost? You must realize that the publication of this work is bound to engender a certain amount of notoriety for its author. Unless you're willing to publish under a pseudonym—"

"No," Lottie said firmly, settling back into her chair. "Absolutely not. I want my name to be the first thing the reader sees when he or she picks up the book."

Mr. Beale shook his head sadly. "I've searched my heart, but I just can't see any way to make this endeavor work."

"Please don't dismiss us so easily," Lottie entreated him, no longer able to hide her desperation behind a gracious smile. "I realize the quality of my writing may not be up to your usual high standards, but I still feel that with some drastic cutting and some extensive revisions . . ."

She trailed off. The publisher was blinking at her as if she'd sprouted a second head. She exchanged a baffled look with Ned.

"You misunderstand me, my lady." Mr. Beale rested a hand gently on top of her manuscript, his rheumy brown eyes going damp again. "This is one of the most profoundly moving pieces of fiction I've ever read. I would dare even the most cynical of our readers to finish it with a dry eye and a cold heart toward his fellow man. I wasn't implying that the book was *below* our standards, but *above* them, suited to a far more prestigious publishing company than ours."

Lottie gazed at him in open-mouthed disbelief, wondering if she'd somehow dozed off and drifted into a dream. She didn't realize tears had welled up

in her own eyes until Ned handed her a handkerchief.

"But if I prefer your company over the others,"
she asked, stealing another glance at his ink-stained
fingers, "would you consider publishing it?"

Mr. Beale nodded, a smile breaking over his long
face. "It would be both a pleasure and an honor."

"Did you hear that, Ned?" Lottie turned to her
friend, laughing through her tears. "I'm going to be
notorious!"

Chapter 20

*I could feel the Devil's icy breath
against the back of my neck . . .*

AN ILL WIND WAS BLOWING AT OAKWYLDE
Manor.

It came whipping across the moors and down the
chimneys, poisoning every breath with its bitterness. It wrested the leaves from the trees with ruthless fingers, leaving them stark and bare. It stripped
away every trace of summer until that brief season
seemed nothing more than a dream.

Some claimed that if you stepped outside and
tilted your head just so, you could even hear the distant tolling of the bell the wreckers had used to lure
unsuspecting ships to their doom on the jagged
rocks a century ago. Others whispered that it was
the same wind that had blown the night the master's
first wife had taken her fatal fall, the same wind that
had carried his agonized cry to their ears.

The servants once again took to locking themselves in their quarters as soon as dark fell. It was no longer a ghost they feared encountering in the gathering shadows, but a man. Although he spent his days barricaded in his study, their master would stalk the deserted corridors of the manor at all hours of the night, his savage countenance and burning eyes making him look somehow less than mortal.

Although no melodies, ghostly or otherwise, emanated from the music room after he sent his wife and daughter away, the maids still dreaded entering the chamber. None of them could shake off the eerie sensation that they were being watched. They would whirl around, their hearts in their throats, only to find themselves all alone with the portrait of the first Lady Oakleigh. One young girl swore that while she was dusting the piano, a choking cloud of jasmine had arisen from the keys, sending her staggering from the room, fighting to catch her breath. After a porcelain figurine went flying off the mantel, barely missing Meggie's head, neither Martha's pinches nor Mrs. Cavendish's threats of immediate dismissal could coax any of the terrified maids into returning to that room.

The footmen began to complain to Giles about icy pockets of cold lingering in certain corridors. They would rush back to warm themselves by the kitchen fire, chilled to the bone and wracked by uncontrollable shivers.

When Martha reluctantly informed Hayden of the servants' growing fears, he suggested that she hire less superstitious servants. He no longer believed in ghosts. Just when he longed for their company the most, they had deserted him.

Although he'd sent Allegra away nearly four months ago, he insisted that the maids keep a lamp burning in her chamber all through the night. He would ease open her door and expect to see her lying there, her cheeks flushed with sleep and Lottie's doll nestled in her arms. But her bed was always cold and empty.

He would linger in the drawing room doorway in the wee hours of morning, hoping to hear the clinking of teacups, the echo of a high-pitched giggle, or a snatch of some ridiculous Scottish ditty. But all he heard was silence.

His aimless wanderings would eventually drive him to the third floor of the house, to Lottie's bedchamber. The first time he'd pushed open her door, he'd been surprised to discover that she had left most of her things behind. Perhaps she had simply packed in haste, he told himself bitterly, desperate to be free of him. He had seen the fear in her eyes when he'd put his hands on her that day on the cliff. It was a fear he never wanted to see in any woman's eyes again as long as he lived. Especially not Lottie's.

He would drift around her room, haunted not by ghosts but by the way she had crinkled her nose when she laughed; the way her hair had gleamed like molten sunshine as she went flying down the drive on the hobbyhorse; the soft, broken cries she had made against his mouth when he had urged her over the crest of pleasure into sweet oblivion. Although he knew he should have Martha and Mrs. Cavendish pack up her things and send them to London, he would simply pull her door shut behind him each night, leaving everything exactly as she had left it.

In the first few weeks after Justine had died, Hayden had learned the dangers of seeking solace in the bottom of a bottle. Yet late one night he found himself stumbling out of a French window in the study, gripping an open bottle of port by the neck.

He picked his way over the rocks, his steps none too steady, until he finally found himself swaying at the edge of the cliff, listening to the sea crash against the rocks below like the last of his dreams. The wind had scattered the clouds, freeing the shimmering orb of the moon to etch the waves in silver. Hayden took a deep swig of the port, then closed his eyes and spread his arms wide, all but daring the wind and the night to take him.

That was when he heard it—the echo of a distant melody drifting on the wind. The song was achingly sweet, irresistible in its simplicity. His blood curdling in his veins, Hayden slowly turned to look at the house. This time he knew there was no Lottie and no Allegra to stroke those piano keys to life.

"Damn you," Hayden whispered hoarsely as that siren song drew him away from the edge of that cliff one inexorable step at a time.

Still gripping the bottle, he stalked through the darkened corridors of the house, both the music and his fury swelling with each step. But when he flung open the door of the music room, he found it exactly as he had expected to find it—dark and silent. He strode to the piano and flattened one palm against its closed lid. He could still feel the faint vibration of its strings, still hear the echo of that bittersweet melody hanging in the air.

He whirled on Justine's portrait, roaring, "I hope to God you're happy now!" Drawing back his arm, he hurled the bottle at the portrait with all of his strength. It shattered against the canvas, the port spattering like drops of blood over Justine's white dress. "Perhaps your intention was always to drive me mad so that you'd never be alone again, not even in death!"

Justine simply gazed down at him, her expression both mocking and inscrutable.

"Hayden?"

Hayden whirled around to find a man standing in the doorway, his face shrouded in shadows.

For one frozen fragment of time, he thought it was Phillipe standing there, young and brash and full of hope. As he waited for his old friend to step out of the shadows, the scorched pistol-ball hole over his heart still smoking, Hayden knew he'd finally gone well and truly mad.

"Hayden?" the man repeated, a querulous note edging his voice. "You haven't gone and scared off all the servants with that frightful bellowing, have you? I knocked and knocked and no one ever came so I finally went around to the back of the house, found an unlatched window in your study, and let myself in."

As his visitor stepped forward, his hair shining silver in the moonlight, Hayden staggered back-

ward and sank down on the divan, going numb
with relief. He buried his head in his hands, a broken laugh escaping him. "Sweet Christ, Ned, I never
thought I'd be so glad to have you barge in unan-
nounced and uninvited."

"That's certainly the warmest welcome you've
given me lately. That was a lovely piece, by the way.
I never realized you played."

Hayden slowly lifted his head, gazing at the piano
keys with a mixture of wonder and disbelief. "Neither did I."

"I'd ask you to offer me a drink," Ned said, slanting the portrait a wry look, "but I much prefer a
glass to having the bottle hurled at my head."

Hayden sheepishly raked a hand through his hair.
"Justine never was much of a port drinker." He
frowned at his friend, realizing for the first time how
odd it was to find him there. "So what brings you to
Cornwall in the dead of night?"

Ned sobered. "My apologies for arriving so late,
but I brought you a gift from your wife—something
she thought you needed to see right away."

"What is it?" Hayden asked, a bitter snort escaping him. "Her petition for an annulment?"

"Not exactly." Reaching into his valise, Ned drew
out a slim leather-bound volume and handed it to
Hayden.

Hayden examined the book, recognizing it as the
first installment of a triple-decker novel. Even before he turned its scarlet cover to the moonlight, he
knew what its florid title would read.

LORD DEATH'S BRIDE *by Lady Oakleigh*.

Disappointment welled up in his throat, more bitter than gall. Although he'd told Lottie to finish the novel, a part of him hadn't truly believed that she would. He'd certainly never dreamed that she'd be so heartless as to throw the book in his face after it was published.

He held it out to Ned. "Thank you, but I don't have to read it. I already know the story . . . and the ending."

Ignoring Hayden's outstretched hand, Ned tossed the other two volumes of the novel into his lap, a cryptic smile curling the corner of his mouth. "I'd read it anyway if I were you. Sometimes even the most predictable endings have a way of catching you by surprise." Snapping the valise shut, Ned yawned. "Although I hate to deprive you of my company, I'll be leaving for Surrey early in the morning. I've promised my dear mum a long overdue visit. So if you'll excuse me, I'm off to find a bed and some pretty maid to warm it."

"You might try waking Martha. She's always had a soft spot for you."

Ned shuddered. "I think I'd rather cuddle up to a warm brick."

After he had gone, Hayden sat staring down at the three volumes in his lap. He could hardly blame Lottie for betraying him, but he couldn't believe that she would betray Allegra so callously. By confirming the worst of what everyone believed of him, she had spoiled any chance his daughter might have had of escaping the sins of her parents, of marrying a decent man and making a life for herself in society.

His anger flaring, Hayden decided to seek out the first fire he could find and toss all three volumes in the flames. As he rose, still a little unsteady on his feet from the port, one of the books slid to the floor, falling open in a puddle of moonlight. He bent down to pick it up, not realizing until he saw the scrawled inscription on the frontpiece that it was the first volume of the set. Lottie's handwriting was every bit as extravagant as he remembered.

He traced the tip of his finger over the graceful dips and loops, murmuring aloud, *"From my heart to yours . . ."*

Unable to bear her mockery, he was about to slam the book shut when, against their will, his eyes were drawn to the very first sentence on the very first page—*I'll never forget the moment I first laid eyes on the man who was to save my life.*

Chapter 21

Was it possible I had misjudged him so badly?

"DID YOU GET IT? DID YOU GET IT? OH, please tell me you got it!" Elizabeth Bly exclaimed, bouncing up and down on her toes in excitement as her best friend came running out the glass-fronted door of Minerva Press's bookshop.

"By Jove, I got it!" Caro Brockway crowed, whipping the thin leather-bound volume out from under her cloak. The girl's breath escaped in white puffs on the frigid air.

Before she could reach Elizabeth, a hulking footman garbed in navy livery stepped into her path. "I'll give you three pounds for that book, miss."

Caro stumbled to a halt, clearly taken aback. "But I only paid half a guinea for it."

"I'll make it five, then." The man stole a desperate

look at the long line of carriages parked just behind them.

The elegant carriages and public hacks were lined up all the way to Gracechurch Street. Swaddled in furs and muffs, their occupants were willing to shiver in the cold for hours, all in the hope of obtaining the third volume of London's latest literary sensation, *Lord Death's Bride.*

"Please, miss, take pity on me," the man begged. "You heard what happened to Lady Dryden's footman, didn't you?"

The girls exchanged a wide-eyed look. All of London had heard what had happened to Lady Dryden's footman. He had dared to return to the countess's carriage empty-handed only to sheepishly confess that he'd let the last available copy of *Volume Two* of *Lord Death's Bride* slip through his fingers and into Lady Featherwick's grasping paws. Some said the countess's outraged shriek was heard all the way to Aldgate. She had beat the poor fellow about the head with her parasol, then stuck her nose in the air and commanded her coachman to drive on without him. The footman had chased the carriage for ten blocks, begging for her forgiveness, before finally succumbing to exhaustion and falling face-first into a pile of fresh horse manure. Rumor had it that he was now seeking employment on the docks.

"I'm terribly sorry, sir, but I can't help you." Clutching the book to her heart, Caro veered around him and backed toward Elizabeth. "I've been waiting in line since dawn and I promised my mother I'd bring the book straight home. She's going to read it to the entire family after supper tonight. They've all been dying to know what happens after the noble duke realizes his new bride has betrayed his trust."

Elizabeth rolled her eyes. "I can't believe what a ninny she's turned out to be." The girl clasped her hands beneath her chin, a dreamy expression softening her features. "Why, I would have realized from the beginning that such a kind, generous, and *incredibly* handsome man would never hurt any woman, especially his wife."

The footman began to stalk Caro, his countenance taking on a more menacing aspect. He stretched out one white-gloved hand. "Come on, gel. It won't kill you to hand it over. Five pounds must be a fortune to a common chit like you."

"Run, Caro, run!" Elizabeth shrieked, grabbing her friend's hand and tugging her out of his reach.

As the two girls sped away, their cloaks flapping behind them, the footman tore off his top hat and shouted, "Seven pounds! I'll give you seven pounds!"

At bookshops and lending libraries all over London, the same drama was being replayed. The author had insisted that an abridged version be published in weekly installments in the periodicals for those who couldn't afford bound books. The second a new edition appeared, the milling crowds would rush the street vendors, snatching and grabbing until the flimsy pamphlets came apart in their grimy hands. Down on the docks where the penny broadsides were sold, even those who couldn't read wept over crude sketches of a noblewoman on her knees begging for her husband's forgiveness as he

turned his sad face away from her and pointed toward the door.

The novel's thinly disguised characters provided
endless hours of speculation and delight among the
ton. They could hardly believe that one of their own
would lower themselves to pen such a thrilling and
touching tale. It was the greatest literary scandal
London had known since a married Percy Bysshe
Shelley had eloped to France with sixteen-year-old
Mary Godwin over a decade before.

When it was announced that the duke of Devonbrooke and Minerva Press would be jointly hosting
a ball in the author's honor at Devonbrooke House,
they set out to beg, borrow, or steal an invitation.
The families who had retired to their country estates
for the winter ordered their footman to hitch up
their teams and headed back to the city. None of
them were willing to miss the social coup of the year
or the chance to ogle the notorious bride of Lord
Death himself.

As Lottie approached the marble steps that spilled
down from the gallery into the vast ballroom of
Devonbrooke House, she felt more nervous than notorious. A crush of guests milled around the ballroom below, eagerly awaiting her arrival. A string
quartet was seated in the corner, their bows poised
over their instruments as they awaited the signal to
strike up the first waltz. Sterling and Laura stood at
the foot of the stairs, looking even more uneasy than
she felt, while George ducked through the crowd

with his head down, trying to elude a persistent Harriet.

Lottie had dreamed of such a moment her entire life, yet now that it had arrived, she felt curiously empty inside.

She touched a hand to her upswept curls, wondering if any of their guests would recognize the girl who had once been known as the Hertfordshire Hellion. With Laura and Diana's help, she'd chosen a gown of emerald green velvet that rode slightly off of her creamy shoulders. A matching choker encircled her slender throat. Shimmering gold banding edged the puffed sleeves and square-cut bodice of the gown. The waist was cut low, hugging the natural curves of her body. The strand of pearls woven through her hair added a touch of elegance to the demure ensemble, as did the whisper of lace peeping through a side slit in the skirt.

Addison was standing at rigid attention at the top of the stairs. The butler gave her a nearly imperceptible wink before clearing his throat and loudly intoning, "The Most Honorable Carlotta Oakleigh, the marchioness of Oakleigh."

An animated murmur swept through the ballroom as all eyes turned to the stairs. Her fingertips grazing the iron balustrade, Lottie slowly descended, a gracious smile fixed on her lips.

Sterling was waiting for her at the foot of the steps. Lottie felt a wistful pang in her heart as she imagined Hayden standing there instead, his green eyes shining with pride.

Her brother-in-law offered her his arm. As she took it, Laura signaled the musicians. They launched into a rousing Viennese waltz and Lottie and Sterling began to glide around the floor.

"No word from Townsend yet?" Sterling asked as several other couples joined the dance, swirling around them in a riot of colors and chatter.

"Not even a whisper. I'm beginning to think Hayden must have tossed him off the cliff along with my book."

Sterling scowled. "Better him than you."

When the first waltz ended, he handed her off to a beaming Mr. Beale. The kindly publisher was only too eager to be seen squiring about Minerva Press's brightest new literary light. The dazzling success of her novel had enriched both his coffers and his reputation. Lottie clutched one of his ink-stained hands, learning quickly that he was a much better publisher than he was a dancer.

"I believe we can pronounce the night a triumph, my lady," he said, peering over the top of his spectacles at the whirl of excitement, "just as we can the seventh printing of *Volume Three* of your book."

He was blissfully oblivious to the sly glances Lottie was receiving from behind their guests' fans and quizzing glasses. It wasn't admiration she saw in their eyes, but rabid curiosity and thinly veiled pity. Smiling at Mr. Beale, she held her head high. If Hayden could endure society's censure for over four years, surely she could survive it for one night.

Occupied with keeping her delicate slippers out from under the publisher's rather cumbersome feet, she didn't realize a marked hush had fallen over the crowd until the music ground to an off-key halt.

Addison's voice rang out in the sudden silence, lacking its usual clipped cadence. "The Most Honorable Hayden St. Clair, the marquess of Oakleigh."

As a stunned gasp traveled through the crowd, Lottie whirled around to find her husband standing at the top of the stairs.

Chapter 22

It seemed the Devil had come to claim his bride . . .

ALTHOUGH EVERY GAZE IN THE ENORMOUS ballroom was fixed on the man at the top of the stairs, he had eyes only for Lottie. The burning look he gave her made several of the women standing nearby fumble in their reticules for their smelling salts.

As he started down the steps, a wave of excited chatter swept the room.

"Is that him? Could it be?"

"Look at those eyes! He's even more handsome than she described."

"Oh my! He looks rather savage and unpredictable, doesn't he? I've always admired that in a man."

For some of the younger guests, it was their first glimpse of the notorious recluse once known as the Murderous Marquess. Others still remembered him as the prized catch who had broken the hearts of their eager young daughters by marrying a penniless French girl. But to all of them he was now the hero of Lady Oakleigh's infamous novel—a man wrongly maligned not only by them, but also by the very woman who stood watching his approach, as pale and silent as a statue. More than a few of them hoped he had come to give her the set-down she so richly deserved.

As Hayden's determined strides carried him across the ballroom, both Sterling and George moved to intercept him. Laura shook her head frantically at her brother and grabbed her husband's arm, digging her fingernails into his sleeve.

Stopping in front of Lottie, Hayden sketched her a crisp bow. "May I have the honor, my lady? Or is your dance card already full?"

"I don't have a dance card, my lord. In case you've forgotten, I'm a married woman."

His eyes smoldered down at her. "Oh, I haven't forgotten."

Mr. Beale stepped aside, eagerly surrendering her. From the glazed look in his eye, Lottie could tell he was already mentally tallying how many copies of her book this fresh scandal was bound to sell. "I'd best hand you over without a fight, my lady. I've heard your husband is the jealous sort. We wouldn't want him to call me out, now would we?"

Giving Hayden a conspiratorial wink, he bowed and backed away, leaving Lottie all alone to face her husband. As the musicians took up the soaring melody where they had left off, Hayden swept her into his arms and into the dance.

Lottie stole a glimpse at the daunting set of his freshly shaven jaw above the snowy folds of his cravat, hardly daring to believe that she was in his arms once again. His hand was splayed at the small of her back, its possessive heat urging her nearer with each dizzying turn around the ballroom.

Gazing straight ahead, he said, "I owe you an apology, my lady. It seems you're capable of maudlin sentimentality after all. You simply weren't going to be happy until you made a hero of me, were you? I just don't understand why you had to do it at your own expense."

"What expense?" Lottie replied, keeping her voice deliberately light to hide how breathless he was making her. "Look around you. I finally have all of the fame and attention I've always craved. Just as you predicted, I'm the literary toast of London."

Hayden did look around, but unlike Mr. Beale, he recognized what he saw. "They didn't come here tonight to honor you. They came to gawk at you. Just look at Lady Dryden. How dare that spiteful old cow look at you with pity in her eyes? She's already driven three husbands to early graves with her incessant nagging." He gave the buxom old woman a fierce scowl, sending her ducking behind her hand-painted fan.

"You really shouldn't be so hard on them. I can assure you that they all enjoyed weeping copious tears when my heroine's redemption came too late and my hero cast her out of his life and his heart."

Hayden lowered his eyes to hers, the look in their dark-fringed depths making her pulse quicken.

"Weren't you the one who told me that it's never too late? Not if you have someone to believe in you."

The music ended in that moment, but instead of letting her go, he drew her even closer. Neither of them realized another startled hush had fallen over the ballroom until Addison made a strangled noise deep in his throat. His voice resounded like a trumpet as he shouted, "His Majesty, the king!"

Hayden and Lottie jerked apart as a fresh surge of astonishment rippled through the ballroom. Sterling and Laura looked as shocked as everyone else. The king's rapidly failing health had driven him into seclusion at Windsor months ago. Some even whispered that he was beginning to show signs of his father's madness, insisting he'd fought at Waterloo alongside Wellington instead of squandering his youth and vigor on excesses of wine, women, and overly rich cream sauces.

As he minced his way toward them, flanked by two of his royal guards, Hayden bowed and Lottie sank into a full court curtsy, her head inclined and her skirts spread on the floor around her. Keenly aware of the vulnerability of her nape, she eyed the guards' swords out of the corner of her eye, just waiting for the king to bellow, "Off with her head!"

Instead, he snapped, "Stand up, gel. Let me have a look at you."

Lottie slowly rose, murmuring, "Your Majesty."

He was more bloated and pasty than she remembered, but not even time or ill health could dim the lascivious twinkle in his eye. As he leaned toward her, his gaze strayed to the deep cleft between the swell of her breasts. "Forgive me for crashing your little party, my dear, but I simply had to pay my respects." To her shock, he drew a lace-edged handkerchief from his pocket and dabbed at his eyes. "Not since the last installment of Harriette Wilson's memoirs have I found myself so engaged by the written word."

"Why, thank you, Your Majesty. I consider that high praise indeed coming from your lips."

Giving her husband a nervous look, the king leaned so close his fruity breath fanned her face. "Your characters were rather thinly disguised, my dear," he whispered. "Perhaps it's just as well that you made no mention of our own little dalliance."

Exchanging a disbelieving look with Hayden, Lottie touched a finger to her twitching lips. "Have no fear. His Majesty can always rely on my discretion."

"Very good, gel. Very good." At that moment, a lovely young woman went bobbing past, her ample breasts swelling over the top of her low-cut bodice. "If you'll excuse me," the king mumbled, already teetering after her on his jeweled shoes, "I believe there are some matters of state that require my immediate attention."

"Two of them, no doubt," Hayden muttered, watching their monarch's beleaguered guards follow his meandering path through the ballroom.

"Well, at least I didn't have to bite him that time."

Hayden shifted his glare to her. "If he had kept ogling you in that shameless manner, I was going to bite him myself."

"Then we'd have both ended up in the Tower."

"I'm not sure that would have been such a terrible idea. At least we'd have had some privacy."

He seized her by the hand, visibly frustrated to find them boxed in on all sides by the milling crush. Not even the king's unexpected entrance had been able to completely distract the crowd from their own little drama. Spotting another door at the rear of the room, he began to draw her toward it.

He'd barely taken two steps when a rotund gentleman stepped into their path. "Oakleigh!" the man boomed, clapping one beefy hand on Hayden's shoulder. "So glad to see you back in London at last. Do hope you plan to linger. The wife and I were hoping you might come 'round for supper one night."

Mumbling something noncommittal, Hayden ducked out of his grip and started in another direction. This time it was a beaming lady blocking their path. Resting a gloved hand on Hayden's forearm, she fluttered her lashes at him. "If you haven't any other invitations, my lord, do consider joining Reginald and me for tea tomorrow afternoon."

Before he could accept or decline, a throng of gentlemen and ladies surrounded them, each struggling to make their voice heard over all the others.

". . . having a hunting party next month at the country house in Leicestershire. Do promise you'll be there!"

". . . an outing to the Lake District in the spring. Everyone who is anyone has vowed to accompany us, but it simply won't be a success without you."

". . . thought you might like to join Lord Estes and me at Newmarket on Sunday. I'm thinking to wager three hundred guineas on a pretty little filly I've had my eye on for the past fortnight."

Hayden jostled and elbowed his way through them, never once loosening his grip on Lottie's hand. When they finally emerged in the corridor outside the ballroom, he flung open one door after another until he finally found what he was seeking—a deserted room with a fire on the grate and a lock on the door. An Argand lamp resting on a satinwood table cast a mellow glow over the chintz-draped walls of the parlor.

Hayden secured the door, then swung around to face Lottie, resting his hands on his lean hips. "Good God, woman, do you see what you've done? Are you happy now?"

"Quite." Settling herself on a brocaded chaise, Lottie smiled up at him. "I've opened every door in England to you. And every door opened to you will be opened to your daughter as well. Thanks to me, Allegra will one day have her pick of suitors."

His eyes narrowed. "I don't suppose you happened to notice that none of their invitations included you."

"And why would they?" She shrugged, pretending the deliberate slights hadn't stung just a little. "After all, I'm the shallow, immature girl whose lack of faith in a kind and decent man cost her all hope of future happiness."

"No, you're not! What you are is the most infuriating creature I've ever met!" Glaring daggers at her, he raked a hand through his hair. "Why, I could just . . . just . . ."

"Kill me?" Lottie cheerfully provided. "Strangle me? Push me off a cliff?"

Biting off an oath, Hayden came striding toward her. As his hands closed over her shoulders, drawing her to her feet, she came willingly into his arms, her mind recognizing what her heart had always known.

She had never been afraid of him. She had only been afraid of her feelings for him. As he lowered his mouth to hers, they swept through her in a raging torrent of tenderness and yearning.

"Adore you," he finished, his voice cracking on a helpless note as he brushed his lips across hers in featherlight strokes. "I could just adore you with all of my heart."

"Then do," she whispered, twining her arms around his neck. "Please."

She didn't have to ask twice. He wrapped his arms around her, plunging his tongue deep into her mouth. As she melted into him, savoring the smoky sweetness of his kiss, Lottie was exhilarated to find herself once again standing on the edge of that dangerous precipice from her dream. Only this time she knew that if she dared to step off that ledge into Hayden's arms, she would not fall, but fly.

Resting his hands on her shoulders, Hayden gently set her away from him. "Now that you've convinced the scandal sheets and all of society that Justine's death really was a tragic accident," he said softly, "don't you think I at least owe you the truth?"

Shaking her head, Lottie touched two fingertips to his lips. "I already know the only thing I need to know—that I love you."

A groan escaped his throat as she slid her hand around to his nape, urging his mouth back down to hers. Between kisses, their shaking hands fumbled with buttons and ribbons, tapes and laces, desperate to shed the crisp layers of clothing that separated them. Hayden reached around to tear at the row of tiny, velvet-covered buttons at the back of her gown; Lottie whipped off his cravat, starving for a taste of him. She ran the tip of her tongue over his jaw, savoring the rich aroma of bayberry soap and the prickly hint of beard-shadow no amount of shaving could ever vanquish.

He dragged off her gown and slid her petticoat down over her hips. She tore at the studs holding his shirt closed, sending them bouncing unheeded across the room.

Shoving her down to a sitting position on the chaise, he disappeared behind her. "If I ever get you into a real bed," he muttered, tugging loose the tangled laces of her corset. "I'm never going to let you out of it."

"Is that a promise?" she asked as his impatient fingers raked the pins from her hair, sending it tumbling around her shoulders.

Lifting that shimmering veil, he grazed the curve of her throat just below the velvet choker with his moist lips, sending a shiver of raw pleasure over her skin. "You have my word as a gentleman."

But it wasn't a gentleman who reached around to cup the breasts he'd just freed from her corset. It was a man, with a man's needs and a man's hungers. He gently squeezed their lush softness in his palms, then captured her aching nipples between thumb and forefinger, tugging and stroking until she was arching against him, writhing with need.

Scattering angel-soft kisses along her nape, he sent one hand gliding over the downy skin of her belly. He didn't waste a single precious moment tearing away the tapes that held up her drawers, but simply continued the downward slide of his hand until his deft fingers breached both the narrow slit in the damp silk and the honeyed cleft beneath.

He slipped two fingers inside of her, groaning deep in his throat. "I didn't think it was possible, but you're as ready for me as I am for you."

"And why wouldn't I be?" Lottie demanded fiercely. She arched against his hand, desperate for the pleasure only he could give. "I've been waiting just as long."

Tearing open the straining front flap of his trousers, Hayden straddled the chaise, then wrapped one arm around her waist and guided her back until she was straddling him. Rising up beneath her, he urged her down . . . down . . . down, until every throbbing inch of him was embedded deep inside of her.

Still holding her from behind, he buried his face in the sweet-smelling softness of her hair, taking deep, shuddering breaths as he fought for control. Despite the surging demands of his body, Hayden would have been content just to hold her forever. Her skin was the warmth his flesh so desperately craved, her hair the golden light that defied the darkness, her heartbeat the music that had been missing from his life ever since she'd left Oakwylde.

Lottie lolled against Hayden's broad chest, murmuring his name over and over in a breathless litany. She could feel all the blood in her body rushing through her veins to that place where their bodies were joined. It took up the rhythm of her heart, pulsing around his thickness until she could no longer bear the exquisite tension.

Bracing the backs of her thighs against the front of his, she eased herself up, then down, riding the rigid length of his shaft.

Hardly daring to believe his wife's delectable boldness, Hayden arched up to meet her on the next stroke, rocking deeper inside of her with each powerful thrust of his hips. He kept one arm fixed firmly around her waist while the greedy fingers of his other hand tore at her drawers, widening the slit in the silk to give him unfettered access to her. Forcing her thighs even farther apart with his own, he gently flicked his thumb back and forth over the taut bud nestled in her damp curls.

A broken sob escaped Lottie's lips. To be taken so thoroughly, yet caressed so tenderly all at the same time was sweet torment. Just when she thought she couldn't bear another moment of it, Hayden cupped his hand hard against her, pushing her downward as he surged upward. His other arm still locked around her waist, he pounded into her in a driving, inescapable rhythm.

As a blinding wave of ecstasy broke over both of them at the same time, something happened that neither one of them had anticipated.

Lottie screamed.

"Allegra! Allegra, wake up!"

Allegra slowly opened her eyes to find Ellie kneeling beside her bed, her round eyes gleaming in the dark. "What is it?" she whispered, sitting up on her elbow.

"You're not going to believe who's here. It's your papa!"

"Don't be silly." Clutching Lottie's doll, Allegra rolled over to her other side. She'd spent the entire evening in her room sulking because Miss Terwilliger had pronounced her and the other children too young to attend the ball. "My father is in Cornwall."

Undaunted, Ellie scrambled around to the other side of the bed. "No, he's not. He's right here at Devonbrooke House!"

Allegra sat up, rubbing her eyes. "Are you sure you haven't been dreaming again? Remember what happened the last time you ate two servings of plum pudding at supper? You swore you saw a giant peering in your bedchamber window."

Ellie shook her head. "I was dreaming earlier, but I'm wide awake now. Aunt Lottie's scream woke me up."

Allegra's eyes suddenly widened in alarm. "Lottie screamed?"

Ellie nodded, her topknot bobbing. "It was a frightful sound. I thought someone was being murdered so I put on my slippers and sneaked downstairs. When I got down there, the guests were all milling everywhere at once and my mama and Aunt Diana were crying and Uncle George and Uncle Thane were threatening to break down the parlor door and my papa was shouting at Addison to bring him his pistols."

"Was he going to shoot Lottie?"

"Of course not, silly! He was going to shoot your papa."

Allegra tossed back the blankets and swung her legs over the side of the bed.

"Don't worry," Ellie said, patting her on the knee. "Before Addison could arrive with the pistols, Aunt Lottie came strolling out of the parlor just as calm as you please, with your papa right behind her."

"Why did she scream, then? Did he make her angry? Was she throwing a tantrum?"

"She claims she saw a mouse." Ellie curved her hands into claws. "A very *large* mouse with blood-red eyes and enormous fangs. It must have embarrassed her to cause such a ruckus over a mere mouse. She was terribly flustered. I've never seen her face quite so pink."

"That's odd." Allegra drew her feet back into the bed, peering nervously into the shadows. "With all the cats around here, you wouldn't think there'd be any mice. So where is my father now?"

"In Aunt Lottie's bedchamber. After they went upstairs together and all the guests left, Cookie made me a warm milk posset and let me sit in the kitchen with her and Addison for the longest time."

Allegra sat chewing on her lip, the furrow between the silky dark wings of her brows slowly deepening. She finally climbed down from the bed without a word.

"Where are you going?" Ellie demanded as Allegra jerked on her dressing gown.

"To see my pa—my father. He needn't think he can come all this way and not even trouble himself to say hello."

"You *were* sleeping," Ellie reminded her.

"Then he can say good-night!" Allegra snapped. Cinching her dressing gown, she went storming from the chamber, her small nose fixed firmly in the air.

Lottie lay with her cheek pillowed on her husband's chest, listening to his thundering heart slowly settle back into an even cadence.

Heaving an enormous sigh, he tightened his arm around her and touched his lips to her hair. "I'm so glad your brother-in-law didn't shoot me. I would have hated to miss that."

"It does rather give one a reason for living, doesn't it?" Still suffering aftershocks of delight, Lottie reached down and drew the blankets over their entwined limbs, then snuggled deeper into the warmth of Hayden's arms. Just as she did, she heard a faint creak coming from the direction of the door.

"Did you hear that?" she whispered, lifting her head.

"Perhaps it was a mouse." Hayden's serious expression would have been more convincing if his chest hadn't started to quake with suppressed laughter. "A really *large* mouse with glowing red eyes and razor-sharp fangs still dripping blood from the mangled throat of his last victim."

Lottie grabbed one of the feather bolsters and swatted him with it. "I was trying to save your life. I thought it was a very impressive effort myself."

"Indeed it was," he admitted, laughing aloud. "But you might have been more persuasive if your corset laces hadn't been caught on the heel of your slipper."

"At least we gave the gossipmongers something new to whisper about. I'm sure it will be in all the scandal sheets tomorrow—'MM and HH Caught *In Flagrante Delicto* After Being Terrorized by Rabid Mouse!'"

As she settled back into his arms, sighing with contentment, moonlight spilled across her bed, bathing them in a hazy glow. Hayden was silent for so long that she thought he might have drifted off. But when she sat up on one elbow, thinking to enjoy the stolen pleasure of watching him sleep, he was gazing up at the ceiling, his expression pensive.

As if sensing the weight of her curious gaze, he slowly turned to look at her. "I need to tell you about Justine."

Shaking her head, Lottie reached to stroke his cheek. "I already know everything I need to know. You don't have to do this."

He captured her hand in his, pressing a moist kiss

to her palm. "I believe I just might. If not for you, then for me."

She slowly nodded, sinking back into his arms.

When he spoke again, his voice was eerily detached, as if he was describing something that had happened to someone else in another lifetime. "After we'd been home from London for nearly three months, Justine realized she was with child. What she didn't realize was that the child was Phillipe's."

Lottie closed her eyes briefly. Thanks to Ned, she didn't have to ask him how he knew the child wasn't his.

"Justine still believed that I was the one who had come to her bed that night in London. I never had the heart to tell her the truth. When she discovered she was going to have another child, she was as happy as I had ever seen her. She spent hours stitching little bonnets and composing lullabies and telling Allegra all about the new baby brother she was to have. She was convinced the child was going to be a boy, the heir she'd always dreamed of giving me. I had no choice but to go along with the charade, to pretend I was as overjoyed as she was."

"What an agony that must have been for you," Lottie whispered, stroking his arm.

"I didn't know what else to do. I could hardly blame an innocent babe for the circumstances of its birth. I was determined to keep Justine secluded in Cornwall until the worst of the gossip died down." His jaw tightened. "But one of the servants brought a scandal sheet back from London and she happened to stumble across it. It was all there between those pages, every ugly word of it—her infidelity, the duel, Phillipe's death."

For the first time, Lottie truly understood the depth of his contempt for those who sold scandal for profit. "What did she do?"

"She lapsed into a terrible depression. It was beyond melancholy, beyond despondency, beyond anything I'd ever seen. She refused to leave her bed except late at night, when she would wander the corridors of the manor as if she was already a ghost. She spent the days locked in her chamber. Although it broke Allegra's little heart, she refused to see either one of us. I think she was too ashamed to face us." He shook his head. "I tried to tell her that she wasn't to blame for what had happened. That I was the one who had left her alone that night, when she needed me the most."

Lottie bit her lip until she tasted blood, knowing it wouldn't do any good to try to convince him otherwise. Not now. Not yet.

"Then one stormy night she vanished. We searched the house, then the grounds. I thought my heart was going to stop when I finally spotted her standing at the very edge of the cliffs. I called out her name, fighting to be heard over the wind and the rain. When she turned and I saw her face, I froze. I knew I didn't dare take another step.

"She stood there without a hint of madness in her eyes—so beautiful, so calm, like an eye in the middle of the storm. I was the one raging like a madman. I begged her to think of Allegra, to think of the child growing inside of her. To think of me. Do you know what she said then?"

Lottie shook her head, unable to choke a single word past the lump in her throat.

"In that one moment of perfect clarity, she looked at me with all the love in the world in her eyes and she said, 'I am.' I lunged for her, but it was too late. She didn't even scream. She just disappeared into the mist without a sound."

A shuddering sob escaped Lottie. "But you told the authorities it was an accident—that she slipped and fell."

He nodded. "I wanted to spare Allegra the scandal of her mother's suicide. I didn't realize until it was too late that an even more damning scandal would arise. And I never dreamed that Allegra would come to blame me for her mother's death. But I didn't do it just for her. I did it for Justine as well. I wanted my wife buried in hallowed ground." He clenched his teeth as his composure began to crack. "I couldn't bear the thought of God condemning her to an eternity of damnation when her brief life had contained so much torment. So I stood on the edge of that cliff, blinded by rain and tears, and I vowed that no one would ever know the truth about her death. And no one has. Until now." He turned to look at Lottie then, his eyes fierce in the moonlight. "Until you."

Lottie leaned over him, wetting his face with her tears. Their salty warmth was the only balm she had to offer for wounds so fresh and so deep. She gently kissed his brow, his eyelids, his cheeks, the bridge of his nose, and finally, his mouth, seeking to draw all the pain and bitterness out of his soul.

Groaning her name as if it was the answer to a long forgotten prayer, Hayden wrapped his arms around her and rolled her beneath him. As Lottie opened both her arms and legs to him, offering him a solace that was beyond tears or words, neither one of them heard the bedchamber door creak softly shut behind them.

Chapter 23

Was it possible, Dear Reader, that one night of scandal could lead to a lifetime of love?

SOMEONE WAS BANGING ON THE DOOR OF Lottie's bedchamber. That might not have been so jarring if the culprit hadn't also been shouting her name at the top of his lungs.

Startled from a sound sleep, Hayden sat bolt upright in the bed, muttering an oath. Lottie simply rolled over to her stomach and moaned in protest, refusing to abandon their cozy nest of rumpled blankets and entwined limbs.

But the banging and shouting showed no signs of ceasing.

Clutching a pillow to her naked breasts, Lottie sat up and raked a tousled curl out of her heavy-lidded eyes. "I do believe it's Sterling. Whatever is the matter with him? Did I scream again?"

Sliding his arms around her waist, Hayden nuzzled the downy skin at the nape of her neck and murmured, "No, but if he's willing to wait, it can be arranged."

The banging persisted.

When Lottie tried to wiggle out of his grasp, Hayden simply shoved her back among the pillows. "I warned you that if I ever got you into a proper bed, my lady, I was never going to let you out of it. You stay right where you are. I'll handle him this time." His expression stern and his hair poking out in all directions, Hayden clambered from the bed, sweeping a quilt around his lean hips.

"Careful," she warned. "He might be armed."

"If he is, then he'd best be prepared to choose his second because this time I have every intention of accepting his challenge."

Lottie might have been more alarmed by her husband's threat if she hadn't been distracted by how scrumptious he looked garbed in nothing but a quilt. Sighing dreamily, she admired the masculine roll of his hips as he swaggered to the door and threw it open.

Sterling opened his mouth, but before he could utter a word, Hayden shook a finger in his face. "I've had it up to here with your meddling, Devonbrooke. Carlotta is not a child anymore. She's all grown up and she doesn't need you poking your arrogant nose in her business. You may still be her brother-in-law, but you're no longer her guardian. She's *my* wife now and she's right where she bloody well belongs and intends to stay—in *my* bed!"

Frowning in bewilderment, Sterling peered over

Hayden's shoulder at Lottie. Warmed by a thrill of pride, Lottie grinned and wiggled her fingers at him.

Sterling shifted his gaze back to Hayden, something in his expression making Lottie's smile fade. "I didn't come here about Lottie. It's your daughter. She's gone missing."

After hastily tossing on their scattered garments, Lottie and Hayden hurried downstairs to find most of the family gathered in the drawing room. Sterling was pacing in front of the secretaire. Laura perched on the edge of the cream-colored sofa, her pretty face etched with strain. Harriet sat on the divan, while George leaned against the hearth behind her, his indolent posture belied by the fitful drumming of his fingernails on the mantel.

Hayden strode directly to the black-garbed figure sitting in the corner. "Where is she?" he demanded. "Where is my daughter?"

Miss Terwilliger looked even more shrunken than usual, as if she was in danger of being swallowed altogether by the overstuffed wing chair. Her gnarled knuckles curled around the head of her cane, she peered up at Hayden over the top of her spectacles, her rheumy blue eyes rimmed with red. "When Allegra failed to show up for her lesson this morning, I went to awaken her. But when I drew back her blankets, all I found was this." She reached into the chair beside her and held up the doll Hayden had given his daughter.

Hayden took the doll from her withered hands, tenderly smoothing one of its shimmering raven curls. "You were supposed to look after her," he said, raising accusing eyes to the old woman. "How could you let this happen?"

"No, Hayden," Lottie reminded him grimly. "*I* was supposed to look after her."

Before he could reply, Cookie came marching into the drawing room with Ellie in tow. Judging from the little girl's swollen eyes and reddened nose, she appeared to have been weeping for a very long time.

"Go on, child," Cookie commanded, tugging the girl in front of her. "Tell them what you know."

"But she made me promise I wouldn't!" Ellie wailed.

Laura swiftly rose and slipped an arm around her daughter's shoulders. "I would never ask you to break a promise, Eleanor, but the marquess here is very frightened for his little girl. He loves her just as much as we all love you and if he doesn't find her soon, it will make him very sad. Can you tell us where she's gone?"

Scuffing the toe of her slipper on the carpet, Ellie gave Hayden a shy glance. "I told her you were here last night. At first she didn't believe me, but after I told her about the mouse and Aunt Lottie turning all pink, she knew I was telling the truth."

Lottie could feel herself turning pink all over again. "What did she do then?"

"She said she was going to see her papa. But then a little while later, she came to my bedchamber and asked for her doll back." Ellie frowned at the doll in Hayden's hands. "When she told me where she was going, I thought she was going to take it with her."

"Where?" Hayden asked desperately. "Where did she tell you she was going?"

"To Cornwall. She told me she was going home to Cornwall."

Relief washed over Hayden's face. "She's only ten years old. If she set off for Cornwall, she couldn't have gone very far." His pleading gaze swept them all, finally coming to rest on Lottie. "Could she?"

"The mail coach," Harriet whispered.

Since her blank expression never changed, it took everyone a minute to realize she had even spoken.

"What was that, Miss Dimwinkle?" George asked, leaning over her shoulder.

"The mail coach!" Harriet repeated, her eyes lighting up behind the thick lenses of her spectacles. "Allegra knew that was how I ran away to Cornwall. She was always asking me questions about my journey. She said it sounded like a fine adventure."

Sterling collapsed against the secretaire, pressing his fingertips to his brow. "Dear Lord! If the child managed to wrangle herself a seat on one of the mail coaches that departed last night, she could be halfway to Cornwall by now."

Hayden raked a hand through his hair, looking dazed. "This still makes no sense whatsoever. If she knew I was here, then why in the name of God would she go there?" Kneeling in front of Ellie, he gently clasped the child by the shoulders. "Think, sweetheart. Think *very* hard. Did Allegra say why she was going to Cornwall?"

Ellie slowly nodded, her bottom lip beginning to tremble. "She said she was going to see her mother."

* * *

The carriage flew across the moor, bouncing through every furrow and rut until Lottie feared her teeth were going to fly right out of her head. Hayden had driven them across England like a man possessed. They had traveled both day and night, stopping only to change horses when the coachman warned Hayden that the animals were in danger of dropping dead in their tracks. When a broken wheel spoke had delayed them for nearly an hour, Lottie had feared Hayden was going to continue the journey on foot.

They had overtaken three mail coaches along the way, but despite Hayden's frantic pleas and threats, none of the drivers reported seeing a little girl trying to book a passage to Cornwall. But the last driver did remember that there would have been another coach ahead of him—a coach that had been scheduled to depart for Cornwall shortly after midnight on the previous day.

Allegra's doll sat on the seat across from Hayden and Lottie, her cool violet eyes and unruffled demeanor mocking their agitation. Lottie tucked her hands deeper into her muff, wishing for her own doll's smug smirk and twinkling eye. But her doll had vanished right along with Allegra.

As the carriage hurtled across the moor, Hayden gazed out the window as he'd done for most of the journey, his profile as bleak as the winter sky. He'd barely spoken a word to Lottie since they'd left London, retreating back into that wary shell where she had first found him. But when she reached for his hand, he took it and laced his fingers tightly through hers.

As they turned into the manor's drive, a winter squall seemed to be blowing in from the sea. Rain scented the chill air and the rising wind whipped the naked branches of the orchard trees into a dancing frenzy.

The carriage rolled to a halt. Before Lottie could even gather her skirts, Hayden had flung open the door and was racing toward the manor, shouting his daughter's name.

Lottie reached the house just as Martha came bustling into the foyer to find her master standing there, hatless and frantic.

"What on earth are you doing here, my lord?" she asked, her round face wreathed with shock. "If you'd have sent word that you were returning so soon, we would have prepared your—"

Hayden caught her by the shoulders before she could finish. "Is Allegra here, Martha? Have you seen her?"

Martha blinked dazedly. "Allegra? Of course Allegra's not here. She's in London with you."

Lottie glanced desperately around the foyer, her gaze finally settling on the mirrored hall tree, where a stack of unopened envelopes lay, awaiting Hayden's return. "The mail, Martha," she said urgently. "Has the mail arrived today?"

"Why, I believe so. I sent Jem to the village to collect it over an hour ago." She waved a dismissive hand. "There was nothing of any import—just a few notices and a letter from your cousin Basil."

Lottie and Hayden exchanged a wild look.

"Allegra!" Hayden shouted, starting up the stairs.

"Allegra!" Lottie echoed, flying down the corridor that led to the kitchens.

They met in the music room a short while later, both hoarse and out of breath.

"I can't find a trace of her anywhere," Hayden admitted, his face reflecting his despair.

"None of the servants have seen her either." Lottie shook her head. "Oh, Hayden, what if we were wrong? What if we're here and she's somewhere in London—lost and frightened and all alone."

Hayden gazed up at Justine's portrait, his hands clenched into fists. "But your niece swore she was coming here to see her mother."

The words had barely left his lips before he slowly turned to look at Lottie, the dread in his eyes chilling her blood to ice.

Allegra stood at the edge of the cliff, her traveling cloak billowing in the wind. She looked very small and very fragile against the roiling backdrop of sky and sea. Making a small, strangled sound in the back of his throat, Hayden started forward. Lottie grabbed his arm, pointing at the loose rocks beneath his daughter's feet.

They crept forward as one, terrified that their approach would startle her over the edge.

When they had drawn close enough to be heard over the roar of the waves crashing against the jagged rocks below, Hayden gently called out, "Allegra."

She turned, the sudden motion making her sway. Hayden's muscles went rigid and Lottie knew it was taking every ounce of his self-control not to spring forward and try to snatch his baby up into his arms. Tears misted Lottie's eyes when she saw the ragged doll Allegra was clutching.

"Allegra, darling," Lottie said, smiling tenderly at the girl, "your father and I have been so very worried. Won't you come here and let us have a look at you?"

Allegra shook her head fiercely, the wind whipping her loose hair across her tear-streaked face. "I don't want you looking at me. I don't want anyone looking at me."

Lottie and Hayden exchanged a bewildered glance. Stretching out one hand, Hayden began to inch closer to Allegra. She recoiled, skittering even closer to that deadly abyss. As he froze, his hand still outstretched, Lottie would have traded ten years of her life to be spared the look she saw on his face in that moment.

"Are you afraid of me, Allegra? Is that it? Are you afraid of me because you think I hurt your mother?"

She shook her head again. "I know you didn't hurt her. I heard you and Lottie talking. I know the truth now. I know exactly who killed my mama."

Hayden could barely choke out the word. "Who?"

Allegra lifted her chin, looking her father in the eye. "I did."

Hayden took two more steps toward her, unable to stop himself. "Of course you didn't! How can you say such a ridiculous thing?"

"Because it's true! I couldn't understand why she loved me so much on some days, but couldn't seem to stand the sight of me on others. One day I stood outside her door for hours and I cried and I begged her to come out and play with me. But she wouldn't. So I got mad and I shouted, 'I hate you! I hate you! I wish you were dead!'" Allegra's chest hitched with a broken sob. "And then she was."

"Oh, honey." Hayden dropped to his knees in front of her, blinking back his own tears. "You didn't kill your mama. You're not to blame for her death. Your mother was very sick and she didn't know any other way to end the pain." He shook his head helplessly. "She loved you so very much. You were the light of her life. If she hadn't been sick, she would have never left you. She would have never left either one of us."

Lottie squeezed Hayden's shoulder, knowing it was the first time he'd ever said those words and believed them. He wasn't only exonerating Allegra; he was forgiving himself for all the sins he'd never committed.

He stretched one trembling hand toward his daughter. "Please come here, sweetheart. Come to Papa."

Allegra's face crumpled. She reached for him, but in that moment, a violent gust of wind caught her cloak and tugged her backward. Her feet began to slide on the loose rocks. As her legs pedaled madly, fighting for balance, Hayden lunged for her and Lottie lunged for Hayden.

Allegra screamed, the shrill sound the stuff of nightmares. Hayden caught the front of her cloak in his fist just as Lottie's doll slipped out of her arms and went plummeting toward the crashing waves below. The three of them teetered there, trapped in a battle with the wind. Digging her fingernails into the back of Hayden's coat, Lottie gritted her teeth and tugged with all of her might, knowing he would never let go of his daughter, not even if he had to go over the edge of that cliff with her.

Terrified that she was going to lose them both, she clenched her eyes shut and whispered, "Please, oh dear God, please . . ."

At that precise moment, a wild surge of jasmine-scented wind propelled Allegra up and into her father's arms. All three of them went tumbling backward, collapsing against the rocks.

"Oh, Papa!" Allegra cried, throwing herself into Hayden's arms for the first time in four years.

Wrapping his arms around her, he buried his face in her tangled hair. "It's all right, baby. Papa's here. He'll never let you go."

Trembling with relief and astonishment, Lottie glanced toward the cliff. The ethereal outline of a woman was drifting in the air. As she smiled and nodded without a trace of mockery in her sparkling violet eyes, Lottie finally understood the message she had returned to deliver—in death she had finally found the peace that eluded her in life.

Lottie slowly nodded back at her, accepting Justine's unspoken blessing to make this man and child her own. By the time Hayden lifted his head, she was gone as if she had never been anything more than a wisp of cloud drifting across the stormswept sky.

As Hayden reached for Lottie, drawing her into their enchanted circle, she smiled up at him through a shimmering veil of tears. "It's all right, Hayden. I understand now that Justine will always be your first love."

He cupped her cheek in his hand, his green eyes both fierce and tender. "Justine might have been my first love, but you, my sweet Lottie, will be my last."

As his lips brushed hers, his kiss flooding her with wonder and hope, the sun broke through the clouds and a merry measure of piano music drifted to their ears.

Hayden froze. "Did you hear that?" he asked, looking around wildly. "Do you think it was a ghost?"

"Don't be silly, Papa," Allegra said, tilting her nose in the air.

Exchanging a grinning glance, she and Lottie finished in unison, "There are no such things as ghosts!"

Epilogue

※

From the society page of *The Times*, London, May 26, 1831:

Lady Allegra Oakleigh, the lovely young offspring of one of our fair city's most respected citizens, made her debut into society tonight at the home of the infamous Devil of Devonbrooke. She began the evening with a performance of Beethoven's "Tempest" on the pianoforte. When the guests, which included the king, were stunned into silence by her brilliance, her proud papa leapt to his feet, shouting, "Bravo! Bravo!," then proceeded to lead the crowd in a round of thunderous applause.

Her delighted stepmother, renowned author of *Lord Death's Bride* and *My Darling Bluebeard*, rarely left her husband's arms during the dizzying round of waltzes and quadrilles. When asked what she was working on next, she simply beamed up at her doting husband and replied, *"A Happy Ending."*

Author's Note

In *One Night of Scandal*, Hayden's first wife, Justine, suffered from bipolar disorder (also known as manic-depression). Until recent decades, it was not known that bipolar disorder was caused by chemical imbalances in the brain—imbalances that can be effectively treated with medication just like heart disease, kidney disease, and diabetes.

Even today, the disease, which affects over two million adult Americans annually, is frequently misdiagnosed as depression or schizophrenia. If you or a loved one are experiencing marked fluctuations in mood, characterized by bouts of depression followed by periods of euphoria, insomnia, irritability, racing speech and thoughts, grandiose delusions, impulsiveness, poor judgment, reckless behavior, and in the most severe cases, paranoia, delusions, and hallucinations, please consult your physician or visit *www.bipolarawareness.com* for more information.

Today, adequate medical treatment can offer something Justine could only dream of . . . hope.

Godspeed,
Teresa Medeiros
December 9, 2002